KILLING KATE

Kate returns from a post-break-up holiday with her girlfriends to news of a serial killer in her home town — and his victims all look like her. It could, of course, be a simple coincidence. Or maybe not. She becomes convinced she is being watched; followed, even. Is she next? And could her mild-mannered ex-boyfriend really be a deranged murderer? Or is the truth something far more sinister?

Books by Alex Lake
Published by Ulverscroft:

AFTER ANNA

Alex Lake is the pseudonym of a British novelist whose first book, *After Anna*, was a *Sunday Times* top 10 bestseller. Alex was born in the northwest of England in the 1970s and now lives in the northeastern US. Having spent a lot of time in the Lake District as a child, he is still in love with going on all-day hikes, as well as swimming, jogging, and learning to play the guitar — which he is enjoying, even if his family members aren't!

You can find him on Twitter @Alexlakeauthor

ALEX LAKE

KILLING KATE

Complete and Unabridged

CHARNWOOD
Leicester

First published in Great Britain in 2016 by
Harper
An imprint of HarperCollins*Publishers*
London

First Charnwood Edition
published 2017
by arrangement with
HarperCollins*Publishers*
London

A catalogue record for this book is available
from the British Library.

ISBN 978–1–4448–3428–4

Published by
F. A. Thorpe (Publishing)
Anstey, Leicestershire

Set by Words & Graphics Ltd.
Anstey, Leicestershire
Printed and bound in Great Britain by
T. J. International Ltd., Padstow, Cornwall

This book is printed on acid-free paper

To TMC-G

Prologue: The Fab Four

They had once been four.

Kate, May, Gemma, and Beth. The Fab Four, their parents called them, with an affectionate nod to the original Fab Four from Liverpool and a wry nod to the fact that their teenage daughters happened to agree that they really were, after all, pretty damn fab.

Four best friends, from their first days at infant school, through the wide-eyed years of junior school and the drama of high school and then on to university and their fledgling careers. Along the way there were fashion fads and music crazes, first kisses and last kisses, tears (lots) and laughter (even more). All of it added layer upon layer to their deepening and — it seemed — eternal friendship.

And then, without warning, it all changed.

Looking back, Kate could pinpoint the night she noticed — they all noticed — that it was going wrong. She had no idea at the time quite how wrong it was going, or how quickly, but she *had* known that something was not as it should have been.

When she fully understood what it was, however, it was too late.

Beth was already lost.

PART ONE

1

She had to get out of there.

There were many thoughts going round in her head — confusion, regret, shame — but that was the overriding one.

She needed to leave. That instant. Kate Armstrong wanted to be anywhere other than where she found herself.

Leaving, though, was complicated by the fact that the man whose bed she was in — what was his name? Rick? Mike? Mack? Shit, she couldn't even remember that — was not there. His side of the bed was empty. Which meant that the option of sneaking out quietly was not available. He was up and about, somewhere in his Turkish holiday apartment, and she would have to face him before she could flee.

Unless there was a window. She knew that leaving that way was unorthodox, maybe even desperate, but she *was* desperate. He might think it was odd when he came in and she was gone, the window wide open, but she didn't really care.

She sat up in the bed, making sure that the sheets were pulled up over her naked torso — God, she was naked, naked in a stranger's bed — and looked around. Her vision was milky — the result of leaving in her contact lenses overnight — and her eyes itched, but she could see through a window that the apartment was not on the

5

ground floor. There were branches of a tree of some kind she did not recognize right outside the window.

So that was that. She would have to face him. Rick or Mike or Mack.

It was Mike, she thought, details of the evening coming back to her. He was called Mike, and she'd met him in a nightclub. She was buying drinks for her friends, May and Gemma, at the bar when some perma-tanned Italian had sidled up behind her and put his arms around her waist, pressing the crotch of his white linen trousers into her bum. He'd muttered something unintelligible — or Italian, at any rate — into her ear and then she'd tried to wriggle free.

She'd managed to turn to face him and he grinned in what she assumed he thought was a charming way, then put his hand on her hip.

Which was when the guy — Mike — showed up.

Hi, he said. He put a hand on her shoulder and smiled. *Sorry I'm late.*

She had no idea who he was, but she knew what he was doing. He'd seen her struggling and had come over to help.

No problem, she said, as though she knew him well. *I was getting some drinks. What are you having?*

A beer. He looked at the Italian. *Who's your friend?*

No one. We just met. She raised an eyebrow and gave her assailant a little wave. *Arrivederci.*

The Italian looked Mike over, took in his taut, muscular frame, then shrugged and walked away.

Thanks, she said. *He was about to become a pain.*

That's OK. I was coming to get a beer and I noticed that you seemed uncomfortable. Anyway, I'll let you get on with your evening.

Let me get you that beer, she said. *By way of a thank you.*

And then, somehow, she'd ended up here. Naked, dry-mouthed, head pounding.

She stared at the tree branches and tried to remember what had happened after that. The memories started to come back, memories of staggering into the apartment and kissing Mike by the door. Memories of him taking her hands and leading her into the bedroom. Memories of him undressing her.

She closed her eyes and groaned. This was *not* what she did. She did not go home with men she'd just met and have sex with them, however drunk she got.

But had they had sex? The seed of a memory formed, then coalesced into something firmer. Into *her* asking *him* if he had a condom.

Are you sure? he said. *Sure you want to do this? We don't have to.*

She was sure. Then, at least, she was sure. Not now, though. Now she was sure only that she wished she'd said *No, let's wait* or *Maybe I should go. My friends will be missing me.*

But he'd shaken his head, kissed her, and said *I think you've had a bit too much to drink. Let's see if you still feel the same way in the morning.*

She'd bridled and mumbled that she was fine, thank you very much, but the truth was she

7

wasn't fine, she was hammered, and thank God he hadn't taken advantage of that.

And how had she got so drunk? She didn't remember having that much. Wine at dinner, then gin and tonics in the nightclub, after which her memory got hazy. They were pretty liberal with the measures here. She'd watched them sloshing the gin into the glass; that must be what had happened. Well, she was going to have to be careful for the rest of the holiday. This could not happen again.

The rest of the holiday. Right then she didn't want it, didn't want to stay here for another two nights. They'd arrived five days ago, her and May and Gemma, on a week away to take her mind off the break-up with Phil, the man she'd been sure she was destined to marry until she'd realized that maybe she wasn't destined to marry him after all, so she'd decided to end it. A decision which she hadn't been sure about when she took it and which seemed even less like a good idea now, as she lay here, mouth dry and head throbbing, having nearly ended up on the wrong end of a one-night stand, a one-night stand that would have been her first ever, had the man she'd thrown herself at not been, thankfully, enough of a gentleman to turn her down.

She'd made *Phil* wait a month before she slept with him. That was more her speed. And it had been well worth the wait. More than worth it. He was the first and — still — only man she had ever had sex with. Her high-school boyfriend. They'd stayed together all through the university years, him at the University of the West of

8

England in Bristol, her at Durham, which were two places about as far apart as you could get in England. A true long-distance relationship, a true test of their devotion, then they'd moved back to their hometown, back to the village of Stockton Heath, where they'd rented a house together, and set off on the final leg of their journey to marriage and kids.

Until she decided that she wasn't ready, that she needed to live a little before settling down. She comforted herself that she could always go back to him, if she needed to. That made the decision a bit easier, although not for him. He hadn't taken the break-up all that well. Truth be told, he'd taken it very, very badly. He called her early in the morning before work and late at night, drunk in his friend Andy's flat, where he was living until he sorted out something permanent, or from outside some nightclub or, once, from the bathroom in the house of a girl he'd gone home with. He'd told her he'd moved on, found someone else.

Why are you calling me from her bathroom at two a.m., then? she'd said, aware that it was mean to mock him, but it was the middle of the night and she was tired and frustrated.

Fuck you, he'd replied, his voice wavering as though he was on the verge of tears. *Just fuck you, Kate.*

So yes, it was fair to say he hadn't taken it very well, which was part of the reason she'd come away. At home he was a constant presence, so she struggled to get any perspective. She needed some space, some distance between them, some

9

time with her girlfriends, doing nothing but relaxing on the beach in the day and going out at night.

Her friends. They'd be freaking out. She leaned over and looked at the pile of her clothes on the floor. A knee-length red summer dress, black lace underwear, strappy high-heels. All bought with this holiday in mind. All bought with the thought that she needed to look good in the pubs and clubs of her holiday destination.

And to look good for what? So she could wake up in a stranger's bed? No, not for that, but, damn it, that was what had happened, and she was not happy about it, not happy at all.

Her bag was next to the clothes. She reached down and grabbed it, then took out her phone. There were a bunch of missed calls from Phil, but then she'd been getting those all week. She'd not answered any of them. She'd come here to get away; the last thing she needed was a long, emotional conversation with her ex. There were also missed calls from May and Gemma, and a bunch of text messages. She scrolled through them.

2:02 a.m., from May:

Where are you?

2:21 a.m., again from May:

For fuck's sake, Kate, pick up your phone! Where are you? We're worried!

2.25 a.m., this time from Gemma's phone.

10

She imagined the conversation, pictured May speaking: *Perhaps my phone's not working, maybe the messages aren't getting through, let's try yours* and then the message:

Did you leave with that guy? You need to message us, now.

And then, her reply, at 2.43 a.m.:

Hi! I'm fine. I'm with the guy from the nightclub, Mike. He's really nice! Don't worry, I'll see you in the morning.

God, she'd been drunk. She didn't remember sending it, couldn't place it in the timeline of the night. Was it before they arrived at his place? After? She had no idea.

She typed another message.

On my way back. See you soon. I feel like a dirty stop-out.

She put her feet on the cold tiled floor and reached for her clothes. Now for the hard part. Now she had to face Mike and then get the hell out of there.

She pulled her clothes on, pushing the thought from her mind that she was going to have to do the walk of shame through the morning streets of this Turkish resort, everyone who saw her dressed in her evening clothes fully aware that she had gone home with someone and was now making her way back to her own accommodation.

She didn't care. She'd never see those people again, and she'd never do this again. All she wanted was to get back, shower, sleep, and forget this had ever happened.

The bedroom door was ajar. She pushed it open and walked into the apartment. It was a typical holiday apartment: an open-plan kitchen and living room, with two bedrooms: the one she had woken up in, and one which still had the door closed. Presumably one of Mike's friend's was still asleep in it.

All the more reason to get out of there.

He was sitting on the couch, a mug of coffee in his hand, one bare foot on the tiled floor, the other tucked under his thigh. He looked up from his iPad and smiled at her.

'Morning, Kate,' he said. 'Sleep well?'

2

'Great,' Kate said. *Awfully badly*, she thought. *And why did I just lie?*

'Would you like a drink? Orange juice? Coffee? Tea?' He raised an eyebrow. 'Beer?'

'What?' she said, her voice little more than a croak. 'Are you kidding?'

He grinned. 'Yes,' he said. 'I am.'

Kate blushed. 'Right. Sorry. Of course you are. I'm feeling a little delicate.'

'Me too. They make strong drinks here.' He drained his coffee, then untucked his foot and stood up. 'I think I need a refill. You want one?'

She didn't. Even though they hadn't, in the end, had sex, she still didn't want to spend a single minute more here. The grubbiness of her hangover mixed with the memory of throwing herself at him had produced a horrible self-loathing. But she also didn't want to be rude; he looked so hopeful. And a coffee *did* sound good.

'Sure,' she said. 'Maybe a quick one. Then I have to get going.'

'If you need to be somewhere, I understand,' he said. He had a neutral accent which was hard to place, although she thought she detected the flat vowels of the north. Lancashire, maybe. 'You don't need to hang around if you don't want to.'

'No,' Kate said. 'It's fine. A coffee would be nice. Thanks.'

13

He crossed the white-tiled floor to the kitchen and took a mug from a cupboard. He filled it from a stove-top coffee maker. He was wearing chinos and an olive green T-shirt and was maybe ten years older than her, in his late thirties, with a lean, wiry body. His movements were precise and deliberate, but graceful — almost balletic — and he was handsome in a severe, school-teacherly kind of way. He was very different to Phil, a stocky, broad-shouldered rugby player who was anything but precise and balletic. His friends called him clumsy; he said he was too strong for his own good. Either way, it was one of the things she had loved about him.

There was a carton of milk open on the worktop. Mike picked it up and gestured towards the freshly filled cup.

'Milk?'

'Yes, please.'

He poured some in and passed her the cup. 'It's that UHT stuff they have here,' he said. 'Not fresh. But the coffee's good. Some local brand. Nice and strong. Perfect after a late night.'

It *was* good. Hot and rich and heady. She only wished she could enjoy it more, that she was drinking it on a café terrace by the harbour with her friends, watching the morning sun glint off the water.

'So,' Mike said. 'Here we are.'

'Yes,' she said. 'Here we are.'

There was an awkward pause. She sipped her coffee. Mike sipped his. After a moment he broke the silence.

14

'Where are you from?' he said. 'Back home?'

She didn't want to tell him. Didn't want him to know anything about her. It wasn't him — he was pleasant enough, considerate and relaxed, and in other circumstances she might have quite liked him — but she didn't want any reminder of the night before.

'Stockton Heath,' she said. 'It's a small town. Village, really. It's near Warrington, in Cheshire.'

His eyes widened.

'No way!' he said. 'Are you kidding?'

'No,' she said. 'Why?'

'Did we talk about this last night? And now you're messing with me?'

'No,' she said. 'We didn't.'

'Are you sure I didn't tell you?'

She would have thought it was impossible for her mouth to get any drier, but that was what happened. She sipped her coffee. 'Tell me what?'

'Where I live.'

She shook her head. 'No. Where *do* you live?'

'I'm your neighbour,' he said. 'I live in the next village along. I live in Moore.'

3

She stared at him.

'Are you serious?'

'Yeah,' he said. 'I'm from Newton, originally. But I live in Moore now. I'm often in Stockton Heath. Where in the village do you live?'

She told him; she was in the centre, and God she was glad he lived a few miles away. It wasn't far, but it was something.

'Amazing,' he said. 'What are the odds of meeting someone from the same neck of the woods over here? I can't believe it.'

Neither could Kate. This was getting worse. She didn't ever want to see him again, never mind have him bump into her in her hometown. It was unbelievable. And there was something familiar about him, now she thought about it, but that could easily be the fact that she knew now that they were from the same place.

'Did you grow up there?' he said.

She nodded. 'Born and bred.'

'I like the area,' he said. 'Quiet, but I like living in a sleepy village where nothing ever happens. It feels safe, insulated from all the craziness in the world.'

Kate bridled at the suggestion that her home was so boring; she thought it could be quite lively, especially on a Friday night, but then he was older, and probably didn't participate in the nightlife of the village to the degree that she did.

Besides, before she'd left for Turkey there had been a big local story.

'It wasn't so sleepy last week,' she said. 'They found that body.'

It was the biggest news in the village Kate could remember. A woman her age had been killed only a few days before she left for Turkey. A dog walker — a magistrate out with his new puppy, Bella — had found a body stuffed into a hedge near the reservoir. It was a young girl, Jenna Taylor, in her late twenties. She'd been strangled, there was speculation that she had been raped, too, although the news reports had been vague, which only served to fuel rumours that something *really* sick had taken place.

'I heard,' Mike said. 'I read about it online. I haven't been following it, though. It happened about a week after I got here, and you know what it's like on holiday. You tend to switch off. One of my friends has been keeping track of it. He said they still haven't found whoever did it.'

'I heard they arrested her boyfriend,' Kate said. 'One of my friends is addicted to reading about it, but she's like that with every news event.'

'Did you know the victim?' Mike said. 'She was about your age, wasn't she?'

'She was,' Kate said. 'But I didn't know her. She moved from Liverpool a few years ago. We would have been at high school together though, if she was from Stockton Heath.'

What she didn't say was what her friends had been teasing her about ever since: she and Jenna Taylor could have been sisters. They had the

17

same long hair, lithe figure and dark eyes. It was no more than a coincidence, but still, she didn't like it. It wasn't the kind of coincidence that you found intriguing; it was the other kind, the kind that you found disturbing.

Mike shook his head. 'Unbelievable,' he said. 'I go away for a few weeks and all hell breaks loose.'

Kate gave a half smile. She wasn't listening any more. She'd had enough of making conversation. All she wanted was to go back to her hotel and her friends.

She finished the drink and put the cup on the counter. 'Thanks,' she said. 'I have to get moving.'

There was a flicker of disappointment on Mike's face. 'You want to meet up later?'

Kate paused. For a second she felt almost obliged to say yes, but she caught herself. She didn't have to be polite. She owed him nothing.

'I don't think so,' she said. She searched for an excuse — what? A prior engagement? Didn't want to leave her friends — but none came. 'I don't think so,' she repeated, simply.

'OK,' he said. 'I understand. From the look on your face, I'm guessing that you won't want to meet up another night, either?'

She shook her head. 'No,' she said. 'Sorry.'

She put her hand on the front door to open it.

'You know your way home?' Mike said. 'Where are you staying?'

She didn't want to give him the name of their hotel. 'Near the harbour.'

'Go out of the main door and turn right,' he

said. 'It's not far. I can call you a cab, though, if you'd like?'

'No,' she said. 'No thanks. I'll walk. I could do with the fresh air.'

'All right,' he said, with a rueful grin. 'Maybe I'll see you round and about in Stockton Heath.'

She hoped not. She really, really hoped not.

4

Phil Flanagan signed the change order on his desk. He'd barely read it; he was a project manager on a residential housing development, but given how he was feeling it was a struggle to muster up the enthusiasm to care about his job. It was a struggle to muster up the enthusiasm to care about *anything*.

Not with Kate gone. It was bad enough that she'd broken up with him, but now she was on holiday, living it up in the sun. Surrounded by men who would be ogling her by day and pawing her in the pubs and clubs by night. God, he couldn't stand the thought of it. Couldn't bear to picture it.

But he couldn't stop himself. All day long images of her in bed with a faceless man, their naked, suntanned limbs passionately entwined, tortured him. Which was the reason he was barely paying lip service to his job.

He stared at his signature on the paper. He hated his name, hated the alliteration of Phil and Flanagan. He'd always had the idea that he was going to change it someday; originally he'd planned for that day to be the day he got married, when, in a grand romantic gesture that would both impress her and get rid of his horrible name, he would take *her* name. But that plan was out of the window now that she'd dumped him because she needed some fucking

20

space, needed to see what life was like without him. Well, he could tell her what it was like, it was rubbish, totally fucking rubbish, just a series of minutes and hours and days all merging into one big morass of him missing her and wondering where she was and if she was in bed with some greasy fucking foreigner on holiday. And at the back of it all, the question: why, why had she done it?

And what was he supposed to do now? His whole life had been planned around her: get married in the next year or so, then kids, then grandkids, then retirement, then their last few years eating soup together in a home somewhere, before dying, her first, then him a few days later of a broken heart.

It wouldn't say *broken heart* on the death certificate, but that was what it would be, and all the people in the nursing home would agree about it. They'd smile at each other and say how lovely it was — sad, but lovely — that he couldn't live without his wife of seventy years.

Well, that wouldn't happen now, and the loss of it *stung*.

He'd known there was something wrong a few weeks back, when he'd suggested that they get started on planning their wedding. They weren't engaged, not yet. Not officially, at any rate. Not in the announced-to-the-world sense. That would come in due course, but he saw no reason not to start at least discussing the main points of their wedding-to-be — possible locations, numbers, all that stuff — because they *were* going to get married, of course they were.

21

Everyone knew that. Everyone had known it for years.

Sure, she said. *We should start thinking about it.*

We should check out some venues. I was thinking Lowstone Hall, or maybe the Brunswick Hotel, if we wanted something more modern.

Yeah, maybe, she said. *Let's think about it.*

So should I contact them? Do you like those places?

Er — let me think about it. I'm not sure.

Not sure? Phil said. *We talked about both those places a while back. What changed?*

She wouldn't look him in the eye. *Nothing. I just — let me think about it, OK?*

He'd thought it was odd, that there was something different in her manner. But he had not been expecting what came a week after that.

Phil, she said. *We need to talk about something.*

And then she told him. Told him that they'd been together since they were teenagers and she wasn't sure he was the right person for her any more. She wanted a break. Wanted some time apart so she could live her life, make sure she knew who she was, that she was not sleepwalking into a bad decision.

So it's a break? He said. *For how long?*

Maybe a break, she said. *Maybe not.*

But if it is, how long for?

I don't know, Phil. I can't say.

He felt his world slipping through his fingertips. *You don't have to be exact, Kate. But what order of magnitude are we talking? A week? A month?*

More, probably. Six months? I don't know. She looked at him, tears in her eyes. *I think it'll be easier if we say it's for good. That'll stop you wondering.*

No, he said. *That's not easier. Not at all. It's a lot worse.*

And that was how they'd left it. Him: broken, devastated, unsure of what to do from minute to minute, staying in his friend Andy's scruffy flat. Her: on holiday in Turkey, living it up with her friends.

On his desk his phone began to vibrate. It was Michelle, a girl he'd met the weekend before. He'd called Kate from her house — from the bathroom — drunk as all get out, expecting her to be sad when she saw how easily he had moved on, to understand what she had lost and to say, *Come over, Phil, leave her and come back to me.*

It hadn't quite ended like that.

To make matters worse, in the morning he'd sat there drinking tea on Michelle's couch and all he could think was *Shit, she looks like Kate, like a pale imitation of Kate.* He hadn't noticed it the night before. He hadn't noticed much of anything with about six beers and a bunch of whisky and Coke swilling around in his belly.

And now she was calling him. He was going to tell her he couldn't see her. He liked her — she was nice enough — but he knew that there was no future with her. It was rebound sex, a way to take his mind off what had happened, and, even if he'd wanted to do it again, he knew it wasn't fair to use her like that. He picked up his phone.

'Michelle,' he said. 'How are you?'

'Good!' She was, he remembered, from Blackpool, and the false brightness in her voice matched the false confidence of the fading seaside resort. 'You?'

'Fine, yeah.'

'What are you doing tonight? Want to meet up?' There was a nervous quiver in her voice.

He was about to say *No, I can't, and I'm not sure we should meet up again, it's not you, it's me, I recently came out of a difficult relationship* . . . But then the image of an evening in Andy's empty flat — Andy was away with work — drinking alone to quiet his thoughts, came to him, and he thought *Why not? It's only a drink. It doesn't have to mean anything.*

'Sure,' he said. 'Sounds great. Where do you want to meet?'

'The Mulberry Tree?' she said. 'Seven?'

★ ★ ★

Just after seven he walked into the Mulberry Tree. It was a popular pub in the centre of Stockton Heath. Michelle was sitting at a table, a half-drunk glass of white wine in front of her.

Phil gestured to the glass. 'Another?'

Michelle nodded. 'I got here a bit early,' she said. 'I came on the bus. It was either arrive ten minutes early or half an hour late.'

She didn't drive. He remembered her telling

24

him; she'd failed her test three times then given up trying.

'I'll be right back,' he said.

As the barman poured the drinks he glanced at her. She was shorter than Kate, and had a rounder, chubbier face, but there was a definite similarity. Long, straight dark hair, dark eyes, a quiet, watchful expression.

Jesus. Hanging out with a Kate lookalike was hardly going to take his mind off his ex.

He paid and took the drinks to the table.

'Here you go,' he said, and raised his glass. 'Cheers.'

Michelle clinked his glass. 'You see the latest on the murder?' she said. 'I can't believe it.'

Phil hadn't. He was too wrapped up in his own misery to pay attention to other people's.

'What is it?' he said. 'I've not been following it. It's only more darkness in the world.'

She looked at him with a teasing smile. 'You're a bundle of fun,' she said. 'Anyway, the cops arrested the boyfriend.' She leaned forward, her tone conspiratorial. 'It's always the boyfriend, or the husband. She was probably sleeping with someone else, or something like that.' She shook her head. 'That kind of violence — it can only come from a strong emotion, you know?'

'I guess,' Phil said. 'I wouldn't really know.'

'I'd hope not!' Michelle said. She leaned back. 'Anyway, enough of that. How've you been?'

'Fine,' he said. 'Fine.'

'That's it?' Michelle said. 'Just fine?'

He stared at her, a feeling of hopelessness washing over him. He could hardly tell her the

25

truth, could hardly confess that he was unable to sleep, his nights filled with obsessive thoughts of his ex, an ex who looked like the woman he was currently out on a date with, a fact which only made matters worse. Could hardly tell her that he didn't want to be here, that he was only here because he had to do *something*, had to find a way to take his mind off Kate, and he had hoped that this might do that, at least a little bit.

Could hardly tell her that it wasn't working, and all he wanted to do was leave.

'Been a tough day at work,' he said.

'What do you do?' Michelle said.

Jesus, she didn't even know what he did for a job. He wasn't ready for this, wasn't ready to make a new start with someone. He was suddenly overwhelmingly tired.

'I have to go,' he said. 'I don't feel well.'

She frowned. 'I just got here! It took two buses!'

'I'm sorry. It's not your fault. I've been fighting something all day — flu, I think, it's been going round the office — and it just hit me. I should have cancelled.' He took a twenty-pound note from his wallet and put it on the table. 'Take a taxi home. On me. Sorry, Michelle.'

'I don't want money!'

Phil ignored her. He got to his feet, his head spinning. He felt faint, nauseous now.

'Are you OK?' Michelle said, her tone switching from anger to concern. 'You do look a bit poorly.'

He waved a hand. 'I'll be all right,' he muttered, and fled.

5

When Kate got back to the hotel room May and Gemma were still sleeping. There were two double beds in the room; Kate and May were sharing one, leaving the other to Gemma. It wasn't a generous gesture; they knew from long experience that Gemma was a very active sleeper who would stealthily colonize your side of the bed, gradually creeping closer and closer to you until she was pushing you over the edge. If you got out and switched sides, she would start to move towards you again; you'd hear her coming and the stress of it would keep you from falling asleep. Allied to the fact that she was a very deep sleeper, who was near impossible to wake up, and she was not anybody's preferred sleeping partner.

Her boyfriend — a maths teacher called Matt — claimed that he had to decamp to the couch five nights a week in order to get some sleep. He had, he said, been collecting data on his sleeping arrangements and was using it to teach statistics to his students. He showed it to Kate once: he'd plotted a bell curve, showing that five nights per week was the mean average, with a standard deviation of three sigma. Kate had no idea what that meant in statistical terms, but she was pretty sure that in the real world it meant that he was not getting enough sleep and was in danger of becoming obsessed with it.

Kate opened the bathroom door and turned on the shower. She stripped off and climbed under the hot water, letting it first soothe and then invigorate her. The shower shelf was crammed with bottles of shampoo and conditioner and she grabbed hers, a tea-tree oil shampoo from Australia. A large part of her was sceptical about the value of these toiletries; Phil always said that they were all just soap anyway so she may as well buy the Tesco value pack for a few pounds, rather than spend a small fortune on the designer stuff. She suspected he had a point, but it wasn't about the chemistry of whatever was in the bottles. It was about the routine, the feeling that she was, in some way, pampering herself, treating herself to something special.

She stepped out of the shower and wrapped herself in a towel. It was a plush, white Egyptian cotton towel and it felt luxurious against her skin. It was these little things that made staying in a hotel so amazing: clean, soft towels every day, a freshly made bed, coffee and breakfast at the end of a phone line.

She went into the bedroom. May and Gemma were still sleeping. May's side of the room was tidy, the carpet empty apart from a small pile of neatly folded clothes from the night before. Her other clothes were either hanging up in the wardrobe or carefully arranged in a drawer. Gemma's side, on the other hand, was a total mess: inside-out jeans hanging off a chair, bras and underwear littering the floor, one of a pair of flats on the pillow next to her head.

It had always been this way: Gemma and May were total opposites. May: organized, precise, together, always on time, following the plan. Gemma: unaware there was a plan, haphazard, confused, totally oblivious that she was supposed to arrive at whatever place she was going to at any particular time.

But they, along with Kate, had been friends forever. Since the day they met as five-year-olds at St Stephen's Primary they had been a unit. They'd been friends for over twenty years: they'd grown up together, seen each other's characters develop and emerge. They knew each other as well as they knew themselves, understood how and why they had become the people they were, and they loved each other in a deep and profound way.

Kate opened the minibar and took out a small, over-priced, glass bottle of orange juice. Normally she wouldn't have spent three pounds fifty — she did the maths to convert the currency in her head — on what was little more than a tiny sip of juice, but she was suddenly overwhelmed by the desire for something sweet. That, she thought, was the price you paid for a hangover, and the reason they had these ludicrously expensive minibars in the first place.

Behind her, May stirred. Her eyes opened and she looked hazily at Kate while she emerged fully from unconsciousness.

'Splashing out?' she said.

'Thirsty,' Kate replied. 'I needed something sweet.'

29

'Me too.' May held out a hand. 'Can I have some?'

'There's not much.'

'Just a sip. I'm feeling a bit delicate.'

Kate swallowed half the contents and handed the bottle to her friend. 'Finish it.'

'So,' May said. 'You arranged your own accommodation last night?'

'I suppose so,' Kate said. 'I wasn't sure where I was this morning.'

'Did you guys — you know?'

'No.' Kate shook her head. 'I tried to, but he told me I was too drunk.'

'Nice guy. Most would have taken advantage.'

'I guess.' Kate paused. 'But nothing about last night feels good. What I remember of it, that is.'

'It's not like you.'

'I know. I feel awful. I can't believe it. I had way too much to drink. Don't let me do that again.'

'We would have stopped you, but you disappeared with that guy.' She sipped the orange juice. 'We were worried, Kate, in case he turned out to be some crazy weirdo, but then you texted to say you were OK, so we left you to it.'

'He was fine. He didn't do anything, thank God. In fact, it was me who suggested we have sex.' She shook her head. 'I can't quite believe it.'

'Are you going to see him again?'

'No,' Kate said. 'He wanted to, but I can't face it. He was nice enough, but I'd rather forget it happened.'

'We'll have to avoid that club, then. In case

30

he's in there. And if we're in other places I suppose we'll have to keep an eye out for him.'

Kate raised an eyebrow. 'That's not the only place we'll have to keep an eye out for him. Guess where he lives.'

'Where?'

'Guess.'

May shrugged. 'London?'

'No. Guess again.'

'Manchester?'

'Warmer.'

May raised her eyebrows. 'Somewhere close to us?'

'Very close.' Kate sat on the end of the bed. 'He lives in none other than Moore.'

May leaned forwards, propping herself up on her elbows. 'You mean Moore? The Moore down the road?'

'The same.'

'You are fucking *kidding* me.'

'I wish I was.'

'You're saying he's from the same pokey part of the world as us? Did you know him?'

Kate shook her head. 'No, although he did seem familiar once I knew. I suppose I might have seen him around. He's older, though, so he wouldn't necessarily hang out in the places we do.'

'How much older?'

'Late thirties. Something like that. I didn't ask.'

'Got yourself a sugar daddy,' May said. 'Lucky you.'

'Don't even joke about it,' Kate replied. 'This

31

is not funny. Maybe I'll be able to laugh about it later, but not now.'

'What's he doing here?'

'Holiday. He's been here a couple of weeks already, hanging out with some friends.'

'And you're not going to see him again?'

'No,' Kate said. 'Definitely not.'

The hotel phone started to ring. May looked up at Kate. 'Do you think that's him?' she said.

'I hope not,' Kate replied. 'I didn't give him the name of the hotel. Shit, I hope he didn't follow me here.'

'I'll get it,' May said. 'If it's him, I'll tell him I don't know you and he's got the wrong number. OK?'

Kate nodded. 'OK.'

May reached out and picked up the phone.

'Hello?' she said. There was a long pause, then she held out the receiver to Kate. 'It's for you,' she said.

'Is it him?'

'No,' May said, and rolled her eyes. 'It's Phil.'

6

Kate took the receiver from May and put it to her ear.

'Phil?' she said. 'What are you doing? Is something wrong?'

His voice was tense, a note or two higher than usual. 'I wanted to talk to you. You haven't been answering your phone. I thought maybe you don't have reception.'

'It's pretty patchy,' she lied. 'I saw some missed calls' — *some*, she thought, *didn't cover it. There'd been dozens of them* — 'but I haven't been able to call back.'

'Oh,' he said. 'I understand.'

'So,' Kate said. '*Is* something wrong?'

'No. I just — I just wanted to talk to you. Check you're OK.'

'I'm fine,' Kate said, her mouth tightening. 'I'm a big girl, Phil. I can look after myself.'

'I know, but — '

'And how did you get this number?' Kate said.

'I asked your mum and dad where you're staying.'

The answer was too quick; she knew Phil and she could tell it was a lie he'd prepared earlier. She wasn't even sure she'd told her parents where she was staying. It pissed her off; this whole phone call pissed her off. She decided not to let him off the hook.

'Are you sure?' she said. 'I don't recall telling

33

them the hotel name. In fact, I'm pretty sure I didn't, now I think about it. So how did you get the number?'

He paused. 'I called around,' he said finally.

'Called around what?'

'The hotels.'

Kate stared at her reflection in the mirror opposite the bed. 'You called every hotel in the resort?'

'No!' he said, a hint of outrage in his voice that she would suggest he was that desperate. 'I knew you were staying near the harbour, so I called those hotels and asked to be put through to your room.'

'Right,' Kate said. 'So you called every hotel near the harbour.' She shook her head, exasperated. Why couldn't he leave her alone, even for one week? One week, so she could enjoy her holiday.

'Well, it's nice to talk, but I'm kind of busy right now,' Kate said. 'We're getting ready to go out for breakfast.' She looked at Gemma, spread out in a star shape, her cheek pressed against the pillow, her mouth half-open as she snored lightly. 'May and Gem are by the door.'

May suppressed a snort of laughter. Kate glared at her.

'I only wanted to chat. I miss you.'

'Can we talk later?' she said. 'I've got to go. They're waiting. And we're hungry.'

'Will you call later?' he said.

'Sure.'

'You promise you'll call?'

'Of course,' she said. 'I promise.' It was a

promise she felt she would be justified in forgiving herself for breaking.

As she put the phone in its cradle, Gemma's eyes opened.

'Who was that?' she said, her voice little more than a croak.

'Phil,' Kate said. 'He tracked me down.'

Gemma frowned. 'Jesus,' she said. 'I know he's hurting, but he needs to get over it. And tracking you down like this is — well, it's kind of fucked up, Kate.'

'I know,' Kate said. 'But he means well. You know Phil, he's — '

'Don't make excuses for him,' Gemma said. 'He can't do this. And you'd think he'd know better, after what happened to Beth.'

There was a long pause. 'It's not like that,' Kate said. 'Beth was a totally different situation.'

'We didn't think so at first, though, did we?' Gemma said. 'And things might have worked out a hell of a lot better if we'd paid a bit more attention to how serious it was.'

'We were young,' May said. 'We didn't know any better.'

'We do now,' Gemma said. 'That's my point, and Phil needs to know he has to give this a rest.' She looked at Kate. 'Anyway, let's not argue. Forget Phil. Which is something you didn't seem to have any problem doing last night. Where *were* you, you dirty slapper?'

Kate reached down and picked up a handful of the clothes that Gemma had strewn around the room. She tossed them to her friend.

'Put these on and I'll tell you over breakfast,'

she said. 'And then let's go to the beach and enjoy the last few days of this holiday.'

7

She was back. Phil knew this because he had been waiting for this day to come the entire time she had been gone, had been thinking about her incessantly every minute of every day, had been hard-pressed not to call her on the hour, every hour, contenting himself with a few — well, maybe a few more than a few — phone calls each evening.

None of which she answered, until, desperate, he had tracked her down by calling nearly every hotel in Kalkan, a place which was, it seemed, littered with hotels. It wasn't very big, looking at it on Google Earth — which he had done at least three or four times every day in the stupid hope that he might see her, even though he was fully aware that Google Earth was not a live feed from a satellite and that the images he was looking at were months or years old — but, small size notwithstanding, there were a lot of hotels.

And all of them full of men looking for someone to have a summer fling with, perhaps a pretty woman in her mid-to-late twenties who'd recently broken up with her boyfriend and was emotional and vulnerable, and would easily fall for their cheesy lines.

Only once in the entire week had he heard her voice and it had been such a relief to know she was alive, to be in touch with her again, to be connected to her in however paltry a form, at least until she had hung up on him and then it had all been even worse than before.

Yes, it had been a long week, but now she was back. She. Was. Back. He'd tracked her flight on the Internet, watched the tiny plane crawl across the screen from Dalaman airport to Manchester airport, then, when it landed, gone online and checked the arrivals board just to be sure.

Of course, he was only sure that the plane had landed, not that she was on it. So, unable to sleep, he got on his bike — a cyclo-cross, designed to work both on and off-road, that he had bought second hand a few months back — and rode to her house — their house — at midnight (when he was pretty sure she'd be through Customs and back home). He used his bike as often as possible these days; riding it cleared his mind. He tended to stay off the roads, preferring the paths and snickets and alleys that connected most parts of the town, routes that most people didn't even know existed, leaving them quiet and unused, which was perfect for the solitude he craved.

As a cloud obscured the moon, he turned into the street their house was on, and there it was.

Her car. Parked outside the house. Proof, absolute proof, of her return.

And upstairs, a light on. Her — their — bedroom was at the front of the house. The house *he* had offered to move out of, even though *she* wanted to break up, an offer he now regretted. He'd hoped it would show her how unconcerned he was, how magnanimous, but all it meant in the end was that he was squatting at a friend's flat.

He stared up at the windows and, as he watched, her silhouette appeared behind the blinds that they had installed together.

Even though it was only a silhouette, the sight of her shocked him, and he gasped. She was safe. She was home. She was back.

And now he was going to fix this.

He was going to fix this, whatever it took.

8

Kate's alarm — a loud, old-fashioned bell sound that she had chosen on her phone as it was the only noise that could reliably wake her at six a.m. — was ringing. She opened her eyes. It took her a few seconds to remember where she was — back home, Monday morning, a week of work ahead.

The first day back from holiday was always a struggle. It was the contrast: the day before you'd been immersed in a free, technicolour life, doing new things, meeting new people, living life the way it should be lived. And then: a six a.m. alarm, and back to normality.

She stared at the ceiling. Her eyes felt swollen. She was very tired; much more than she would have been on a normal Monday. It was amazing how exhausting holidays were. Late nights, too much to drink, bad sleep (on one night in someone else's bed, which was a memory she was glad she could leave behind. What happens on holiday, stays on holiday, after all), and then, on the way back, a delayed flight which meant she had finally got home shortly after midnight.

And discovered that she didn't have her house key.

Before leaving for holiday she'd detached her house key from her key fob — on the grounds that she wouldn't need the back-door key, electronic pass for work, keys to her mum and

dad's house or any of the other things she had
attached to it — and then stashed it in a side
pocket of her bag and forgotten about it, in the
expectation that it would be there when she got
home.

Well, it wasn't. Under the dim glow of the
interior light in her car, she'd emptied her bag
onto the front seat and scrabbled around.

No key.

Then she'd unpacked her suitcase, spreading
the contents all over the inside of the car.

Nothing.

So she'd slammed the car door in frustration,
which had woken her neighbour, Carl, an
engineer in his fifties, who, on hearing the
commotion, came downstairs.

Need a hand? he said.

*I've lost my key. Left it in Turkey. It must
have fallen out of my bag somewhere.*

Oh. Want me to help you break in?

Can you do that?

*Sure. It's easy. All you have to do is tell me
which window you don't mind being broken and
we'll be away.*

Ten minutes later, she was in, with a broken
kitchen window and a promise from Carl that
he'd call a friend of his in the morning who
would be able to replace it.

So, all that, less than six hours' sleep, and now
back to work.

Back to the slow commute along the M56 into
Manchester, back to hours lost to the ridiculous
traffic, back to the panic when you saw the red
lights of the cars ahead as they braked and you

thought *Oh shit, what's happened? Don't let this be a delay, I want to get home and eat and read and go to bed.*

Back to the offices of her law firm; a solid, well-respected regional company that offered a good salary and career prospects in return for your life and soul. Back to her boss, Michaela, a forty-two-year-old woman who thought she should have done better than merely reaching the level that made her Kate's manager, especially since she had worked and worked and waited and waited to have kids and then found that she couldn't, that it was too late, that although there were articles and advice out there claiming that pregnancy and childbirth were options for women well into their forties, they weren't options for her.

And she resented Kate having already reached the rung below her, along with the obvious fact that she would rise further still, maybe making partner by her mid thirties, which would leave her with plenty of time to have a couple of kids and the life that Michaela thought should have been hers.

Back, in short, to the daily grind.

Kate swung her legs out of bed. She felt groggy, jet-lagged almost, which she supposed she was: her body clock had adjusted to late nights and lie-ins, and here she was, dragging herself out of bed hours earlier than she was now used to.

It was going to be a long, painful day.

She walked along the landing to the bathroom. Her feet were tanned, a white V splitting at her big toes and running up to her ankles tracing where the straps of her sandals had been. She smiled as she remembered walking through the markets in the sunshine, evading the traders who tried to get her and May and Gemma into their bazaar with the promise of cheap leather bags or real gold jewellery or — this was her favourite — the offer of genuine fake watches. She'd laughed out loud when the man, a young Turkish guy with wide eyes and an infectious smile, had stepped in front of them and gestured to his stall.

Come in, he said. *Only for a look. Best watches in Kalkan. Genuine fakes!*

And then he laughed, and they laughed, and went in. Gemma bought a Rolex — a real, honest to God, no messing genuine fake Rolex — for Matt. Kate would have got one for Phil, in a different life. There was a Tag Heuer that he would have loved, and she almost bought it, but no: it would have sent mixed signals, and she had enough to deal with where Phil was concerned already.

The shower took a few minutes to warm up. She wondered briefly whether the boiler was broken — *Have to get Phil to look at it*, she thought, then remembered that Phil was no longer an option for that kind of thing, so she'd have to call someone. She thought they — she — had a service contract, but Phil had dealt with it, so maybe she'd have to call him to find out, unless there was paperwork somewhere — in the kitchen drawer, maybe . . . Then the hot water came and she relegated the boiler service

43

contract to a mental note — that she would ignore — to check it later.

When she was done she switched off the shower and grabbed a towel. It was odd to emerge to a silent house. Phil was an early riser and, by the time she finished her shower, he was normally downstairs, dressed, with the radio on, so that she dried herself and put on her make-up to the sound of the *Today* programme, mostly, or sometimes Radio One, the smell of coffee wafting upstairs.

Not today. Today the house was silent and scent-free.

The holiday had been fun, a blur of movement and action and laughter with her friends. Apart from when Phil kept calling — which had stopped after the morning he'd called the hotel — it had been simple to forget the break-up and all the implications it had. And that had been exactly what she needed.

But now the holiday was over, and reality was about to hit. And the reality was that this was not going to be easy.

9

She was at her computer, a large coffee on her desk, not long after eight.

A couple of minutes later, her neighbour, Gary, an overweight father of three in his mid thirties, arrived. The office was open-plan, each person having a small desk — paperless, which was the new office policy — divided from whoever sat next to them by a low screen. There were booths scattered around the office where you could go if you needed to have a private conversation, or concentrate on something for a while, but generally speaking you were at your desk in full view of anyone who happened to be passing. Kate didn't mind it that much; she'd joined the workforce at a time when that kind of office arrangement was more or less the norm, but some of the older people hated it.

Gary was one of them. Prior to the move to open-plan, he had been the proud occupant of a small, windowless office which he had worked for years to obtain, and the loss of it still rankled. Kate suspected that he would have been less bothered by a pay cut than the loss of his office; there was something about the visible reduction in status that he found particularly hard to take.

He made up for it by swearing a lot. In the open-plan area everyone could hear, and it showed his younger colleagues how, even though he had been stripped of his office, he would not

45

be cowed by the management.

'Welcome back,' he said. 'Fucking traffic was abysmal as usual this morning.'

'Not too bad coming from my side,' Kate said. 'The normal slow-moving car park.'

'It was total shit coming from Glossop,' Gary said, shaking his head. 'Total fucking shit. Anyway, no bother. How was your holiday?'

'Great. Really good.' She would have said that if it had been a shocking disaster; it was how you responded in an office, especially to people who you didn't know outside of a professional setting. It was odd; she sat with Gary every day, heard him talk to his wife about the bills they had to pay for private schools, heard him arrange beery nights out with his friends, knew that he was a fan of Leeds Rhinos in rugby league and Sheffield Wednesday in football and hated Arsenal with a passion, but, for all that, she didn't know him at all. Despite the time they spent in close proximity to each other, they never shared more than pleasantries, general chit-chat. He didn't even know that she and Phil had broken up.

He probably didn't know they'd been together. She left her private life, as many of her colleagues did, at the door.

'Good week to be gone,' Gary said. 'It was mad. An audit blew up.' He puffed out his cheeks. 'I was in here all hours. Got home Friday and I was fucking whacked. Then I had to wake up early on Saturday to take the kids to some fucking party.'

'Hope it's calmer this week,' Kate said,

suppressing a smile at his horrendous swearing.

'Doubt it. Anyway, welcome back to the jungle.' He tapped his login details into his computer. 'I'm going to the canteen, get a bacon butty. You want anything?'

Kate nodded at her coffee. 'That'll do me. Thanks, though.'

She watched him walk off, his trousers loose and saggy around his buttocks, shirt partially untucked, shoulders round and slumped. Was that her future? Was this what life had to offer? Rotting away in an office, doing a job she hated, or, at best, found repetitive and boring?

That was what she feared. Maybe it was because she had just come back from holiday, but watching Gary walk away she thought, *I don't want to be like that. There has to be something more.*

There had to be. Surely she could do something she found more inspiring. Become a cider-maker or a pilot or a photographer.

And the thing was, it felt possible, now that she had broken up with Phil. With him, her life had been mapped out for her, a gentle progression from wife to mum to grandma. Now though, she could do what she wanted. She had some money saved up; she could go travelling for a year. Or two. Or three. Maybe go to Nepal, meet someone and stay there, or move to New Zealand to work on a sheep farm. Who knew what would happen? That was the beauty of it. No one knew. All she had to do was make the decision to go and then the world would change from this — she looked around at the rows of desks — to an endless series of possibilities. She could end up *anywhere*.

But before that, she had work to do, emails to read, contracts to review. She looked at her inbox. Six hundred and twenty-four emails. She almost groaned.

She was about to sort them by sender so she could read the ones from her boss first when her phone pinged. It was a text message from Gemma.

Check out the news.

She typed a reply.

What is it?

They found another body in Stockton Heath.

It took Kate a few seconds to understand what Gemma was getting at, then it clicked. There'd been another killing. Another murder.

There was a link in the text message. She tapped it with her finger and watched as the story came up.

The body of a woman was found this morning near Walton Reservoir, on the outskirts of the village of Stockton Heath. Police were called to the scene by a local resident who spotted something unusual when out running.

This is the second body of a young female to be found in the vicinity of Stockton

48

Heath. It follows the discovery ten days ago of Jenna Taylor, 27, not far from the location where the latest victim was found. Speculation is mounting that the two killings may be linked. When asked about the possibility that there was a serial killer at work, the police said it was too early to comment, but they would be pursuing all lines of inquiry.

A police spokesperson said that the woman was in her mid to late twenties, and named her as Audra Collins.

She blinked at the screen. She read the name again to be sure.
Audra Collins.
She *knew* Audra Collins.
She knew her because she knew everyone who was around her age and who had been at high school with her. That was how small towns worked.
But she also knew her because people had always said that Audra Collins could be her sister. *Or your secret twin,* they joked. *Proof of human cloning.*
May and Gemma had joked that the first victim — Jenna Taylor — looked like her. She was dead, and now Audra Collins — her secret twin, her clone — had joined her.
And the joke wasn't funny any more.
She picked up her mobile phone and scrolled to May's number. She was about to press call when a voice interrupted her.
'Welcome back.'

Kate looked up; it was Michaela, her boss. She put her phone down, screen to the desk. She always felt guilty when she was caught reading the news or sending texts at work.

'Hi,' she said. 'Just checking the news. Someone sent me something.'

'Oh? Anything interesting?' Michaela said.

'Did you hear about the body they found a week ago?' Kate said. 'Near Stockton Heath?'

Michaela nodded. 'Did they find the killer?'

'No. They found another body. Another woman in her twenties.'

Michaela's mouth opened. 'You're kidding? Is it the same person, do they think?'

'They don't know.' Kate raised an eyebrow. 'But it seems a hell of a coincidence if it isn't.' *Too much of a coincidence,* she thought, *especially since they look so similar.*

'Well,' Michaela said. 'I wouldn't be wandering around on your own, if I was you.'

'Right,' Kate said. 'That's what I need to hear when I'm newly single.'

'Speaking of that, how was your holiday?'

'Great.' She repeated the bland formula from earlier. 'Really great.'

'Good,' Michaela said. 'It was a busy week. Glad you're back. Are you free at ten? There's some stuff I need you to work on. We can meet in the conference room.'

The small talk was over. Michaela was back in business mode.

'Of course,' Kate said. 'See you then.'

10

At four p.m. — an hour or so before his normal departure time — Phil shut down his computer. He watched the screen go black, then put his laptop in his bag. He was leaving work early. An idea had come to him during the day. And it was a good one. An *excellent* one. It could not go wrong.

It went like this:

Kate had come home from holiday at midnight, after a week away, a week in which whatever food she had in her house would have gone off. OK, there might be some pasta and sauce and packets of soup and things like that, but there would not be any fresh stuff: no fruit, no vegetables, no bread, no milk, no cheese, no meat, no fish.

So he would take her some. Yes, they had broken up; yes, he knew that he was not handling it well; yes, she had made it clear that she wanted some distance between them, but this was different. This was merely a friendly, thoughtful gesture to help her transition from holiday to home. He'd knock on the front door, hand over a bag — or bags — and then, if she wanted him to, he'd leave. No problem.

Of course, if she saw that he was a standout guy, a caring, resourceful, loving partner and decided to ask him in to share the meal, then he would accept. As a friend. To provide some company; nothing more, nothing less.

And if they ended up having amazing, mind-blowing make-up sex, then that would be OK too.

Phil stopped himself following that train of thought. It was simultaneously too exciting and too upsetting for him to handle. He took a deep breath, and walked out to his blue Ford Mondeo.

Or his Ford Mundane-o, as her dad had called it. He was into cars and he always teased Phil for his choice. As Phil pointed out, it was practical and good value for money, and — above all — safe, which you would have thought would appeal to a father, but her dad had shaken his head and told him to get a Triumph Stag or something with soul. He knew he was only teasing him — Kate's dad teased him all the time — but Phil hated it. It had probably contributed to Kate dumping him. He felt his resentment rise.

No — enough of that. That was the past. For now, he had a job to do.

★ ★ ★

Kate was normally home around six thirty — Phil knew her routines well, since he had been part of them up until a few weeks ago — so he timed his arrival at about fifteen minutes after she returned. He parked behind her Mini — British Racing Green; her dad had insisted that she get that colour — picked up the two Sainsbury's shopping bags from the passenger

52

seat, and walked to the front door.

He knocked. He didn't want to use the bell; it was somehow too formal.

The door opened. And there she was.

Looking beautiful. Looking like Kate. She was barefoot. He glanced at her feet. They had tan lines from her flip-flops. They reminded him of the holiday they'd taken the year before in Mallorca. She'd had them then, as well as other tan lines in more intimate places. Despite her pale skin, Kate tanned heavily in the sun and he had a clear image of her white buttocks contrasting with the golden brown of her legs and lower back.

'Hi,' he said. 'Welcome home.'

She stared at him. She looked tired, her eyes a little red. 'Phil,' she said. 'Hi.'

'I brought you some provisions,' he said, and held out the shopping bags. 'I thought you might need some fresh food. You probably don't have anything in, coming back from holiday. This might help.'

She didn't take them. 'That's so sweet,' she said. 'But you didn't have to do it.'

'I wanted to. Got to keep your strength up!'

'For what?'

'I don't know,' he said. 'I just — I just said it.'

And I should have said nothing, he thought, *but I'm so fucking nervous, which is ridiculous, this is Kate.*

'How was the holiday?' he asked, his tone bright.

'It was good.'

'You didn't call me back that day.'

'We were busy. And I was enjoying myself, Phil. The point was to get away.'

'I know, but I'm your — ' He stopped himself. He'd been about to say 'boyfriend', a status which would have given him the right to expect a call from his girlfriend when she was on holiday, but that was no longer correct. 'I'm your friend,' he finished.

'I know. But I have lots of friends who I didn't call from holiday.'

'Right. So what did you do all week?'

'Hung out on the beach. Went out at night.' She shrugged. 'Usual holiday stuff.'

'Did you — did you meet anybody?'

'We met lots of people.'

'Right.' There was a long, awkward silence. They both knew what he was asking, and they both knew that she wouldn't answer. They both knew that it would be better if he didn't ask again, but they both knew he would.

'Did you meet any — you know — any guys?'

'Phil, if you're asking me whether I met any men, then the answer is yes. We met lots. If you're asking me whether I went out on dates with them or kissed them or did whatever, then the answer is that it's none of your business.'

'It sounds like you did.'

'Fine. Think what you like.'

This was not going well. He needed to get it back on track. He held the bags out to her. 'Are you going to take them?'

'I'm not sure, Phil. You don't need to feed me.'

He opened one of the bags and showed her the contents.

'Look,' he said. 'Smoked salmon. And crab pâté. And some white wine. Asparagus. A baguette.'

'Phil,' she said. 'I'm tired. I don't have the energy to make — '

He put the bag down and opened the other. 'Vegetables: carrots, potatoes . . . parsnips — your favourite. They're organic. And two steaks. Filet mignon. They'll be delicious.'

She folded her arms. 'Why *two* steaks, Phil?'

He stared at her, speechless.

'I thought this was something to welcome me back, to make sure I had food in the house?'

'It is.'

'Then why two steaks? I only need one.'

He blinked. He didn't need to answer the question. They both knew why there were two: one for each of them. Which meant that this wasn't a kind, selfless gesture, after all, but a desperate attempt to get back together with her.

He put the bags on the stone step. The bottle clinked.

'Do whatever you want,' he said. 'Sorry I tried to be helpful.'

'Don't guilt-trip me, Phil.'

He looked at her, at the woman he loved more than anything else in the world, and he realized that it might be over, after all, that this might be for real, that he might be losing — have lost — her for good.

That couldn't happen. Not under any circumstances. He had to get her back. Had to.

He turned and walked back to his car. Behind him, he heard the door shut. As he drove away, he saw that the bags were still outside.

11

Kate watched him leave from the window, saw him glance back at the bags on the front step.

It *was* a kind gesture — typical of him, in many ways. He was thoughtful and caring and she loved him, she did, but not enough. Not in the way she once had. And, more to the point, the more this went on, the more she lost respect for him. She understood that he was hurting — she was, too, she missed him — but he needed to accept it and move on.

And so she hadn't taken his bags of food; if she did, she worried that it would create an expectation on Phil's part that she owed him something. But now they were sitting on her front step. *This is stupid*, she thought, *there's no point wasting it. And I can't leave it outside, littering the street. It'll end up attracting foxes.*

She opened the door and picked up the bags. In the kitchen, she texted Phil.

> Sorry if I was short. I'm really tired. Thanks for the stuff — it's very kind.

Then she unpacked the bags, poured a glass of wine and switched on the television. It was the local news, and they were reporting on Audra Collins.

★   ★   ★

Kate hadn't seen much of Audra for a few years. She was a nurse, and, with her boyfriend, had a three-year-old daughter, so she wasn't out and about all that much.

God, her daughter. Kate had met her once. A sweet, blonde, curly-haired girl called Chrissie with large, soulful eyes and a quiet smile.

She would never see her mum again. She'd grow up knowing that her mum had been out running early one morning before her shift started, and had been killed — dragged into the bushes and strangled to death — by some sick bastard. She would learn from an early age that the world was not safe, that she could never be sure that someone would not reach out and grab her and put her life to an end like they'd done to the woman — who she would barely remember — who had brought her into this sick world.

The police were pursuing all lines of inquiry, and asked that if anyone had seen anything, however small, that might be of interest to them, they should come forward.

Which meant that they had no idea what was going on.

A reporter was on location at the reservoir, speaking to camera. She turned up the television so she could hear.

Tonight, people are left wondering whether these two brutal murders are linked. The police are not confirming this, yet, but it certainly seems to be a strong possibility, especially when the similarity in the way the

two women were killed is taken into consid-
eration. It is also notable that the victims
share some physical resemblances . . .

So the media had picked up on it too. It was
hard not to. On the screen there was a photo of
Jenna Taylor alongside one of Audra Collins.
They shared the same appearance: long, straight,
near-black hair, dark eyes, pretty. Slender build.
A slightly exotic, ethereal look.

Her grandma — who was from Youghal, in
County Cork — had called it the 'Irish look'.
She said it came from the old country.

She said Kate had it.

And looking at the photos of Jenna Taylor and
Audra Collins, they had it too.

Kate picked up her phone and called May. She
needed to find out what was going on. May's
fiancé, Gus, was a newly minted police
constable, and would have the inside scoop.

'Hey,' she said, when May picked up. 'I'm
watching the news. About the latest murder.'

'God, I know,' May said. 'It's horrendous. I
feel so sorry for Chrissie.'

'Do they have any idea who's behind it? Did
Gus hear anything?'

'He was telling me about it earlier. After the
first one, they thought it was the boyfriend — it
normally is — but he's off the hook now. He has
an alibi for this one.'

'Do the police think they're linked? Is this a
serial killer?'

'They're not saying so publicly. Gus said that
they don't like to start throwing around words

like 'serial killer' until they're absolutely sure, but privately they're working on the assumption that it's the same person. There were a lot of similarities between them.'

'Like what?'

'Both strangled. Gus said that there was a lot of bruising on the bodies, which suggests there was a high degree of violence. And they were both raped . . . ' May hesitated. 'Post-mortem.'

'Oh my God. You mean he had sex with their corpses?'

'Seems so. Sick bastard.'

Kate tried to clear the image from her mind. She sipped her wine. This kind of thing was both repellent and fascinating at the same time; she had the kind of morbid curiosity that she always had when there was some disaster in the news, only this time it was all the more intense — and came with a frisson of worry and fear — because it was right on her doorstep.

'If it *is* a serial killer,' she said. 'There might be more.'

'That's what they're worried about.' May paused. 'It's so fucking weird that there's someone out there right now who's raping and killing women of our age in our town. I mean, it could be anybody. It could be your neighbour, the barman, your boyfriend. You just don't know.'

'And the next victim could be anybody.'

'Not according to Gus. He — they assume it's a he — will have a pattern. A type that he goes after. There'll be some kind of thing that links them all.'

59

'Jesus, May,' she said, her phone to her ear. 'Don't say that. They both look like me. You know everyone always used to say that about Audra.'

May hesitated. 'She'd changed over the years,' she said. 'I don't think she looked so much like you now.'

'I saw the photo on TV, May. She's not changed at all.'

'Well,' May said, her hesitation a clear indication that she agreed. 'The first one wasn't that much like you.'

'May!' Kate said. 'It was you who said Jenna Taylor looked like me in the first place!'

'I know, but that was a — look, it's a coincidence, nothing more. You don't need to worry. Honestly.'

She was not convincing, and her discomfort was all the proof Kate needed that May did not think it was a coincidence at all, not for a minute. And, for that matter, neither did Kate.

Which meant she did need to worry.

'Holy shit,' Kate said. 'I don't think I'll be able to sleep tonight.' She was only half-joking. In fact, she wasn't joking at all. She would make sure that the door was locked before she went to bed — and thank God that Carl had got his friend to fix the kitchen window — although even so she doubted she'd get much sleep.

'You can come over here, if you like,' May said.

Kate hesitated. 'Thanks,' she said. 'I might take you up on that later. But for now, I'll stay here.'

'You're welcome anytime,' May said. 'But maybe you need to take some precautions. Gus bought me a personal alarm. And some cans of mace. You spray it in someone's face and it stings. Blinds them. He bought me a few, said it was a good idea to keep one in every bag I use, so I'll always have one. I'll bring some over. OK? I'll come over now.'

Kate thanked her and hung up. As she did, May's words rang in her ears.

He'll have a type, she'd said, and it seemed he did.

A type that Kate recognized.

She recognized it because she was it.

12

Thirty minutes later there was a knock on the door. Kate pushed the curtains aside and peered through the window: it was May. She let her in and they sat on the couch. May took a canister with a nozzle from her bag and passed it to Kate.

'Mace,' she said. 'Be careful with it. And there's this as well.' She reached in and pulled out an alarm that looked like a tiny megaphone. 'Rape alarm. The mace is not exactly legal, so don't tell anyone where it came from, but if either of us do end up spraying some serial killer with it, I doubt anyone will be bothered about that.'

Kate pushed the button on the alarm; she jumped back. The sound was deafening. She imagined using it, on a lonely, dark street, the sound echoing into nothing.

She wouldn't be on a lonely, dark street anytime soon. Ever, probably.

'You sure you don't want to stay with us?' May said. 'You're welcome, if you do. I can make up the spare bed.'

Kate shook her head, in part because she didn't want to put her friend to the trouble and in part because to run to her house would be to accept that this was real, and once she did that, what came next? Live with May for ever? Move back to her parents' house? No: she would stay in her home.

'I'll be fine,' she said.

★ ★ ★

She was, sort of. If waking up every hour at the slightest noise — the creak of a radiator, the pop of floorboards settling, the bark of a neighbour's dog — and then being unable to get back to sleep because of the adrenaline coursing through her body, was fine, then she was fine.

At work the next morning her eyes were puffy, dark circles underneath them.

'You OK?' Gary said, as he sipped his coffee. 'You look like me. Big night last night? Out giving it fucking large? Hitting the clubs?'

'No,' she said. 'I wish. Bad night's sleep, sadly.'

She sincerely wished that all she was dealing with was a hangover, and not the prospect of more sleepless, terrified nights. This was a bad time to be newly single. Trust her luck: the moment she broke up with Phil, someone started killing women who looked like her. There would be no boyfriend when she got home from work, no peck on the cheek, no enquires about how her day had been, no cuddling on the sofa, no shared bottle of wine followed by an early bedtime and leisurely sex. No comforting presence next to her in the bed at night.

Just silence, and insomnia, and a sense of worry, an unsettling feeling that she was vulnerable, and not only when she was home alone. On her way to work that morning she had found herself checking her rear-view mirror as she drove so she could make sure no one was following her. To be on the safe side, she was planning to stop at a supermarket in a different town on the way home. Paranoid, she knew, but she couldn't help it. Everyone was a potential threat; the world was no longer a safe place. It was going to be a long week.

★ ★ ★

And it was, but thankfully, as the week went on, the fear diminished. It didn't disappear, but normal life intruded and staked a claim on her attention. She, like most people, was a creature of habit. She had her routines: wake up, coffee, toast, upstairs to shower and brush teeth, dress. She did them in that order, every day. It meant she didn't have to think. She just did. It was easy, reassuring. Most people were like that: it was why, the first time someone stayed in a hotel they were unsettled; the next time, it was familiar, almost like home.

On Friday afternoon, she was wrapping up a meeting with a client. It had been a difficult few hours. The client had been sued for continuing to make a toaster despite having been given reports that it could catch fire and they were not happy with the work Kate and her colleagues had done. Michaela was there — probably enjoying Kate's discomfort — along with a woman, Claire, whom she had worked with before, and a man, Nate, who she had seen around, but not met. He was a contract specialist who had been drafted in to answer some specific questions.

The client had spent most of the meeting pointing out what they considered to be mistakes. At first Kate had gently tried to argue that she had done the best she could, given the circumstances — they were in the wrong and they were going to have to pay a large sum of money — but there was no point. They were upset and, rather than look at themselves, they were blaming their lawyer, and all Kate and her colleagues could do was to take it.

At the end of the meeting she headed for the coffee machine. She poured herself a cup of black coffee and leaned against the wall. She had not been looking forward to the weekend — she had no plans — but now she was glad it was Friday afternoon. Saturday and Sunday could take care of themselves; all she wanted now was to get out of here and go and have a drink.

'Tough meeting.' Nate appeared in the doorway. 'Not the most pleasant bunch.'

'I know,' Kate said. 'They were so unreasonable.'

'Ach,' Nate said. 'They were pissed off because they're going to lose. That's all.'

'I mean, what do they expect from us?' Kate said. 'We're lawyers, not miracle workers. They're in the wrong: nothing we can do will change that. If they want someone who can do that then they need to go to Hogwarts and see if Harry Potter wants to work for them when he leaves school.'

Nate laughed. He was thin, with high cheekbones and sharp features. He wore gold-rimmed, delicate glasses, and had an intense, searching gaze. 'You should have suggested that as a strategy.'

'Right. Michaela would have loved that.'

He nodded. 'You have a point. Perhaps better that you kept it to yourself.'

'It's a shitty case,' Kate said. 'How did you get roped in?'

'I asked if I could,' Nate said. 'I wanted to work on it.'

'Seriously?'

He smiled at her. 'Seriously.'

'Why?'

'Because it's interesting. And I've heard that you do good work.'

'I wouldn't get your hopes up,' she said. 'What I do is pretty bog-standard stuff, I'm afraid.'

'Not what I heard.'

She rolled her eyes. She wasn't sure Nate was telling the whole truth, but still, it was flattering to hear that she had a good reputation. Kate blew out her cheeks. 'Well, it's been quite a week. And that was the perfect end.'

Nate nodded at the coffee mug in her hands. 'Sounds like you could do with something stronger.'

'You can say that again.'

'Sounds like you could do with something stronger,' he said, then laughed. 'Sorry, couldn't help it. I'm famous for my crap jokes.'

'With good reason, it seems,' Kate said. 'I'm not sure what's worse — that client or your sense of humour.'

'You want to get out of here? Go for a drink?'

66

He looked at his watch. 'It's pretty much clocking-off time.'

Kate hesitated. Was he asking her out on a date? It was a long time since she'd been single, and the etiquette of dating — even of what passed for a date — was a mystery to her. Could you go out innocently with a colleague you barely knew? Or was there more to it?

She glanced at his hand. No wedding ring. Not that she was interested. He was not her type.

She shrugged.

'Why not?' she said. 'Where do you have in mind?'

★ ★ ★

They went to a tapas bar in a converted cellar under a railway station. They ordered some chorizo, a smoked mackerel paste of some kind and a plate of Spanish cheeses, none of which she knew the name of. She had a glass of Ribera del Duero; he had two bottles of Spanish beer. He was — when he was not indulging his passion for crap jokes — witty and engaging and good company, but she knew immediately that it was going nowhere, at least not in a romantic sense. Although she liked him and would have happily done it again some other Friday, there was no spark, no frisson of excitement. She didn't have any sense of being intrigued by him, of wanting to know him better, of wanting to impress him, to make him like her.

But still, it was fun, and great to get out. She couldn't see herself with Nate, but she could see herself in places like this with *other* people.

She looked back at him. He was staring at her; he blinked, caught out, and a pink flush spread up from under his collar. There was an awkward silence. For a moment she wondered whether he was going to comment on it, but then he smiled, although the smile did not quite reach his eyes. They looked a little sheepish; nervous, even.

'Another drink?' he said.

She shook her head. 'No. I'm driving. Aren't you?'

'Nope. I bike in on Fridays.'

'Oh? Is that new?'

He patted his stomach. 'Need to keep an eye on this. So I got myself a bike and some tight shorts.'

'I don't know what you're worried about,' Kate said. 'You're hardly carrying a lot of weight.'

'I don't know,' he said. 'All the sitting around in meetings, at the computer — it's starting to bother me. It might be as much in my mind as anything else, but still — I want to nip it in the bud.'

'Well,' Kate said. 'I'm impressed. Where is it you live?'

'Sale. Not too far.'

Kate looked at her phone. She was planning to curl up in front of the TV with a glass of wine. 'I'd better be going. Thanks. This was fun.'

She signalled the waiter. When he brought the bill. Kate reached for her bag.

He put his hand over the bill. 'I'll get it.'

She shook her head. 'Thanks, but I'd prefer to split it.'

'OK,' he said. 'Your call.'

She opened her bag and took out her purse. As she did, the canister of mace fell out onto the table.

Nate looked at it. 'Is that the stuff you spray on people?' he said. 'It would have come in handy today. You could have used it on the clients. That would have shut them up.'

'I wish I'd thought of it.'

He picked it up. 'Why do you have it? Are you worried about something?'

'I live in Stockton Heath.'

'Oh,' he said. 'I see.'

'I've got an alarm too.' She tapped her fingers against the table. 'Although — touch wood — I hope I'll never need them.'

'Yeah,' he said. 'Let's hope so. Are you parked at the office? I'll walk you back.'

13

She was on the M56 near the airport when Gemma called. She answered on her hands-free.

'Hi,' Gemma said. 'Are you in the car?'

'Coming back from work.'

'At this time! It's nearly nine p.m. It's Friday night, for God's sake. You need to take it easy.'

Kate laughed. 'I went out for a drink after work.'

'Oh? With who?'

'Nate.'

'Who's Nate?' she said. 'Someone special?'

'No. Just a colleague.'

'But you went out for a drink with him.'

'Yes,' Kate said. 'I did! He asked and I thought, why not? And it was only a drink.'

'It's *never* only a drink.'

'OK,' Kate said. 'I admit it. When he asked I did wonder if there might be something there, but there isn't. He's lovely, but he's not my type. Apart from anything else he tells awful, goofy jokes. Sweet, but awful.'

'Fine,' Gemma said. 'I'll believe you. Millions wouldn't, but I will. So, have you got plans for the weekend?'

'I'm getting an early night tonight,' Kate said. 'I'm exhausted. And I haven't thought beyond that.'

'Want to get together tomorrow? Matt's going to Anfield — a friend of his got some tickets for

70

the game — and they'll be going out in Liverpool afterwards.'

'Sure,' Kate said. 'I was thinking of going to the Trafford Centre. I need an autumn coat.'

'And then we could go out. Maybe eat in the Thai place in the village?'

'Sounds great. I'll pick you up? Three?'

Arrangements made, she hung up, and pulled off the motorway onto the A49. Ten minutes to home, a bath, pour that glass of wine, then bed and sleep, a sleep that would not be interrupted by a six a.m. alarm, a sleep that would leave her fresh and invigorated and restored.

Half a mile from her house she turned off the main road onto a street lined with red-brick Victorian terraced houses. A left, a right, a left and she'd be home.

A car pulled out from one of the narrow alleys that ran behind the warren of terraced houses. It was moving quickly and, within a second or two, it was only feet from her rear bumper. She looked in the rear-view mirror and, before she could make out the driver's face, the high beams came on.

They were dazzling; the reflections from the wing-mirrors blinded her and she narrowed her eyes to shield them from the brightness.

She sounded her horn; the car behind came closer.

Her first thought was that she had done something wrong, cut the guy up — she assumed it was a guy — or was driving too slowly, or had committed some other offence, but she hadn't, she knew she hadn't. He'd pulled out behind

71

her, at speed, and quite deliberately.

And now he was trying to intimidate her. It was almost as though he had been waiting for her to pass so he could follow her, lights blazing, to her house.

She felt the first fluttering of panic, and then, shortly afterwards, the real thing: heart-racing, palms sweaty, mind struggling to focus.

It was him. The killer. No one else would be waiting for her like this. She was the next victim. She scrabbled in her bag for the alarm. If he ran her off the road, she would open the door and press it as hard as she could.

Had he done this to the other victims, too? Was this part of his sick routine? She knew from TV shows and films and books that these kinds of people did things in a certain way, a way that allowed them to reap the full pleasure they got from their twisted activities.

She was approaching her street, but she couldn't go home. Even in the panic, she knew that. She couldn't lead him straight to her door.

She carried on past her street, then turned towards the village centre.

Where there were people. Pubs. Restaurants.

And a police station.

She wasn't going to take this. She wasn't about to let this bastard — serial killer or drunk fool or casual bully — intimidate her. The station would be closed at this time, but there would be cops around, policing the village. She'd park right outside it and go and find one.

The car behind her flashed its lights, on and off, on and off. She tried to make out what type of car it was, but it was impossible to see through the dazzle of the high beams. She turned right, back onto the main road. For a moment she thought about accelerating, about putting some distance between her and the other car, but she decided not to. She was not going to show fear. She was going to drive at a steady, measured pace to a safe location.

But God, she was frightened. It was all she could do to stop herself dissolving into a tearful, gibbering wreck.

And then, the lights went out. She looked in the rear-view mirror. The car — a dark saloon of some description — was turning into a residential street, and then it was gone.

* * *

She parked by the police station — closed, as she had thought — and dialled 999. The operator picked up and Kate asked for the police.

'I've been followed,' she said, when the dispatcher came on the line. 'In my car.'

'Where are you now, madam?' asked the dispatcher, a woman with a neutral BBC accent.

'I'm outside the police station in Stockton Heath,' Kate said.

'And can you explain what happened?'

Kate took her through it: the car pulling out, dazzling her with its high beams, and then leaving her alone when she headed for the village.

'I think he was hoping I'd go home,' she said. 'So he could follow me there. I live alone,' she added.

'You did the right thing not to return to your residence,' the dispatcher said. 'Are you going home now?'

'I think so. Should I?'

'That's up to you. But if you do plan to, let me know. We'll send an officer round to take a statement. They'll be with you shortly.'

'Like five minutes?'

'Maybe thirty minutes,' the dispatcher said. 'And try not to worry. I'm sure it will all be fine.'

'Thanks,' Kate said. 'I'll meet them there.' She recited her address, and hung up.

14

She had driven the route from the village to the house hundreds — maybe thousands — of times, but it had never felt like it did this time. It looked the same, but every turning, every house, every alley was now a threat, a possible hiding place for a faceless man who wanted to kill her. As she passed each one she glanced at it, waiting for a car to pull out.

None did.

She parked outside the house. Fortunately, the spot right outside her front door was free so she did not have to walk far from the car to the house. She opened the door and stepped onto the pavement.

And realized someone was watching her.

She didn't know how she knew, but she knew. She'd read once that the feeling you got when you were being watched or followed was the result of your subconscious picking up clues that your conscious mind didn't notice. It felt like it was a sixth sense, a paranormal or telepathic ability, but it wasn't. It was simply that the mind took in a great deal more information than it could process at the conscious level and, when some of that information represented a threat, it made itself known by creating the uneasy feeling of a prickle on the back of the neck that said *You are not alone.*

Whatever her subconscious had noticed was at

the end of the street. There was a large yew tree — some said that it meant there had once been a graveyard there — at the corner, under which there was a bench. It was mossy now, and rotten, so nobody ever sat on it, but there was someone on it now, hiding in the shadows.

She turned and looked. It was hard to make out anything specific, but she was sure that there was a patch of darkness that was darker than the rest, a kind of stillness under the tree which was different from what surrounded it.

'Who's there?' she shouted. 'Who are you?'

There was no answer. 'Leave me alone!' she shouted. 'I don't know what you want, but leave me alone!'

The door to the house next door opened. Carl stood there, framed in the light.

'You OK?' he said. 'What's all the shouting about?'

The relief at seeing him, at not being alone, left her dizzy.

'There's someone out here,' she said, her voice wavering. 'Under the tree. They've been following me.'

'You sure?'

'Totally sure. They were driving close to me, flashing their lights. And now they're stalking me.'

Carl gave her a sceptical look, then shrugged.

'All right,' he said. 'I'll go and check it out.'

He walked outside. As he did, there was a metallic noise from under the tree, then, seconds later, a hooded figure appeared, pushing a bike. It jumped on and rode away, legs pumping.

'Bloody hell,' Carl said. 'You were right.'

★ ★ ★

Ten minutes later the police — two male officers, one in his twenties, the other late thirties — were sitting in her front room, taking notes as she told them what had happened. Carl was home; he'd sat with her until they arrived, then left her to it. They were going to talk to him afterwards and get his account.

'It sounds very unusual,' the older one said, when Kate had finished. 'Although we don't know at this point that the two episodes are linked. It could have been nothing more than an aggressive driver, and maybe a teenager hiding away to have a smoke. You can't be sure it was the same person both times.'

'I know,' Kate said, totally convinced that it was the same person. 'But what if it is? What if it's the man who's killed two young women? If there's a serial killer out there, I think I need to bear that in mind.'

'It's not officially a serial killer,' the police officer said. 'We're still not sure about that.'

'Serial killer or not, two women are dead,' Kate said. 'Which is enough for me. I don't want to be next.'

'Of course,' the younger cop said. 'We understand that, madam.'

The older officer got to his feet. 'I think we have all we need,' he said. 'There isn't all that much we can do, I'm afraid. We'll circulate the details of both incidents to see if they match any others. And I'm pretty sure that a detective is going to want to talk to you about what happened, in case it does have any bearing on the murder investigations. Do you have a number they could call? Perhaps a mobile?'

Kate gave her number. 'Who should I expect to call? So I know it's the real thing?'

'Detective Inspector Wynne,' the older cop said. 'It'll probably be her. And if there's anywhere you can go tonight — a friend, maybe — you might want to think about doing that. Just in case. It'll be nice to have company, especially if you're a bit shaken up.'

'My parents,' Kate said. 'I'll go to them.'

'Good idea,' the officer said. 'We'll be in touch if anything comes up, Ms Armstrong.'

Kate showed them to the door. Then she picked up her car keys. There was no way she was staying alone in the house for the night, no way.

15

He couldn't believe he'd been seen.

He was sure that he was invisible under the tree; he'd looked from every angle before choosing it as his hiding place, but somehow she'd known he was there.

He'd hoped that she would go inside, so he could sneak away, but then Carl — his old neighbour — had come out and he'd had no choice but to flee.

Which meant that he would no longer be able to use the tree if he wanted to watch what his ex-girlfriend was up to. He'd have to find another place to hide, but for the moment he couldn't think where.

He'd find somewhere, though, if he had to.

He biked along the canal towpath in the direction of the London Bridge pub. He needed a beer to calm his nerves, and maybe a cigarette. It had been years since he'd smoked, but all of a sudden the craving was back.

He had to get a grip of himself. He was falling apart: all day long all he could think of was Kate. He had a constant low-level nausea, a sinking sensation in his stomach that was part anxiety and part disbelief that this was happening. Even worse was the feeling of lacking control; sometimes he felt like he wasn't himself, that he wasn't there, that it wasn't him making decisions.

Like that evening. He'd decided to go and see her after work. He needed to explain what he was going through, not in a desperate, please-have-me-back way, but so that she would know how bad this was for him.

She *needed* to know: if this was a temporary thing, a break while she lived her life a little, then she had to understand the price he was paying for that break. If it was permanent, then so be it. But they needed to talk.

Except she wasn't there. And then he started to wonder where she was. Out with someone else? Another man? He couldn't bear the thought of that, couldn't accept it. He *had* to know, and in the end, like an addict with his dope, that need took over.

So he ended up hiding under the tree, waiting for her to come home, imagining her walking down the street with her arm around another man, kissing him on the front step, then unlocking the door and going into the house.

He was frantic the entire time, drumming his fingers on his knees, tapping his shoes on the ground, jiggling his legs, standing up and sitting down. If it wasn't for the fact that he was hiding, he would have paced the street.

And then she came, alone, and he was caught out, and he fled.

Now it was over, he couldn't believe he'd done it. Couldn't believe that he'd acted so crazily. It scared him; the whole thing felt like a dream, like it was a different person. He thought about the time he'd spent under the tree. It was almost like he'd been watching it all unfold, an observer, but now, afterwards, he knew this was not the case. He had done it. He shuddered. It was very troubling.

He walked into the pub and stood at the bar. The pub was warm and busy with the Friday-night crowd. He waited his turn. He ordered a pint of strong bitter and a double whisky, Bells. He felt faint, and dizzy.

The barman looked at him. 'You all right, mate?'

'Yeah,' Phil said. 'I think so.'

'You *think* so? You look a bit pale.'

'I had a rough day.'

'All right. Well, let me know if you need anything.'

He paid and took his drinks to a table in the corner. He drank the whisky in one swallow, then swigged the beer.

Even now, he couldn't stop the thoughts coming. Where had she been? Was she planning on going out tonight? Alone? He wanted to go and see, go and knock on her door and lay himself at her feet, pour out everything he was going through, throw himself on her mercy.

It wouldn't work. He needed to pull himself together.

But he couldn't. He knew that she was there, that she was in the house, that she was available. All he had to do was go and knock on the door and he'd be with her. And knowing that — well, it was impossible to resist. He *had* to go and see her. It didn't matter if it was a good idea or a terrible idea. He had to do it.

He finished the last of the beer and got to his

feet. His legs felt weak, drained. No wonder; he'd barely eaten all week. Most of his calories had come from the wine he'd been drinking himself to sleep with every night.

He got on his bike and retraced the route to their — Kate's, he had to stop thinking of it as theirs — house. He felt a mounting excitement: for the first time in days he felt almost happy. He was going to see her, face to face. They could sort this out, once and for all.

A few minutes later, he turned into her street, and stopped dead.

There was a police car outside the house.

She'd called the cops. What had she done that for? Because he'd been under the tree? It was a bit of an overreaction, surely. Whatever — he couldn't go there now.

As he watched, the door opened and two cops came out. He turned and pedalled back towards the pub. The last thing he needed was to be spotted again. He shook his head. Seeing the police at the house brought things into focus: this wasn't a game.

He had to stop this. He absolutely had to stop this.

The only problem was that he wasn't sure he could.

16

Her parents, of course, overreacted.

'Move in with us,' her mum said. 'Don't go back to that house. You mustn't go back there. It's not safe.'

'It's perfectly safe,' Kate said, her teenage self bridling at her mum's attempt to limit her freedom, to suggest that she couldn't take care of herself.

'Then why are you here?' her dad said. 'Your mum has a point, Kate.'

'I need to stay tonight,' Kate said. 'That's all.'

Her dad didn't reply, which was what he did when he didn't agree but didn't want to say so and risk being accused — as he often had been — of imposing his views on everyone else. He was a man of strong opinions, and at some point had realized that one of his more unattractive traits was his inability to change them. In an attempt to mitigate this, he had developed the strategy of remaining silent when he disagreed with someone, which, in many ways was worse. Kate had been on the receiving end many times. She remembered when she had declared that she was planning to buy her Mini, a plan that required getting a car loan.

You should never borrow to buy something, unless it's a house, her dad said.

Dad, it's fine. Everyone does it. I can afford the payments.

No response. Not a *Well, I'm sure you'll be OK, no doubt you've thought it through.* Just silence, which — ironically, since it was an attempt to say nothing — said a great deal. It said *You're totally and utterly wrong and probably not even functionally intelligent, but it's your funeral and don't come crying to me when it all goes to hell in a handbasket.*

Which was what the silent treatment she was now getting meant. Fortunately, her mum had no such inhibition about expressing an opinion.

'No,' she said. 'You're staying here. And that's it.'

'We'll talk more tomorrow,' Kate said. 'But I'll probably get Gemma to stay with me, or something like that.'

Her mum shook her head. 'Under no circ — '

'Mum!' Kate said. 'Please!'

'I'm only trying to do what's best for you, darling.'

'I know, and I'm grateful. But can we discuss this later? I'm tired. I think I'm going to go to bed.'

'Do you want something to eat?' her mum said, which was her default question.

'A drink?' her dad said, which was his default question. 'There's white in the fridge. I think there's a red open as well.'

'No thanks,' she said. 'I think I'll have a bath, then bed.'

★ ★ ★

Lying in the bath, she googled serial killers. There was a *lot* of material out there on them. She scanned it, clicking between websites. It varied, but there were some key themes, one of which she found particularly troubling.

There was, a lot of experts claimed, a strong ritualistic element in the activities of most serial killers. Often they were repeating the same murder over and over, each time trying to perfect it, each time getting a greater and greater thrill from it.

There were other themes that emerged: many serial killers liked to engage in a game of cat-and-mouse with law enforcement agencies — often trying to insert themselves into the investigation in some way — in an attempt to prove their superior intelligence; the level of violence towards the victims often increased as the killer's confidence grew; the serial killer would purge the desire to kill before it started to build again to the point where they needed release.

But the one that stuck with her was the presence of ritual.

Was the appearance of the victims part of the ritual in this case? She wasn't sure, but it certainly seemed possible.

Which gave her an idea. A way to put a stop to all this.

★ ★ ★

The next morning she made some phone calls. Most places were busy, but eventually she found one that had an open slot.

'Mum,' she called, sipping the last of her tea. 'I'm just popping out. I'll be back for lunch.'

Her mum came into the kitchen.

'Where are you going?'

'Out. And then at three I'm meeting Gem to go to the Trafford Centre.'

'But where are you going now?'

She didn't want to tell her mum. She couldn't face the conversation, didn't want to have to explain what she was doing and then listen to her mum's objections. It was easier to do it and deal with the fallout later.

Gemma had a saying: *Beg forgiveness, don't ask permission.* Kate thought it applied here.

'Out. Maybe go grab a coffee somewhere. But mainly anything to get out of the house.'

'Go *and* grab,' her mum said. 'Not *go grab.* You aren't American, darling. I know you like to watch those television shows, but you don't need to speak like them.'

God, her mother annoyed her sometimes.

'And anyway,' her mum continued, her expression sceptical. 'You had a cup of tea five minutes ago.'

'Mum! I'm old enough to go out for a coffee!'

'I'll come with you. I could do with an outing.'

'Mum, please. I'm only popping out. OK?'

Her mum shrugged, evidently not believing a word she said. 'See you at lunch, then.'

★   ★   ★

She was back shortly after midday. Her dad was sitting in the living room, watching the news. She walked in and stood, waiting for his reaction. He studied her before he spoke.

'Bloody hell,' he said. 'Bloody hell.' He called into the kitchen. 'Margaret, come and see your daughter.'

Her mum appeared in the door frame. She blinked a few times, then smiled.

'Gosh,' she said. 'That's quite a change.'

17

It was. Kate had explained what she wanted to the hairdresser; he had asked if she was sure, absolutely sure, and she said yes, she was. So he went ahead. He cut her long, black hair into a close-cropped fuzz, which he dyed a dark red.

She hated it. Hated seeing her hair on the floor, hated how big her head looked, hated seeing herself shorn in this way. She was not vain, but she had always been proud of her hair. She had been told a million times that it was *gorgeous* and *lovely* and the compliments had stuck. Some portion of her self-esteem was wrapped up in her hair, and now it was gone. But she had a good reason for having done this, and, when it was safe to do so, she could always grow it back.

On her way home she went to a costume shop. It was a place she'd used before, when she and Phil had gone to a Halloween party in fancy dress. That time she'd bought bright red contact lenses; this time, she got green ones.

With them in she looked nothing like herself. More importantly, she looked nothing like Jenna Taylor or Audra Collins.

⋆　⋆　⋆

Gemma's reaction was far less muted than her parents' had been. She screamed, clapped her hand over her mouth, then burst into laughter.

'Oh. My. God!' she said. 'What have you done?'

'That's a nice reaction,' Kate said. 'Don't you like it?'

'I dunno,' Gemma said. 'I suppose so. It's — well, it's a pretty big change, Kate. It's not your usual style. It's not what *you* do. I mean, it's kind of like if Kate Middleton did it. A bit of a surprise.'

'I know,' Kate said. 'And I hate it. Not as much as I did this afternoon — I suppose it's growing on me . . . '

'Literally,' Gemma said. 'Although it's still got some growing to do.'

' . . . But I have my reasons.' She took out her phone and typed a search into Google. A picture of the two murdered women came up. 'They look like me,' she said, handing her phone to her friend. 'Remember you guys teasing me about that? We laughed, but it's not so funny now.'

Gemma studied it for a second or two. When she looked at Kate she was pale.

'They don't look like you now,' she said.

'Right,' Kate said. 'And it's going to stay that way until this is over.'

★   ★   ★

They spent the afternoon at the Trafford Centre. Kate had never noticed before, but it was a place that, between the glass shopfronts and the mirrors inside the shops, was full of reflections. She saw herself everywhere, saw this stranger with the short, red hair and green eyes walking side by side with the familiar form of her friend, and each time was surprised anew at the realization that it was her.

It was interesting to see how the shop assistants treated her. When they suggested clothes for her they were different to the clothes she was used to being offered: more urban, more punk, more edgy.

She wasn't quite ready to embrace her new style fully yet, not least because those scruffy-looking punk clothes came at designer prices. It cost as much to dress down as to dress up.

She was glad, though, that they saw her that way. It meant that the transformation had been a success. Whatever the type was that the killer was targeting, she no longer fit it.

★   ★   ★

That evening they went out for dinner, and then for a drink at a wine bar. Gemma had agreed to stay over, and they had drunk a bottle of wine with their meal. They were now drinking gin and tonics, and Kate was feeling the effects.

It was a nice feeling, though. Relaxing and warm. A great way to end a difficult week.

'Well,' Gemma said. 'I'm starting to get used to your new look. And I have to say, I kind of like it.'

'You're only saying that,' Kate replied. 'And there's no need. This is temporary. You don't have to make me feel good about it.'

'I'm not, I promise. It's cool. And you're so

90

pretty that you can get away with it. Especially with those green eyes. I might get some myself.' She sipped her drink; it was getting low. 'One more?'

'Why not?' Kate stood up. 'It's my round. And I need the loo.'

In the Ladies she used the toilet, then, after washing her hands, took a small bottle of eye drops from her purse. The contact lenses were irritating her eyes. She wasn't used to wearing them and she was looking forward to taking them out when she got home.

She stared at herself in the mirror. It was like looking at a different person. She smiled, and headed to the bar.

As she waited her turn, someone bumped into her back.

'Sorry,' a voice said. 'Excuse me.'

The voice was familiar, and she turned round. It took her a moment to realize who it was.

It was Mike, the guy from Turkey.

'Sorry about that,' he said. 'It's a bit of a tight squeeze.'

She grinned; it was clear he didn't recognize her, which was exactly what she wanted. 'That's fine,' she said. 'No problems.' Then she added: 'Mike.'

He paused. 'Do I know you?' he said. He stared at her, then his mouth opened. 'No way,' he said. 'It's you! It's Kate?'

It was half-question, half-exclamation.

'That's right,' she said. 'How've you been?'

'Great,' he said. 'Same as usual. Nothing new.' He gestured at her hair. 'Can't say the same for you. It looks great, by the way. You look great.'

'Thanks, but I didn't do it for looks.' The wine and the gin and tonic were making her more loose-lipped than usual. 'I did it for tactical reasons.'

'Oh? Like what? You joining the SAS?'

She laughed. 'No, not exactly. It's kind of a disguise.'

'It's a pretty good one. Can I ask why?'

She took out her phone and showed him the picture she'd showed to Gemma earlier.

'Wow,' he said. 'I see. Good idea. It's a bonus that it looks pretty awesome too.'

'That's kind of you to say. Anyway, what are you doing here?'

He pointed to a group of men at the end of the bar. 'Cricket club. I used to play and I came to watch a game today. Been having a few beers with the boys.' He looked at his watch. 'But I have to go.'

'Hot date?' She was surprised at her forwardness; maybe she'd think again about another drink.

'Something like that.'

She was intrigued to find that she was — a little — jealous.

'Well,' she said. 'Enjoy. And I'll maybe see you around?'

'Yeah,' he said. 'See you around.'

★ ★ ★

When she got back to the table, Gemma gave her a knowing look. 'Was that who I think it was?'

'Who do you think it was?'

'The guy? From Kalkan? What was his name?'

'Mike. And yes, it was. And guess what? He didn't recognize me.'

'He's kind of cute. In an older way.' She raised an eyebrow. 'And you obviously thought so when we were on holiday.'

'He's OK. But I'm not interested. Not at the moment.'

'At the moment,' Gemma said.

'Ever,' Kate replied, although she wasn't sure that she meant it.

18

Gemma gestured around the pub.

'It's so weird,' she said. 'Look. This place is full of people talking, drinking, falling in love. There are probably people meeting each other tonight who'll get married. Others are having affairs. It's full of life and warmth and fun . . . ' She paused and leaned forward. 'And any one of these people could be a serial killer. It makes you think, doesn't it?'

'It makes me sick,' Kate said.

'I mean, it could be *anyone*,' Gemma said. 'It doesn't have to be some oddball loner. It could be someone's husband, or father, or a teacher or a judge. You have no way of knowing.'

That was the reason serial killers were so fascinating, Kate thought. An ordinary killer — if there was such a thing — was easily explained, banal almost. It was a matter of normal emotions or situations that got out of hand. Someone screwed his wife and a husband got jealous; a robbery went wrong; a brother wanted all of an inheritance to himself. Grubby human life, writ large: jealousy, lust, greed.

And then there was gangland stuff, revenge killings, assassinations. That was more interesting, but it was a different world. It didn't spill over into most people's lives.

Not so with a serial killer. They were there, amongst us, monsters in our midst, hidden in plain sight. They were one of us, but also separate, and we could be their next victim. It was both terrifying and utterly compelling.

'It might be him,' Gemma said, pointing to a tall man with long, wavy red hair who was drinking alone at the bar. 'Maybe he's angry at the world for teasing him about his hair colour.'

Kate knew that her friend was joking, but she felt suddenly uneasy. It really was the case that one of these people could have killed Jenna Taylor and Audra Collins, and the thought made her want to get out of there.

'Let's go,' she said. 'I've got a bottle of wine at home — Phil brought it round the day we got back from holiday — we can drink that.'

Gemma shrugged. 'Sounds good to me.'

★   ★   ★

'So what are you going to do?' Gemma said. 'Are you looking for a new boyfriend?'

'I don't think so,' Kate said. She sipped her wine, then balanced the glass on the arm of the couch. 'I don't want anything serious. Maybe date a bit. Meet some people. See what happens. But I don't want to go straight into another relationship. I've been with Phil for over ten years.' She shook her head. 'More than a *decade*. It's hard to believe. It'll be nice to be single for a while.'

'Do you miss him?'

'Yeah. Sometimes a lot, but that's inevitable, I think. The weird thing is that sometimes I don't miss him at all. I feel the opposite: I'm glad we

95

broke up. I feel almost like I had a narrow escape, like I was blindly following a path without ever considering any other options. I could have been making a terrible mistake without even knowing it. At least now I'll find out.'

'And you can always go back to him.'

'You know, that's what I thought, but I don't think I would. It's strange: I can hardly picture us together now.'

'It's funny how that happens,' Gemma said. 'My mum and dad were together for twenty-five years before they got separated. For a month or so I hoped they'd get back together, but pretty soon it was obvious that they wouldn't. They were so different. I stopped wondering whether they'd get back together and started wondering how they'd ever got together in the first place.'

'That's kind of how I feel.'

Gemma grinned. 'Then it looks like you are ready to start dating,' she said. 'You should try an Internet dating site. Let's set up a profile.'

'No. I don't need that right now.'

'Why not? It can't do any harm. You can check it out, then, when the time comes, you'll know what to do. And you don't have to accept any invitations. Come on. It'll be fun.'

'I don't think so,' Kate said.

'What's the harm? And you never know, you might meet your dream man. A sensitive, caring dolphin trainer. Or a rugged fireman.'

'I doubt it.'

'Then find out. And I won't take no for an answer.'

She wouldn't. Gemma was, if nothing else, persistent. They had all learned over the years that once she had an idea she would never give it up. It was why they had ended up stuck in the snow on Snake Pass one New Year's Eve: Gemma had heard that there was some nightclub in Sheffield that they absolutely *had* to go to. Never mind the weather, never mind the distance, never mind the old Mini Metro that she drove. They were going to that nightclub. So go they did. Except they never actually got there, instead spending the evening waiting for a tow truck to come and rescue them.

And now she had that look in her eyes again.

'Fine,' Kate said. 'I'll try it.'

19

Phil stood in the kitchen, filling two wineglasses — one for himself, one for Michelle — and wondered how the hell he'd let himself get into this situation.

It had started on Friday night, after he got back from staking out Kate's house. He was alone — Andy was away at his brother's house in Lancaster — and feeling sorry for himself, so he'd called Michelle. He'd also had a large portion of a bottle of malt whisky that his sister had bought for his last birthday — a twelve-year-old Macallan — before he did so, which, looking back was a larger part of the reason for the call. Until recently, he hadn't been much of a drinker; his father had been more than partial to a drink, a fact which had contributed to his seemingly unending anger. He had taken out his frustration on their mother, at first by belittling her with his words and then, when that wasn't enough, by bringing her down to his level with his fists.

Phil heard it many times, heard the thuds as his father threw his wife around the living room, heard her sobs when he stomped off to bed or to the drinks cabinet for some more anaesthetic. He heard it, but it was never spoken about. It was as though his mum thought that, by taking the punishment but not acknowledging it, the damage done would only be to her, and not to her family.

It was a vain hope, and it ended one day when Phil walked into the bathroom as she was getting out of the shower.

Her stomach and ribs were dark with bruises. *Was that Dad?* he said.

His mum shook her head. *I fell.*

I hear him, Mummy, Phil said, aware even at eight years old that he was crossing into dangerous territory. *I hear him a lot. Why does he hit you? Is that what dads do to mums?*

She didn't reply for a long time. When she did, she had tears in her eyes. *No,* she said, *it isn't. And he won't ever do it again.*

A week later he was gone. Phil was pretty sure that his mum found a way — and the strength — to get rid of her husband because she didn't want whatever it was that drove him to violence passing to her son any more than it already had. Phil saw him once, maybe six months after that, when he showed up on a Sunday afternoon with a bunch of flowers and a sheepish grin. He was there for five minutes, and then he was gone for ever.

So Phil had avoided alcohol, largely. Avoided the binge-drinking at university, avoided the casual slurping of a glass or two or three on a weeknight. He saw what it could do if it took hold in someone, and he feared that he had inherited his father's propensity to let it take hold in him.

But Friday night, he needed it, so he had opened the Macallan and accepted the numbness it offered.

And then at some point he had called Michelle and suggested she come over for dinner Saturday night. When he woke up, he had forgotten; it was only when she sent a text message asking what time she should come to his house and whether she should bring anything — wine, maybe? — that he remembered calling her.

She came over, with a bottle of red wine and a hopeful look in her eyes. They'd eaten the lamb tagine he'd made, and had moved to the couch to discuss whether they had room for ice cream.

Michelle had made it clear that she had other plans, too, sliding closer to him and resting her head on his shoulder. They'd had sex the night they met, but not the second time they'd gone out, the night that Phil had fled the pub. Now he wanted to flee again, but he couldn't: he was already in the place he would flee to.

And now, to buy time, he was refilling her wineglass in the kitchen. He walked back into the living room and handed her the glass. She glanced at the empty space next to her on the couch; at the last second, Phil went to sit in the armchair.

She looked at him, head tilted, her expression quizzical.

'Sit with me,' she said. 'Why've you moved?'

'I prefer it here,' he said, the real reason not something he felt he could pass on. 'This is my favourite chair.'

She put the wineglass on the table and folded her arms.

'Is everything OK, Phil?'

'Fine,' he said. 'I just like sitting here.'

'Right,' she said. 'Of course you do. Look, I don't know what's going on, but if you don't want to be with me then at least do me the courtesy of telling me. I'm a big girl. I'll survive.'

'It's not that. It's . . . ' Phil paused. ' . . . I'm sorry. I had a difficult break-up with my last girlfriend.'

My last girlfriend. It made it sound like he'd had a lot of others. And it made it sound so final.

'I get it,' Michelle said. 'You're on the rebound and you're not sure how you feel about me.' She leaned forward. 'I've been there, Phil. A few years back I had my heart broken. I felt so lonely, like there was a cold space inside me, and when I met a guy — I was drunk, of course, my sorrows needed some drowning — I went home with him. The next day I knew that I didn't want to see him again, but then, a day or two later, the loneliness set in and I gave him a call. And then I saw him, and I realized that I didn't want to be with him after all, because I was still in love with my ex, but I felt guilty for leading him on. I ended up seeing him five or six more times, and it was awful. Joyless, awkward, depressing. Eventually, I told him it wasn't working, and that was that. My one regret is that I didn't do it earlier.'

She stood up, and reached for her coat.

'It was nothing to do with him,' she said. 'It was all to do with me. And so don't worry that I'll take it personally. I won't. But this is not going to work out, so let me make it easy for you and call it a day.'

Phil looked at her, nodding. 'OK,' he said.

'Thanks. And I'm sorry.'

'Don't be,' she said. 'What you're feeling now is one of the worst things you can go through. But it gets better, Phil. It takes time, but it gets better. And I don't blame you. You're a good man, and I like you. I enjoyed spending time together. It's a shame we didn't meet in a year or two.'

'Maybe I'll give you a call sometime?' he said.

'Don't. It wouldn't work.' She put on her coat. 'Bye, Phil.'

He got to his feet and followed her to the door of the flat. 'You want me to call you a cab?'

'It's OK,' she said. 'I could use the walk.'

'I'll come with you. Make sure you get home safely.'

She shook her head, firmly. 'I'll be fine.'

'No,' Phil said. 'There's — you know. There've been the — '

'The murders? I know. But I can take care of myself. And honestly — I don't feel all that great right now, and it's kind of thanks to you. So you'll forgive me for saying that I don't want to spend any more time with you than is strictly necessary.'

'OK,' Phil said. 'I get it. Be safe.'

'Thanks, Phil. And goodbye.'

He closed the door behind her and stood there, waiting. After about twenty seconds had passed, he grabbed his keys, put on an old baseball cap and followed her out of the apartment.

20

Kate poured a coffee from the fresh pot she had made. Mornings were impossible without coffee; often, she went to bed looking forward to waking up refreshed and relaxed and having a quiet mug of milky coffee before the chaos of the day began. It was an addiction, for sure, if an addition was defined as something you believed you couldn't do without and which caused physical symptoms of withdrawal if you didn't get it. And if she didn't get coffee in the morning, she'd end up with a headache that would increase in intensity until she satisfied her craving.

This morning's headache, however, was not the result of coffee non-consumption; this one was the result of red wine and gin and tonic consumption. She took an ibuprofen, then curled up on the couch.

Her iPad was on the table in front of her. She picked it up. She had new emails; a few from colleagues who didn't know when to stop working, one from May, and two from Dating Harmony.

She was about to send them to her junk mail folder when she remembered.

Under Gemma's supervision, she'd set up a profile on a dating website the night before.

The first email was to welcome her to the site and thank her for joining. It was time-stamped at eleven minutes past midnight, which must have been when they set up her account. The second was to tell her she had a message from a user called Tony–Adcock17.

This one was time-stamped at seven minutes past two a.m., which in itself put her off. Who was up at that time, looking on dating websites? Tony–Adcock17, apparently.

She clicked on the link. Tony–Adcock17 was forty-two, liked football and eating out, golf, going to the gym.

She deleted the message. Forty-two? She was twenty-eight, for God's sake. She opened her profile. She was, it seemed, looking for people in the age range twenty-five to forty-four. Well, that could change. She adjusted the upper limit to thirty-four. Even that felt a bit older than she wanted, but it would do for now.

She read her profile. They'd taken a photo in the living room. It was a shot of her face, turned slightly to the left, looking away from the camera and smiling. Gemma had experimented with different lighting levels, and, in the end had taken a photo of her that didn't really look like her. It made her a little uncomfortable, as though she was engaged somehow in false advertising, although no doubt everyone did the same.

She'd selected an age range — twenty-five to twenty-nine — rather than putting her actual age. She liked theatre, the outdoors, good food and wine, and reading — which was true, sort of. She didn't actually do all that much of those things — although she liked the idea of them

104

— but then what were you supposed to put? That you liked sitting around in your pyjamas drinking tea, watching crap films, going to the pub with your friends, and checking Facebook on your phone? That was the reality of what 99 per cent of the people out there were doing, but look on a dating website and you'd think that the UK was crawling with super-fit rock-climbing enthusiasts who spent the little time they had left over after their Highland expeditions in Stratford watching the latest offering from the Royal Shakespeare Company, after which they went home to clarify a consommé, prepare a duck quenelle, then bake the perfect soufflé.

She closed the browser. She'd check it later, maybe. She wasn't sure about this whole enterprise. She had nothing against Internet dating, but she wasn't sure she had the energy for it, especially not when she had a hangover on a Sunday morning. What she needed now was more coffee and some toast with butter and Marmite.

She went into the kitchen and put two slices of white bread — it had to be white bread when your stomach was feeling delicate — into the toaster. As she poured another mug of coffee, her phone rang.

It was May.

'Morning,' she said. 'How's it going?'

'Good,' May said. 'Did you and Gem have a good night?'

'Great. Nothing extraordinary, but fun.' Kate paused. 'I tell you what did happen, though. I ran into that guy, Mike.'

'From holiday?'

'From holiday.'

'Oh my God. Was it weird?'

'Sort of.'

'Only sort of? Did you talk to him?'

'A bit. He was on his way out.'

'Well,' May said. 'Changing gears for a second. Have you seen the news?'

'What news?'

'I'll take that as a no.' There was a long pause. 'They found a body this morning. Woman, late twenties. There's been another.'

It took a few seconds for her meaning to sink in.

'Another murder?' Kate said.

'Another murder.'

'Who?'

'They don't know yet. Or if they do, they're not saying.'

'Jesus,' Kate said. 'This is fucking unbelievable. Are they saying it's a serial killer?'

'Not yet,' May said. 'But that conclusion seems inescapable.'

That conclusion seems inescapable.

May's words echoed in Kate's head as she clicked through to the website of the local newspaper.

BREAKING: THIRD BODY FOUND IN STOCKTON HEATH

Reports are emerging that the body of a woman found this morning near Ackers Pond may be the third case of murder in the

106

village of Stockton Heath in as many weeks.

Police have yet to name the victim, but did not rule out the possibility that her death may be linked to those of Jenna Taylor, 27, and Audra Collins, 28. If so, it seems certain that speculation about a serial killer targeting young women in and around Stockton Heath will increase.

More to follow.

That story was from eight fifty-five that morning, a full hour before Kate had got out of bed. When she navigated back to the home page, there was a link to another story. This one was new: from a few minutes ago.

Name of latest murder victim released.

Kate clicked on the link and began to read.

Police have named the woman found dead this morning near Stockton Heath as Michelle Clarke. Miss Clarke, 28, a junior school teacher, lived in Latchford, Warrington. She was originally from Blackpool.

It seems increasingly certain that the murders are the work of a single individual. Police are advising women to take additional care, especially if travelling at night, and especially if they are unaccompanied.

There is a press conference at noon during which the police will release further details.

There was a picture of Michelle Clarke

alongside the text. Kate felt goosebumps form on her arms as she looked at it.

Long, straight, near-black hair. Dark eyes.

Her grandmother's 'Irish look'.

Her look. Or, at least, her old look.

She ran her hand over her newly cropped hair. Thank God she'd done that. Thank God she hadn't gone out last night looking like the other victims.

Or — and it seemed barely credible that this could be the case — it might have been her photo in the papers that morning.

21

Kate ordered her drink — a skinny macchiato — and joined Gemma and May on a wide couch in the corner of the café.

It looked, at first glance, like a normal Sunday in a normal coffee shop anywhere in the country. Small groups of people chatting over large cups of steaming latte; single men cradling mugs of strong tea, newspapers splayed out in front of them, couples staring at their phones, the last bite of a shared cake waiting on a crumb-laden plate in front of them.

It was anything but normal.

The apparent absorption in conversations or phones or newspapers was paper-thin. Each time the door opened, eyes flickered over to see who it was. Any single men were subjected to suspicious glances, the subtext clear: *Is that him?*

Because now three women were dead, all killed in the same way, all sharing the same appearance. There was no doubt — whether the police confirmed it or not — that this was the work of a serial killer. He — and no one thought it was not a man — already had a name.

The Stockton Heath Strangler.

'What does Gus have to say about it?' Kate said. 'Has he heard anything?'

'Not much,' May said. 'Other than that it's definitely the same guy. Sometimes they get copycat killings, but apparently there's no chance of that in this case.'

'Any suspects?' Gemma said.

'They've got one, according to Gus. But he doesn't know who it is. They don't tell the run-of-the-mill cops. It's a pretty good lead, though. At least, that's what he heard. He's working this afternoon, so he'll probably hear more then.' She leaned forward. 'He swears me to secrecy on this stuff, by the way, so you can't tell anyone. OK?'

'Of course,' Kate said. 'I've not got anyone to tell, anyway.'

'She might have soon,' Gemma said, looking at May. 'She signed up for a dating website last night.'

'Really? Which one?'

'Dating Harmony,' Kate said. 'We'll see what comes of it. I'm not convinced.'

'Did you get any interest?'

'One creep,' Kate said. 'At some ridiculous time of the night.'

'Could be the Strangler,' Gemma said. 'Looking for his next victim. Searching the Net for lonely, single women he can — '

'Gem!' Kate said. 'That's not helping! I'm already having second thoughts about this. And all you're doing is giving me third thoughts and fourth thoughts.'

Before Gemma could answer, Kate's phone rang. She did not recognize the number.

'I'm not answering,' she said. 'I don't know who it is. I'm paranoid now, thanks to you' — she glared at Gemma — 'so they can call back some other time.'

'I think you're getting carried away,' Gemma said. 'You don't put your phone number on the website, so there's no way anyone could be calling you. It's probably some marketing crap.'

The ringing stopped. Seconds later, Kate's phone buzzed. There was a voicemail.

'I guess I'll find out,' she said, and put the phone to her ear.

It was a woman's voice. Flat, tired, authoritative.

'Miss Armstrong, this is Detective Inspector Jane Wynne from the Cheshire Constabulary. No doubt you are aware of the recent' — she paused — 'the recent events in Stockton Heath. There's a matter I'd like to discuss with you, if possible. It's a question of some urgency, so if you could call me back at your soonest convenience, I'd greatly appreciate it.'

DI Wynne gave her number, then hung up.

Kate looked at her friends. 'It's the cops,' she said. 'They want to talk to me.'

★ ★ ★

Gemma and May stayed on the couch; Kate went to sit at a table by the window. She'd called DI Wynne and arranged to meet her at the coffee shop in thirty minutes.

The fact that the detective — who must have been just about the busiest copper in the UK at that moment — was prepared to drop everything to come and see her was the most worrying thing about this whole situation.

As soon as she walked through the door it was

111

obvious who she was. She was wearing a pair of dark jeans with a jacket over some kind of shirt, but like most cops, it didn't matter whether she was in uniform or not. There was no hiding the fact she was police. It was hard to say what it was — the stiff back, the watchful expression, the wary smile — but there was an essential police-ness about her that could not be hidden.

Kate nodded. 'DI Wynne?'

'Yes. Miss Armstrong?'

'Kate, please. Would you like a drink?'

'I'll grab a coffee. I could do with the caffeine.'

She went to the counter. May waved to Kate; Kate replied with a surreptitious thumbs up.

When DI Wynne came back, she smiled.

'I'm sorry to interrupt your coffee with your friends,' she said, and gestured to May and Gemma. 'We'll make this as brief as possible.'

Kate blushed; the detective must have spotted her thumbs up to her friends, despite the fact that she had her back to Kate when she had done it.

'Sorry,' Kate said. 'We were already here when you called.' She shrugged. 'So they stayed. Is that OK?'

'That's fine.'

'I'm surprised you noticed them.'

'It's my job to notice things, Miss Armstrong.'

'You had your back to me.'

DI Wynne pointed to a large mirror behind the counter. It was emblazoned with the name of a brand of coffee. 'In my experience we're always being observed, one way or another. Which is one of the reasons this investigation is proving so challenging. We have no witnesses. Nothing. No one saying they heard the noise of a struggle, no one saying they saw a suspicious person late at night, no one saying they noticed a vehicle in the morning near the places the bodies were left.'

'Is that unusual?'

'Very.' DI Wynne sipped her coffee. 'But what's more unusual is that you think you might have been followed by the killer?'

'I didn't say that,' Kate said. 'I was followed by someone, and then there was someone outside my house. But it might not have been the killer.'

'Talk me through what happened. Every detail you can remember.'

Kate recounted the events, the car pulling out behind her, full beam lights on so that she was blinded, sensing that there was a person under the tree at the end of the street, the person riding away on their bike when Carl appeared.

DI Wynne listened and took notes. When Kate was finished, she drummed her fingers on the table.

'Did you recognize the person under the tree?' she said.

Kate shook her head. 'No. They were wearing a hoodie. And they were some distance away.'

'They were on a bike?'

'Yes.'

'Did you recognize the bike?'

'No. I know nothing about bikes.' Phil was more into them, but they had never interested Kate. He'd bought her one, once, but she rarely used it. It was somewhere in the cellar. She paused. 'Do you think it was him? The person

113

who's been killing people?'

'I don't know,' DI Wynne said. 'It's possible he did this to the other women, but there's no evidence to support that. And then there's the appearance. The victims look alike. You don't share that.'

Kate gave a half-smile. 'I do,' she said. 'Or at least, I did. I changed. Cut my hair.' She gestured at her eyes. 'Not naturally green, DI Wynne. These are contact lenses.'

DI Wynne's reaction was almost imperceptible. A narrowing of the eyes, a stiffening of the back.

'I see,' she said. She put her notebook down.

'Miss Armstrong — Kate — you recently broke up with Mr Phil Flanagan, is that correct?'

'Yes.'

'After a long relationship?'

'Ten years, more or less.'

'Would you say it was you or Mr Flanagan behind the break-up?'

'It was more me.'

The detective nodded. 'Did he take it well?'

'No,' Kate said. 'He didn't.' She looked at DI Wynne. Why was she asking this? What could her break-up with Phil have to do with the investigation? And then it came to her: the detective thought it was Phil following her in the car and hiding under the tree. She thought it was a jealous ex-boyfriend, and nothing whatsoever to do with the killings.

'You think it might have been Phil in the car?' she said. 'Or hiding under the tree?'

'Do you?' DI Wynne said.

114

'No,' Kate said. 'I mean, I doubt it. Do you suspect Phil?'

DI Wynne ignored the question.

'Were you aware that Mr Flanagan had started a new relationship?' she said.

'No,' Kate said. 'I had no idea.' She shook her head. 'I knew he'd . . . you know, met some women out. He phoned me once from one of their houses at about two a.m., but I had no idea he had a girlfriend.'

DI Wynne nodded slowly. 'Does the name Michelle Clarke mean anything to you, Miss Armstrong?'

'Of course. She was one of the victims. The one that was found this morning.'

'She was also in a relationship with Phil Flanagan,' DI Wynne said. 'Michelle Clarke was his new girlfriend.'

22

Kate stared at the detective. After a few seconds she became aware that her mouth was open and that she was shaking her head. She wasn't sure what was more of a shock: that Phil had a new girlfriend or that his new girlfriend had been murdered.

Scratch that: it was *much* more of a shock that she had been murdered.

And that she looked like Kate; or at least, like Kate used to look.

Which, even to someone who knew nothing about murder investigations, meant one thing was obvious.

Phil was a suspect, which was why DI Wynne had been so keen to see her.

'I don't know what to say,' Kate said, then added. 'Do I need a lawyer?'

'Do you?' DI Wynne said. 'Feel free to consult one if you wish. You're not under arrest, or even under suspicion.' She folded her arms. 'But if you would be happier making this more formal, we can go to the station?'

'No,' Kate replied. 'I'm just . . . I'm shocked. We can do it here. I mean, you don't think Phil had anything to do with this, do you? He wouldn't — he's not that kind of a person. I know him, and he isn't — he *couldn't* do this.'

'I don't think anything,' DI Wynne said. 'I'm merely exploring all avenues. But at the

116

minimum, Mr Flanagan is going to need to answer some questions. Miss Clarke was with him last night, according to her friends. She was planning to stay the night, but that evidently didn't happen. We need to find out what happened to her, and Mr Flanagan is the person we most need to speak to about that.' She paused. 'Has Mr Flanagan seen you since you changed your appearance?'

Kate shook her head. 'Why?'

'Michelle Clarke looks like the other victims. And she looks like you used to look. Although Mr Flanagan may think she still looks like you.'

'No. It's not Phil. It can't be. Why would he do it?'

The detective shrugged. 'Resentment at your break-up? To scare you? If someone is killing people who look like you, then you might be so terrified you'd get back together with him.'

'He wouldn't do that!' Kate said. 'He wouldn't murder people to get back with me. No way. No one would.'

'People do all kinds of things for all kinds of reasons, Miss Armstrong,' DI Wynne said. 'But this is all speculation. There is another reason I needed to see you.'

'Which is . . . ?'

DI Wynne fixed her with a steady gaze. Her eyes were dark and unreadable, the result, no doubt, of years of dealing with murderers and rapists and child abusers and whoever else she encountered in her job. It couldn't have been easy to spend your life assuming the worst of people, and then finding out that your assumptions were correct. It was bound to skew your view of humanity somewhat.

'Which is that I don't know where Mr Flanagan is. I was hoping you might be able to tell me.'

'What do you mean?'

'We've been unable to locate him. As you no doubt know, he has been staying with a friend, Mr Andrew Field. Mr Field is away this weekend, but we managed to talk to him and he said that he was unaware Mr Flanagan had plans. However, when we went to Mr Field's residence, there was no one there.'

'I don't know where he is,' Kate said. 'I haven't spoken to him.' She took her phone from her bag. 'I can call him, if you like.'

'That would be very helpful.'

She selected Phil's number and called it. It rang once, then went to voicemail.

Hi, Phil's recorded voice said, *you've reached the voicemail of Phil Flanagan. I can't get to the phone right now, but leave me a message and I'll get back to you as soon as I can.*

Kate swallowed. Her mouth was dry. 'Phil, it's me. I need to talk to you. Call me back as soon as you can.'

She looked at DI Wynne. 'Voicemail,' she said.

'Thank you for trying.' The detective picked up her notebook. 'Have you noticed anything odd recently? About Mr Flanagan's behaviour?'

'It's all been odd,' Kate said. 'We recently broke up. It's hardly a normal time.'

'Anything specific? Anything worrying?'

'I don't know,' Kate replied. 'I don't know

what normal is in this kind of situation.'

DI Wynne finished her coffee. 'Well,' she said. 'Thank you for your time, Miss Armstrong.' She handed Kate a card. 'And please don't hesitate to call me if anything comes to mind.'

Kate watched her go. By the time she was on the pavement, Gemma and May were standing at the table.

'So?' May said. 'What did she want?'

'It's Phil,' Kate said. 'They think it's Phil.'

Gemma pulled out a seat and sat down. 'Are you serious? They think it's Phil?'

'He's disappeared,' Kate said. 'They can't find him. And he was with the girl last night.'

'Which girl?' May said.

'The one who was killed — Michelle Clarke.' Kate massaged her temples with her thumb and forefingers. 'Michelle Clarke was Phil's girl-friend. And he was with her last night.'

'She was his *girlfriend*?' Gemma said. 'I thought he was pining after you, wasting away from unrequited love. *That* didn't last long.'

'I'm not sure that's the point,' May said.

'I know,' Gemma replied. 'But still. It's a bit rich.'

Kate looked at her friends. 'She looked like me. Like I used to. And Phil hasn't seen me, so he wouldn't know I'd changed.' She paused. She felt like everything had shifted beneath her, like everything she knew had changed. If this *was* Phil, then her world was not what she had thought it was.

'What if it *is* him?' she said. 'What if Phil's killing these women?'

'It can't be,' May said. 'It can't. We've known him for ever. Almost as long as we've known each other. And he isn't capable of doing this. You both know that.'

'Yeah,' Gemma said. 'But people change. Look at Beth. What about what happened with her? None of us saw *that* coming.'

PART ONE: INTERLUDE

Five Years Earlier

1

'Beth,' May said. 'What are you doing?'

'Taking a photo,' Beth replied. She stood in front of her three friends, holding a tray with four glasses of Coke on it.

'Why do you have four Cokes?' Kate said. She gestured at the four wineglasses and half-empty bottle of wine on the table. 'We already have drinks. And why are you taking photos of them?'

'Give me a second,' Beth replied. 'There's something I need to do.'

Kate, May and Gemma watched as their friend moved their wineglasses to an adjacent table, along with the half-empty bottle, then replaced them with glasses of Coke. She smoothed her jacket over her bum as she did so; it was a gesture that she often made, born of self-consciousness at what she considered to be too-wide hips.

She sat behind the table, then took out her phone and lined up a photograph of the four soft drinks.

'There,' she said. 'Done. You can take your drinks back now. So, how were your weeks?'

Gemma raised an eyebrow. 'Er, before we discuss how shitty our jobs are and how much we fancy the hot guy in the finance office, could I ask a question?'

'Sure,' Beth said.

'What the fuck just happened?'

'I needed to take a photo,' Beth said. 'That's all.'

'Of some drinks we're not drinking?' May said. 'What for?'

Beth shifted uncomfortably on her seat. 'For, erm, for' — she tapped her foot on the floor — 'for something. Never mind, OK?'

'Never mind 'never mind',' Kate said. 'What's going on?'

So Beth told them.

★ ★ ★

'The weirdest thing happened tonight,' Kate said, when she was back at the house she and Phil had not long moved into. 'Beth took a photo of four glasses of Coke on our table.'

'Why? Is she some kind of drink photographer now?'

'No. And she got super uncomfortable when we asked why, but in the end she told us. It's kind of disturbing.'

Phil turned and looked at her. Beth was the only other girl he had ever dated, just the once, when they were thirteen. He claimed they'd kissed; Beth always said that it was more of a brief touching of lips. 'Oh?'

'She said that she has a new boyfriend and he doesn't like her drinking. He likes her to prove she isn't by taking photos of her drinks and sending them to him throughout the night. She did it a few more times before we left.'

'That's pretty fucked up,' Phil said. 'She wants to get out of that relationship ASAP.'

'Apparently it's a guy from work.'

'Who?' Phil and Beth worked in the same place in town; he was a trainee in project management, she was in marketing. 'Maybe I know him.'

'He's a bit older. Moved here in the last couple of months. He's called Colin Davidson.'

'Yeah,' Phil said. 'I know of him. Seen him around. He's some kind of Internet marketing guru. Seems a normal enough chap.' He picked up the remote control. '*Match of the Day*'s on,' he said, then added, as an aside. 'She needs to be careful.'

2

'OK,' Kate said. 'I'll try them on. Wait here.'

Until recently, her favourite clothes shop in the Trafford Centre had allowed two people into the changing rooms at the same time. That had changed; apparently it made it easier to steal things if potential clothes-lifters had an accomplice, so Beth had to wait outside before she could pass comment on the skinny jeans that Kate was almost certain she would be buying.

Kate pulled off her old jeans — she was already thinking of them as her old jeans — and put on the new ones. She knew immediately that they were for her. There was a feeling of rightness when something fit well, and she had it now. She buttoned them up, looked in the mirror, then turned to see the view from the back.

Perfect. She loved them. Beth would love them. Phil would love them.

She pulled back the curtain and stepped out, smiling and ready to see confirmation of her choice in her friend's eyes.

Beth was not there.

Kate looked around. She couldn't see her anywhere.

She had the same unsettling feeling that she'd had the night that Beth had taken photos of her fake drinks. She'd had it when Beth failed to show up for the regular Friday-night post-work drinks with May and Gemma, first for one week, then two, then three — which was the reason Kate had called her and arranged to meet at the Trafford Centre in the first place.

And now she was gone.

She looked around again, taking a few steps away from the changing rooms to see if Beth was looking at some clothes, or talking to a friend she'd bumped into.

Nothing.

She couldn't go too far, not wearing the jeans; she didn't want to be arrested for shoplifting, but she had to find Beth. Something was wrong, and she had to find her friend.

She headed back for the booth.

'They look lovely.' A girl with spiky hair and a nose stud was folding the clothes others had tried on and discarded. 'They really suit you.'

'Thanks,' Kate said.

'Are you taking them?'

Taking, Kate noted. *Not buying.*

'Not today,' she said. 'Something came up.'

'You sure? They look amazing.'

' 'Fraid so,' Kate said, and went into the booth. She changed into her old — current — jeans and left, handing the unbought ones to the spiky-haired girl. She pulled her phone from her bag and called Beth.

It rang once, and then went to voicemail.

'Hey, it's me. Just wondering where you are. Call me back.'

She hung up and walked briskly through the store, retracing their steps. Where the fuck was

Beth? And why had she left without saying goodbye?

She called Beth again. This time, she answered.

'Hey,' Kate said. 'Where are you?'

'I had to go,' Beth said, her voice businesslike and matter-of-fact.

'You don't have a car. I drove.'

'I'm getting a lift.'

'From who?'

She hesitated. 'Colin. I bumped into him.'

'Colin? What was he doing here?'

'Shopping. He needed something. It was — it was a coincidence. And he — he said he'd give me a lift.'

'We were going to have dinner. And a drink.'

'I know,' Beth said. For a second, Kate thought she was about to say something, but she sniffed. 'Plans changed. Sorry, Kate. I have to go.'

3

They always — *nearly* always — had sex on Sunday mornings, and they always — *always always* — took their time about it. On a weeknight, the worries of work and the pressure of early mornings and the need for a decent sleep meant it was more hurried, more frantic, but on a Sunday they could lose themselves in each other. All they had to do afterwards was drink tea, read the papers and maybe have sex again.

They lay in their new bed in their new house. Rented, but their first place together; it felt like a treasure chest of possibilities.

Phil had his head on her chest, his hand on her stomach. He had started doing that after sex recently. Kate loved it.

'I'm worried about Beth,' she said, after a while. 'I don't like the vibes I get from that guy she's seeing.'

'Like what?'

'Like, I think he's controlling her. Not letting her drink, making her take photos on a night out, 'accidentally'' — she made air quotes — 'bumping into her when she's shopping and taking her home without even letting her say goodbye to me.'

'Maybe they're madly in love. You know how it is. You meet someone and then you retreat into your own world for a while. Perhaps he

131

genuinely was in the Traffic Centre' — Phil called it that, in an attempt to be dismissive that Kate hated — 'for some reason, and they saw each other and couldn't wait to get it on.'

'She would have said goodbye,' Kate replied. 'Do you know anything about the guy? Heard anything at work?'

'Apparently he's super smart. I've been in a few meetings with him and he seems pretty nice. Well put together. But he operates above my pay grade.'

'OK.' Kate swung her legs out of bed. 'If you hear anything, let me know.'

★ ★ ★

She sat by the window, a mug of tea steaming in her hand, and called Beth. Straight to voicemail.

Hi, this is Beth. Leave a message and I'll get back to you.

'Hi, Beth,' Kate said. 'I was thinking of going to the gym this afternoon. Let me know if you're interested.'

At lunchtime she received a text.

Got yr msg. I'm busy this afternoon. Maybe next week?

It was weird; Beth never used text speak. Never wrote *txt* for *text* or *U* for *you*. Either way, her phone was on, so Kate dialled her number. She wanted to hear her friend's voice, see if there

132

was something wrong. Ask her outright what was happening. She'd know if Beth was lying to her.

It went straight to voicemail. Again.

This time, Kate didn't leave a message.

★ ★ ★

She sent an email from work on Monday morning.

Beth. You good? You left so suddenly on Saturday. Just checking in. Everything OK with Colin? K. xxx

Beth replied immediately:

Everything's fine. Better than fine. Colin's awesome. Sorry if I haven't been available. He and I are spending a lot of time together.

Glad to hear it. How about all meeting up? Me, you, Gemma, May, Phil, Gus, Matt and Colin? Would be good to get to know him. How about this Saturday?

I'll ask him. I'll let you know.

She didn't hear from Beth until Friday afternoon, when an email popped up:

Hey, this Saturday's not going to work. Colin has to go and see his parents.

Kate's neck prickled. She typed out a response:

No problems. Hope everything's OK. How about Sunday lunch in the pub? We can be flexible. I'd love to meet him.

Beth replied half an hour later:

Colin's not very social. And he's uncomfortable hanging out with people from work, especially more junior people. Maybe another time.

Kate didn't reply.
Which, looking back, was a mistake.

4

How do you force someone to talk to you?

Not talk as in an exchange of pleasantries — *How are you? Fine, you?* — but talk as in telling the truth, sharing information, discussing what's happening *behind* the pleasantries. How do you force someone to do that?

Answer: you can't. You can send text messages, emails, leave voicemails. You can ask your boyfriend to buttonhole someone at the coffee machine at work. You can invite them to your house, the pub, the gym. But if they tell you they're OK, evade your questions, decline your invitations, then what can you do?

Answer: nothing. But it doesn't stop you feeling guilty as hell when the shit hits the fan.

★ ★ ★

Beth and Colin left three months later. He had a job in Gateshead; she went with him. Apparently they were engaged, or so Phil had picked up from the work gossip. Kate didn't know first-hand. She hadn't seen or spoken to Beth since the day they'd been shopping at the Trafford Centre. Neither had Gemma or May.

Kate was concerned. May was confused. Gemma was pissed off.

That guy, Kate said. *We've still not met him. I don't like that. It's not right.*

135

Maybe she's infatuated with him, May said. *But I don't see why she would ditch us like this. I can't believe she doesn't want to be friends any more.*

If that's what she wants, Gemma said, *then so be it. My guess is we'll never see her again.*

But Gemma was wrong.

Very wrong.

PART TWO

1

Kate left May and Gemma in the coffee shop and went home. She'd made up her mind: the change in her appearance wasn't enough. She was going to pack a bag and move in full-time with her parents until this was over. There was too much going on: the car, the person under the tree, her resemblance to the victims, and now Phil's — potential — involvement.

It was *his girlfriend* that had died. His girlfriend that looked like her. She had a horrible feeling about this, and, even though she found it hard to believe that Phil was in any way involved, she was not going to take any risks.

Upstairs, she picked out a week's worth of work clothes and folded them into a suitcase. She packed some make-up and then went into the bathroom to grab some tampons; she was due on in a few days. Then she went into the spare bedroom, which she and Phil had used as a study, to pick up some files she needed for Monday morning.

Their computer — an old desktop — was on the desk, plugged into the mains. She nudged the mouse to wake the screen so she could quickly check her emails.

The screen didn't come alive.

Kate frowned. She always left the computer on. Phil had complained about it. It was a waste of electricity, he claimed. Even though it wasn't much, it added up over time, and if everyone did it then it was a huge waste.

Be the change you want to see in the world, he used to say.

A load of pious crap, she used to reply.

One day, he'd say, *there'll be someone who uses up the last drop of oil, and he or she will look back on you and wonder how you could have been so wasteful.*

But, whether he was right or wrong, the fact they had argued about it meant that it was something she always noticed, and she knew that she hadn't switched the computer off.

She felt the power cord to see whether it had become detached from the back of the computer, then checked the plug socket. Both fine. Then perhaps the computer had died; Phil had also warned her that being constantly on wasn't good for it.

She pushed the on button. There was a whirring sound, then the screen flickered on and the login prompt, asking her to press CTRL + ALT + DELETE, appeared.

So, no problem there.

A feeling of unease corkscrewed in her stomach. She was aware that her heart was beating faster.

If she hadn't shut the computer down, then someone else had. Someone had been in the house.

Someone had been in this *room*.

She looked around, searching for anything that was out of place. She examined the pictures on the wall, the photos on the desk, the books on the shelves. Everything seemed OK. She pushed the chair back from the desk — it was one of those office chairs on castor wheels — and took in the whole of the desk.

There was something different. She studied it for a few seconds. Then it came to her.

There was a filing cabinet under the desk that Phil had brought home from work. It was faulty and going to be scrapped, so he had rescued it. He'd had a plan to fix it, but it had proved more difficult than expected, so they had been left with a faulty filing cabinet. It didn't matter too much; it was a pretty minor fault, so they had put their files in and forgotten about it.

The filing cabinet had two drawers: a large one on the bottom and a smaller one on top. The fault was that, for some reason, both would not close at the same time.

The day before, Kate had opened the top drawer to take out a pen, then left it partly open.

Now, it was the bottom drawer that was partly open.

She leaned forward and pulled it all the way open. It looked like it always did, but then, since there was no index, she had no way of knowing if an individual file or document had been taken.

What she did know, however, was that somebody had been in the house, checking her computer and looking through her files.

And it could only be Phil. The door was locked when she got here and there were no signs of a break-in. He had a key; it made sense.

Fuck, Phil. What the hell was he up to?

She grabbed her suitcase. The sooner she got

141

out of here, the better.

★ ★ ★

Her dad handed her a cup of tea. She had just finished telling him about her conversation with DI Wynne and her suspicions that someone had been in the house.

Her dad sipped his tea. 'Phil's not the killer,' he said. 'I know that boy and he didn't kill those women. He might have been in your house — he's pretty upset, by all accounts — but he's not a killer.'

'Isn't that the point, Dad?' Kate said. 'You don't know. Some mild-mannered accountant turns out to be a psychopath, playing with his kids by day and slaughtering people by night.'

'Well,' her dad said, 'if it is Phil — which I doubt — he'd have to be a bloody good actor. I mean, to portray himself for such a long time and so convincingly as a genial, slightly hapless bloke while beneath it all he was really a cold-blooded killer? Brando would have been proud of that performance.' He shook his head. 'No. I don't see it. Remember, this was the man who called you when you got your first mobile phone and sang — shouted, I should say — 'Angels' at the top of his voice as soon as you answered.'

'Except I didn't answer,' Kate said.

'He didn't take the time to find that out, though, did he? He launched right in, top of his lungs. He was quite surprised when he finished and I said I'd go and get you. Surprised and apologetic. It would take a certain kind of genius to go to such lengths to hide his evil psychopathic nature. So no, I don't see it.'

In all honesty Kate didn't see it either, but then those closest were often the last to know. Did Ian Brady's mum think he was an evil killer? Or Peter Sutcliffe's? They probably doubted it until the very end, until the jury pronounced its verdict. Even then they probably had some doubts.

And maybe they were reasonable doubts. Maybe their sons had been fine and dandy and well adjusted all through their childhoods until, at some point in their lives, something inside them had changed and they had embarked on a killing spree. Perhaps it had always been in them; perhaps some event had brought it on, but Kate was prepared to bet that the people that knew them were more astonished than anyone when it came to light that they were the culprits.

On the kitchen counter, her phone buzzed. Her dad picked it up. He read the screen and passed it to her.

'Well, well,' he said. 'It's Phil.'

Kate took the phone and walked across the kitchen to the back door. On the patio, she lifted the phone to her ear.

'Hello,' she said. 'Phil?'

'I got your message,' Phil said. It sounded like he was in the car. 'What's up? Are you OK? You sounded a bit upset.'

'Have you seen the news?'

'What news?'

'Phil,' Kate said. 'Where are you?'

143

'Ingleton. I went for a hike, on Whernside.'

'And you've not read the news?'

'No. I thought my phone was in my rucksack, but I left it in the car.'

'Something happened to Michelle,' Kate said. 'The woman you've been seeing.'

There was a long silence. 'How do you know about Michelle?'

'The police told me.'

'What? Why would the police be talking to you about Michelle?'

'Can you pull over?'

'I'm on hands-free,' Phil said. 'I don't need to pull over.'

'It's not that. This might be — it might be a shock. It'd be better if you weren't driving.'

'I'm fine,' Phil said. 'Tell me what the hell is going on, and why the cops are talking to you about Michelle.'

'Phil,' Kate said. 'Pull over, please. For me.'

'Fine,' Phil said, his tone exasperated. 'There's a lay-by up ahead. Hold on a second.'

There was a pause. A minute later he spoke again.

'Right. I've stopped. This better be good.'

Good isn't the word I'd use, Kate thought.

'Phil,' she said, 'I've got some bad news.' She paused, and stared through the window. Her dad was reading the newspaper. 'Michelle Clarke is dead.'

There were a few beats of silence.

'I'm sorry,' Phil said. 'The line's not great. Say that again?'

'She's dead. She died last night.'

'I don't understand,' Phil said. His tone was flat and disbelieving. Her dad's words came back to her: if he was acting, he was doing a good job of it. 'She died? How?'

My God, Kate thought. *Why does it have to be me who tells him this?*

'She was killed,' she said. 'They found the body this morning.'

2

The sun was setting as Phil drew up outside Andy's apartment. There was a red Honda Civic parked near the front door, and as he pulled on the handbrake, two people got out: a woman in her forties in an ill-fitting suit and a younger man in dark jeans and some kind of leather jacket. They were obviously cops. Only cops dressed so badly. What was it about joining the force that destroyed your fashion sense? He was hardly a snappy dresser himself, but even he could see that DI Wynne — this must be her — and her partner could have done with a makeover. Maybe he'd call Susannah and Trinny, or whatever their names were, when this was all over and suggest that they help these detectives with their image.

'Mr Flanagan?' she said, when he got out of his car. 'I'm Detective Inspector Wynne. This is Detective Sergeant Chan.'

'Nice to meet you,' Phil said. 'Come in.'

He opened the front door and climbed the stairs to the apartment door. Andy was lying on the couch, his hand in a large bag of crisps. There was a cup of tea on the carpet and a rerun of *Top Gear* on the television.

'Hey,' he said. 'You're back. We need to talk. The cops called me. They — '

Phil nodded. 'I know.' He gestured for DI

146

Wynne and DS Chan to enter the room. 'They're here.'

Andy straightened up on the couch. 'Holy shit,' he said. He glanced around, looking, Phil thought, for weed or porn or anything else illegal or embarrassing, 'I mean, hi. I'm Andy Field.'

DI Wynne waved him back down. 'Please, don't move on my account.' She looked at Phil. 'Is there a room we can talk in?'

'Kitchen,' Phil said. 'Would you like a drink? Tea? Coffee?'

DI Wynne shook her head. 'No, thank you. I had one at the station. You go ahead.'

'It's OK,' Phil said. 'I'll wait. But let's go to the kitchen. Leave Andy to his *Top Gear*.'

They sat at the kitchen table, DS Chan to Phil's left, DI Wynne opposite him. Phil moved an egg-stained plate onto the worktop. There were quite a few other plates to keep it company.

'So,' DI Wynne said. 'You were with Michelle Clarke last night? At least, according to her friends you were.'

'That's right. She came here.'

'What time did she arrive?'

'Around seven,' Phil said. 'We had a drink, then a meal.'

'What did you eat?' DS Chan said.

'Lamb. A Moroccan thing.'

'Good?' DS Chan said. 'Tasty?'

'It was,' Phil replied. 'Not bad, anyway.'

'Did you make it?' Chan said.

'I did.'

'Some kind of tagine?'

Phil ignored the question and turned to DI Wynne.

'Is this really what you need to know, Detective?'

'Detective Inspector,' DI Wynne said. 'And yes, it is. That's why we're asking these questions. We'll be checking the contents of her stomach.' She paused. If she was trying to shock him, it was working. He had a sudden, graphic image of Michelle on some kind of autopsy table.

'Had you been drinking?' Wynne asked.

'Yes. Wine, mainly. I had a Scotch before she arrived. A Macallan.'

'Do you drink a lot, Mr Flanagan?' DS Chan said.

'No. Not normally.'

'Not normally? What about at the moment?'

'At the moment, I'm drinking more than usual.'

'Why is that?'

'I think you can probably guess,' Phil said.

DI Wynne smiled a thin smile at him. 'We're not in the business of guesswork,' she said. 'It tends to cause problems in our line of work.'

'Because of the break-up,' Phil said. 'With Kate. You spoke to her today.'

'I did.' DI Wynne paused. 'Are there any other changes in your behaviour as a result of the break-up? Beyond the drinking?'

'No,' Phil said. 'There aren't.'

'You haven't been — how should I put this — paying Miss Armstrong more attention than normal.'

148

'In what way?'

'Following her. Waiting — hiding — near her house?'

Phil hesitated before answering, wondering whether he needed to tell the detectives about the night he had nearly been caught outside Kate's house. By the time he decided he didn't, it was too late; the hesitation had answered the question for him.

'Yes,' he said. 'Look, it's been difficult and I wanted to see her — '

'Let's keep to the facts, please,' DI Wynne said. 'What happened?'

Phil told her: watching so he could catch a glimpse of Kate, make sure she was not with another man; Carl coming outside, him fleeing.

'And earlier?' DI Wynne said. 'Was there another incident, earlier that evening?'

'Like what?' Phil said.

'Nothing,' DI Wynne said, although it was clear to Phil that she was not telling the truth. There was something else, something specific that she was getting at. Before he could push her on it, DS Chan started speaking:

'Let's talk about last night. Miss Clarke left this apartment at what time?'

'Around ten.'

'That seems early. For a Saturday night.'

'We'd — well, I'd told her that I wasn't over Kate. And so she left. I offered to get her a cab, but she decided to walk. She doesn't drive.'

'You let her walk?'

'She insisted,' he said. 'I tried, but . . . we'd

149

had a difficult conversation. She wanted to be alone.'

DI Wynne raised her eyebrows and he realized his mistake.

'You had a difficult conversation? An argument?'

'No,' he said. 'Not like that. I told her about Kate, that I wasn't ready for a relationship. So she left.'

'And you let her,' DS Chan said. 'Despite the murderer running around.'

'What did you do after Miss Clarke left?' DI Wynne said, after a pause.

'I stayed here.'

'Can anyone confirm that?'

'No.'

DI Wynne nodded. 'How about the night that Audra Collins was killed?'

'Which night was that?'

DI Wynne gave him the date.

'I was with Michelle,' he said.

'Unfortunately, she's unable to corroborate,' DI Wynne said. 'Very inconvenient for you.'

'Her friends will, though,' Phil said.

'Was she with you the whole night?' DI Wynne said.

'No. We went for a drink — lots of people will have seen us, we were in the Mulberry Tree, so there'll be CCTV footage, for sure — then she went home. She took a cab, I think, so there may be some record of that. You should check.'

'Thank you for the suggestion,' DS Chan said. 'And then?'

'I came here.'

'Can anyone confirm that?'

'I — I don't know,' Phil said. 'Andy — Andy was at his girlfriend's place for the night.' He closed his eyes. 'So no, they can't.'

'And the night Jenna Taylor was killed?'

'Remind me of exactly which night that was,' Phil said.

DI Wynne reminded him. A Wednesday night, almost three weeks ago.

'I don't know,' Phil said. 'It was a normal night. I got back from work, hung out here with Andy.'

'Andy? Can he verify your statement?'

'Ask him. But yes, I'm sure he will.'

DI Wynne held Phil's gaze. He felt like he was being weighed up, evaluated, examined, and, to his shock, she had a look in her eyes of total and utter mistrust.

There was more to this than he had thought, and he had the feeling he was about to find out what it was.

Eventually she spoke:

'Of course, even if he confirms you both stayed in, you could have gone out after he was asleep.'

'I could,' Phil said. 'But I didn't.'

'Do you ever?'

'Ever what?'

'Go out late at night?' DS Chan said. 'Go for a walk? Or maybe a bike ride?'

Phil hesitated.

'No,' he said.

'Miss Clarke left here around ten p.m., alone,' DI Wynne said. 'She was killed around midnight,

151

a mile and a half from here. She bears a significant resemblance to two other recent victims of a killer in this area, and to your ex-girlfriend. The last person to see her alive was you — or the killer, I suppose.' She paused, studying him. Folded her arms. 'And then there's the CCTV footage from the all-night garage on Wilderspool Causeway. Can you guess what that footage might show, Mr Flanagan?'

Phil blinked. He felt weak and had to struggle to focus. He *could* guess — in fact, he knew — what it would show.

'Look,' he said. 'It's not what you think.'

'Stick to the facts,' DS Chan said. 'What do you think that footage shows?'

The detective held up his hands. 'Don't bother,' he said. 'I'll answer for you. It's you. It's you, on your bike, stopping for some water. But you said you were at home. That you didn't go out. Help us understand, Mr Flanagan. Because a bike is a good way — stealthy, quiet — for a killer to get about.'

Phil nodded. He put his hands on his thighs so the cops wouldn't see them shaking. 'I followed her,' he said. 'I didn't want her to walk home alone. Because of the killings.'

'Very noble of you, Mr Flanagan,' DS Chan said.

DI Wynne gestured to her partner to let Phil speak. 'Go on, Mr Flanagan,' she said.

'I wanted to be sure she was OK, so I followed her. But she stopped to make a call, so I hid. By the time I looked again, she'd gone. I rode around for a while, but I couldn't find her.'

'Why did you lie?' DI Wynne said. 'If it was as innocent as you say? Help me to understand that.'

'Why do you think?'

DS Chan laughed. 'You don't want to know what I think.'

'Listen,' Phil said. 'I'd hardly have gone to an all-night garage, would I? If I'd killed someone a few minutes earlier.'

'Mr Flanagan,' DI Wynne said, 'would you be prepared to give a DNA sample?'

'Have you found DNA on the bodies?'

'We may do.'

'Then yes, I would. Because you won't find mine. Maybe on Michelle's body, but not the others. When would you like it?'

'Now? As you can imagine, we are very busy, so the sooner the better.'

'Fine. Now is fine. Where?'

DI Wynne gave him an address.

'I'll be right there. I'd like to have a quick shower before I come, if that's OK.'

'That's fine,' DI Wynne said. 'But be sure you *do* come.'

'I will,' Phil said. 'I have nothing to hide, Detective.'

'I hope so,' DI Wynne said. 'For your sake, I hope so.'

3

POLICE: WE ARE LOOKING FOR A SERIAL KILLER

Cheshire police confirmed yesterday that they believe the recent murders in Stockton Heath were all committed by the same person.

A third body, that of Michelle Clarke, 28, was found on Sunday morning near to Ackers Pond, a local beauty spot. As with the earlier victims, Ms Clarke had been strangled and sexually assaulted. The police did not confirm whether the sexual assault was pre- or post-mortem.

The manner of the murders has led to the killer being given the name 'The Stockton Heath Strangler'. Dr Michael Groton, an academic who has written extensively about serial killers, said that the pattern of the killings is typical of such cases.

'There is a strong compulsive element to many serial killers,' Dr Groton said. 'This means that the killing itself is only part of what they do: the selection of the victim, the planning, reading about it afterwards — all of these give the killer pleasure and form part of what they view as their work. These murders show all the hallmarks of a typical serial killer: the victims are all women, all in *their mid to late twenties, all of similar appearance, and the method is the same in each case. There will be some significance to the selection of victims of this type, but what that is is hard to say.'*

The detective in charge of the case, DI Wynne, said that they have no one in custody, but there are a number of leads which they are currently following up.

Kate closed the browser. She felt sick, both because this was happening and because Phil was one of those leads.

There was a tap on the divider that separated her desk from her neighbour. It was Nate; in one hand he held a file, in the other, his wallet.

'Jesus,' he said. He gestured at her hair. 'I know we have an HR policy that we shouldn't comment on people's personal appearance, but — wow. You really went for it.'

It was a reaction she had already experienced many times that morning: from the receptionist, the security guard, her colleagues.

'I wanted a change.'

'You certainly got one.' He shrugged. 'I like it. It's modern. Bold. Something like that. Anyway, I'm going to get some coffee. We'll need it before our Monday-morning meeting with the compliance folks. Takes a big jolt to keep awake through that one. Want to join me?'

'I already have one,' Kate said, pointing to the large Styrofoam cup on her desk. 'But I'll come down for the walk.'

They crossed the office to the lifts. There was

155

one open and they took it down to the ground floor, where Costa Coffee had set up a franchise. Nate went to get a coffee; Kate found a seat by the plate-glass window that separated them from Manchester's busy Deansgate.

He came back with a cup of coffee and a large blueberry muffin, which he set between them and cut into two halves.

'There you go,' he said. 'Tuck into that.'

Kate broke off a small section. Even though she hadn't eaten breakfast, she wasn't very hungry.

'Don't feel like eating?' Nate said.

'It's all this serial killer stuff,' she replied. 'It's kind of getting to me. I'm always looking over my shoulder, checking I'm not being followed. I've even moved back in with my parents.'

Nate raised an eyebrow. 'That seems pretty extreme.'

'It is, but then — well, there were a bunch of incidents over the weekend.'

'Like what?'

Kate didn't want to go into it. It was unsettling enough as it was; she didn't want it to permeate her work life as well.

'Nothing specific,' she said. 'But I got spooked, so I ran to Mum and Dad. Guess we never really grow up, after all.'

'Not until they die,' Nate said. 'That's what I found, anyway.'

'Your parents passed away?'

'When I was younger.' He sipped his coffee and looked away. 'And it's probably not a bad idea for you to move back. Whoever this guy is,

156

he must stalk them, figure out what routes they take to places, understand their routines. You're better off breaking yours up.'

'God, it's so awful,' Kate said. 'I can't quite believe this guy is out there.'

'I know,' Nate replied. 'Although I must admit I've got a kind of sick interest in it.'

'Everyone has,' Kate said. 'It's all over the news.'

'People love a good serial killer,' Nate said. 'They make a great story.'

'Yeah, unless you're one of the victims,' Kate said. 'Or the same age and gender, and living in the same village.'

'Apparently the killer leaves the bodies on their backs,' he said, 'arms folded across the chest, legs straight out. He'd have to arrange them like that after he'd strangled them — presumably there'd be some struggle beforehand.' He sipped his coffee. 'There's one other thing he does. It's pretty horrible.'

'I'm not sure I want to hear this,' Kate said.

'I don't have to tell you, if you don't want.'

'How bad is it?'

'On a scale of one to ten?' He wagged his head from side to side, as though considering the matter. 'Nine.'

'Then no, I don't want to hear it,' Kate said.

'No problem.'

Kate looked at him. 'OK,' she said. 'Tell me. I need to know or my imagination will run riot.'

Nate nodded. 'He removes their eyes,' he said. 'He cuts off their eyelids while they're alive, then scoops out their eyes after he's killed them.'

157

'Jesus,' Kate said, her voice a whisper. 'That's sick. *Beyond* sick.'

'The cops think it's some weird fetish. He wants them to have to look at him, so that he is the last thing they see before they die. They're keeping that to themselves, though, to stop the false confessions. Believe it or not, there are people weird enough to confess to high-profile crimes so that they can have their fifteen minutes of fame. Crazy, or what?'

'Not as crazy as the people who are actually doing it.'

'You don't think? In some ways it's even weirder. Anyway, they keep certain details out of the public eye so that if someone does confess they can check whether it's for real or not. If they don't know the details of the killings, then the cops can tell they're a glory hunter.'

Kate took another small bite of the muffin. 'So how do you know?' she said. 'If they're keeping it hidden?'

'Because I'm the Strangler,' Nate said. 'And this is all part of my sinister game.'

Kate froze, then relaxed as he grinned.

'Sorry,' he said. 'Another of my crap jokes. The truth is a bit less dramatic. I know a cop. He's a forensic tech in Cheshire, working on the case. He filled me in over a beer.'

'Who is he? I might know him.'

'A friend. I can't say more.'

'Should he be telling you this stuff? If they're keeping it secret, I'm surprised he would, to be honest.'

'He probably shouldn't,' Nate said. 'But we go

158

way back, and I'm a lawyer, so he can trust me, right?'

'Millions wouldn't, Nate.'

'Keep it to yourself, OK?'

'I will.' Kate hesitated. 'Did he say if they have any idea who did it? Any suspects?'

'He said there was one, but he wouldn't elaborate. That kind of information he *really* can't share.'

★ ★ ★

Back at her desk, Kate saw that she had an email from Dating Harmony.

Toby–Turner342 wanted to send her a message. According to his profile, he was thirty-two, a teacher, musician and an active member of a mountain rescue unit in the Lake District. He was interested in travel and new experiences and disliked people who brought him down.

But haters gonna hate, he said. *The rest of us just gotta smile and walk on by.*

He sounded very pleasant.

But there was no way she was going on a date with anyone she didn't know right now.

No way.

She deleted the email. When this was over — when the Strangler was behind bars — she'd maybe look him up, if he was still on the website. And if he wasn't? Well, then it wasn't meant to be, and she was fine with that.

4

By Wednesday, Kate was having second thoughts about staying at her parents' house; by Thursday she was trying to think if she had any colleagues or friends who needed someone to share their house with; by Friday afternoon, sitting at her desk with a weekend of cups of tea and not very subtle questioning from her mum ahead of her, she was ready to move in with the Strangler and take her chances.

OK, maybe not that, but not far off.

It wasn't that she didn't love her parents — she did, of course she did — but that didn't mean she wanted to live with them. Kids left home at a certain point; late teens for some, early twenties for others, thirties, forties, maybe fifties for a few. And they left because they were ready to live their own lives. There was a period of transition, of coming home on weekends for a meal and to get clothes washed, of mentioning that money was a bit tight that month in the hope that a parental cash donation might be made, of borrowing Mum's more reliable car when a long journey was in the offing, but that period came to an end, and when it did the chick was fully fledged.

Kate was finding that moving back in after having gone through that wasn't like going back to how it had been before: it was much worse. She was not the person she had been when she had last lived there — a person, remember, who had decided to leave — she was someone totally different, someone fully formed, an adult, who came home when she wanted or stayed up late watching trashy movies or had the occasional cigarette when her friends came over and they drank too much wine.

Home was the same, though. *It* had not changed. Her mum and dad were still in bed by ten, the lights off downstairs; her mum still tidied up all clutter and wiped down every surface and hoovered the floor at the end of every day; her dad still couldn't resist passing comment on the television programmes she watched.

Rubbish, he'd say. *These people are talentless. These Pop Idol shows are glorified karaoke.* Or: *Why anyone would want to watch a bunch of idiots in a house is beyond me.* Or: *Why don't you read a book? Or play the piano? Surely it's better than watching this junk.*

It made her want to scream and run back to her house and never mind if the Strangler came and murdered her in her bed.

And, as luck would have it, she had no plans for that Friday night. May was going out for dinner with Gus, who wasn't working a Friday night for the first time in three weeks, and Gemma had sent a reply to her request for a Friday-night drinking buddy.

Sorry! Going to Matt's mum and dad's place. It's their fortieth wedding anniversary.

Forty years. It seemed almost impossible that

anyone could be married for that long. Her parents weren't far behind: they'd shared thirty-six years of marital bliss, although not all of it had been bliss. Kate remembered some pretty big arguments when she was a teenager; aged thirteen or so, she'd been convinced that her parents were going to split up, so much so that she'd asked her dad when the divorce was.

Eh? he said. *What divorce?*

You and Mum. You seem to hate each other.

He put his arm around her. *Seem,* he said. *That's the word that matters. We're having a rough patch, but every husband and wife do. Think about it: if you're with someone for thirty years and you're unhappy ten per cent of the time — and ten per cent's not bad — that's three years. And when you're in one of those years it can feel like a long time. So don't worry, petal. We're not getting a divorce. We'll muddle through this and things'll be back to normal.*

A few months later, they were — if normal was defined as a low-level mutual exasperation.

She wondered whether her generation were less pragmatic than her parents, whether they wanted more, wanted instant and total happiness and turned tail at the first sign of anything less than that. Maybe, maybe not. What she did know was that she had nothing to do but sit around with her mum and dad on a Friday night after a long week at work.

She replied to Gemma.

Enjoy. Forty years is amazing. Give them my

162

congrats. I'll be at my mum and dad's living the dream . . .

She checked the time on her phone. A few minutes after four p.m. Another half an hour in the office and she'd get out of there, go home to her wild Friday night, to her mum pouring her a small glass of white wine at dinner and then watching to see if she drank another, or, heaven forbid, one after that.

Have you not had enough, darling?

No, Mum, or I wouldn't be having more.

And then she'd feel guilty and a bit stupid, because, after all, why *did* she need more? Why not settle in for a quiet night, get a good sleep, wake early and go for a run? Why not settle for Phil, for a *good enough* life? Because, a voice told her, good enough might be as good as you get.

A bird in the hand is worth two in the bus, she thought, then smiled.

That's what her and May and Gemma used to say. *Bus*, not *bush*. They liked to do that: make subtle changes to familiar sayings then use them in everyday conversation and see if people would pick them up on it. Most people didn't; those that did met with fierce resistance to their suggestion that the girls were incorrect.

It's true, they'd say. *It's bus, not bush. And a rolling stone gathers no mush. You'll be saying that's wrong next.*

But no. Right now, a bird in the hand was *not* worth two in the bus. She wouldn't settle. She decided to see if Nate wanted to grab a drink

163

after work. She knew that he was interested in her, and that she had to be careful not to lead him on, but she couldn't go home, not yet.

She moved the mouse to shut down her computer.

She had an email from Dating Harmony. Someone had seen her profile and wanted to get in touch. For a second she considered it, but no — she'd made up her mind. With the Strangler out there it was too risky.

She glanced at the photo of the person who had sent her the message, then froze.

It looked like Mike.

Surely not. She peered at her screen.

It was him. MikeSadler79.

She clicked on the link and accepted the request. She typed a message.

Hey, you didn't mention you were on this site.

The reply came a few minutes later.

Neither did you! But since you are, I thought I'd say hi and see if you want to meet up sometime.

Damn, Kate thought. She'd made up her mind that she wouldn't meet up with anyone she met through the website until this Strangler thing was over.

Except Mike wasn't the Strangler. He'd been in Turkey when the first victim was killed.

So she could — if she wanted — bend the rules. And she had thought he was kind of charming when she'd bumped into him in the pub. Attractive, was the word. Not handsome — that only described an appearance — but attractive. That described the effect he had: there was something about him that attracted her.

OK. Why not? When?

He replied instantly.

Tonight? I'm not doing anything. I know it's short notice and you're probably busy, but worth a try.

Kate grinned.

As it happens, she wrote, my date cancelled at the last minute, so I'm looking for a replacement. We could meet for a drink?

5

They arranged to meet at a pub not far from Kate's parents' house. At dinner her mum tried — and failed, miserably — to conceal how avid her interest was in Kate's plans.

'Are you sure you want to go out with someone you don't know? With everything that's going on?'

Her dad nodded sagely in agreement.

'I told you. I do know him,' Kate said, aware that, while not exactly a lie, she was not quite telling the truth. 'I met him on holiday. In Turkey.'

Her mum rolled her eyes and puffed out her cheeks. 'Well, that's all right then,' she said. 'I feel a lot better knowing that my little girl is going out with a man she met in some bar in a foreign country.'

Kate gritted her teeth. 'I. Am. Not. Your. Little. Girl,' she said. 'I'm twenty-eight and a successful lawyer.'

Then why do I feel like I'm fourteen and a hormonal teenager? she thought. *Parents are like time machines: they take you back to your adolescent self.*

'You'll always be my little girl,' her mum said.

'And mine,' her dad added. He coughed. 'You said you met him in Turkey? You didn't mention him.'

'It wasn't a big deal.'

'Must have been quite a big deal, to stay in touch,' her mum said.

'We didn't. He found me on a website.'

Too late she realized her mistake.

'Did you say a website?' her mum asked. 'Not one of those dating websites, surely?'

'Yes, Mum, one of those dating websites. There's nothing wrong with them.'

Her mum's expression was somewhere between shock, disbelief and disgust. 'You might think that, but as far as I'm concerned it's — well, it's a bit obscene, advertising yourself out there, like you're for sale in a shop.'

'It's not like that,' Kate said. 'It's not like that at all.'

'Hmm.' Her mum looked away. 'I hope no one finds out. I'd be ashamed.'

Kate pushed her plate away from her. There was no point in trying to convince her parents that dating websites were not the same as escort agencies, and that she hadn't, driven mad after the break-up, become a prostitute.

'I'm going to get dressed,' she said. 'Thanks for dinner.'

★ ★ ★

He was sitting at a table in the corner of the pub. She hadn't been there for about a decade and the place had changed from a dark-panelled drinkers' haunt into a modern, anytime, any-place gastropub of the type that had proliferated all over the country. No doubt they were beloved of accountants and bankers who

167

salivated over the *diversified revenue streams* and *brand value creation*, but there also was no doubt that something had been lost in the transformation.

Not the hardcore drinkers, though. They still sat at the bar, passing occasional comment to the other regulars, but communing in any meaningful sense only with the drink that sat before them.

'Hey,' he said. 'Great to see you. You look well. And I have to say that I still like the new haircut and eye colour.'

He was wearing dark jeans and a fitted, well-made shirt that highlighted how lean and muscular he was. Kate guessed that he had not been one of the boys in school who all the girls had a crush on — but he had aged well and had a lively, inquisitive look in his eyes.

Attractive, she thought again. *That's what he is.*

'You too,' she said. 'What are you drinking?'

'I'll get it.'

'It's OK. I'm on my feet. What do you want?'

'I'll have a glass of red wine, then. Thanks.'

'Anything in particular?'

'No. The cooking stuff's fine. I don't drink much, so anything good's wasted on me.'

She came back with two small glasses of house red and put them on the oak table. Pubs no longer contented themselves with shiny dark wood tables that were easy to wipe down and didn't show stains. Now it was Scandinavian-inspired hardwood furniture that looked good with a triangular bowl of feta, rocket and peach salad on it.

'Good week?' he said.

'Busy. Thank God it's the weekend.'

'Where do you work?'

'In Manchester.'

'Ouch. So you have the commute on the M56.'

'Or the M62. Either one can be a nightmare. What about you?'

'My office is in Chester, but I work from home a lot. I travel quite a bit.'

'What do you do?' It was strange to be having this getting-to-know-you chat when they had already slept in the same bed, although Kate was surprised how unselfconscious she felt. Of course, since she didn't remember most of the night they'd spent together, she could well have already asked about his job.

'Consulting,' he said. 'IT stuff. I advise companies on what kind of IT strategy they could put in place — you know, if they have dated architecture or underlying systems, how to modernize, that kind of thing. Pretty boring.'

'Sounds exciting,' Kate said, not meaning it.

'You don't mean that. You're being nice.'

Kate blushed. 'No!' she said. 'I mean the travel, that must be kind of good . . . ' her voice tailed off. 'OK,' she said. 'It does sound a bit boring. But my job's not much better! I'm a lawyer.'

'That *is* interesting,' he said. He put on a stentorian voice. 'Where were you on the night of March twenty-second? I put it to you that you were in fact engaged in the robbery of the

169

Warrington branch of Barclays Bank, along with your co-conspirators Scarface, Lefty and Short-stuff.'

Kate laughed. 'Sadly, I'm not a barrister,' she said. 'Or involved in criminal law at all. All my stuff is corporate: breach of contract, liability, intellectual property disputes.'

'Oh,' he said. 'Then I take it back. That's as boring as my work.'

'We do get some perks,' Kate said. 'Some of the lawyers have contacts with the police, so we get the inside scoop on stuff.'

'Like?'

'Like the Stockton Heath Strangler.'

He frowned. 'That's the guy who's been killing women, right? I've read some stuff about it. To be honest, though, I try to avoid reading too much. I don't want to know about some sick idiot. And I find all the interest a bit distasteful. It only encourages these people.'

'I know,' Kate said, thinking *Shit, why did I bring that up? Now I look like one of those people with an unholy interest in the Strangler.* She sipped her wine then got to her feet.

'Ladies room,' she said. 'I'll be right back.'

★ ★ ★

They had one more drink; she had another glass of red, he had a ginger ale. Their conversation flowed easily, slipping from topic to topic. She noticed that they were laughing a lot; when they finished their drinks, she found it hard to believe that it was already ten p.m.

170

And she realized that she was sad the time had passed so quickly.

'Sorry to be a party pooper,' he said. 'But I have an early start tomorrow. Properly early. Like five a.m.'

'What are you doing?'

'I'm going swimming,' he said. 'The Great North Swim, in Windermere. I need to get up early and get going.'

'God,' Kate said. 'I never do anything like that. I'm always too exhausted. I don't know where you get the energy.'

'The more you do, the more energy you have,' he said. 'At least, that's what I find. And I sleep better if I'm tired; if I've been sitting around all day I can't go to bed.' He reached behind for his coat. 'You need a lift home?'

'It's OK. I drove.'

'You OK?' He looked at the empty wineglass. 'To drive?'

'I should be. We've been here a while, and I only had two glasses.'

'Two glasses might be over the limit, especially with pub measures.' He raised a hand. 'Sorry. None of my business. I'll shut up.'

He was so sensible. So responsible. Like the night they'd met and he hadn't taken advantage of her. It wasn't what she imagined she would be looking for when she thought of an ideal partner — *I'd like to meet Mr Sensible, please* — but she liked it. A lot.

She liked *him* a lot.

'You have a point,' she said. 'But I think I'm OK.'

'Good.' He smiled at her. 'I'd love to see you another time. This was fun. *You're* fun.'

'You too,' Kate said. 'We should definitely do this again.'

'What's your mobile number?' He took out his phone and Kate gave him her number. He typed it in and called her; in her bag, her phone rang.

'There,' he said. 'Now you have my number. Call me.'

6

Phil sat at a metal table in a windowless room and waited for DI Wynne to show up. She'd called that morning — a Saturday, for God's sake — asking to see him. He'd suggested that they meet in Costa Coffee. She said no: she wanted him to come to the station.

He hadn't seen her since the previous Sunday, when she and DS Chan had interviewed him; nearly a week later, the detective had red blotches on her cheeks and looked tired and irritated; DS Chan looked hungover.

'Mr Flanagan,' she said. 'I'd like to talk to you about the evening you spied on Ms Armstrong.'

'What about it?'

'Could you describe your state of mind that evening?'

'I was . . . ' Phil paused, searching for a suitable word, ' . . . upset.'

'Upset? Is that all?'

'More or less. It was a difficult time for me.'

'How upset were you, would you say?'

Phil nearly laughed. 'My girlfriend of ten years had broken up with me, more or less without warning. I'd expected the next big change in our relationship to be marriage. It was a shock to find out that it was termination. So I was — I would say — pretty bloody upset.'

'Do you normally react in that way when you are upset?'

173

'In what way?'

'Acting secretively. Spying on people. Would you, for example, spy on your boss if you lost your job?'

'I don't know. It's never happened before.'

DS Chan nodded. 'So the one time it has happened, this is how you reacted?'

'Evidently,' Phil said. 'But I'm not sure what this has to do with anything.'

'It's of interest,' DI Wynne said. 'I'm not wasting your time, you can trust me on that.' She sipped her water. 'Would you say that there was anything unusual about your state of mind? Apart from being upset?'

'I'm not sure what you mean by unusual?'

'Did you feel in control of your actions, Mr Flanagan?'

'Yes!' Phil said. 'Of course!'

He thought back to that night, to when Carl had come outside and he had been forced to flee, and, as he ran, he had thought *What the hell am I doing?* There had been a moment of clarity, a moment when he realized that he was acting a little bit crazy, that he was being driven on by something outside of himself.

But he wasn't going to tell the cops that. It would only make things look a lot worse.

The detective seemed to sense his uncertainty. 'Sometimes, Mr Flanagan,' she said, 'people can enter a state in which they are not themselves. I wonder if you recognize that sensation at all?'

'No,' Phil said. 'Not at all.'

'Before the incident outside the house, Ms Armstrong claims she was followed by someone

174

who drove very closely behind her and dazzled her with their high beams. Do you know anything about that?'

Phil shook his head. The last time they had spoken, the detective had referred to an earlier incident on that night. Was this it? 'No,' he said. 'Was someone harassing Kate?'

'She says so. I wonder if it might have been you?'

'I said it wasn't,' Phil said.

'Mr Flanagan, let me explain how it appears from our point of view. We know you were in the area that evening, waiting for Ms Armstrong to return. We know you were in a state of high emotion — upset, as you termed it — and we know that you spied on her. It is not a huge leap to wonder whether you also followed her in her car. Perhaps to scare her.'

'No,' Phil said. 'It wasn't me! I don't know what else I can say. I only found out when you told me. And why would I want to scare her?'

'Why *would* you?' DS Chan said. 'Good question. How about because, if she felt frightened and vulnerable, she might be keen on having her boyfriend back in the house?'

'That's ridiculous,' Phil said. He looked at DI Wynne. 'You must see that.'

DI Wynne smiled. It was not a warm smile.

'Let's move on,' she said. 'Mr Flanagan, there have been three very troubling — very vicious — murders recently. They started after your girlfriend broke up with you, all the women killed resemble your girlfriend, and you were the last person known to be with the third victim.

You have no alibi for any of the murders, and you have admitted to some erratic behaviour, namely spying on your ex-girlfriend. Then there's the CCTV footage at the all-night garage and the lies you told about that. You can see how this looks.'

DI Wynne paused. DS Chan spoke up.

'Now would be a good time to confess, Mr Flanagan. If there is anything you think that we should know, then telling us now would certainly help your case.'

Phil didn't reply. He pushed his coffee away.

'I need to see a lawyer,' he said.

★ ★ ★

The lawyer he found — a bespectacled man in his sixties called Edward Marks — sat on the shabby couch in the front room of Andy's apartment holding his mug of tea with a look of some distaste. Tea, clearly, was meant to be served in more elegant cups.

'Thanks for coming on a Saturday,' Phil said.

'Not a problem,' Marks said. He took a file from his briefcase. 'Let's get started. Here's where we are. The police evidently view you as their number one suspect, in part because they have no others.'

Phil felt the blood drain from his face. 'But I didn't do it,' he said. 'This is so unfair. They're going to pin this on me!'

'No, they aren't,' Marks said. 'Let me be clear with you: the police think you did this. But all they have is circumstantial evidence. Now, you

176

can get a conviction with circumstantial evidence, but it's damn tricky, and they'd need more than they have here. Yes, you have a motive. Yes, you have no alibi. But that means — pardon my language — bugger all. In an English court of law, they need proof beyond reasonable doubt, and that is, as it happens, a very high standard of proof. It is one of the glories of our legal system, and what it means right now is that they won't arrest you or take you to a trial until they have evidence.' He leaned forward, putting his untouched tea on the table in front of him. 'And at the moment they don't have any. Your DNA was not on any of the murder victims, which is good news. The bad news is that no one else's was, either. The killer did not leave any traces, at least not that the forensic folks have been able to find. Which means you are not ruled out.'

'So what do I do?'

'You wait, Mr Flanagan. You wait until they clear you or they catch you.'

7

Kate had *that* feeling. The feeling of possibility, of newness, of growing excitement that something might be getting started.

She had a smile on her face when she left for work on Monday morning, and a smile on her face when she sat down at her desk. She grinned at the man in the sandwich shop at lunch and hummed as she worked through her emails in the afternoon. She felt a thrill go through her when she saw she had an email from Mike.

How goes the battle? Drink this weekend? Maybe Friday evening?

She typed a reply:

Yes! Sounds good. How was the swim?

She swapped *great* for *good*, then sent the message. Moments later he answered:

Awesome. Really good fun, although it was a bit choppy so I swallowed about half the contents of the lake. 7 pm on Fri?

Seven p.m. on Friday. It felt a long way away.

★ ★ ★

On her way home, her phone rang. It was DI Wynne.

'Miss Armstrong,' she said. 'How are you?'

'Fine. You? How's the investigation going?'

'We're making progress.'

'How can I help?'

'Could we meet? I have some questions I'd like to ask.'

Kate gave her parents' address, and said she'd be home by six.

★ ★ ★

She was late; when she pulled up outside her parents' house it was closer to six twenty, and DI Wynne's dark red Honda civic — old, but very clean — was parked on the street.

In the living room the detective was perched on the edge of the floral patterned couch with a cup and saucer balanced on her knee. In her hand she held a piece of shortbread. Kate's mum was hovering by the door.

'There's someone to see you,' she said, then lowered her voice and raised her eyebrows. 'She says she's a detective.'

'I know her, Mum,' Kate said. 'It's OK.'

She went into the living room and closed the door. There was no doubt whatsoever that her mum would listen outside it.

'Detective Inspector,' she said. 'How are you?'

'Good, very good.' DI Wynne flashed her a brief, mirthless smile. 'Miss Armstrong, could I ask you some questions about the car that followed you?'

179

'Of course.'

'Could you describe it?'

'I didn't get a good look. But it was a pretty normal car.'

'Could you explain what you mean by 'normal'?'

'Four-door family car. That kind of thing, you know?'

'A saloon car? Or a hatchback, like a Golf?'

'Saloon, I think.'

'Colour?'

'Dark. Black. Maybe grey.'

DI Wynne nodded. 'Or dark blue?'

'Could have been,' Kate said. 'But I only got a glimpse, so it could have been a purple Jeep, to be honest.'

'But you don't think it was. If pressed, you would say it was a dark-coloured saloon car of some type?'

'I guess I would, yes.'

'Mr Flanagan drives a dark blue Mondeo,' DI Wynne said. 'Could it have been that car?'

Kate hesitated. The last thing she wanted was to get Phil in trouble. 'Look,' she said. 'You need to talk to Phil about this.'

'We have. But — '

'What did he say?'

'He said that it wasn't him, but — '

'Then it wasn't him. He admitted to hiding outside the house, so why wouldn't he admit to the car?'

DI Wynne sipped her tea, then put the cup and saucer on the coffee table.

'I am trying to establish whether it could have

180

been Mr Flanagan's car,' she said. 'That's all.'

'It *could* have been,' Kate said. 'But it could have been lots of cars.'

'It could,' DI Wynne said. 'One other thing, Ms Armstrong. Is Mr Flanagan a keen biker?'

'Keen-ish. He likes to ride his bike from time to time. Why?'

'We've found tracks from bike tyres near the murder scenes.' She shrugged. 'Probably nothing, but we're keeping an open mind.' The detective stood up. 'Thank you, Ms Armstrong. That's very helpful. I'll see myself out.'

* * *

Kate followed her to the front door and watched her drive away. Why were they trying to prove that Phil had followed her in the car? Even if it was him, what did that have to do with the murders? He was simply upset — very upset — at the break-up.

And the bike? It was only a bike, surely. Millions of people had them. It didn't mean anything.

She closed the door and went upstairs. She had a horrible, uneasy feeling that something was very wrong.

Maybe Phil had followed her and was lying about it, but that didn't make sense. If it was Phil, then why would he lie? If it was because he didn't want to piss her off it was too late for that: that ship had sailed when he confessed to hiding at the end of the street.

Unless he was covering up something worse.

Unless he *was* the Strangler. And it made sense, in a way. She could see the press stories now: *MAN DRIVEN MAD BY BREAK-UP KILLS WOMEN WHO REMIND HIM OF HIS EX.*

Kate sat on her bed and hugged her knees. All the optimism of her fresh start with Mike drained away. She felt guilty — which was ridiculous, this wasn't her fault — and scared. If it was Phil, then was he coming after her? Who the fuck knew? Who the fuck knew *anything* in this kind of situation?

But it couldn't be Phil. It couldn't. She knew him as well — almost as well — as she knew herself, and he wasn't a killer. She was sure of it.

Almost sure, that was.

8

Kate looked at her phone, her finger hovering over the green 'call' button. She'd been hesitating for a few minutes, but was close to making up her mind.

She didn't want to speak to Phil, but she had to know what was going on, and she had to hear it from him. She'd known him for a long time, and she was sure that he would not be able to hide the truth from her. If he was lying, she'd know.

At least, that was what she told herself. A voice in the far corner of her mind whispered that she was being naïve, that we never truly know anybody, and that, even if we do, people change, and they can change quickly, pivot on a sixpence, be knocked onto an entirely new trajectory if something powerful and unexpected enough happens to them.

Like an out-of-the-blue break-up with the love of their life.

She dismissed the thoughts, and called him. He answered immediately.

'Kate?' he said. He sounded hoarse, and, she couldn't help notice, hopeful. 'Hi. What's up?'

'Can you talk?' Kate said.

'I'm at work,' he replied. 'But yes, of course. What is it?'

'I'm sorry to bother you with this, Phil, but I

need to know . . . ' she paused, 'I need to know what happened the night you were outside my house. I need to know if you followed me in your car.'

'Have you been talking to that detective?' he said, his voice suddenly harder. 'I told her it wasn't me. Did she get you to call me?'

'No. And if she had, I wouldn't have done it, for the record. I want to know for my own peace of mind.'

'Like I said, it wasn't me.'

'Phil, this is important. If it was you, I need you to tell me. I won't talk to DI Wynne about it, I promise, but I need to know.'

There was a long pause.

'Let's talk face to face,' Phil said. 'Now's not a good time.'

Kate tensed. 'You said you could talk.'

'I could, for a bit, but this will take more time.'

'I'll call you this evening.'

'No. It needs to be in person. That way you can look me in the eye and know that I'm telling the truth.'

'Phil, I'm not sure it's a good — '

'Then don't. But I'm not doing it over the phone.'

Kate paused. She could meet him in a well-lit, public place at a busy time. Maybe in the town centre, on a bench outside.

'OK,' she said. 'How about this evening?'

'Sure,' he replied. 'Just tell me when and where.'

* ★ *

184

He was already there when she arrived, sitting on a bench in the Golden Square shopping mall, shoppers and workers streaming around him. He had his arms folded, and he needed a shave.

She sat on the other end of the bench, facing him.

'Wow,' he said. 'You look different.'

Kate ran her hand over her hair. 'Yeah. It was . . . you know. Because of the women. They all look the same.'

'Good idea,' Phil said. 'I like it.'

She could see that he was lying, but she didn't care. 'So. I wanted to talk to you.'

'And this is honestly where you want to meet?' he said.

'It's fine. As good a place as any.'

'Nice and public,' he said. 'I can't hurt you here. That's why you chose it, isn't it?'

'No!' Kate said, then sighed. 'Yes. I suppose so. I'm worried, Phil.'

'You don't need to worry about me. I would never hurt you. Never. You know that.'

The sudden intensity in his voice startled her; she flinched away.

'What?' he said, his voice rising. 'Why are you scared of me?'

A man in a suit turned to look; Phil lowered his voice.

'So what do you want?' he said, deflated. 'What do you need to know?'

'There's been a lot of weird stuff happening lately. Three things, mainly.'

'One of them was me under the tree, right?'

'Right. The other was the car following me — '

185

Phil interrupted. 'Which wasn't me.'

She ignored him. 'And there was another. I think someone was in the house. I came back and the computer was shut down. I *never* shut it down.'

'I know. It used to piss me off.'

'Which is how I know that it wasn't me who shut it down. Someone else did.'

Phil stared at her. 'Are you saying that was me?' he said. 'As well as the car?'

'Who else could it be?' Kate replied. 'You have a key. You might have needed a file from the computer, or something like that.'

'I would have asked.' He laughed sarcastically. 'Unless of course I was spying on you, or whatever it is you're going to accuse me of next.'

'Look, Phil, you've been upset. You're not yourself.'

'It wasn't me, Kate,' Phil said. 'I know what the cops — and you, it seems — think. I know they have some idea that I'm losing my mind and doing this stuff in some kind of a trance, but I'm not. I miss you, I love you, my heart is totally broken and I don't know how I'm going to live the rest of my life, but that does not mean I did these things.'

'Then who did?'

The words hung between them. Eventually, Phil shrugged.

'I don't know. Maybe you imagined it. Maybe you did switch off the computer, or knock the plug out, or something else.'

'I didn't.'

'Then it was someone else. But it wasn't me.

The Strangler, maybe.'

Kate closed her eyes to fight the tears that were threatening to come. Was she making this up? Was it her who was going crazy?

When she opened her eyes, Phil was standing up.

'I have to go,' he said. 'It was nice seeing you.' He gave a little wave. 'Bye, Kate.'

9

Friday afternoon. Phil had read a study somewhere claiming that the average time that people stopped being productive on a Friday was two fourteen p.m. After that, they entered weekend mode and mentally switched off. They might be physically present in their workplace, but they might as well not have been, because they got nothing done.

In happier times — when he'd been a relaxed, charming, fun member of the team — he'd suggested to his boss that they recognize this by instituting a two fourteen p.m. finish time on Fridays.

No point is keeping people here if they're doing nothing, boss, he'd said.

Yes, she replied, *but it's not two fourteen that's important. It's that two fourteen is about two hours before everyone normally goes home. If we made the official end of the day two fourteen, then everyone would mentally clock off at twelve fourteen. Then you'd come to me with a study showing that to be the average time people stopped being productive, and the working day would end then. We'd end up cancelling Fridays altogether.*

Sounds good to me, Phil said. *Should I put it on the agenda for the next staff meeting?*

Sure. And how about preparing a proposal for a mini-weekend in the middle of the week? We

188

could have Wednesdays off too.

I'm on it, boss.

It hadn't happened, of course, but at least he'd been the kind of person who could joke about that kind of thing.

Now he was watching the clock, hungover, and waiting for the moment he could go home and have a nap. Or a cup of tea. Or a beer, maybe.

He was going out with Andy, to some bar in Liverpool where there was, according to his friend, wall-to-wall pussy, whatever that meant. For Andy, going out was still about getting smashed and picking up women, although his picking up women bore a close relation to his fishing: lots of time and money invested in it, but not many actual fish caught or women picked up.

Phil hadn't done that since he and Kate had got together when he was sixteen, and it wasn't like he'd done much of it before then. A few discos, some nights sneaking into pubs that didn't worry about the age of their punters, evenings drinking illicitly procured cider in the park.

Now, though, that was what he had ahead of him. He was a late twenties single man who went drinking and picking up women in bars in Liverpool which had wall-to-wall pussy.

He looked at the clock. Three twenty-nine. He was well past the end of his productive phase for the day, although the truth was that he had barely been in onc at all; he'd arrived late with a nasty headache. Cheap red wine clearly didn't agree with him, although in the quantities he and

Andy had drunk the night before, it was doubtful it agreed with anyone.

He logged off. He had to go. Maybe go for a run. Clear his head.

★   ★   ★

As he crawled over the Thelwall Viaduct — the busiest, or one of the busiest, motorway bridges in Europe, or so he'd heard — the traffic report came on the radio.

There was a major tailback on the M62 between Leeds and Manchester; the motorway was closed. Apparently a badly attached surfboard had fallen off the roof of a car and caused chaos behind it. The driver was probably oblivious; he'd only find out when he got home that he had left something behind.

Shit. Andy was coming back from Leeds. He'd be late, and Phil didn't feel like staying in on his own. He dialled his friend.

The phone went to voicemail.

'Hey, mate,' he said. 'I hear there's traffic on the M62. Let me know your ETA.'

Ten minutes later Andy called back.

'Mate, it's fucked,' he said. 'No way through. I'm aborting the mission.'

'Which means?'

'I'm going to see my buddy, Chaz. You know, the one that married that hot Polish chick, Elsa.'

'The one you went to uni with?'

'No. A guy I met skiing.'

Phil shook his head. This was typical of Andy; he had seemingly random friends all over the

190

place, the result of his easy-going, open character, and his complete lack of any boundaries. He thought nothing of showing up for the night unannounced at the home of one of these distant friends, which meant that, over time, he kept in touch with them.

'We can go to Liverpool tomorrow night,' he said. 'Unless you've got plans?'

'No,' Phil said. 'No plans. Tomorrow it is.'

'All right. It'll be great. Wall-to-wall pussy, mate, remember that. Wall-to-wall pussy.'

* * *

By six p.m. he was half-drunk and feeling sorry for himself. He didn't want to go to the village; he didn't want to sit in a busy Friday-night pub on his own, drinking away his sorrows in full view of the people he'd known all his life.

But he couldn't stay in. He'd go crazy. What he really wanted was to see Kate, to curl up on the couch in front of a crappy movie with her, but he knew that wasn't going to happen. Even catching a glimpse of her would be good enough, though. Just seeing her would do.

But even that was not going to happen, and it was driving him crazy. He had another large swallow of whisky.

He pushed the glass away. This was a disaster. He had to get out, had to do something. He grabbed his bike helmet and headed for the door.

10

Kate's mum's car bumped along the cobbled street that led to the Feathered Egg. The pub had a thatched roof and was supposed to be one of the oldest in the country; at one time it had been a coach house and there were stories of murders and robberies and dark dealings accumulated over the centuries.

The name came from one of those stories: in the time of the witch trials, a chicken had begun laying eggs with feathers on them, which was not, in itself unusual. It was the fact that the feathers were growing through the egg shells, and when they hatched they did not contain fluffy little chicks but baby wyverns.

This was taken as a sign of witchcraft, and, as there was a known witch in the area, it was obvious that it must be her work.

No proof was required; there was no other possibility. It was the work of witches, and everyone knew who the witch was. The Witchfinder General himself stayed at the coach house and oversaw the trial, which was swift: he declared her to be guilty.

No matter that the young — and beautiful — witch claimed to be with child as the result of intercourse (some called it rape) with Earl Belvoir, and suggested that he had staged the whole affair in order to rid himself of her and the babe. No matter that the Witchfinder General was a friend of his. No matter that the wyverns — the only pieces of real evidence — had disappeared.

She was executed by drowning that very day. Very convenient for the Earl.

But then, a week later, the Earl's horse threw him. He died of his injuries. Witchcraft from beyond the grave, some said. Bad luck, others said.

But justice had been done.

Her mum pulled up underneath the pub sign. There was a large, feathered egg in the foreground. Behind it stood a confused-looking chicken, a distant witch and a man lying at the feet of a horse.

'Shall I pick you up?' her mum said. 'Ten o'clock?'

'I might be a bit later than that,' Kate said. 'I'll make my own way home.'

'Don't get a taxi,' her mum said. 'It's not safe. Give me a call. I'll come and get you. But no later than eleven. I'll be in bed by then.'

Kate leaned over and kissed her mum on the cheek. 'Thanks, Mum. Love you.'

'Love you too. Have a nice time.'

She watched her mum drive away and walked into the pub. It was dark and warm and full of quiet chatter. It was not the usual Friday-night crew that you got in town; the clientele here was older, less frantic, but she noticed that there were fewer than usual. Perhaps fear of the Strangler was keeping people at home.

Mike was standing at the corner of the bar. He waved and she walked over.

193

'Hey,' he said. 'Happy Friday.'

'You too.' She felt a strong urge to touch him, to hold his hand or hug him or kiss him. She put her hand on his elbow. 'Good to see you.'

'What are you drinking?'

She ordered a gin and tonic; when it came they went to find a table. Mike passed her a menu.

'You want to eat?'

Kate nodded. 'I'm starving. Have you eaten?'

'Not yet. I'm going to have steak and ale pie. I always have it.'

'You come here a lot?'

'No. But I always have steak and ale pie, whatever pub I eat in.'

'Not very adventurous.'

'I'm a creature of habit. Plus, I don't like to waste time deciding. Easier to get something you know you like.'

Kate laughed. 'Does that only apply in pubs? Or other restaurants too?'

Mike wagged his head from side to side. 'Lasagna in Italian restaurants, crispy duck in Chinese, lamb jalfrezi in Indian.' He grinned. 'Keep it simple.'

'Don't you want to try different stuff?'

'I've tried plenty. And I've decided that the best way is to find something you really, really enjoy and stick with it.'

'All right then,' Kate said. 'I'll have steak and ale pie too.'

'Glad to hear it. I'll go and put the order in.'

Mike went to the bar to place the order. While she waited, Kate picked up one of the beer mats from the table. It had the picture from the pub sign on it. She turned it over; there was a web address and a message.

Interested in more tales from the bloody history of the Feathered Egg? Go to our website and click on the 'Gory Stories' link.

When Mike came back, Kate tapped the beer mat.

'You know the history of this place?' she said. 'How it got its name.'

He shook his head. 'No. I did wonder, though.'

'Look at the picture. It pretty much tells the story. It's the usual: powerful man, vulnerable woman. Apparently, there was a local girl who caught the attention of the Earl. He — '

Kate was interrupted by the sound of a glass breaking. It came from the bar. The pub fell silent for a moment, then there were some ironic cheers and a smattering of applause. Kate looked up to see who was the unfortunate person at the centre of attention.

'No way,' she said. 'I don't fucking believe this.'

11

'What is it?' Mike said. 'What's wrong?'

Kate turned to face him. 'Nothing,' she said. 'Well, nothing for you to worry about. I'll sort this out. Stay here.'

She started to get to her feet. Mike put his hand on hers to slow her down.

'Is everything OK?' he asked. 'Can I help?'

'No,' Kate said. 'I'll be fine.'

'At least tell me what it is.'

'Not what,' Kate said. 'Who. My ex-boyfriend showed up and smashed his glass on the floor.'

★ ★ ★

When she got to the bar, Phil was bending down, picking up shards of broken pint-glass while a barman with a dustpan and broom tried to persuade him not to.

'It's OK,' the barman said. 'I'll do it.'

'No,' Phil mumbled. 'It's fine. I'm sorry.'

'Seriously, mate, I'd prefer that you let me do it. I don't want you to cut yourself. It'll be a health and safety nightmare if you do.'

Kate reached down and grabbed Phil by the arm.

'Stand up,' she said. 'Get to your feet.'

Phil staggered into a standing position and stared at her, his eyes glassy and unfocused.

'Kate?' he said. 'What are you doing here?'

196

Kate had to fight to stop herself screaming. She could not remember when she had last been this angry. First, he showed up at the pub where she was having a date with her new boyfriend — well, with someone who may, one day, be her new boyfriend, but not if he thought he'd have some crazy ex to deal with — and then he had the gall to pretend he didn't know she'd be there.

'Outside,' she said. 'Now.'

'Let me get my drink,' he said, then looked down at the puddle on the carpet. 'Oh. I'll get another.'

'Are you drunk, Phil?'

'No,' he muttered. 'Not very. A bit.'

She steered him towards the front door. 'You're leaving.'

'I don't want to! You can't make me!'

'Don't make this worse than it already is,' Kate said, as she pushed him through the door. When they were outside she let go of him and folded her arms.

'What the hell are you doing here?' she demanded, struggling to keep her voice down.

'I wanted to get out,' he said. 'I was supposed to be going to Liverpool with Andy but he got stuck behind a surfboard . . . ' he paused, 'No, a surfboard fell on the motorway and so he had to stay in Leeds.'

'What the fuck are you talking about? Why are you making this shit up, Phil?'

'It's true! Check the news.'

'Whatever.' Kate shook her head. 'You need to leave me alone. Understand?'

197

'I didn't know you were here! I wanted a pub where there wouldn't be a load of people, so I chose this place.'

'That's such bullshit, Phil, and you know it.' She looked at him, noticed his bloodshot eyes. 'You *never* come here. What's happening to you? You're falling apart.'

'I miss you,' he said. 'I can't stop thinking about you and it's driving me crazy.'

How crazy? she thought. *Exactly how crazy is this driving you?*

'You're going to have to stop,' she said. 'You're going to have to move on.'

'I can't,' he said, a look of utter desperation on his face. 'Kate, I can't.'

'I'm sorry,' she said. 'But I can't help you, Phil. Only you can do that. And please, stop following me.'

'I didn't! I swear I didn't know you were here!'

'So this is sheer coincidence?' She gave a low, sardonic laugh. 'Until you start being honest, you're never going to get over this.' She paused. 'And more to the point, how *did* you know I was here?'

'I didn't.' He looked at her, his expression utterly wretched. 'Kate, I promise.'

Kate shook her head in disgust. 'Go home,' she said. 'And from now on, leave me alone.'

He backed away from her, tears in his eyes. She was surprised that he didn't head for the road; instead, he walked around the side of the pub.

'What are you doing?' Kate called.

He reappeared, pushing his bike in front of him.

'Getting this,' he said.

His bike. She stared at it. He'd been riding his bike a lot, it seemed.

'What are you looking at?' Phil said.

'Nothing. But you shouldn't be riding a bike,' Kate said. 'You've had too much to drink. And you're not wearing a helmet.'

He shrugged. 'I don't care,' he said. 'And don't pretend you do.' He climbed on his bike and started to ride away, bumping over the cobblestones.

Kate watched him go, then turned to go back inside, to Mike and her gin and tonic and steak and ale pie.

All of sudden, it felt a lot less inviting.

12

'Thanks,' she said, when she sat down.

Mike cocked his head to the side. 'What for?'

'For letting me deal with that. For not feeling you needed to come outside and protect me.'

'Oh. Well, thanks for thanking me, but' — he held up his hands — 'that's all between you and him. I take it he's your ex? And he's not handling the break-up that well?'

'No. Not well at all. It's been a while, but he can't seem to move on.'

'I can understand him being upset. There aren't too many people like you around.'

'Yeah, right,' Kate said. 'Flattery will get you everywhere.'

'I mean it!' He shrugged. 'But if you don't know how to take a compliment then that's fine. I won't waste any more on you.'

'I wouldn't go that far, Mike.'

'How long's it been since you broke up? Since before you went to Kalkan?'

'Yeah. That trip was partly to get away from' — she gestured in the direction Phil had taken — 'all this. I mean, I don't know how he even knew we were here.' She shook her head. 'I'm sick of it, you know? Sick of it.'

'Has there been a lot of trouble with him?'

'I'm not sure.'

'How so?'

'There's been a lot of trouble, but I don't know if it was all Phil.'

Mike leaned forwards. 'What kind of trouble?'

'There was someone who followed me in the car. And then someone was hiding on the street and watching me — that one *was* Phil — and then someone was in my house.'

His eyes widened. 'Were they there when you were in there?'

'No. I came home and the computer was switched off. And my filing cabinet had been messed with.'

'You think it was Phil?'

'I think it's likely.'

Mike nodded. He looked thoughtful. 'Maybe that's how he knew you were here.'

'What are you saying?'

'Do you leave your email logged in on your home computer? So when you open it you don't need the password?'

'Yes.'

'Then maybe he checked your mail.' He paused and held up his hands, as though apologizing. 'I don't want to accuse him of something he didn't do, but if he *was* in your computer then he could have set it up so that it automatically forwards your emails to him. That way, he'd see whatever plans you were making. Like tonight?'

'Is that possible?'

'Sure. It's pretty easy.'

Kate closed her eyes. This was getting more and more disturbing. 'Can I check? And change it?'

'I could take a look for you, if you want?'

'I think,' Kate said, 'that that would be a *great* idea.'

13

Phil pedalled furiously, the rushing air whipping up tears in his eyes and blurring the passing cars and people and trees.

It was so fucking *unfair*.

It wasn't like he'd had many hopes left that they'd get back together, but the few he *had* had were now gone for good.

It was over. *Over*. Such a small word; such huge implications. He wanted to howl and scream; instead he pedalled harder. He knew now beyond all doubt that this was not a break while she figured out who she was and what she wanted. That was what she'd said, that was how she'd softened the blow, but it wasn't true. It might have started like that, but it was emphatically not the case now. She had moved on. She had left him behind.

He should have known it would come to this. He should have known that if she was happy she would not have broken up with him in the first place. He'd tried to tell himself that she was just curious, that she'd been with him since they were teenagers so it was natural that she'd want to see what life apart was like. He'd even reconciled himself to the fact that she might have sex with other men.

And it was all fine, if at the end she realized that what she had with Phil was special and unique and irreplaceable and came back to him.

But that was off the cards now. He could see that as clear as day. She was almost a different person; she'd grown somehow, and even he could see that they no longer fit together.

Moreover, she had a new boyfriend. He hadn't seen him up close, but he'd caught a glimpse of his back. It was why he'd dropped his pint. She was out on a date. Already. Bitch.

So what now? He had nowhere to go. Andy was in Leeds, his parents were down in Dorset, in the cottage they'd retired to. Most of his other friends were in relationships with Kate's friends — Matt and Gus, for example — which was what happened when you stayed in your hometown and lived with your high school sweetheart.

He was going to have to start again. Maybe move to a new town. Get a job in London or Cornwall or Timbuc-fucking-too. Somewhere far away where he didn't know anyone and he could become whoever he wanted. Get a new girlfriend, a hot twenty-two-year-old fuck bunny. Have affairs with her friends. Take drugs and use prostitutes. Do whatever he felt like.

He'd tried to be a good, solid citizen. The kind of person who made a good husband and father. He'd worked hard and stayed sober and treated Kate with nothing but love and respect and care. And look where that had got him.

Well, it was time for a change. He was going to do what he wanted. Be irresponsible and free and have some fucking fun.

But that was the future. What about now, what about this evening?

204

The answer came to him and he grinned. Yes, that was it. If today was the end of the old Phil and the start of the new, then he needed to recognize that. Do something symbolic to mark his transformation.

And he knew just the thing.

★ ★ ★

She'd changed the lock.

Of course she had: she thought he'd been in the house and she wanted to make sure he didn't come in again.

He withdrew his key and headed around the side of the house. What she had forgotten — if she had ever known — was that the window in the downstairs bathroom had a broken catch and he was pretty sure she wouldn't have had it fixed. Either way, it was worth a try.

He felt strangely calm about breaking into his ex-girlfriend's home, although since she was staying at her parents' house he didn't think there was much chance of being caught. Still, he'd have expected his heart to be racing, adrenaline pumping, but it wasn't. He was emotionless.

Not himself, almost.

And he wasn't feeling guilty, either. He didn't care what she thought of him now. She'd made her position clear enough, so now he had nothing to lose.

He glanced around. No one there. He pushed the window open and levered himself off the ground. A few seconds later he was in.

Oh God, the smell. He had barely noticed it when he lived there, but now it hit him and a wave of nostalgia threatened to overcome him. He inhaled deeply, a look of near ecstasy on his face, then he shook his head and walked softly through the kitchen and living room to the hall.

He walked up the stairs, checking that his shoes were not leaving marks on the cream-coloured carpet, then pushed the door to the main bedroom open.

The bed was unmade. He put his hands on the sheets — so familiar, so comfortable — and lowered his face to the soft cotton. Again, he inhaled deeply, drinking in the scent. *Her* scent.

He stood up and crossed the room to the chest of drawers. He opened the top one and looked inside. It was half-full — she'd taken a lot of stuff to her parents — but he picked through the jumbled contents, letting the underwear slide through and over his fingers. He took out pairs of her knickers at random, remembering her wearing them, remembering peeling them off, pulling them over her hips and down her legs and throwing them onto the bedroom floor.

He was getting an erection. For a moment he considered masturbating, but he stopped himself; this was about moving on, saying goodbye, not returning to the past.

He wanted to though, desperately wanted to, but not as much as he wanted to have sex with her one more time, lie next to her and kiss her breasts and stomach and thighs, feel the softness of her skin, be with her like that, one last time.

But that would never happen. Some other guy

was fucking her now. He bit back a wail of anguish, and left the room.

He walked around the rest of the house, letting his memories flood over him, letting himself be swallowed up by his grief, letting all his emotions come to the fore. It felt good, cathartic, a way to finally move on. When he was done, he went back to the kitchen and stood in front of the sink.

He was thirsty. Very thirsty. Hangover-on-the-way thirsty. He turned on the tap and cupped his hands under the stream of water, lifting them to his mouth and drinking, again and again.

He heard a noise.

Hands halfway to the tap, he froze, and listened.

It was the front door, opening. Someone was here. Kate, it had to be, probably bringing her new man back here for a quick screw before she went back to her parents' house.

Fuck. He had to get out of there. He turned off the tap — the water sounded incredibly loud as it gurgled down the drain — and headed for the downstairs bathroom. The window squeaked as he pushed it open and he winced at the noise. He shrugged; it was too late to do anything about it now. He climbed out and grabbed his bike.

As he rode away he saw the lights go on in the living room.

Shit, he thought. *That was close.*

14

Kate switched on the light in the hall. It was not yet dark outside but the sun was dipping below the horizon.

'Did you hear that?' she said.

Mike shook his head. 'I didn't hear anything.'

'It sounded like a door shutting.' She gestured to the rear of the house. 'Or a window. It came from the kitchen.' She paused. 'Unless I'm hearing things, which isn't surprising after Phil's performance this evening. It's making me paranoid.'

'I'll go and check,' Mike said.

Kate followed him through the living room. He flicked on the kitchen light. It was empty.

'No one here,' he said.

Kate looked around. 'The sink's wet,' she said. 'Look.'

As she spoke, a large drip fell from the tap onto the brushed metal base of the sink.

'Leaky tap,' Mike said. 'That's all.'

He reached out and turned the tap. It moved about a quarter turn. 'It wasn't fully off,' he said. 'Probably been dripping like that since you left.'

Kate opened the fridge. It was pretty bare. 'Drink?' she said. 'I think there's some red wine around.'

'I'll have water,' Mike said. 'I'm in the car. Or tea, if you have any.'

Kate frowned. 'No milk,' she said.

'Water it is then,' Mike said. 'Now, let's have a look at this computer.'

* * *

'Well,' he said, a few minutes after he sat down at the monitor. 'Two things are pretty obvious.'

'OK,' Kate said, sipping a glass of wine. 'Go ahead.'

'One, you need a new computer. This thing's not much more advanced than a Spectrum Forty-eight K.'

'A what?'

'Never mind. Before your time. But the point stands: this is pretty badly out of date.'

'And the second thing?'

'Someone has been reading your emails.'

Kate sat up. 'How do you know?'

'Every email you receive or send is forwarded to another email address. ADPUNM776xc@gmail.com, to be exact. Ring any bells?'

Kate shook her head. 'None.'

'The thing is, your email would normally alert you to the fact that it was forwarding, but this was done outside the application.'

'What does that mean, in English?'

'It means that there's a program on your computer which is running in the background, intercepting your emails and sending them on. As long as you're logged into your email on this computer — which you always are — then every email you send or receive is getting read.'

'And how the fuck would that get on there?'

'Someone would have to install it.'

'Someone like Phil. Someone with a key for my house.' She banged her fist on her knee. 'That's how he knew where we were. That bastard's been spying on me.'

'It certainly seems that way.'

'Can you remove it?'

Mike nodded. 'Yeah. Pretty easy, once you know it's there. You want me to?'

Kate thought for a few moments, then shook her head. 'Not yet. Let's give that shithead a taste of his own medicine.'

'Sounds interesting. What are you thinking?'

She told him, and he laughed.

'You,' he said, 'have an evil mind.'

★　★　★

Ten minutes later they were ready.

Mike gave her a thumbs up. 'Should be in your inbox now,' he said.

Kate checked on her phone. There it was, an email from Rod–Granthorpe4537.

Hi babes, Rod — an entirely fictitious character whose email account Mike had set up — wrote. Great to see you this week. Want to meet up tomorrow?

Kate typed her reply:

Yes! I'm so glad we hooked up on Tinder. I've never done that kind of thing before and I wish I'd started earlier. Like I said when we met, I feel I've missed out on so much — and the sex was amazing! Better than any I've had before. I was sore for two days afterwards, but then I'm not used to such a big dick as yours. God, I nearly fainted when I saw it. I didn't know they made them like that! I can't wait to see it again! Tomorrow's perfect. How about the afternoon? Your place? I'm not sure I want my parents to hear the kind of noises I was making last time . . . and even if they're out, the neighbours will probably lodge a noise complaint with the council!

She hit send; a few seconds later Mike laughed. 'Wow,' he said. 'That's quite the reply.'

'Send something back,' she said. 'In the same vein.'

Tomorrow it is, you hot bitch. I'm getting hard already. I'll be ready, bumcakes.

Kate looked up from her phone. 'Bumcakes?' she said. 'Where did you get that from?'

Mike blushed. 'It's something I picked up. From a song.'

'A song?' Kate said. 'With 'bumcakes' in it?'

'It was in a film. *Spinal Tap.*'

'Spinal what?' She shook her head. 'Right. I'm rethinking this relationship.'

Mike tilted his head to one side. 'It's a relationship?'

It was Kate's turn to blush. 'You know what I mean.'

'Do I?' Mike said.

'Forget it,' Kate said. 'Forget I said it.'

Mike raised his hands, palms facing her.

211

'Forget you said what?' he said, raising his hands in mock innocence.

'That's right,' Kate replied. 'Forget I said what.' She looked at her phone. 'I need to call Mum,' she said. 'Ask her to come and pick me up.'

'I'll give you a lift,' Mike said. 'If you want?'

'That would be great. It'd save her the trouble. I'll send her a text and let her know.'

'You want to leave now?'

'I probably should. She'll be waiting up.'

Mike laughed. 'I feel like I've gone back in time,' he said. 'To when I was sixteen and my friends and I had to worry about getting in trouble with our parents for coming home late.' He paused, then added, almost as an aside, as though he was speaking to himself. 'At least my friends did. My mum and dad wouldn't have noticed.'

'Your parents weren't bothered if you came home late?' Kate said.

'It wasn't that, exactly,' Mike said, his tone brisk. 'It was no big deal. It was kind of a complicated situation. A long time ago now.'

Kate didn't press him; it wasn't any of her business, and if he wanted to share then he would, when the time was right. She started to shut down the computer.

'Hold on,' he said. 'I still need to take off the app, if you want me to?'

'Of course.'

He tapped away on the keyboard for five minutes or so. 'I've set up a password screen,' he said. 'So if he comes back here again he won't be

212

able to get on. This computer is safe as houses now.'

He passed her the keyboard, and turned away.

'Put in your new password,' he said. 'I won't look.'

★ ★ ★

They pulled up outside her parents' house. Mike put on the handbrake.

'That was fun,' he said. 'Even if Phil did show up. I enjoy spending time with you.'

Kate nodded. 'Me too,' she said, and smiled. It was refreshing to be with someone who was so open emotionally, who was able to express his feelings in a simple, plain way. With Phil, it was either nothing, or, if he had been out with his friends, drunken outpourings of love. Perhaps it was because Mike was older, but she didn't think so. It was just his way; he was not ashamed of showing how he felt, did not have any sense of pride or fear that his feelings might not be reciprocated. She had the impression that if she had told him she liked him as a friend and a friend only he would have accepted it; there was none of the puppy-like desperation that she saw in Phil.

And it made him all the more attractive.

She leaned over and put her hand behind his neck, spreading her fingers through his hair. There was a moment of hesitation on his part, then he kissed her. They kissed for a long time with an increasing level of passion; Kate felt a powerful desire for him grow in her.

She pulled away. 'Shall we drive somewhere?' she said.

He looked at her for a long time, then shook his head. 'I'd love to,' he said. 'But let's take our time. Make sure we get it right.'

For a moment she felt the sting of rejection, but then a surge of affection overcame it.

'OK,' she said. 'Good idea. What are you doing the rest of the weekend?'

'On Sunday I have to drive to London,' he said. 'I have a client meeting early on Monday.'

'And tomorrow?'

'I volunteer for a local charity,' he said. 'Help them with handyman stuff. I need to go there tomorrow.'

'Which charity?'

'A place in town,' he said.

'Which one?'

'It's a kind of . . . ' he paused, 'shelter. On Bridge Street.'

Kate realized why he was being evasive. She knew that shelter. Not many people did, but she — briefly — had been involved with it a few years back.

'Do you mean the shelter for women?' she said. 'Who need a place to get away from — stuff?'

'You know it?' he said.

'I had a — ' Kate stopped herself. 'I know of it.'

'That's the place,' Mike said. 'I try and help them when I can.'

'They don't like to have too many men around there,' Kate said.

214

'I know. But I go back quite a way with them. They know me pretty well.' He shrugged. 'So I'll be there in the morning. But I'm free in the afternoon, if you want to catch up?'

'Sure,' Kate said. 'I'll give you a call.'

15

LOCAL BUSINESSES 'STRANGLED' BY KILLER FEARS

With the serial killer known as the Stockton Heath Strangler still on the loose, local businesses are reporting that they are suffering a downturn in their fortunes.

Taxi firm Pritchard Cars have seen business drop by around a third since it was confirmed that a serial killer was targeting young women.

'They don't want to get in taxis alone — or even in groups,' Jeff Pritchard, the proprietor said. 'Even if a few get in, there always has to be one who gets dropped off last, and no one wants to take that risk.'

Other businesses are also feeling the effects. Bars and restaurants are reporting a significant drop in takings as people choose to socialize in the safety of their own homes.

The owner of one local restaurant — who preferred not to be named — is upset with the efforts of the police. 'They need to catch him,' he said. 'And if they can't, they need to make people feel safe. There should be officers on every street corner, so people know there's no threat.'

A police spokesperson declined to comment, saying only that the investigation was

*proceeding and that the police were making
every effort to catch the killer.*

The pun in the title was, Kate thought,
particularly insensitive, but the local paper finally
had something to write about — other than
planning consent issues and minor infractions
— and they were going to town on it.

Her mum came into the living room with a
cup of tea.

'Here you go,' she said. 'This'll make you feel
better.'

'I feel fine,' Kate said. 'But thanks.'

Her mum ignored her. 'And a bit of breakfast
will pick you up. I could make you a bacon
sandwich?'

'I don't need picking up. I only had a couple
of drinks last night.'

'How did you get home? You were going to
text me to let me know. Did you get a cab?'

Shit. She'd forgotten to text her mum. Now
she was back home — temporarily — she was
going to have to get back into the habit of
informing her parents where she was. 'Sorry,
Mum. I got a lift in the end.'

'From the man you met on the Internet? Was
that safe?'

Kate sipped her tea. Missed text or not, at her
age she did not need an interrogation first thing
in the morning. 'Yes,' she said. 'It was him, and it
was perfectly safe. You can tell because I'm here,
alive and well. In fact,' she added, 'I'm seeing
him again today.'

'Gosh?' her mum said. 'That's a bit sudden.

You don't need to rush into anything, you know.'

'I'm not rushing. I happen to enjoy his company, that's all.'

'I hope Phil doesn't find out. He'll be very upset.'

'He showed up last night,' Kate said. 'At the pub. He was totally drunk. I think this is tough for him, especially with the police treating him as a suspect.'

Her mum scoffed. 'He didn't do anything,' she said. 'He's a nice lad.'

'He's certainly having a hard time.'

'Well, don't make it worse for him,' her mum said. 'Be kind to him, Kate.'

★   ★   ★

She met May and Gemma for lunch and told them what had happened the night before.

'So Phil was reading your emails?' May said. 'That's fucking awful.'

'I feel bad for him,' Gemma said. 'I'm not saying that what he did was right — or even OK — but I do kind of understand. I mean, he must be so heartbroken — I can't help feeling bad for him.'

'I do, too,' Kate said. 'But he has to get a grip. He can't be following me around in his car or lurking outside — or inside — the house. Especially not with what's going on. And there was the girl he was seeing — '

'Michelle Clarke,' May said. 'Gus said the cops think Phil might have done it — he was the last person to see her alive, she looks like you, all

218

the rest of it. I told him there was no way. Of course he went for a girl that looks like you — he's on a massive rebound — but he didn't kill her. Not Phil. He wouldn't be able to.'

'You say that,' Kate said, 'but I don't know. I mean, I agree that it's a long shot, but' — she shrugged — 'you can't say for sure. He might not even be aware of what he's doing.'

'Anyway,' Gemma said. 'What about your date?'

Kate smiled. 'I like him,' she said. 'I'm not sure if he's the one, or anything like that, but I like him. For now.'

'Are you going to see him again?' Gemma asked.

'I am.'

'When?'

Kate looked at her phone. 'In about two hours.'

16

Mike was wearing paint-splattered work boots, a pair of dusty jeans and a black T-shirt that showed the sinewy muscles of his arms and his flat stomach. He was carrying a duffel bag over his shoulder.

'Sorry for the outfit,' he said. 'It took longer at the shelter than I thought. I didn't have a chance to get home and change.'

'That's fine,' Kate replied, thinking *I'm glad you didn't. Sexy doesn't do it justice.*

'So what do you want to do?'

'Well,' Kate said. 'I thought about an early evening drink and then something to eat, but I'm not sure that you're quite dressed for it.'

'Yeah,' he said. 'That'd be about right. How about I run back to my place, shower and change, then we meet up?'

* * *

They arranged to meet at Kate's house. On the way there she stopped and bought some basics: bread, milk, crisps, fruit and a bottle of Prosecco. It felt strange to be there alone after staying at her parents' house; she made sure that she locked the door, even though it was early evening on a Saturday.

You never knew. That was what she was learning; you never knew.

She resisted opening the Prosecco. That could wait until Mike arrived, if he was interested. She didn't want him to show up and find her halfway through the bottle while all he wanted was water or mint tea or some kind of healthy protein shake.

She liked him, she realized, more than she was comfortable with. In the first place, she didn't want a boyfriend at the moment, at least not a serious one, and in the second, she didn't want a boyfriend who was ten years older than her. Not that she had anything against it in principle; it was more that they were at different stages of their lives. She wanted to travel, try new things, be free to up sticks and move if she so desired. He — although he hadn't said as much — was more than likely looking to settle down, have kids, start the serious business of life.

She'd had enough of the serious business. She wanted to have some fun. But — like it or not — she was falling for him.

★ ★ ★

Half an hour later there was a knock on the door. Kate looked out of the window; it was Mike. She let him in. His hair was wet and slicked back; there were still paint-flecks in it. He had a bottle in one hand and a bunch of flowers in the other.

'Never show up to someone's house unarmed,' he said. 'That was what my aunt told me.'

'Your aunt?' Kate said. 'That sounds like a piece of mum advice.'

221

'Yeah. My aunt dished out most of the advice in my case. Mum wasn't one for that kind of thing.'

This was the second time he had made a cryptic, negative reference to his mum. Although she knew it was prying, Kate was desperate to ask for more information. She contented herself with a statement.

'She sounds an interesting character.'

'She was.'

'Was? Is she . . . ?'

'She died a few years back. Both my parents did.' He held up the bottle. 'Anyway, I know you don't have much in, so I brought this.'

Kate laughed. 'Prosecco,' she said. 'How lovely. Great minds think alike. I bought the same thing. Should I open one of them?'

'Why not?' he said. 'It's been a long day.'

★   ★   ★

Kate took two champagne flutes from the kitchen cupboard and unwrapped the foil and the wire cage from the cork. She twisted the cork; it turned slowly in the neck of the bottle. It took a few attempts to open it, but Mike didn't step in and try to take the bottle from her. She liked that, liked the assumption that she was capable and did not need immediate assistance with every basic physical task.

She poured the pale liquid into the glasses, then handed one to Mike.

'Cheers,' she said. 'Let's go and sit down.'

He stepped aside to let her pass; as she did,

her hip grazed his and she turned to face him. They looked at each other for a few moments, then they leaned into each other and their lips met.

Kate was aware of his scent, his freshly showered clean smell, and of her own mounting desire.

She put the glass on the worktop and put her arms around him, feeling the thick cords of muscle in his back; his free hand ran down from her shoulder to her buttocks and she shuddered.

Suddenly, he pulled away.

'We have to stop,' he said. 'Before we get carried away.'

Kate took the Prosecco from him and put it next to hers. She took his hands and pulled him towards her.

'I want to get carried away,' she said, and led him towards the stairs.

★ ★ ★

Afterwards they lay in her bed, side by side, silent. She and Phil had bought the bed together and only she and he, assuming he hadn't ever had an affair — which she was pretty sure was a fair assumption — had ever had sex in it, a state of affairs which she had once assumed would last forever, but which had now, suddenly, irrevocably, changed.

She was aware of Mike's warmth, of the heat coming off him after the exertions of the last half an hour or so. He was lying on his back, one arm around her, his eyes closed. Was this what he did after sex? Phil did one of two things: he got out of bed and took the condom to the bathroom or he lay with his head on her chest, one hand resting protectively on her stomach. She had never figured out what made him do one or the other; she'd always meant to ask but she doubted she would get the chance now.

She and Phil had a routine that they went through when they had sex. That wasn't to say that it was dull, or repetitive, but they knew each other so well, knew what gave each other pleasure, and they tended to focus on those things. It was different with Mike: it was all new. All uncertain. All to come.

It was thrilling.

She was going to discover all these things, make new routines, find new ways of getting and giving pleasure. It was, in so many ways, the perfect metaphor for her life after Phil.

Other people must go through the same thing, she thought, people who were married for twenty years, watched their kids grow up then realized they had nothing left in common and went their separate ways and found other people to share their lives with. They too must go through this exact process of discovery, of getting to know a new partner: what they liked to eat, how they drove, whether they brushed and flossed or only brushed. And what they like to do in bed.

Kate looked at her alarm clock.

'Whoa,' she said. 'It's eight. We need to eat.'

Mike opened his eyes. 'Yeah,' he said. 'I'm pretty hungry. I didn't eat all day.'

'And you've been on your feet at the shelter. That's tiring work.'

'And then there was the last hour or so. That took the dregs of my energy.'

'Hour?' Kate said. 'Don't get carried away with yourself, Mike. But I agree, you must be tired.' She paused. 'What did you do at the shelter today? It looked like you were painting.'

'Some painting,' he said. 'And I put in some new windows. Ones with extra security. They have to be very careful.'

'I know,' Kate replied. 'They deal with some tough cases.' She propped herself up on her elbow. 'You don't have to say anything if you don't want to, Mike. But I'm interested in how you became involved.'

'Well,' he said. 'It's kind of a long story.'

'We've got all evening,' Kate said. 'If you want to tell me, that is. You don't have to.'

Mike shrugged. 'No problem,' he said. 'But how about we order take-out first? I'm starving.'

They went downstairs and ordered Thai food; Kate poured two fresh glasses of Prosecco while they waited.

'So,' Mike said. 'The shelter. It was my mum. She spent a lot of time there when I was a teenager. My dad, he was' — he sipped his drink — 'well, he was very fond of this stuff, for a start. And he was an angry, disappointed man, who thought he should have done more with his life. And maybe he would have done, if he hadn't blamed everyone else for what went wrong. In particular, my mum.'

'What did he blame her for?'

225

'For wanting a baby. For trapping him in a conventional family. For giving him responsibilities which meant he had to get and keep a job so he could pay the mortgage. In his mind, she had stolen his chance to be someone by forcing him to fit the mould.'

Kate leaned against him, her head on his shoulder. 'What did he want to be?'

Mike laughed. 'Nothing. Everything. He didn't know: he just wanted to be someone other than who he was. Nowadays, shrinks would say he suffered from chronic low self-esteem and anxiety, which manifested as self-hatred — or something like that. All I know is that he drank it away, and when he did he got rid of that self-hatred by beating the shit out of my mum. Badly.'

Kate sat next to him still and silent, letting him talk.

'We're talking black eyes, broken ribs, internal bleeding. More than once she came to me, apologizing, needing me to go and get her painkillers from the chemist because she was in too much pain to go herself. That was me aged twelve: buying pills for my mum and feeling guilty that I couldn't stop it.'

'God,' Kate said. 'That's awful. And that's when you found the shelter? She went there?'

'Oh no,' Mike said. 'It got a lot worse before that happened.'

17

Wall-to-wall pussy.

That was one way of thinking about this place. Phil stood, back to a wall, and watched the pub as it filled up. It was only loosely describable as a pub; it was more accurately a large city-centre drinking palace, serving sugary, sticky drinks high in alcohol content or cheap, strong beer. Standing room only, all the better to pack more people in.

Phil's main problem was that he didn't like this kind of thing. Didn't enjoy the drinking — although he seemed to be doing plenty of it — didn't like the atmosphere or the fact that half the people there — the male half, mainly — were only out to pick someone up for casual sex. He'd tried that with Michelle and discovered that all he wanted was to have sex with Kate, and Kate alone. Some people wanted to play the field before they settled down, find out what was available, explore different opportunities, but he didn't. He wanted to be with Kate. But he couldn't.

And he couldn't forget it.

He checked his phone for the tenth, twentieth, fiftieth — who was counting? — time, hoping, as he hoped each time, even though he knew there was no chance it would happen, that there would be a message from Kate.

Come round. We need to talk.

Then he would go there and see her and they would sort this mess out.

There were no messages, not from her or anyone else, which was something else he was coming to realize. He didn't really have any friends. Andy, yes, but beyond that there was no one. He'd invested his entire life in Kate, and now that it was over, he found himself very isolated. He had work colleagues, but he'd kept them at arm's length, turning down most opportunities to socialize with them.

No texts from her, no texts from anybody.

He looked up. Andy was weaving his way through the clientele, four bottles of some drink in his hands. Behind him was a group of women about Phil's age — which was old for this place — wearing angel's wings on their backs and red devil horns on their heads. They were in white; one of them had L plates around her neck and the words 'Dirty Angle' printed on her forehead.

Andy grinned. 'Found you a dirty Angle,' he said. 'I'd have preferred a Saxon, but what can you do?'

'Hiya,' the woman said. 'I'm Dawn.' She was, in a way, pretty, but she was wearing too much make-up and too few clothes.

'She's getting married,' one of the other women shouted. 'We're on a hen night.'

'Is that so?' Phil said. 'I never would have guessed.'

'She's got to get off with twenty-one guys tonight,' another shouted. She was holding two shot glasses. 'A snog and a shot. Your mate said you'd be up for it.'

'Twenty-one?' Phil said. 'Twenty-one shots and twenty-one snogs?' He wasn't sure which was more shocking — the idea that someone who was shortly going to get married was prepared to kiss twenty-one strangers in a pub, or that she was able to consume twenty-one shots and not die of alcohol poisoning.

The woman with the shot glasses thrust one at him. She gave the other to Dawn.

'One, two, three,' Dawn said, then poured the shot down her throat.

'Go on,' Andy said. 'Get it down you.'

Phil looked at the liquid in the glass. It was green. He had no idea what it was. Maybe something minty. He'd had something like that once; when he was a teenager, someone had stolen a bottle of crème de menthe from their parents' cupboard and passed it round after school one Friday. Maybe it was that.

He drank it. Whatever it was, it wasn't crème de menthe. He couldn't tell from the taste what it was supposed to be — maybe some kind of fruit, or maybe pistachio, or maybe marzipan — but he did know that it was foul.

When she kissed him Dawn tasted of it, mingled in with cigarette smoke and something slightly rotten. He got the sense that she did not take much care with her dental hygiene. As she kissed him, she put her hands on his back, then felt down to his buttocks.

After a few seconds he pulled away. Dawn's friends all cheered. One of them passed him a red marker pen, and Dawn turned round.

There was a list of names written on the back

of her white dress. He counted seven — so he was the eighth person she'd done this to. For some reason he'd thought he was the first. He felt nauseous; God knew what germs she'd picked up.

'Sign her back,' someone said. 'Write your name.'

He leaned forward and read the names:

Elvis Presley
Simon Cowell
Your Dad
Jeremy Clarkson
The Elephant Man
David Cameron
Donald Trump

Phil thought for a second, then made his contribution.

Phil Flanagan, he wrote.

Then he handed the pen to her friend and picked up his drink.

★ ★ ★

Outside, there was a cold wind coming off the Irish Sea. Andy was still in the pub, standing in a corner fondling one of the hen party women. Phil was dizzy, and sick, and he wanted to go home.

He leaned over, his hand on a lamppost. On the pavement below his face was a congealed pizza and a half-eaten wrap of chips and mushy peas. They gave off a pungent, vinegary smell.

He retched, and a stream of watery vomit splattered the tarmac, splashing back onto his shoes and trouser legs. He put his hands on his knees and groaned.

'Mate,' a voice said behind him, 'that's fucking disgusting.'

There was a sharp push in his back and he fell forward, his temple slamming against the lamppost. He staggered to his feet; three broad-shouldered kids — maybe seventeen, eighteen — were laughing at him. They walked off, flashing V-signs.

He put his fingers to his temple. They came away wet with blood. Great. Perfect for Monday at work. He'd look like he'd been in a drunken bar brawl.

A private-hire taxi was waiting outside a pub fifty yards up the road. He walked up and knocked on the window.

The driver, a thin man with a pinched face and thick stubble, shook his head.

'I'm booked, mate,' he said.

'Fifty quid,' Phil replied. 'On top of the fare. Going to Warrington.'

The cab driver glanced around, checking that no irate punters were on their way. He nodded.

'All right,' he said. 'Get in.'

18

They sat at the table, pad thai, massaman curry, spicy beef salad in front of them.

'She did end up at the shelter,' Mike said. 'But before she did, Dad got a lot worse. He started drinking in the day, lost his job. Drank more. And the more he did, the more he beat Mum.'

'Did he hit you?'

'Yeah. But only if I got in his way, and only enough to clear me out of it so he could get to Mum.' Mike paused. 'Tell me if I'm over-sharing,' he said. 'I don't want you to think I'm some kind of fuck-up. I'm not. I came to terms with this a long time ago.'

'I don't think that,' Kate said. 'And tell me as much as you like. I'm fine.'

'All right,' he said. 'Well, like I was saying, it got worse. He started to hurt Mum. Snap the bones in her fingers. Burn her with cigarettes. Beat the soles of her feet with a tyre iron.'

'Didn't she see doctors? Or tell the police?'

'She didn't dare. She thought he'd kill her. And she was right. He would have done. He thought she was something less than human, treated her like she was a piece of dirt. And then, one night, he showed up at the house, as drunk as I'd ever seen him — which was saying something — with a friend, although when I say a friend, it wasn't anyone I'd ever seen him with before. I think it was some fellow drunk he'd run into, another shambling, angry, foul-mouthed version of him.

'Anyway. They raped Mum. He went first, then he let his new friend have a go. I heard it all. And I did nothing to stop it.'

'You couldn't have done anything,' Kate whispered. 'You were only a kid.'

'I could have. And I should have. Even if they killed me, I should have. But that's history now. The next day, I *did* do something. I asked a friend's mum — who was a magistrate — where women like my mum could go, and she told me about the shelter. Told me that she couldn't give me any details — she couldn't risk people like my dad finding out — but that she would give me the number of a woman — Carol — that Mum could call.'

'And did she?'

'I took her the next day to a phone box and made her do it. Carol — if that was her name — told her that she would pick her up at the phone box and take her there and then.'

'What about you?'

'I went to the magistrate's house. Mum made Carol promise that I wouldn't have to go home. I was sixteen by then; a few months later I was living with a friend who had a flat in Winwick.'

'And then what?'

'I didn't hear from Mum for a year, until Dad was in prison for stabbing a guy in a fight. He never came out. Liver cancer. Which was better than the bastard deserved. Anyway, Mum got in touch and we met up. She was a different person, more whole — although the scars were

233

still there, if you knew where to look. She moved into her own place. Lived another six years before she was killed by a stroke. The happiest years of her life. After she died, I inherited some money from her, and I donated it to the shelter. They'd given her life back, what was left of it, and I wanted to make sure they could do the same for other people. The magistrate arranged it. And then, over time, I became more and more involved. And now, I help them out. Give money. Do odd jobs. Because there are plenty of women out there who are suffering like my mum did, and if I can help in any way, then I will.'

Kate wanted to cry, both for his story and for his compassion. She hugged him.

'That's an amazing story,' she said. 'You're amazing. And I know what you're talking about.'

'You said you knew the shelter,' he said. 'I was wondering what you meant.'

'Well,' Kate said. 'This too is a long story.'

'Like you said,' Mike replied. 'We've got all night.'

PART TWO: INTERLUDE

Five Years Earlier

1

Kate walked to the lift with her work bag in one hand and a bottle of champagne in the other. It was the last day of work before Christmas and Trevor, the partner in charge of the new graduates, had given them all their Christmas gift from the firm: a bottle of Veuve Clicquot's finest.

Which was great, other than the inconvenient fact that the champagne wouldn't fit in her bag, which meant she'd have to carry it around the pub where the graduates were meeting for Christmas drinks. Worse, she'd have to keep it safe from all the drunks on the train home; it would be a miracle if it made it back. She could picture the scene, a bunch of bespectacled lawyers and accountants full of bottled beer.

Open it! Don't be mean! Come on, love, it's Christmas!

Still there were worse problems to have.

She walked into the lobby, and headed for the main door of the office. Outside, she turned left. The bar was about fifty yards down the street.

She heard a voice say her name.

'Kate.'

It came from a bench a couple of feet away. She turned to see who it was.

It took a moment to figure it out. She was twenty pounds lighter and with hair cropped close to her skull, but there was no doubt it was her.

'Beth?' Kate said. 'What are you doing here?'

2

'Where can we talk?' Beth said. She had an empty look in her eyes, and each word seemed to cost her a great effort.

Kate looked around. She couldn't take Beth into the office without signing her in, and she didn't want to do that.

'I'm supposed to be meeting people,' she said. 'For a drink. You're welcome to join us. But first — give me a hug, stranger.'

She was achingly thin, Kate realized. Under the bulky winter clothes there was not much of her left.

'Are you OK, Beth?' she said.

Beth shook her head.

'No,' she said, and started to cry. 'I'm not.'

'Let's go home,' Kate said. 'Forget the pub. We can get a cab, even.'

'No,' Beth said. 'I can't go to your house.'

'Why not?'

'Because' — she looked at Kate, her eyes glistening — 'because he might be there.'

Kate guessed immediately who 'he' was. 'Colin?' she said.

Beth nodded. 'Colin.'

'Beth,' Kate said. 'What the fuck is going on?'

★ ★ ★

They went to Kate's parents' house. Her mum

and dad were out at a retirement party, so there were no awkward questions about Beth's sudden reappearance and radical change in appearance.

Beth slumped on the couch. She looked tiny and her eyes were red with exhaustion. She'd barely spoken on the way home.

'So?' Kate said. 'What's the story?'

'Morning glory,' Beth said. It was what they had said as teenagers when they were into Oasis, although by then Oasis were past their best. For them it had been an ironic after-the-moment embrace of the band. Beth smiled. 'Long time ago, eh?'

'Yeah. Seems that way. So what *is* the story?'

Beth stood up. She shrugged off her coat then pulled up her sweater.

Her ribs stuck out, each one visible beneath the pale, puckered skin. That was shocking enough, but it was nothing compared to the dark blue and black bruises that covered every inch of her torso.

'Oh my God,' Kate said. 'Beth, what happened? You poor thing. Did he do this to you?'

Beth nodded. 'And worse. You don't want to know the worse.'

'I do,' Kate said. 'Tell me it all.'

Beth shook her head. 'Maybe later.'

Kate wrapped her arms around her friend. 'How did this happen?' she said. 'What did he do to you?'

Beth pulled away. 'At first it was — it was stupid shit like the photos of the drinks. And most of the time he was fine. Loving.

Considerate. He told me how beautiful I was, how intelligent, how he could see that I was special, that other people didn't know, didn't love me like he did.' She gave a wry smile. 'It was horseshit, but anything is easy to believe when you want to.'

She sniffed, then continued.

'Then he changed. Became more possessive. Jealous. If I went out with you, he shouted at me. He always apologized, mind you.'

'That day, at the Trafford Centre — '

Beth shook her head. 'I was so fucking embarrassed. He showed up when you were in the changing room, grabbed my arm. Tugged me out of the shop, hissing in my ear about what a slut I was, about how you were corrupting me, making me into a slut like you. He *hated* you — Gemma and May, too, but mainly you.'

'Why? What did I do? Not that I care what that bastard thinks.'

'Because you were a threat, I guess. I always felt closest to you, and so he saw you as the one person who might get between me and him.'

'Fuck,' Kate said. 'I knew there was something going on at the time. I knew it. I should have *done* something.'

'You tried. I remember. But he wouldn't let me call you, he read my emails, sent replies from my account telling you I was OK.' She put her hand on Kate's thigh. 'This isn't your fault, Kate. Not your fault at all. It's on me.'

'No, it isn't. It's on *him*, and no one else. Don't you dare say it's your fault.'

And then, over wine and tears and pizza, it all

spilled out. The hitting, the rape, the grovelling apologies, the promises that it was all over, that it would never happen again, and then, of course, it did, each time worse than the last, until she felt like she deserved it, like she was making him do it, like there was no way to stop it, no way out other than one way, the final way, but she didn't even have the courage to do that, at least not directly. She was choosing the slow way: starvation.

When she had finished, Kate hugged her.

'You're going to be OK,' she said. 'I promise. I will take care of you. Between me and Gem and May and Phil and Gus and Matt and all of the people we know, we will take care of you.'

'Thanks,' Beth said. 'But you don't know him.'

'I don't need to. I *will* keep you safe.' Kate paused. 'I do have one question, though. How did you get away?'

'I decided to. Funny, isn't it? That was all it took. I simply decided to. Decided that I had to get out of there, decided that I would come to you, decided that I had to leave, before it was too late. He watched me, closely, but I found a way. Walked out of work this afternoon, found a hairdresser and took a train to Manchester. The real question is *why* I decided to.'

'And? Why did you?'

The colour that had been returning to Beth's cheeks, fed by the wine and pizza and love of her friend, drained away.

'Because,' she said, 'I'm pregnant.'

3

'Holy shit,' Kate said. She looked at Beth's stomach, assessing how far along she was. She couldn't be very far; with so little body fat, any swelling would have been obvious and there was nothing.

Then she looked at her friend's wineglass. It was her third, it was half-empty, and she showed no signs of slowing down.

'Six weeks,' Beth said. 'Still early.'

'Does he know?'

'Of course. He knows everything. He saw that I'd missed a period and made me take a test.'

'And so you left, because you know you have to protect the baby,' Kate said. 'You have to keep it safe from him.'

'God, no,' Beth said. 'I left because I want to get rid of it.' She sighed, and reached for the wine. 'It's complicated, Kate. Like everything at the moment.'

'It sounds it.' Kate raised her hands. 'But whatever you do is fine by me. I assumed — '

'I know what you assumed.' There was a slight edge in her voice; this was hard for her, Kate saw, which was no surprise. 'But here's how it is: that bastard wanted me pregnant for months. He kept a close eye on my cycle and when I was ovulating he pinned me down and fucked me every morning and every evening. He wanted me pregnant because he thought

244

that way he would own me for ever. How could I leave with a kid — or two, or three — and no money?'

'This just gets worse,' Kate said. 'I feel so sorry for you.'

'Don't. It won't change anything. So, when he found out I was pregnant, he was ecstatic. Absolutely over the moon. He isn't much of a drinker — thank God — but he opened a bottle of champagne and we toasted our good news. Or he did: I had water, some folic acid, and a hearty meal. He was going to make sure I was healthy for his baby, he told me.'

'And that was when I knew I had to go. Had to go and get rid of his baby. I don't want it, don't want anything of his in my life, don't want a reminder of him staring at me every day. I need to start again, and how could I do that if I had his child? And there was no way I could have had an abortion.'

Beth laughed, a bitter, acid laugh.

'He would have killed me. He's a very religious man — or he says he is, but I see none of the warmth of religion in him, only its fanaticism — and he is implacably opposed to abortion. In his eyes, I would have been a murderer, and that would demand justice. An eye for an eye, a tooth for a tooth. It's one of his favourite sayings.'

'How did he do this?' Kate said. 'How did he ever convince you to go out with him in the first place?'

'He's a very charming man,' Beth said. 'Funny, warm, attentive. Until the mask slips — because

245

that's what it is: a mask. And behind it is a monster.'

'OK. So what do we do?'

'I don't know. Get rid of the baby. Then find a place I can hide from him.'

Kate's phone rang. It was Phil.

'Hi,' she said. 'Sorry — '

Phil interrupted. He sounded tense. 'No problem,' he said. 'Have you seen Beth?'

Kate straightened in her chair. Something was wrong; she could tell from his voice. And why was he asking about Beth?

'No,' she said. 'Not for ages. You know that. Why do you ask?'

'That guy Colin's here. Says she's disappeared. Says she was very upset — he didn't say why — and he's worried she's done something rash. He thought she might have sought you out.'

Thank God she'd said no. 'I haven't seen her. I can try calling, if he'd like?'

Phil passed on the message. Kate heard a voice replying. She couldn't make out the words.

'He says don't bother,' Phil said. 'She'll turn up. Hold on a sec.'

She listened as Phil said goodbye to Colin and promised to let him know if they heard anything from Beth, then she heard the sound of the front door shutting.

Phil came back on the line. 'Where are you, anyway?'

'At Mum and Dad's. Can you come over?'

'Why?'

'I'll tell you when you get here.'

246

'What's going on, Kate?'

'Just come over.'

'All right,' Phil said. 'By the way, that guy Colin. He's a bit weird.'

'You don't know the half of it,' Kate said.

4

'Phil's on his way,' Kate said. 'Colin was at the house.'

Beth shook her head. 'Tell him to stay put.'

'Why?'

'Colin will be following him.'

'He doesn't know you're here. I said that I hadn't seen you.'

'It doesn't matter. He doesn't trust anyone.' Beth pressed the heel of her hand into her forehead. 'You don't understand. He's not like you and me. He won't believe what Phil said and he'll want to check. So Phil can't come here. If he does, I'm leaving. Right now.'

Kate could see that she was serious. She picked up her phone and called Phil.

'Don't worry,' he said. 'I'm on my way. You don't need to check in.'

'Change of plan. You need to go back home.'

'What? You said to come to you.'

'Not any more. I'll explain later, I promise. But you need to go home.'

There was a long silence. 'Fine. But you need to tell me what's going on. Now. I'm getting worried.'

Kate took a deep breath. She looked at Beth, who nodded. 'OK. It's Beth. She's with me. She's hiding from Colin. She left him, he isn't taking it well and she's worried about what he might do. He has' — she looked at her friend — 'he has a history of violence.'

'Against her?' Phil said. 'He's been violent to her?'

'Very,' Kate said. 'But we can talk later.'

'I don't like the thought of you alone,' Phil said. 'I'm not going home. I'm coming to you.'

'No!' Kate replied. 'Beth thinks he might be following you. So go home, and wait. I'm going to see if she can stay here for a few days. It's the safest place; Colin doesn't know my parents from Adam.'

'All right,' Phil said. 'But call me immediately if anything happens. OK?'

'OK. And thanks. I love you.'

'Love you too.'

'You're lucky,' Beth said. 'Phil's a lovely guy.'

'I know,' Kate said. 'And all this makes me realize how lucky I am. We have some figuring out to do.' She raised an eyebrow. 'What *do* we do? Mum and Dad will be back soon. How do we explain this to them?'

'Tell them the truth. Or part of it. Tell them that I've left Colin and need a place to stay for a few days.'

'They'll ask why you don't stay with me. Or Gem, or May.'

Beth shrugged. 'I don't know,' she said. 'I'll think of something.'

'Leave it to me,' Kate said. 'I'll talk to them.'

★   ★   ★

When her parents' car pulled up outside the house, Beth went upstairs. Kate waited in the kitchen.

'Hello, love,' her mum said. 'What are you doing here?'

'I need to talk to you about something.'

Her dad frowned. 'Everything OK?'

'With me, yes. But something came up today. I saw Beth.'

'Oh,' her mum said. 'How lovely. It was such a shame you two lost touch. How is she?'

'She's good enough. But she needs a favour. She's broken up with Colin — that's the guy she was with — and she needs a place to stay for a few days.'

'Right,' her dad said, drawing out the word. 'Is she staying with you?'

'She can't. I was wondering whether she could stay here.'

Her parents exchanged a glance. 'She's more than welcome,' her dad said, 'but wouldn't she be better with you?'

'No. Phil's busy at work. It'd be a distraction.'

'It's the weekend,' her mum said. 'What work is he doing?'

Her dad folded his arms. 'Look, petal,' he said. 'We're happy to help. But we need to know what's going on.'

'It's kind of private. It's Beth's business. But she needs to stay here.'

'It's fine.' Beth appeared in the doorway. 'I'll tell them.' She stepped into the kitchen. 'Hi, Tony. Hi, Margaret.'

Kate watched her parents struggle not to react to the change in Beth's appearance. Eventually, her mum walked to Beth and hugged her.

250

'Hello, love,' she said. 'Would you like a cup of tea?'

A wide grin spread over Beth's face. 'I knew you'd say that,' she said, as the tears came again. 'It's so great to see you. I've missed you. All of you.'

★ ★ ★

Beth sat down at the kitchen table, a cup of tea in front of her. Kate's dad sat opposite her; Kate was to her left, her mum to her right.

'So,' her dad said. 'First things first: you can stay here as long as you like, and you don't need to tell us anything that you don't want to. But if you do want to, then we're ready to listen.'

'Thank you,' Beth said. 'I'll tell you. But it might be easier to show you.'

She lifted her jumper to expose the bottom of her ribs.

Kate's dad stiffened. An expression Kate had never seen before came over his face.

She realized what it was: it was fury.

'Was that your boyfriend?' he said, his voice low.

Beth nodded.

He leaned over the table, and put his hand on hers. 'Whatever's been going on,' he said. 'It's over now.'

'I hope so,' Beth said. 'I hope so.'

★ ★ ★

They talked for a long time, about Colin and

251

what he had done, about how she had felt, about her options now she was free.

'What about the police?' Kate's dad said. 'What about informing them, and letting them deal with it?'

Beth shook her head. 'I don't want to. I want to be done with him, for good.' She sipped her tea. 'He'll get to me,' she said. 'There'll be a court case and it'll drag on and he'll get to me.'

Kate's mum leaned forward. 'But then the police will know he did it, and he'll — '

'He doesn't care. He'll find me and kill me and then go to jail. He's a . . . ' she paused, 'a psychopath. At least, I think so. He has no feelings. It's weird. He can be so charming, but it's an act. He can turn it on and turn it off. Underneath, all he cares about is himself. And you can't hurt him. He's not scared, of anything. Of pain, of prison, of punishment.'

'He'd be scared of me, if I got hold of him,' Kate's dad said. 'That bastard would — '

'He wouldn't,' Beth said. 'Whatever you did to him, he wouldn't care. Or the police. And when he finally got to me, he'd take it out on me. So I don't want the cops involved or anything like that. I just want to be free from him for good.'

'But how?' Kate's dad said. 'How do you disappear?'

Her mum sat back, upright in the kitchen chair.

'There's a way,' she said. 'There are people who can help.'

5

It moved quickly after that.

A phone call that night; a meeting the following morning, and then Beth was gone. She stayed for a few weeks in a shelter in the town centre, an innocuous building that used to house a small school but which had been shuttered for years, until it was bought by a charity and quietly converted into a place where women could seek refuge. There were no signs outside. A keen-eyed observer may have noticed that only women entered or left, but other than that, there was no way to guess who used the building and why.

Kate only went inside once; even though she was a friend of Beth's, the people who ran the refuge didn't like to have any more people than was strictly necessary go there. They made an exception the day that Beth had her abortion; Kate went to see her afterwards. It was odd; she seemed more troubled than upset. Thoughtful. Either way, it was done, and a few weeks later, Beth was gone. She had a new name, a new address and a new start in life.

It was years before Kate heard from her again, but this time she did not regret her friend's absence. She knew that it was the only way she could move on.

PART THREE

PART THREE

1

'Jesus,' Mike said. 'That's such an awful story. Thank God she got away from him. At least she's alive.'

Kate shook her head. 'It's ridiculous that we live in a world where a woman needs to be grateful that she's alive, that her husband or boyfriend didn't actually kill her. It's so fucked up.'

'I know. And I watched my own mum go through it. It made me hate my father, you know? That's how fucked up it is: it made me hate my own father. I was glad when he died. I didn't feel empty or angry or sad, unless you count sadness that I didn't kill him myself.'

'Well,' Kate said. 'She's happy now.'

'What happened to her?' Mike said. 'Did you stay in touch?'

'Not for years, but then I got a friend request on Facebook. Different name, but I recognized the photo. We exchanged the occasional message, but that's it.'

'Good for her,' Mike said. 'Good for her.'

★ ★ ★

After dinner they lay on the couch and watched *Love Actually*.

'Phil would never watch this with me,' Kate said. 'He said it was garbage. And it is, but

257

sometimes garbage is what you want.'

'It's harmless enough,' Mike said. 'And I don't care what we watch, as long as we're watching it together.'

He looked at his watch. 'Although it's getting late. Are you staying here tonight? Or at your parents'?'

'Parents'. I need to go home. I still don't feel safe alone.'

'I could stay. If you want.'

'It sounds very appealing, but I think Mum would have a heart attack.'

He pushed out his bottom lip in mock disappointment. 'OK. Do you want me to drive you over there?'

'Yes,' Kate said. 'But there's something else I want first.'

'What?'

She turned her face to his and kissed him. 'This,' she said.

★ ★ ★

Her mum was still awake when she got home.

'So,' she said. 'Two nights on the run. Getting serious.'

'Mum,' Kate said. 'Not now. And it's not getting serious. Not yet, anyway.'

'Do you like him?'

Kate caught her mum's eye. 'Yes,' she said. 'I do.'

★ ★ ★

She slept better than she had since the break-up. When she woke up she had the feeling of renewal and hope and energy that a deep, natural sleep can bring.

It didn't last long. When she checked her phone there was a text message from Phil.

Don't worry about me. I'm having a great time! Really great!

It was time-stamped two thirty-three a.m. God, that boy was falling apart. Drinking, picking up women. He needed to stop the slide before it became too late. And what was he thinking, sending her a text like that? Did he think it would make her so jealous she'd go running back to him?

More likely he hadn't thought anything at all. He was nothing other than drunk and unable to control himself.

Her phone buzzed again. This time it was Gemma.

OMG. Have you seen the news?

Kate's pulse rate increased.

No. What is it?

The reply came.

There's been another.

Kate opened the web browser and navigated

to the local newspaper. There it was:

BREAKING NEWS: STRANGLER —
ANOTHER VICTIM

Reports are emerging that the body of a woman found by the Bridgewater Canal near Stockton Heath may be the latest victim of the serial killer that has been operating around the village over the last month.

Police have yet to confirm the identity of the victim or the manner of death, but fears are increasing that this may be the fourth woman to be murdered in the vicinity.

More to come as the story develops.

Kate lay back in bed. She scrolled through her text messages to the one Phil had sent.

Don't worry about me. I'm having a great time! Really great!

Sent at two thirty-three a.m. She didn't want to jump the gun, but it was hard not to at least ask the question.

Was it Phil? Was it Phil who, mad with grief, was killing these women? If so, then he'd sent that text message after he'd murdered his latest victim, which didn't make sense. Why would he do that? It was asking for trouble.

But then, none of this made sense. Even if it wasn't Phil, even if it was some random person, the fact that someone wanted to and was capable

260

of doing this made no sense. And maybe Phil didn't care about getting caught — maybe he even *wanted* to be caught — in which case why not send the message?

Shit, this was an unholy mess. She wished it would all go away. But there was one more question she had to deal with before that could happen.

Should she tell the police about Phil's message?

Kate closed her eyes. She had no choice.

2

Phil kicked off his covers. He was hot, and it was making him uncomfortable, and he wanted to go back to sleep. The thought of getting out of bed and facing a Sunday without Kate and with a stinking hangover was not exactly appealing.

But now he *was* awake, and his mind was starting to turn over. Images from the night before formed and played out before him. The dark nightclub — *wall-to-wall pussy*, Andy had said, over and over, until Phil was sick of hearing it — the sweet, sticky drinks, Dawn, the woman on her hen night, Andy going off with her friend, then him, stumbling, alone, out of the pub and into the street.

Where he'd vomited, cut his head on a lamppost and bribed his way into a taxi, then, finally home.

What else had he done? Amazingly, he'd poured a glass of whisky when he got back, which was the last thing he'd needed before he passed out. He shook his head. This had to stop.

He scrabbled on his bedside table for his phone to see what time it was.

Shit.

On the screen was a message he'd sent to Kate. He read it and cringed. It was ridiculous.

Don't worry about me. I'm having a great time! Really great!

It was time-stamped two thirty-three a.m. He didn't remember sending it. He must have poured the whisky then got the bright idea that he should send his ex-girlfriend a sarcastic message.

Because he had meant it sarcastically, he assumed, had meant it to convey how shit a time he was having, presumably in the hope that she would read it and feel such sympathy that she would call in the morning and suggest a reconciliation. Reading it now, though, it did not come across like that at all. It came across as the stupid rambling of a bitter drunk.

That was it. He'd had enough. He was going to stop all this. Stop the drinking, stop the disregard for his responsibilities, stop the adolescent self-indulgence in his own heart-break. Yes, he was sad, yes, he would take time to get over this, but that was no excuse for this pathetic, maudlin self-pity. It was time to grow up and deal with this in a mature way.

Never mind that it pissed her off. It was becoming a matter of self-respect.

And it would start with an apology. Sincere, grown-up, from the heart. He picked up his phone and began to type an email.

Kate — I'm sorry for the text message I sent last night. It was foolish and immature and unfair to you. I want you to know that I realize that I have been behaving badly and it is going to stop. I was — and am — very upset that we broke up. However, that is no excuse for my behaviour. Please accept this unreserved apology, along with a promise that this is the last time I will behave in this way.

Yours, Phil

He read it through, once, twice, then, after a brief hesitation, hit send. Happy — or at least, at peace — for the first time in weeks, he rolled back into bed, and closed his eyes.

★   ★   ★

He was woken about an hour later by the intercom buzzing. He got out of bed, mouth dry, and walked to the door, rubbing some life into his eyes. He pressed the button on the intercom.
'Hello?'
'Mr Flanagan?'
He recognized the voice of the detective immediately.
'Yes?'
'This is DI Wynne. I was wondering whether we could talk.'
'I'll buzz you in. Give me a few minutes to put some clothes on.'
'Why don't you come down, Mr Flanagan? It'll be better if we talk at the station.'
'What about? I already answered your questions.'
'We can talk at the station,' DI Wynne said. 'I'll wait outside.'
Phil headed for the shower. On the way, he checked the news. As soon as he had, hands trembling, he called Edward Marks. He had a

feeling he'd be needing his lawyer.

★ ★ ★

He sat in silence until the door to the interview room opened and Edward Marks came in. Marks had promised to get there as soon as he could, which turned out to mean nearly ninety minutes, and told him to say nothing until he did. Phil took him at his word.

For the entire time, DI Wynne and DS Chan sat opposite him. Wynne read through a thick file. Every so often she paused to dwell on a photo, making sure, Phil could tell, that he could see them.

They were photos of the victims. One showed Jenna Taylor at the scene, her neck ringed with a purple bruise, a sheet over her face. One was taken from a distance, of a body lying by a bush. One was a close-up of Michelle, two dark holes where her eyes had been.

He looked away, studying his feet.

Marks pulled out a chair and sat next to Phil. 'Detective Inspector,' he said, with a nod. 'Detective Sergeant. I understand you would like to question my client?'

DI Wynne gave a patient smile. 'That's correct. We have a few questions.'

'Go ahead,' the lawyer said. He turned to Phil. 'I'll let you know if you shouldn't answer.'

Wynne ignored him. 'Mr Flanagan, could you tell us your whereabouts last night?'

'I was in Liverpool.'

'Alone?'

265

'With Andy Field. The guy whose flat I'm staying in.'

'Where did you and Mr Field go in Liverpool?'

'A bunch of pubs. Then Caspers.'

'What is Caspers?'

'A big pub.' *Wall-to-wall pussy*, Phil thought. *Although it didn't turn out like that. Wish it had: I'd have an alibi.*

'What time did you leave Caspers?'

'I'm not sure. Probably around one a.m.'

'Alone?'

'That's right.'

'Where was Mr Field when you left?'

'He'd met someone. Went home with them.'

'But you did not?' DI Wynne said. 'Meet someone, that is?'

'No.'

She gestured to his temple. 'How did that happen?'

'Someone pushed me into a lamppost.'

'Where?'

'Outside Caspers. I'd vomited on the pavement. They were laughing at me.'

She nodded. 'We can check that, on CCTV. I hope you're telling the truth.'

'I am.'

'And then? After vomiting in the street? What did you do?'

'I came home. In a taxi.'

'And what time did you arrive home?'

'Probably two-ish. I wasn't checking the time.'

'Why was that?'

'I'd had quite a bit to drink.'

'Would you say you were intoxicated?'

Phil nodded. 'Pretty much.'

'How much?' DS Chan said. 'You said you'd vomited?'

'That's right.'

'So highly intoxicated would be a fair description, wouldn't it?' Chan said.

'Please don't put words in my client's mouth,' Marks said. 'He can speak for himself.'

'Yes,' Phil said, aware that there was, as a result of the CCTV footage of him throwing up into a bin, no point trying to hide it. 'You could say that I was highly intoxicated.'

'So,' DI Wynne said. 'You arrived home — highly intoxicated — at around two o'clock in the morning. What did you do then?'

'I went to bed.'

'Immediately?'

'Yes,' Phil said. 'Immediately.'

DI Wynne opened her ring binder and consulted a piece of paper. She frowned, then ran her finger along it, as though concentrating on reading something that was hard to understand.

'Hmm,' she said. 'That raises a question. Do you recognize these words, Mr Flanagan?' She began to read from the paper in front of her: '*Don't worry about me. I'm having a great time! Really great!*'

It was his text message. So Kate had gone to the cops. He could hardly believe that she had done it, both because of the betrayal, but also because of what it meant: it meant she thought he was guilty.

'It's a text message I sent to Kate last night,' he said.

'At two thirty-three a.m.,' DI Wynne said. 'Although you said you were in bed by that time.'

'I said about that time. I must have sent the text first.'

DI Wynne gave him a thin smile. 'Yes. You must have done.' She coughed. 'What did you mean by that text, Mr Flanagan?'

'Not that it matters,' Phil said. 'But I was actually being sarcastic. Because I wasn't having a great time at all. I haven't been, lately, in case you hadn't noticed.'

'Could it have meant something else?' DS Chan said. 'Maybe that you *were* having a great time?'

'I suppose it *could*,' Phil said. He was about to tell them that he couldn't actually say what it had meant as he didn't remember sending it, but he decided to keep that to himself. 'It didn't, though.'

DI Wynne tapped her forefinger on the table. 'Do you know Angela Wood, Mr Flanagan?'

Phil tensed. The cut on his temple started to throb. 'Angie Wood?' he said. 'From Stockton Heath?'

DI Wynne nodded.

'She was a couple of years behind me at school.'

'At Bridgewater County High School?'

'Yeah. I don't know her all that well,' Phil said. He started to get an uncomfortable feeling. There had been no name in the news report, but

268

now he had an idea about who the victim might be. 'But I know who she is. Why?'

'Ms Wood was killed last night,' DI Wynne said. 'Around two a.m. Around the time you were sending that text message.' She looked at him. 'You can see the implications, Mr Flanagan.'

'Are you accusing me of killing Angie Wood?'

There was a long pause before DI Wynne spoke. 'Mr Flanagan,' she said. 'Are you entirely sure that you did not leave the house after returning last night?'

'Yes,' Phil replied. 'Entirely.'

'There is no possibility that you did go out, but that you don't remember doing so? You were, as you admitted, highly intoxicated.'

'I . . . ' Phil paused. *Had* he gone out? He didn't remember going to bed, didn't remember sending the text message. What else didn't he remember? He was suddenly overwhelmingly relieved that he hadn't mentioned that he had no memory of sending the text; they would have assumed he had blundered around in a drunken stupor doing God knew what.

Which maybe he had.

'Look,' he began. 'I don't — '

Edward Marks gestured to him not to answer. 'Detective Inspector Wynne,' Marks said. 'Do you have any evidence to suggest that my client is responsible for the crimes of which you seem to suspect him? If not, then I'm going to suggest that we leave.'

DI Wynne gave a regretful shrug.

'Not yet, I don't.'

Outside the police station, Marks turned to face Phil. A cold wind pushed his hair into a fan-like shape.

'What happened last night?' he said. 'Is there anything you need to tell me?'

Phil met his gaze. 'No,' he said. 'There isn't.'

3

LATEST VICTIM NAMED

The latest victim in the string of murders in Stockton Heath has been named.

Angela Wood, 26, was a lifelong inhabitant of the village. Her body was found early on Sunday morning. It had been concealed under a bush by the towpath of the Bridgewater Canal.

A police statement said that the manner of the killing 'bore the hallmarks of the three earlier incidents. As such, we are treating this as the work of the serial killer known to be operating in this area in the last two months.'

This is the fourth victim of the killer, who has become known as the Stockton Heath Strangler.

Kate sat at her desk and read the story with mounting disbelief. If, at first, this had been a story that gave a thrill of vicarious interest, that was no longer the case. Now it was simply terrifying. Four women had been killed within a mile of her house. Four. Strangled, their eyes scooped out. The police had no idea who had done it — unless, that was, it was her ex-boyfriend, in which case she was going to have to deal with the fact that a) she had been

271

dating a serial killer and b) the trigger for him getting started on his killing spree was her breaking up with him.

She knew this victim well. Angie Wood was Stockton Heath through and through. She lived on Bedford Street, in the terraced house her dad had grown up in. Her brother was a few years older. He was in the army; Kate had had a crush on him when she was twelve. In a weird circle, Angie had confessed — when drunk, aged fourteen — to having a crush on Kate. Not long after gay marriage was legalized she'd married a woman from Iceland; they had adopted twin girls.

She'd bumped into Angie in Morrisons supermarket shortly after she and her wife had brought the twins home.

Kate jerked upright at the memory. Her eyes widened. No. This was not happening.

Angie had been pushing a trolley, her eyes red-rimmed with tiredness.

How's it going? Kate said.

Tough. Not getting much sleep. But we love the girls.

I almost didn't recognize you, Kate said. *That's quite a change.*

I know. But I needed one less thing to have to deal with. Quite a lot of new mums do it.

Angie had been famed for her thick, long, dark hair. She could have been a hair model, people said.

But it was all gone. Close-cropped for convenience.

Kate put her hands to her mouth. Angie didn't

have the green eyes, or Kate's lithe build, but she had the hair.

Kate had changed her appearance and the killer had killed a woman who shared the most obvious change she had made. In amongst the maelstrom of emotions that swirled around her, one stood out.

This was *her* fault. A mother was dead. A lifeless body, by a canal. And she was to blame, at least in part. She couldn't have foreseen this would happen, she knew that, but she also knew that if she hadn't tried to throw the killer off then Angie would be alive today.

And it also meant that the killer was *not* targeting women who happened to look like her.

He was targeting her.

And he was out there, uncaught, planning his next attack.

★ ★ ★

At lunchtime, Nate came to her workstation.

'Grab a bite?' he said.

Kate nodded. 'Maybe a sandwich,' she said. 'I have to get back to this brief.'

They walked to the lift. When the doors closed, Nate pressed the ground-floor button.

'See the news?' he said. 'About the killing?'

'Sure,' Kate said. 'It's on my doorstep.'

'That's four now,' Nate said. 'It's getting serious.'

'Getting serious?' she said. 'You don't think three women dead was serious?'

He raised his hands in a defensive gesture.

273

'That's not what I meant,' he said. 'I meant this is getting out of control.'

'What does your police friend think?' she said. 'Does he think it's out of control?'

Nate nodded. 'I spoke to him this morning.'

'Anything interesting?'

The lift stopped and the doors opened. They walked across the lobby to the main doors. When they were outside — and not in earshot of anyone else — Nate answered.

'Yes. He said that they've been looking further afield, checking other open cases to see if there are any that bear a resemblance to this one. Apparently, these people often move around.'

'And?'

'There's nothing exactly the same. But there was a series of murders a couple of years ago in Sheffield. They never found the killer.'

'Were they similar to these ones?'

'Not exactly.'

They walked into a sandwich shop and joined the queue. When they had their food they sat by the window.

'Not exactly,' Kate said. 'But somewhat similar?'

'According to my friend,' Nate said. 'The method wasn't the same — not strangulation and no eye-removal — but the victims were all women, all in their early thirties, and all childless. They were killed in their houses, at home alone.'

He leaned forward. 'Whoever did it knew what they were doing. They waited until they knew the

274

routines of the victims, when their husbands or partners would be out, then . . . ' he paused, evidently relishing telling the story, 'they got into their houses and suffocated them.'

'And they think it's the same guy?' Kate said. 'He moved here from Sheffield?'

'Maybe. It's possible. Or he could have travelled to Sheffield. From here.'

'So what are they doing?'

'They're going to compare evidence. See if there's a link.'

Which would get Phil off the hook, Kate thought. *Or not. Maybe he went over the Pennines and killed those women. But at least I could check the dates and see if he had an alibi.*

'OK,' she said. 'Keep me posted.'

'I will.'

'Who is your friend, anyway?' Kate said. 'I know a policeman in Stockton Heath. He might know him.'

Nate froze, mid-bite. 'You can't say anything,' he said, his tone urgent. 'Don't mention my name.'

'OK,' Kate said, taken aback by the strength of his reaction. 'I was only asking.'

'Sorry,' Nate said, back to normal. 'But I can't tell you who it is. He probably shouldn't be passing all this on, you know?'

'I know.' *And it's strange that he is,* she thought, *and that you were worried about your name, and not his.* 'But you will let me know about the other murders, right?'

'Sure. I guess you have an interest, living in the vicinity.'

'Except that I'm staying with my parents at the moment.'

'Oh,' Nate said. 'You are? I didn't know that. Where do they live?'

Kate told him.

At least, she told him the name of the town. She decided to keep the address to herself.

4

Back at her desk, she looked up the story of the Sheffield killings. There was plenty of information about them.

Four women killed over three months. It was clearly the work of a serial killer; they were all killed in the same way, in the same area, and, to cap it all, they all looked alike.

Nate had failed to mention that.

She studied their pictures. They all had short, blonde hair. Charlotte Walton, Melissa Jones, Lisa Wallace and, the last victim, Claire Michaels. The killer had broken into their houses, suffocated them, then taken them upstairs and arranged them in their beds.

By the time that Claire Michaels died, the way the killer operated must have been widely known. Kate pictured her boyfriend coming home and finding her, lying in bed, thinking at first she was asleep, wondering why, in the early evening, she was already in bed, then the mounting fear that she was the latest victim and the frantic scramble to feel her pulse, shake her awake, call an ambulance, call the police.

He was called Mark Stevens, her partner. Thirty-six years old, IT professional. Probably, at that age, getting ready to settle down, pop the question. Maybe that day. Maybe he came home with a bottle of champagne and a ring, expecting to end up with a fiancée. What he ended up with was a corpse.

Then it had stopped. Suddenly, without warning, the killing had stopped.

There was plenty of speculation online, ranging from the practical — the killer had moved elsewhere, the killer had died — to the unlikely — the police had found him and killed him and were covering it up — to the frankly absurd — it was not a serial killer at all but a bizarre suicide pact among short-haired blonde women.

She ended up on a website dedicated to the murders. There was a discussion — closed now — about the victims. One thread caught her eye: it was under the heading *Claire Michaels*, and it was called *Mark Stevens*:

I knew Claire well, and in the last few months of her life she was miserable. I used to see her a lot, but since she'd met her boyfriend — Mark Stevens — I saw less and less of her. When I did, she was unhappy. She pretended not to be, but I could tell she wasn't right. My guess is that he was hitting her. After she died, I told the police but they weren't interested. They couldn't go after him for it now she was gone, and it wasn't like he had killed her. It was the serial killer who had done that.

God, Kate thought. *The poor woman. An abusive boyfriend and then killed in your own house.*

She looked back at the screen.

At least he got what was coming to him, the friend of Claire Michaels wrote. *He killed himself a few weeks later. Glad the bastard died in misery.*

It was a bit harsh, Kate thought, to wish a miserable death on someone, although if he'd been anything like Colin Davidson, she could see why someone might. She typed in his name, and a news story came up, from a local paper in Lytham St Annes, on the Fylde coast.

MURDER VICTIM
BOYFRIEND SUICIDE

The boyfriend of Claire Michaels, victim of the serial killer who has recently been operating in the Sheffield area, apparently killed himself on Sunday.

Mark Stevens was a lifelong lover of the Lytham area, and, according to a suicide note found by friends, planned to kill himself by drowning in the seas off his favourite beach.

He was said by friends to be distraught over the death of his girlfriend. When he did not show up for work on Monday, they attempted to contact him, and found the letter in which he outlined his plans.

No body has yet been recovered, although the search is ongoing.

Kate rubbed her eyes. He was the fifth victim of the serial killer, in a way, driven to take his own life by the grief. She wondered whether the

279

murderer had read the reports of Mark Stevens' death, whether he had taken pleasure in the knowledge of what he had driven him to. Maybe, maybe not: it was hard to know the mind of someone capable of doing the things he had done.

A voice interrupted her.

'Kate.'

She looked up. It was Michaela. 'Hey,' she said. She minimized the web browser. 'I was checking on some news. What's up?'

'How's the Osborne brief coming? My meeting was brought forward to nine a.m. tomorrow. Any chance you can do it for then? If the news is not too riveting?'

Shit. It was going to be a push, and now she'd been caught wasting time on the Internet she would have no excuse if she was late. Still, she wasn't going to give Michaela the satisfaction of knowing that.

'Sure,' she said. 'No problem. It'll be ready.'

★ ★ ★

She was going to need help. It was a financial fraud case and there were some complicated accounts to go through. Moreover, this one might go to trial, so Michaela would want to know what had happened in similar cases in the past, and that meant she'd need to review the case law. She wouldn't have time to do it all on her own.

She picked up her phone.

'Nate?' she said. 'Do you have plans tonight?'

'No,' he said. 'Are you asking me on a date?'

'Not exactly,' she said. 'But I will buy you dinner.'

⋆ ⋆ ⋆

They ordered sushi and ate it in a conference room, legal books and documents spread over the table. On the surface, it looked like a scene from a legal thriller; in reality, all it meant was a lot of careful reading to make sure nothing was missed.

'All right,' Nate said, tidying up the sushi containers. 'Let's do it.'

⋆ ⋆ ⋆

At eight thirty, he stood up.

'How are you getting on?' he said.

Kate shrugged. 'Fine. If I keep cranking through it, I reckon I'll be done in an hour or so.'

'I think I'm nearly there too,' Nate said. 'There's one more question I need to dig into.' He picked up a handful of files. 'I think I'll go through these somewhere else. Get a change of scene. I'll be back in a bit.'

'OK,' Kate said. 'See you soon.'

⋆ ⋆ ⋆

He was back forty-five minutes later, as Kate was wrapping up.

'Did you get it done?' she said. 'And thanks, by the way. I appreciate it.'

281

'No problems, team mate,' Nate said. 'And yes, I did get it done. But I also found out something much more interesting.'

'Oh?' Kate said. 'About the case?'

He shook his head. 'Not about our case. About the Strangler.'

Kate's pulse sped up.

'What?' she said. 'What did you find out?'

'It's out,' he said. 'The press think the Sheffield killer and the Strangler are the same person.'

5

'Where are they getting that from?' Kate said.

'I'm not sure,' Nate replied. 'But if the press is saying it, then there must be something. They won't reveal what, but there'll be a reason.' He raised an eyebrow. 'I think it's the same guy.'

'Can you ask your friend?'

He shook his head. 'I'll try. But check out the news.'

STRANGLER: DONE IT BEFORE

The mystery around the serial killer known as the Stockton Heath Strangler deepened this evening. In a shocking development, speculation emerged that the police are investigating evidence that the perpetrator of the recent string of murders in Stockton Heath is the same person who killed four women in Sheffield in the summer of 2013.

The four women — Charlotte Walton, Melissa Jones, Lisa Wallace and Claire Michaels — were all suffocated in their houses. They were all in their early thirties. When the murders ceased, there was widespread speculation that the killer had moved, either to another part of the country or to a different country entirely.

Although the methods are different, a police spokesperson said that there may be

283

evidence linking the two sets of murders.

At this point, the police still do not have a suspect in custody. The spokesperson said that they are actively following leads and that the public should rest assured that they are doing everything possible to find the killer.

John Strettle, a former investigator, says this means they know that the killer is the same in both cases. 'The evidence is there that it is the same person, but not who it is, or they'd have arrested them by now. Of course, they can start to look for links, but if the perpetrator selects victims at random then it might be hard to find any. It's the element of randomness that makes these cases so hard to solve. It could literally be anybody.'

In the meantime, the people of Stockton Heath continue to wonder who will be next.

'Unbelievable, isn't it?' Nate said. 'This is going to be a huge story.'

'It is,' she said. It was also going to answer some questions, like where was Phil when the Sheffield murders happened? Although she was desperate to figure it out, she didn't want to do it in front of Nate. She closed the browser. 'But we have to get this finished.'

★ ★ ★

In the taxi on the way home — paid for by the firm, if you worked late — she looked up the dates of the Sheffield murders.

The first one was 11 August 2013.

She felt suddenly dizzy. It was hard to concentrate.

They'd gone on holiday that summer, an epic three-week trip to Thailand. She knew the dates; it was the best and longest holiday they'd ever had and she'd spent weeks planning it. They'd left on 20 July and come back 9 August.

The day after, in the midst of post-holiday blues, they'd had the biggest blow-out argument of their relationship. They'd both said things that should not have been said, and Phil had left. Went to a hotel, he said.

He came back a couple of days later. On 12 August.

The day after the murder.

So was it him, then? Had he reacted badly to the argument — it had felt like a break-up at the time — and worked out his anger by killing a woman? And now that they *had* broken up, he was doing it again? The pattern fit, she had to admit it.

But not Phil. Surely not Phil. He wasn't capable of it. And if he was, how could she have missed it?

Because she had never broken up with him before, that was why. And the one time she almost had, a woman had been killed.

By the same person who was killing women now. And who else would be targeting women who looked like her? Specifically like her — whether she changed her appearance or not?

And the dates, the timing: it all made a

sickening sense. Michelle Clarke had been killed the night she had changed her appearance.

Which was before Phil had seen her and found out that she no longer looked like he thought she did. That she no longer looked like Michelle Clarke.

This was awful. Beyond awful. She looked out of the taxi window. The cars and houses and telegraph poles rolled by and she felt sick. Dizzy and sick and disbelieving.

6

Phil looked at the lettings agent. She was smiling with the kind of grin that contestants in a talent show wore and which, apparently, people starting out in the lettings business thought would reassure prospective clients. She was young — maybe twenty-one, twenty-two — and was quite pretty.

Apart from her short hair. Her short, close-cropped hair. He didn't like short hair, and he hated it on Kate. He couldn't believe it when he had seen it. It was horrendous.

'I'll take it,' he said. 'Six months at first.'

'It' was a two-bedroom terraced house on Miller Street in Latchford. It was furnished and available immediately — *As soon as you can take a look and sign the paperwork, Mr Flanagan* — and so Phil had made a call and arranged an appointment to see it.

'That's wonderful!' The agent — Carly, he remembered — grinned even more widely. 'Are you available to come to the office to complete the paperwork?'

'I took the morning off,' Phil said. 'So no problem.'

'OK,' Carly said. 'I'll see you there. You go out first. I'll lock up behind you. It's not yours yet!'

★ ★ ★

Phil wound down the car window. He wanted to feel the air on his face. He wasn't over Kate yet — that would take a long time — but he was moving that way, and it felt good. No, it felt great. It was funny how that one thing, that one decision to pick himself up and move on, had put so much more in motion. A new place to live, a new attitude at work, a new approach to life. He hadn't decided yet what he would do — stay here, move, change jobs; all were options — but whatever it was, it would be good.

His phone rang. He looked at the screen.

His good mood drained away.

It was DI Wynne.

Shit. What did she want now? She needed to leave him alone. She had no evidence — she couldn't have, because there wasn't any; and if there was, she would have done something with it by now, like arrest him. There was some speculation as to whether he had a compelling motive — which he could admit looked bad — and some bike tracks that could have been anybody at any time, but other than that, nothing. And right now, he didn't want to speak to DI Wynne.

So he didn't answer.

The phone went silent. A few seconds later, it rang again.

DI Wynne, the screen said, again. Why wouldn't that damn cop leave him alone?

His mood darkened. Fine, he'd answer, and this time he'd give her a piece of his mind.

He answered the call. 'Look,' he said. 'I don't know what you want, Detective, but I've had enough of you harassing me.'

'Mr Flanagan,' DI Wynne said. 'I'm sorry you feel that way. But I have some questions I need to ask you.'

'What questions? I told you that I didn't do this.'

'I appreciate that. Have you been following the news, Mr Flanagan?'

'No.' He had been steering clear. It was part of his fresh start.

'We learned yesterday that whoever is responsible for the current series of murders in Stockton Heath is also responsible for a series of four murders in Sheffield, two years ago.'

'I remember them,' Phil said. 'I remember reading about them. We were in Thailand, I think.'

'Were you, Mr Flanagan? If you were, then that would be very good news for you. Nevertheless, I'd like you to come to the station. We can go through the dates of the murders and you can give details of your whereabouts.'

'What was the date of the first one?' Phil said.

'August eleventh, 2013,' DI Wynne said.

Phil thought for a moment. They'd got back sometime in early August, he was sure of that, but he wasn't sure of the exact date.

'Fine,' Phil said. 'I'll come in.' He hung up and scrolled through his contacts. He chose Kate's mobile.

'Hi,' she answered. 'How are you?'

'Same as usual,' Phil said. 'Except I got a call from Detective Inspector Wynne.'

'Oh?'

'And she wants to know where I was when some killings in Sheffield happened, back in 2013.'

'Right. Because it's the same person who's killing people now.'

'Which isn't me. I told her I thought we were in Thailand. The first murder was August eleventh. Do you remember when we got back?'

'We got back on the ninth,' Kate said.

Phil ran his fingers through his hair. Shit. That was his alibi gone.

'And then,' Kate said, 'you stayed out for a few days. We had that argument, remember?'

He did remember. He'd gone to a hotel in Chester and moped around until he couldn't stand it any more, then come home.

'Did you tell DI Wynne about that?'

'No,' Kate said. 'She hasn't asked.'

'Well don't,' Phil said. 'It'll only make things worse.' He pulled up outside the lettings agency. 'I have to go,' he said. 'I'm signing for a house. I'm going to move into a place in Latchford.'

'OK.' Kate paused. 'Good luck, Phil.'

'You too,' Phil said. 'Stay in touch.'

7

It was strange to think about Phil.

He had been such a big part of her life, but from now on their lives would travel in separate directions. He'd meet someone, change jobs, move somewhere, get a dog, do new things, and each time he did, the gap between them would grow, inch by inch, until it was a chasm. He would be part of the past; the man who had once been the most important thing she could ever imagine would one day be a memory. An ex-boyfriend. The answer to a question her daughter or son would ask when they came across a photo of her, in her twenties, with a strange man who was not their dad.

Who's that, Mum?

That's Phil.

Who's Phil?

A boy I used to go out with. My first boyfriend.

Was it serious?

I suppose so, at the time. But it's a long time in the past now.

I wonder what he's doing, they might add.

Me too, she'd reply, and for a moment she'd think of him. Fondly, she hoped. Then she'd move onto something else and he would once again be forgotten.

Unless he was a mass murderer, in which case

even the years of therapy she'd have to have to get over it wouldn't be enough for her to forget him.

She doubted it would come to that. For now, she was ready to move on.

★ ★ ★

She called Mike from work and suggested it.

Suggested that they go out on Friday and that he spend the night at her house. She'd agonized about whether to do it. She wasn't planning to move back, not yet, and certainly not now that she knew the Strangler had a track record of breaking into houses and suffocating women who were alone at home, but why not stay there with Mike after a night out? It was better than getting a lift home to her parents'. That made her feel like a teenager again. It was embarrassing.

She was aware that this was a step towards a relationship — not a big one, not moving in together or anything like that — but a move in that direction. She hadn't planned to end up in a relationship this quickly, but maybe she was a serial monogamist. Or maybe not. She didn't know. There were a lot of things about herself that she didn't know, that she had not needed to think about while she was with Phil. Then she had been Kate, half of Phil and Kate, kind, sensible, hard-working, small-town, instantly forgettable. Now she had a chance to rewrite that list of adjectives, and it would be fun figuring out which ones, from the thousands out there, were going to fit her.

'Are you sure?' Mike said. 'I'd love to, but I'm happy either way.'

'I'm sure. Let's meet at my house at seven. We can go out from there.'

'All right,' he said. 'That sounds great. But how about this instead: I'll pick you up at your office at six. I've got a plan.'

'What is it?'

'Wait and see.'

'Should I dress up?'

'No. Nothing special. See you then.'

She hung up. Friday — three days away — couldn't come soon enough.

★ ★ ★

When Friday finally came he pulled up outside her office shortly after six. She was wearing work clothes, but only just; a close-fitting knee-length dress was not her normal office attire. Nate had teased her about it — *Going on a date after work? Anyone special?* — but she had batted away his questions. She could tell that his interest was more than that of a friend. She wasn't sure that it was desire or lust, not exactly. She didn't get the sense from him that he fancied her, didn't catch him looking her up and down, but there was definitely something, and so she wanted to keep their relationship as professional as possible. No more late nights working together, no more after-work drinks, no more sharing what was happening in her private life.

'Jump in.' Mike looked at her. 'You look amazing.'

'Thanks,' she said. He was in dark jeans and a brown leather jacket. 'You too. Where are we going?'

'The Lowry.'

Kate smiled. 'To do what?'

'See a play. *Rosencrantz and Guildenstern Are Dead*. It's been getting amazing reviews. I grabbed some tickets. You don't mind, do you?'

'Mind? It's a fab idea. It's years since I went to the theatre.'

'It's a great play. Kind of a play within a play within a play. Lots of layers; it's complicated. My kind of thing.' He paused. 'And then dinner afterwards? There's an Ethiopian restaurant nearby that's supposed to be good.'

'Can't wait,' Kate said. 'And thank you for doing this.'

★ ★ ★

They stood in the foyer of the theatre, guessing the stories of the people they saw.

'Russian oligarch,' Mike said, pointing at a man who was clearly a geography teacher.

'Plays football for Manchester United,' Kate said, nodding at a man in his fifties with a prodigiously large beer belly.

'No way,' Mike said. 'He plays for City.'

'Excuse me.' A young Asian woman interrupted them. She was holding her phone. 'Would you mind taking a photo of me and my friends?'

294

Kate took the phone. 'Of course not.'

They assembled themselves and Kate held up the phone. 'Ready? Say 'cheese'!'

She handed it back to the girl.

'Would you like one of you two?' she said.

'It's OK,' Mike said. 'That's fine.'

'Come on,' Kate said, and put her arm around his waist. 'Smile for the camera.'

'Let's not bother them,' Mike said. 'The play's nearly starting.'

'It's no bother,' the girl said. She took Kate's phone. 'Smile!'

They linked arms; Mike seemed stiff. The girl handed Kate's phone to her.

'Thanks,' Kate said. Mike merely nodded, and led her into the theatre.

They watched the play, thighs pressed together, arms linked. He had his hand on her knee; the touch on her bare skin sent a thrill through her. She was hyper-aware of his presence, of the heat he gave off, of his scent.

This was what she wanted to do, the reason why she had broken up with Phil. They had a routine, a way of doing things, and it didn't involve going to the theatre. It could have, of course, if she had made him, if she had bought tickets and dragged him there, but she didn't want to have to do that. She wanted it to be the norm, the kind of thing that they often did. And with Mike, it was.

When the play was finished, they filed out of the theatre. He was behind her, his hands lightly resting on her hips.

'You want to go and eat?' he said.

She shook her head. She wanted to be with him and with him alone as soon as possible. 'No,' she said. 'Let's go back.'

8

The next morning she woke up, for the first time in what seemed like an age, in her own bed in her own house.

She looked over to her left; Mike wasn't there. His jeans were on the floor, so he was presumably — unless he was running around Stockton Heath in his underpants — downstairs. She got out of bed and walked to her wardrobe to grab some clothes. This was very different to the last time she'd woken up in a bedroom after spending the night with him; that time all she'd wanted to do was get away. Now, she wanted to do the opposite.

She heard footsteps approach the bottom of the stairs.

'Hey,' Mike called. 'Do I hear you wandering about up there?'

'I'm coming down,' she said. 'Give me a moment to make myself decent.'

'Don't bother,' Mike said. 'Indecent is good. And don't come downstairs. I'm making breakfast. I'll bring it up.'

'What are you making? There's no food in the house?'

'I popped out.'

'In what? Your jeans are up here.'

'Shorts. I brought a pair so I could go on my morning run.'

Was this guy for real? Evenings at the theatre?

297

Up half the night having energetic sex? Breakfast in bed? Morning run?

'Stay in bed. Read the news. I'll be up in a bit.'

'Fine,' Kate said. 'Sounds good to me.'

And when breakfast is over, she thought, I'll have to think of a treat for you, which is probably why you're doing this in the first place, you sly dog.

★　★　★

She picked up her phone. There was a text from Gemma.

Check this out — from the Sheffield case.

Typical Gemma. Obsessed with the news, as usual. Kate clicked the link.

STRANGLER: POLICE APPEAL FOR INFORMATION

Police investigating the recent murders in Stockton Heath today released an appeal for information from the public.

Detective Inspector Jane Wynne, who is leading the investigation, said 'We would like to ask the public to come forward with any information they have about the victims of the Sheffield murders, their partners, and any links they might have to the recent killings in Stockton Heath. If they think of anything — however insignificant or incidental it seems — they should contact the police immediately.'

There was a series of photos attached, showing close-ups of the faces of the victims next to their boyfriends and husbands.

Kate scanned them. A set of young people, their lives ended — in the case of the women — or ruined — in the case of the men — by the killer. And in the case of Mark Stevens, both.

She studied his photo. Stevens had a shaved head and a beard. He looked out of shape, the shadow of a double chin starting to appear while the line of his jaw disappeared. He had very intense, very blue eyes. They were a bit like Mike's; in some ways, Mark Stevens resembled him. Kate chuckled. When she was a teenager there was a TV show that found normal people who looked like overweight versions of famous people; they called them fat lookalikes. It probably wouldn't pass the PC test now, but it was quite funny in its day. She imagined the presenter holding the photos up.

Mark Stevens, ladies and gentlemen, the fat lookalike of Mike Sadler.

Same initials, too. M.S. She looked at the photo again.

The eyes really were the same. They had the same cool, slightly distant look. Mark Stevens and Mike Sadler could almost have been brothers. It was uncanny.

Not the same, she said to herself. *Similar, but not the same.*

299

It was something her dad always said when, as a teenager, she'd say *May and me have the same shoes* or something like that.

Similar shoes, he'd say. *You can't have the same shoes. It's impossible; if you're wearing a pair of shoes, May can't be wearing the same ones. And it's May and I, by the way.*

So the eyes were similar, but not the same.

If Stevens had been thirty-six when he died they'd be a similar age too, give or take. And in the same field — they both worked in IT, if she remembered correctly.

Her leg twitched nervously. She studied the photo, imagined Mark Stevens with no beard, with thick, brown hair, with the thick brown hair she'd run her hands through the night before. She mentally stripped away the nascent double chin.

And she had Mike.

She shook her head. This was ridiculous. Mike Sadler, the man downstairs in her kitchen making her breakfast in bed, was not Mark Stevens. Mark Stevens was dead. He'd committed suicide after his girlfriend had been killed.

She typed *Mark Stevens Sheffield* into Google and scanned the results. There it was — the story she'd read about his death.

MURDER VICTIM
BOYFRIEND SUICIDE

The boyfriend of Claire Michaels, victim of the serial killer who has recently been operating in the Sheffield area, apparently

300

killed himself on Sunday.

Mark Stevens was a lifelong lover of the Lytham area, and, according to a suicide note found by friends, planned to kill himself by drowning in the seas off his favourite beach.

He was said by friends to be distraught over the death of his girlfriend. When he did not show up for work on Monday, they attempted to contact him, and found the letter in which he outlined his plans.

No body has yet been recovered, although the search is ongoing.

There it was, in black and white. Stevens had left a note for his friends and then drowned himself in the sea off Lytham.

Except there was no body, so technically — and she knew this from law school — there would be no death certificate. You had to wait seven years to declare someone dead without a body.

This was getting stupid. Did she seriously think that Mark Stevens had faked his death? And that he was somehow related to Mike? Not a brother, obviously, because they did not share the same surname, but a cousin, maybe?

Because the resemblance *was* there, and the more she looked at the photo, the stronger it became.

It was a coincidence. It *had* to be. She needed another photo of Stevens; that would settle this once and for all. She clicked on the 'images' tab.

Other than the photo from the police appeal,

301

there was nothing. Mark Stevens had not been on Facebook, Twitter, LinkedIn. He'd kept his online presence to a minimum.

Maybe the police had another. She opened her email and typed in Gus's name. His email address auto-populated the To: field. She clicked on the message body and typed:

Hey, could you try and find out if the police know anything about Mark Stevens? I'm looking at the photo of him, and he reminds me of someone I know. Not urgent. Email me back if you have anything. Ideally another photo, if possible. Thanks, K. xxx

She hit send.
And in Mike's leather jacket a phone buzzed.

9

Kate paused. She rarely saw Mike's phone; he wasn't one of those people who constantly had it out on the table or in his hand. It was normally stashed away in the inside pocket of his leather jacket, the jacket that was now hanging on the handle of her bedroom door.

Her phone buzzed. A fraction of a second later, Mike's did the same.

She looked at her email. It was Gus.

Sure, I'll take a look. You OK?

Kate looked at the screen, blinking, then replied:

Yes, fine. Enjoying a Saturday morning lie-in.

She hit send. Mike's phone buzzed.

Her mouth went dry. In her mind, pieces began to arrange themselves. As they did, a picture emerged. It was like a part-finished jigsaw; there were holes, but there was enough there to give her a picture of something that she didn't like.

Mike had told her that Phil had installed something on her computer that forwarded all her emails — incoming and outgoing — to him. They'd had some fun with it — sending dirty emails to a fictitious lover — and then he'd

303

removed the software.

Phil had never mentioned it, which, she'd assumed, was because he was ashamed. She'd half-expected an apology, but she'd let it slide. She didn't feel the need to rub his face in the dirt. She'd been surprised, though: he was a pretty honest guy and it was a bit out of character for him to say nothing.

But maybe he'd said nothing because he hadn't done it. Because he hadn't known about it, hadn't been getting the messages at all. Maybe it was because Mike had been on her computer and *he* had done what he said Phil had done.

He had put some kind of software on her computer. Which meant that *he* was reading her emails.

But then who had been in her house and turned off the computer, who had messed with the filing cabinet? It couldn't have been Mike; he'd have had to break in, and there were no signs of that. It was Phil; only he had a key.

So this was all a coincidence. People received lots of emails; it was easy to imagine that two people could have emails arriving at the same time.

But not three, not all at the exact moment.

There was a way to find out. She typed an email to herself, titled *test*. If he was getting copies of every email she sent or received, his phone should buzz twice when she sent this, once when it left her outbox and once when it arrived in her inbox.

She sent it.

His phone buzzed. Then buzzed again.

304

She sent it again, and again, and again.

His phone buzzed and buzzed and buzzed and buzzed.

Kate stared at her phone, blinking. In her inbox she saw the emails she had sent herself.

test. test. test. test.

Those emails — she knew this now — were also in Mike's inbox. The man she had had sex with last night in her own home — in her own bed — was reading her private communications. All of them.

She thought of what she had said to her friends about him. What she had said to her friends about herself. Her private thoughts.

And he had read all of it.

She didn't know why, or how, or what he wanted, but she did know that this was not good. She had to get out of the house as soon as possible and — she shuddered — she needed help. She needed someone to know about this.

She opened Gus's email and started to type a reply.

As she did, the bedroom door opened.

10

'Hey,' Mike said. He was in a pair of running shorts, his legs long and muscular. Not like the legs of pudgy Mark Stevens. He was holding a tray, on which were two cups of coffee and two plates of scrambled eggs on toast. They smelled delicious; Kate could see cracked black pepper and chives on them.

She stared at him, phone in her hand. She was pale, she knew that. She could feel that the blood had drained from her face. He frowned. 'What's wrong?'

She couldn't think of what to say. All she knew was that she had to get out of the room, then out of the house, naked or not.

'I . . . I . . . I . . . ' she stammered. 'I have to go to the t . . . t . . . toilet.'

He stepped backwards to block the door. 'What's going on, Kate? What's wrong?'

'Nothing,' she replied. 'Nothing's wrong.'

Her legs felt weak; her head spun. 'Mike,' she said, unable to raise her voice higher than a whisper. 'I feel a bit sick. I need to go to the bathroom. Now.'

He shook his head. His expression was cold, emotionless. It was as if he had taken off a mask.

'What's going on, Kate? A few minutes ago, you sounded happy. You said you were coming down. You didn't mention feeling sick.'

'It came over me suddenly.' Her voice was

faint, the words a struggle to get out. She felt, she noticed, no hatred towards him, no anger, no resentment.

Only fear. Sheer, unadulterated terror. Terror so all-encompassing it left no room for any other emotions.

'Kate? What's happened? You can tell me.'

Her phone buzzed in her hand. In his jacket, his did the same. She glanced at it; as she did, she realized it was a mistake.

Understanding spread slowly over his face. 'I see,' he said. 'Oh, I see. It looks like you might have worked it out after all.'

She swallowed, hard. 'I haven't worked anything out,' she said. 'I promise.'

'Don't try to fool me,' he said. 'It won't work.' He pushed the door shut and stood in front of it. 'Just me and you now, Kate.'

There was no way out. She was trapped. She felt cold inside, disconnected from herself.

But there was one thing she could do. She picked up her phone and began to type.

11

The reply to Gus was already open, so she didn't have to worry about that. All she had to do was type.

In trouble, she wrote, then there was a loud crash. She glanced up; Mike had dropped the tray and was reaching out to grab her. She lifted her legs and kicked at him to keep him away; he grabbed her calf and twisted. She cried out in pain as something in her knee gave way.

She scrambled across the bed, her knee agony, holding her hands away from him. She ignored everything else — him, the pain, the fear — and focused on holding the phone still enough so that she could get the email — her only lifeline — to Gus.

She tapped send with her thumb; as she did he slammed his body on top of her and wrenched the phone from her hands. She closed her eyes. She wasn't sure that it had gone.

His phone buzzed.

Yes, she thought. *Yes, yes, yes.*

He tossed her handset onto the floor and walked to his jacket. He took out his phone and read the emails.

'Your message to Gus went through,' he said. He was like a different person. His voice was flat and impersonal, his face expressionless. All the warmth and animation was gone. The play was over; the actor had taken off his costume. 'But

308

that won't make any difference. All it means is that I'll speed things up. And, as of this morning, I have what I need, so the end was coming anyway.'

'You have what you need?' Kate said. 'What's going on?'

He ignored her and continued to read the emails she had been sending.

'You hacked my emails,' she said. 'I can't believe you did that.'

'I did,' he said. 'You're right.'

'Why?' she said. 'I trusted you.'

He continued to scroll through her messages.

'Well,' he said, ignoring her question. 'You're not as stupid as I thought. You linked me to Mark Stevens. To my former self.'

'What?' Kate said. 'What do you mean, your former self?'

'Exactly that,' Mike said. 'Mark Stevens is my former self.'

'But that means . . . ' Kate paused, staring at him, 'that means you and he are — you and he are — '

'The same person,' Mike said.

She had thought that she had reached her capacity for being afraid, but as she understood the implications of what he had said, she discovered that she was wrong. She made a kind of mewling, whining sound; all that was left of her, it seemed, was fear.

If he was Mark Stevens, then Mark Stevens had not committed suicide. Mark Stevens had faked his suicide, so that he could disappear.

And he would only want to do that because he

had killed his girlfriend and all the other women before her. She forced herself to focus. She needed time, time to think.

'So you're Mark Stevens,' she said, struggling to comprehend what he was telling her. 'You're Mark Stevens.'

'I used to be,' Mike said.

'He's not dead?'

'In a sense he is, yes. He no longer exists. People who knew him think he vanished, unable to bear the grief. But not dead.' He spread his arms. 'As you can see.'

'And he — you — killed the women in Sheffield?'

'Yes. And since he's gone, he can't be linked to me.' He smiled. 'The perfect crime.'

Kate stared at him. Even though she had already figured it out, it was still a shock to hear him admit that it was him, that *he* had killed those women.

And, of course, all the women in Stockton Heath.

Because if he was the Sheffield killer, and the Sheffield killer was, according to the cops, also responsible for the murders in Stockton Heath that meant that he — the man standing in her bedroom, blocking her way out — was the Strangler.

12

Phil unpeeled his key from the key chain and tied it to the side of his right trainer. That way he wouldn't have to worry about it falling out of the pocket of his shorts as he jogged. Unless he took off his shoe, there was no way he could lose it. It was a trick he had learned from Andy, in the days that Andy went running.

He looked at his watch. Nine thirty a.m. He was planning a trip to Manchester to buy some new clothes; it was time to smarten up. Not because he was interested in meeting someone new; he was still too raw from the break-up with Kate for that, not to mention Michelle's murder. He had a feeling of guilt that he couldn't shake, although he felt a bit fraudulent complaining about it. There were plenty of other people — her family, friends, work colleagues — who were suffering much more than him, but nonetheless he had been the last person to see her alive, and if he had insisted on her taking a cab home, she might not have been killed.

On the shelf by the door his phone rang. He ignored it. Whoever it was could leave a message. He bent down and tied his other shoe.

His phone rang again.

Kate, he thought, *it might be Kate*, and he picked it up and looked at the screen.

It was Gus.

Gus never called him, and now he had called

311

twice in a minute. Phil felt a sense of — not worry, exactly, but a keener interest than normal in what this was about.

'Gus,' he said. 'What's up?'

'You still got a key to your old place?' Gus said. 'Kate's place?'

'No,' Phil said. 'She changed the locks.'

'Any other way in?'

'There's a window at the back.' He blushed a little at the memory of the last time he'd used it.

'OK. Can you meet us there? May and I are on our way now.'

'Short answer, yes,' Phil said. 'I was about to go running, but that can wait. What's going on?'

'Tell you when you get here. See you then.'

Gus sounded brisk and professional.

Phil started to worry. There was a reason for this, and whatever it was, he didn't think it was anything good.

★ ★ ★

When he arrived, Gus was looking through the front windows. May was hammering on the door.

'Her car's here,' May said. 'But she's not. Or if she is, she's not coming to the door.'

The neighbour's door opened. Carl came out.

'Everything OK?' he said, then noticed Phil. 'Hey, stranger,' he said. 'Long time, no see.'

'Hi,' Phil replied. He looked at Gus. 'What's going on?'

'Kate's gone.' He looked at Carl. 'Have you seen her this morning?'

Carl shook his head. 'There was a car here last night.'

'Whose car?' Gus said. 'Did you see anyone?'

'No,' Carl said. 'I didn't see him. Or her. Can I help?'

Gus shook his head. 'It's fine.' He turned to Phil. 'Let's try the back.'

As they walked around the side of the house Phil felt a mounting panic.

'What's going on, Gus?' he said.

'I got a strange email from Kate,' Gus said. 'First she asked me if I knew anything about Mark Stevens, who was involved with one of the victims in the Sheffield case. That was a pretty random request in its own right, but then I got this . . . '

He handed his phone to Phil. The message was short and to the point:

In trouble

Phil's throat constricted. 'Jesus,' he said. 'What the hell is that?'

'Looks like she was in a hurry,' Gus replied. He caught Phil's eye. 'So we got down here ASAP. Which window?'

Phil pointed at the bathroom window. Gus gave him a leg up, and he climbed inside. The key was in the back door and he unlocked it.

'Kate?' Phil shouted. 'Are you there? You OK?'

Gus and May joined him and they walked through the kitchen into the living room. There was a bottle of red wine — about two-thirds drunk — on the coffee table, along with two

313

glasses and a small booklet.

Phil picked it up.

'Programme for a play at the Lowry,' he said. 'She went to the theatre.'

'Kate?' Gus called. 'Can you hear me?'

They looked in the front room — empty — they headed up the stairs. Phil ignored the bathroom and spare room and headed straight for the master bedroom. He pushed open the door.

'Holy shit,' he said. 'You guys better come and see this.'

13

He had forced her to get dressed, a flick knife — a fucking flick knife, this was real, this was actually happening — at her throat, and then told her to get in his car and not to say a fucking word or scream or run or do *anything* at all, because if she did he would fillet her and leave her to bleed to death on the pavement, and then he would disappear, which was what he did, and he would never be caught so she shouldn't worry about that.

She sat in the passenger seat. He opened the glove compartment and took out a pair of handcuffs, which he put on her wrists. She realized she had never worn handcuffs before.

Mike — Kate thought of him as Mike still — certainly kept the new experiences coming.

Like dating a serial killer. That was a new one, too.

A serial killer who had been killing women who looked like her. Stalking them at night, then strangling and raping them.

But this was different. This was the morning. This was her boyfriend. And he was about to drive away with her. The fear washed over her again.

'Where are you taking me?' she said.

'You'll find out.'

Kate felt like she was going to vomit. 'Are you the — are you the Strangler?' she said, fighting to keep her voice calm.

'Yes,' he said. He started the engine and looked in the mirror. Mirror, signal, manoeuvre. He was so responsible. It was what she had liked about him. She had wondered if it might get a bit tedious, his non-drinking, exercising, responsible behaviour, but, as it turned out, she didn't have to worry about that. She had something else to worry about.

He was a serial killer.

'Is this what you did to the others? Got to know them? Spent the night with them?'

He shook his head. 'No. You're different.'

'I'm different?' she said.

'Oh, yes. The others were nothing. They were cover. You're the target.'

The target? This time she did vomit, a warm gush that spread over her thighs and onto her bare feet.

'Bloody hell,' he said. 'That's going to be a bugger to clean up. I can't have any trace of you in here.'

'Why not?' she said, panic mounting. 'Why can't you?'

'Because I'm going to kill you,' he said. 'At least, the Strangler is. I'm going to play the part of the grieving boyfriend. I'm good at that, as you know. I might commit suicide, like Mark Stevens.' He paused. 'I'm guessing your friend Gus — he's the cop, right? — will be at the house pretty soon,' he said. 'Which is why we had to leave so quickly. Still, he won't find anything. Only the mess the breakfast made and an empty house.' He shrugged. 'No problem. My

316

plan won't change.'

'You said the others were cover?' Kate said. 'That I'm different. Why am I different?' She started to cry. 'I don't *want* to be different. I want to be back home.'

He paused, hand on the gear stick, suddenly excited, like a kid about to show a new trick to his parents. 'The cover,' he said. 'That's the best part of it all.'

Kate had the feeling that she might not agree with that assessment, but she nodded. 'Why?'

'Because it gets me off the hook.'

'Off what hook?'

He put the car in gear and pulled away. 'Think about it. If I befriended you, dated you for a while, then killed you, I'd be the number one suspect. It's always the boyfriend, right? That's why they went after Phil — which, by the way, was part of my plan. I killed that slut he was fucking — if he *was* fucking her, which I doubt as he's too pathetic and lovelorn about his lost bitch to get it up for anyone else — even though you'd changed your appearance. I knew he hadn't seen you, so if he was the killer he would still have been targeting women who looked like you.'

'No,' Kate said. She couldn't believe that these innocent women had been killed like that, as though they were nothing. 'No. That's sick. It's unbelievable.'

He held his hands up in a show of fake modesty. 'I know, I know. I'm a genius. And, as a result of my genius, they're looking for a serial killer. The Strangler started killing before I met you, and, as far as anyone knows — you included — we have no prior connection. So when you die, it'll be the Strangler that they look for, not the guy who you met on holiday. Especially after the weird stuff that happened — the victims resembling you, the car following you, all that.'

'That was you? In the car?'

'Of course it was. I wanted you scared, and I wanted the police not to be surprised when you turned up dead. It would all support the theory that the Strangler got you. And then he would disappear.'

Kate couldn't look at him. 'Like in Sheffield.'

'Yes!' he said. 'That was when I got the idea. I had to deal with that bitch Claire. She wouldn't do what I wanted, you know? I wanted to love her, to be with her — that was all. Not too much to ask, right? But she told her friends bad things about me, didn't want to let me take care of her. And then she tried to leave! Can you believe that? Ungrateful slob. So that's when I came up with the plan: make her the victim of a serial killer. That way, the police wouldn't be looking at boyfriends and husbands. Then all I had to do was wait a while before Mark Stevens killed himself.'

'You invented a serial killer so that nobody would think you had a motive?'

'Exactly. Brilliant, no?' He paused. 'Sometimes I think I would have been a good — a *great* — novelist. Or a playwright. You know, the thing with Shakespeare is that he *understood* people. He knew what made them tick. Never mind all the fancy language: what makes him special is

318

that his people are *real*, and you know what you need to be able to understand people like that? You have to be better than them. *Superior.* Which is me. I know how you lot will react before you do, which is why *I'm* in control. Yes, I could be a playwright, like him. I'd be better, though.'

He meant it. This was not some comical flight of fancy; he actually believed what he was saying. Mike Sadler, Kate now saw, was a total fantasist. It was chilling to get a glimpse into what passed for his inner life. He was inhuman, lacking something very profound. However he viewed the world — and she could not truly imagine how that was — it was utterly different from any normal person.

There was, though, one thing that didn't make sense about his story. Kate shook her head. 'What about Turkey?' she said. 'You can't be the Strangler. You were there when the first murder happened.'

'Oh God,' he said, as matter-of-fact as if they had been discussing his late arrival at a party. 'That's what I told you so you'd think I had an alibi. I got there the day before you.'

'But that was why I trusted you.'

'Yes,' he said. 'I know. One of the things I've noticed about people is how easily they trust other people. I mean, trust is probably the most valuable thing you can give someone, but you lot throw it about like confetti. It's almost like you assume — '

'Shut up,' Kate said. 'Just shut up. I don't want to hear your voice any more. Kill me now,

319

if it means I never have to hear your stupid preachy sanctimonious voice ever again.'

'I can't,' he said. 'Kill you now, that is. The Strangler kills at night, so I have to wait until then. Or I would. Trust me, I've been looking forward to killing you for a *long* time.'

She stared out of the window. He had driven down a back road that led to the Cheshire countryside and she watched the hedges roll by. He'd been looking forward to killing her for a *long time?* Why? What had she done? He had killed the women in Sheffield so that he would not be a suspect after he killed his girlfriend; fine, she understood that — although she wasn't sure that *understood* was the right word — but why her?

And if he did want to kill her, why go to all this trouble? Why not simply kill her? There was no link between them. It wasn't as if the police would suspect him; it would appear to be a totally random killing.

So why? Why do all this? It made no sense.

There was a missing piece in this puzzle, and she could not for the life of her work out what it was, although there was something lurking at the back of her mind. Something he had said, back in the bedroom, when he had seen that the message to Gus had gone through.

But that won't make any difference. All it means is that I'll speed things up. And, as of this morning, I have what I need, so the end was coming anyway.

He'd said he had what he needed.

But what *was* that?

She took a series of deep breaths. They didn't work very well — nothing was going to keep her calm right now — but they allowed her to get some sense of sanity.

'You said you had what you needed,' she said. 'Back at the house. But I thought you wanted me dead?'

'I do,' he said. 'I do want you dead. But that's not all I want.' He gave her an odd look, as though questioning why she would be insulting his intelligence. 'If that was all I wanted, I could have killed you already. A completely random murder. It would have been untraceable.'

Which is what I figured, Kate thought. 'So what is it?' she said.

'You don't need to know,' he said. 'And I operate on a need-to-know basis.'

Kate didn't say anything. She sensed that Mike liked to withhold information, in order to prove his superiority; fine, she'd go ahead and burst that bubble.

'Sure,' she said. 'You operate on your need-to-know basis. Where did you learn that, by the way? Watching *G.I. Joe*? Or playing with your Action Men?'

He glanced at her, his eyes narrowed.

'I didn't have Action Men,' he said.

'What did you have? My Little Ponies?'

'Be careful,' he said. 'Be careful what you say to me, Kate.'

'Or what? You'll abduct me and kill me? Too late for that, G.I. Joe.'

'Don't call me that,' he said. 'That's not my name.'

321

'It's as good as any,' Kate said. 'Are you Mark Stevens? Or Mike Sadler? How am I supposed to know? And I prefer G.I. Joe. It's got a ring to it. Sexy, kind of.'

'Don't. Call. Me. That.'

Kate laughed. She was aware she was walking a fine line, but she had to find out what was going on. It was the only way she could get out of this. 'Touched a sore spot? Did someone steal your G.I. Joe dolls when you were a little boy?'

'You are going to call me by my name,' he said, his knuckles white as he gripped the steering wheel. 'I will MAKE you, you fucking bitch.'

He reached over and slapped her, hard, across the face, then he lowered his hand and grabbed her breast and squeezed. She took a sharp breath.

'Not so tough now, are you?' Mike said. 'From now on you use my name. OK, bitch?'

'Fuck you,' Kate said, clenching her teeth. 'G.I. Joe.'

He squeezed harder and she cried out in pain.

'Use. My. Name,' he said. 'Last chance.'

'Sure thing,' she said. 'G.I. Joe.'

He let out a strange, high shriek, his face red with anger.

'You will do what I say!' he shouted. 'You will stop calling me that and you will call me by my name!'

'I don't know it,' Kate said. 'I don't know your fucking name!'

He glared at her, the car swerving on the road.

Go on, she thought, *crash. Crash and this'll be over.*

But he didn't. He looked ahead and straightened the wheel. He was grinding his teeth.

'What is your name, G.I. Joe?' she shouted. 'What the fuck is your name?'

His answer shocked her. It was the last thing she had expected to hear. A name — a name that she had hoped never to come across again — from the past.

'My name,' he said, his face screwed up in anger, 'is Colin. Colin Davidson.'

14

'*Colin Davidson?*' Kate said. '*Beth's* Colin Davidson?'

He smiled. As he did, his whole body relaxed, his posture changed, his eyes took on a kind of sparkle. He was, Kate saw, a brilliant actor.

'Colin Davidson,' he said. 'Nice to meet you.'

His expression changed again; the look of fury was back. 'Lucky that I never met you back then,' he said. 'Or you'd have recognized me and I wouldn't have been able to get away with this.'

So this was the man who had beaten Beth, driven her to the brink of suicide, driven her to the point where she had changed her name and moved to a new place so she could be free of him. And now he was back. But why? What on earth was he up to?

'I still don't get it,' she said. 'What do you want from me?'

'That's easy,' he replied. 'I want Beth.'

'Beth?' Kate said. 'That's what all this is about?'

'Yes. Beth. I want to find her.'

'I don't understand,' Kate said, struggling through the fear to think straight, to think at all. 'I don't see how this helps you find her.'

'Let me explain,' he said. 'She's been *very* hard to find. At first I tried everything, but there was no way I could get to her. Of course, I couldn't ask the police, or make enquiries through the

324

authorities — not that they would have told me — or even go to a private detective, because I couldn't leave a trace. Not with what I planned to do. So, pretty soon I made a new plan. Took a long view. After all, I was in no hurry.'

Kate didn't reply. She didn't know what to say. She had no reference point for this situation.

'So I hid out. Became Mark Stevens. Met that slut Claire. She reminded me a lot of Beth — fat, needy, easy to control — and gradually Beth faded from my mind. But then Claire tried to leave! Which was another way she was like Beth.' He shook his head. 'Obviously, I'd learned from what happened with Beth, so I had to stop her. And what better way than to kill her? So I came up with the serial killer idea — a *brilliant* idea — and got rid of her. The thing is . . . ' he paused thoughtfully, 'once she was dead, I had the free time to think about Beth, and I realized that I still loved her. I'd been wasting my time with Claire; I wanted Beth back. She was my one true love.'

'You don't know what true love is,' Kate said. 'You're only capable of some sick, twisted version.'

Mike tutted. 'You're jealous,' he said. 'Because I love Beth but I was only using you. Anyway, once I understood that it was Beth I wanted, two things came to me: the first — I'll tell you about the second later — was that I had to figure out a different way of finding her. Which is where *you* came in. I had a suspicion that Beth would be in touch with you, in some way or other. If I could get close enough to you, then I could get to her.

Hence going to Turkey to meet you.'

'How did you know I was going?'

'Facebook,' Mike said. 'You people plaster your lives on that thing: birthdays, travel plans, all kinds of personal information. It's an open invitation for people who are up to no good to get up to no good.' He laughed. 'It's so much easier these days.'

These days, she thought. *He's done this before, God knows how many times.* 'So you went to Turkey, picked me up in the bar.' She fought another wave of nausea. 'Why Kalkan? Why not do it here?'

'Because here there would be too many people watching. And you're not the kind of girl who does that kind of thing. Your friends would have stepped in. On holiday, though — all bets are off. You have to be even more careful on holiday than you are at home, but the strange thing is that all you idiots do the exact opposite.' He shrugged again. 'Bad for you, good for me.'

'Fuck, I wish I hadn't had so much to drink that night.'

'You didn't,' he said. 'I gave you a little something to help loosen you up. Popped it into your gin and tonic. That's why your memories are a bit hazy.'

'You drugged me,' Kate said, her voice flat. 'You bastard. You absolute bastard.'

'I needed you to think that I was a gentleman,' he said. 'And what better way than to not take advantage of your drunkenness?'

'And the text message? To May and Gemma, saying I was fine?'

'I sent that,' he said. 'I couldn't take any chances. The thing is, I was hoping you'd fall for me, but in case you didn't — which you didn't — I needed a plan B.' He grinned. 'So I told you I lived near Stockton Heath.'

'You don't?'

'No, of course not. That would be a ridiculous coincidence. But it gave me the excuse for bumping into you, if I needed to. I wasn't sure I *would* need to; I thought that I might find what I needed in your house, but it wasn't there.'

Kate stared at him, his words barely registering. 'In my house? Were you in my house?'

'Of course. I got into your house while you were at work. Had a good look around. But I couldn't find any trace of Beth. She's not in your address book, for example. Or your diary.'

'You went through my *diary*?' Kate said. 'Please, no.'

'It was pretty fucking boring, I have to say. *Phil this, Phil that, got a crush on a guy at work, flirted with someone in a bar and feel a bit guilty but also proud of myself for not doing anything.* God, you're like a crap version of Bridget Jones. At least she had some *spirit*.'

'Fuck you,' Kate said. 'How's that for spirit?'

'Very good!' he said. 'Bit late, though.'

'So it was you? Who switched off the computer? And went through the files?'

'Yes,' he said. 'It was very convenient that you had Phil and his key to blame it on.'

'How did you get into the house?'

'I let myself in.'

327

'How?'

'With the key I stole from you in Turkey.'

Kate sank back into her seat. The memory came back: her, standing outside the house the night she came back from Turkey, realizing she had lost her key somewhere. And all the while Mike had it.

'I found it when you were sleeping,' he said. 'Helpfully stashed away in your bag. Anyway, back to the story — this is a good bit. When I couldn't find any trace of Beth, I realized that I needed you to tell me where she was, which meant I was going to have to bump into you. Which would be a lot easier if I knew what you were up to.'

'So you fucked with my emails?' she said. 'Is that it?'

'Got into your email account and set it up to forward me your emails. It's easy, if you know what you're doing, and I know exactly what I'm doing. That's how I knew where you'd be, and that you had a profile on the dating website.' He smiled. 'Then we met and you fell for me — and for my story about the shelter. I *knew* that would get you to share with me.'

'Was that bullshit, too?' Beth said.

'Oh yes. Total rubbish. My parents are alive and well in Scunthorpe, living the most boring life you could imagine. Dad's a Methodist teetotaller. I made all that up so you'd think I was someone who understood what Beth had been through and could be trusted to be told about her.'

'I would never tell you about Beth,' she said.

'Oh,' he replied. 'But you already did.'

'I didn't. I didn't tell you anything about Beth.'

'You did,' he said. 'You told me everything.'

The nausea hit her again. Kate shook her head. 'I don't get it. I said nothing.' As she spoke she started to feel a growing nervousness. What had he said? *And, as of this morning, I have what I need, so the end was coming anyway.* Had she given it away somehow? Had he drugged her again?

'You said that she had contacted you on Facebook,' Mike said. 'That she kept her profile hidden and didn't post pictures, but that you'd been in touch.'

'So? You can't see her. Her public profile is hidden, and there's nothing on it anyway. She's very careful.'

'Right, but if I had access to your computer, then I'd be fine. Because you don't log out of your Facebook account. Anybody who can use your computer can see whatever they want. So I was very pleased when you gave me all the access I needed.'

'I didn't give you anything. No passwords. Nothing. I'd remember.'

'Oh, but you did.' He paused. 'I was reading your emails, but I didn't have access to your Facebook account. The night Phil showed up at the pub and you told me you thought he'd been on your computer — which was me, of course — I saw an opportunity. We set up password protection, but remember how I turned away when you put in your new password? Well, I was

329

watching. It's a skill I have. And, since you're stupid enough to stay logged in to your Facebook, all I needed was a chance to spend half an hour alone on your computer, and I'd have what I needed.'

Kate let out an involuntary moan. What had she done? How had she been so stupid?

'So this morning — which was my first opportunity, since you changed the locks — while you slept I took a look through your friends. Found one that was added around three years ago, who shared minimal information. And there she was. Andrea Berry.'

He wagged his head from side to side, as though thinking to himself.

'Interesting that she swapped this shithole of a town for Wolverhampton,' he said. 'Useful to know that. She shouldn't have told you, but there it was, right in front of my eyes in a message she sent you a couple of years ago.' He tapped his fingers on the steering wheel. 'That's all I need. And it means I don't need you.'

'So all this was a sham?' Kate said. 'A scheme to find out where Beth is?'

'Yes,' Mike said. 'Exactly. I was pretty sure that she would have been in touch with you — she's a loyal soul, Beth — and so all I needed to do was to get the information from you somehow. And, thankfully for me, you obliged.'

'So now what?' Kate said. 'Where are we going?'

'To a place I have where I can keep you hidden until I kill you. The Strangler's last victim. Then I disappear, and, after a while, go

330

and re-introduce my Beth to the only man who ever truly loved her.' He grinned. 'Then kill her, the fucking bitch.'

'So that's it?' Kate fought back tears. She didn't want him to see her cry. 'After all this, you're going to kill me? Just like that?'

'No,' he said. 'Not just like that. First I'm going to make you suffer, the way you made me suffer.'

15

She was silent while the words sank in.

'What do you mean, like I made you suffer? I've never done anything to you.'

'Oh, you have,' Mike said. 'And that's why this is only half about Beth. If all I needed was information about Beth, I could have got it and then dumped you. But the other half is about *you*. The other half is the reason *you* have to die, and the reason the Strangler had to exist.' He grinned. 'That was the second thing that came to me after I killed Claire. I could use the same method to deal with you. Once you'd led me to Beth, I could create a new serial killer — which is always *tremendous* fun — and get him to kill you.' His grin vanished and his face twisted into a scowl. 'That way, I'd get Beth *and* my revenge. So Claire turned out to be very useful, in the end.'

Claire, Beth, revenge: Kate had the sensation that he was spinning out of control; it was a struggle to keep track of his mood swings and the different directions the conversation was going in. She tried to focus.

'But why?' she said. 'How is it about me? What did *I* do?'

'You don't get it, do you?' Mike said. 'You don't even know what you did.' He banged his fist against the dashboard, hard, with a loud, shockingly loud, report. He turned to her, his

332

face screwed up in fury. 'You don't even know what you did,' he shouted. 'That makes me so fucking angry!'

'OK,' Kate said. 'OK. I'm sorry. I probably do know. Tell me and I might remember.'

'I love her!' Mike screamed. His face was puce, his eyes bulging. 'That's what you don't get! I love her! Still! So much that I have to kill her. Don't you understand?'

Kate didn't get it. She didn't get it one little bit. She had no idea what kind of love would prompt her to want to kill the person she loved, but then she wasn't crazy. And Mike — or Colin, or whatever he was called — was clearly as crazy as they came.

Suddenly he was calm again, the smile back on his face, the light back in his eyes.

'So,' he said, his tone calm and rational. She almost preferred the shouting, out-of-control version. At least with that she knew what she was up against. 'This is why it's about you. I love Beth. And she loved me, back then. Back then she loved me and we were together and she was going to have my — our — baby, a baby which would have cemented our love for each other.' He turned and stared at Kate, not even remotely watching the road. 'And then *you* interfered,' he said. 'You turned her against me and got her to kill my child. You might not have wielded the knife — that was some shithead of a doctor — but you are responsible. You're a *murderer*, Kate. A *child* murderer.'

'That's not what happened,' Kate said. If she was going to die — which looked, she had to

333

admit, not unlikely — then she was going to damn well tell the truth before she did do. 'She hated you. She came to me for help.'

'That's your story — ' Mike began, before Kate interrupted.

'That's *the* story,' she said. 'I saw the bruises. I saw what you did to her.' She laughed sarcastically. 'You know, the funny thing is — like I told you — I thought she'd fled you so she could have the baby, but it was the opposite. She hated you so much she was prepared to give up her child to make sure she wasn't reminded of you. *That's* the truth, Mike — or Mark or Colin or whatever your fucking name is. She would have found a way to leave you, you know,' Kate said. 'You can't blame me. She *hated* you.'

'We'll never know, will we? But what I *do* know is that you took her — and my child — from me. And you're going to pay for that. Don't you see? That's why this is the perfect plan. I get to find my Beth and I get to destroy you.' He grinned at her. 'It was very hard to fuck you, Kate. Very hard. It was like fucking an animal. But I did it because I had to. Because it was in the service of something beautiful.'

'There's nothing beautiful about you, or anything you do,' Kate said.

'Come on,' he said. 'Don't say that. You *know* it's not true.'

They were driving along a country road, passing high hedges and farm gates. Kate looked around, seeking something familiar. If she did get away from him, she needed to know where she was.

334

'Nearly there,' he said.

'Where are we going?'

'To my barn. I rent it from a farmer. He thinks I keep vintage MGBs and MG Midgets in there, that I restore them. I've had it for a while; he's used to me coming and going. Not that he's around much.'

'You're sick,' she said. 'You know that, don't you? You are sick. Anyone who wants to do something like that — God, it's disgusting. I don't know what goes wrong with people like you, but you are very, very ill.'

'Does it make you feel good, to try and hurt me?' Mike said. 'I hope so, because you're going to pay for it. You're going to pay in pain.' He drummed his fingers on the steering wheel. 'Maybe I'll try waterboarding,' he said, back in his grandstanding mode. 'You know? The torture thing they do? Where they hold your face underwater just long enough that you think you're drowning, you're sure you're drowning, you know it's about to happen, and they pull you out at the last second. Then they do it again. Doesn't even leave any marks. You can do it as many times as you want.' He gave her a friendly grin, as though they were two friends discussing some high jinks they'd got up to. 'Of course, they don't need to, when they're using it to get information out of someone. Apparently, after one or two rounds, hardened terrorists are begging to tell their secrets rather than face it again. Doesn't apply to you, though, does it? I already have your secrets, so I'll be doing it purely for fun.'

335

He sniffed. 'But you can't die by drowning. You have to die by strangulation. Then I — the Strangler — will cut out your eyes and fuck your dead body and dump you somewhere.' He leaned towards her, his face contorted in a leer. 'And you know what? I think I'll enjoy that more than fucking you when you were alive.'

This time she did vomit again. She retched three, four times, until what little had been left in her stomach was gone.

He tutted and shook his head. 'What an awful mess,' he said.

16

The barn was at the end of a rutted farm track. Kate had lost all sense of where they were — somewhere in the Cheshire countryside was all she knew. She had never noticed how rural it became so close to Stockton Heath; once you were south of the urban belt that ran from Liverpool to Manchester there was a lot of empty space.

More than enough to hide someone for a while.

The barn doors were open; they drove in and, as they slowed to a stop, Mike reached onto the back seat. He grabbed a roll of bungee cord, which he fastened around her ankles. He climbed out of the front door and threw his leather jacket onto the empty seat.

'You'll be staying in the car,' Mike said. 'I don't want traces of the barn on your body. Too many clues for the police.'

Kate ignored him. She ran through the situation in her mind. It was pretty hopeless; Mike/Mark/Colin had spent weeks — years, maybe — planning this. For her, it was hours old. And she had no idea what to do. She didn't have even the first idea what her options were; as far as she could see, she didn't have any.

She stared at the dusty walls of the barn and the reality — the absolute undeniable reality — of the situation hit home: she was going to die here.

And she was overcome with a feeling of utter terror.

'Understand?' he said. 'Stay here, and don't try anything. You'll only make it worse for yourself.'

Then he got out and closed the barn door and, for a moment, it was pitch-black.

* * *

She heard his footsteps cross the barn and then a light fizzed on. It was a naked bulb, hanging from a thick, grimy beam. There was a smell of sawdust and animals and manure. Mike walked across the barn to the shadows at the back. Kate tried to see what he was doing, but she could not make it out.

Not that it would help. Ankles tied and handcuffed, there was not a lot she could do.

And then, on the seat next to her, in the pocket of his leather jacket, his phone started to buzz.

His phone. This was her chance. If she could answer it, she could ask whoever it was for help, to call the cops.

She imagined it: some worker in a call centre making the two hundredth call of the day:

Hello, I'm calling about your credit card. Don't worry, there's no problem —

There is a problem, she'd say. *I've been kidnapped, by the Stockton Heath Strangler, and I need you to do something, right now.*

Enough daydreaming; Kate leaned forward and bit the shoulder of the jacket. The leather was salty and smelled of Mike. She gagged, then yanked her head back so that the jacket was in her lap. Even though she was handcuffed, she could reach into the pocket with her fingers for the phone; she grabbed it and took it out.

And her eyes widened.

It wasn't a call centre.

It was *her* number calling.

17

'Look at this mess,' Phil said. 'What the hell happened in here?'

There was a tray on the floor, upside down and surrounded by two plates, two coffee mugs and an array of cutlery. Dark stains had spread across the carpet; scrambled egg was scattered in a wide radius.

'Looks like there was a struggle,' Gus said. 'I'm calling this in. This is bad news.'

They heard footsteps in the corridor. It was May. 'What's happening?' she said, then clapped her hand over her mouth. 'Oh my God.'

'Wait,' Phil said. 'She left her phone.'

It was on the floor by the bed. He picked it up.

'It has fingerprint recognition,' he said. 'We set it up to recognize both of ours. I doubt Kate changed it.'

He pressed his thumb to the button. The screen switched on. Phil scanned her emails.

'This is the one she sent to you,' he said to Gus. He scrolled through the others. 'Might be a clue about what she was up to. There's a lot from this guy Mike Sadler.'

May couldn't look him in the eye. 'She said she'd been seeing someone.'

'It's fine,' Phil said, even though he wasn't sure that was how he felt.

'I'm calling the station,' Gus said. 'In this kind of operation time is critical.'

'Wait a second. Let me look at the photos. Maybe there's a clue there.'

He opened the photo album.

There was one from last night. It showed Kate and a man — presumably Mike Sadler — in the foyer of the Lowry theatre. They must have asked someone to take it for them. The perfect couple.

Phil stared at it. So this was the guy that was going to take his place. It was hard to take, hard to accept, but right now there were more important things to worry about.

'I have to call this in,' Gus said.

'Let me speak to Mike Sadler first,' Phil said. 'See if he knows where she is. If not, then we can tell that to the cops when we call them.' He tapped the screen and lifted the phone to his ear.

It took five or six rings before it answered.

'Hello?' a woman's voice said. She sounded breathless, but Phil recognized her immediately.

'Kate?' Phil said. 'Is that you?'

'Yes,' Kate said, she sounded panicked and Phil's heart began to race. 'Phil, thank God it's you. Oh shit, he's coming back. Phil, it's Mike Sadler, the guy I've been seeing. He's Colin Davidson and he's after Beth and he's got me in some barn and he's going to kill me and he's the Strangler and oh shit — '

The phone went dead.

Phil stared at Gus and May.

'What the fuck is going on?' he said. 'That was Kate. She's with Sadler — who's Colin Davidson and he's after Beth — and she said he's going to kill her.' He paused. 'And then the phone cut off.'

341

18

Mike snatched the phone from her with his left hand; with his right he punched her in the side. She bent over, winded.

'Who was that?' he said. 'Who did you call?'

She groaned, unable to answer. He looked at the screen.

'*They* called *you*,' he said. 'From your phone. Shit.'

'It was Phil and he knows who you are,' Kate said. 'And if he knows who you are then your plan is shot. You can't pretend that I'm the latest victim of the Strangler and then disappear. He'll be looking for you. He'll figure this out.'

He rubbed his fingers against his temples. 'This is like in Harry Potter,' he said. 'Have you read those books?'

It didn't seem much like Harry Potter to Kate, but she nodded; yes, she had read them. *Everyone* had. Even serial killers, apparently.

'Their problem in those books is that they never do what Voldemort wants,' Mike said. 'He makes his plans and they don't ever do WHAT HE WANTS!'

He slammed his hands on the headrest then walked around to her side of the car, opened the door, and pulled her out onto the dirt floor of the barn. She lay on her side, her ankles and wrists bound.

'Doesn't matter if there's a trace of you now, does it?' he said. 'Because now your stupid little boyfriend knows who I am! He knows I'm the Strangler.' He kicked her in the thigh, hard. 'I can leave as many traces of you as I want. Which I suppose is kind of convenient.' He walked around her and lifted his foot, then brought it down on her cheek. She felt something break and pain spread across her face. Blood started to flow from her nose.

He was, she realized, going to kill her there and then.

'Stop,' she said. 'Please. Stop.'

'Why? I have nothing to lose now, Kate. All I want to do is kill you. Once I've done that, I can get to Beth, and then this will be over. But you're no use to me now.' He kicked her in the stomach. 'You RUINED EVERYTHING,' he shouted. 'All you had to do was follow instructions, but you couldn't even do that.'

He took a step back, getting ready for another kick — maybe the last one, Kate thought, maybe the one that killed her or left her unconscious — but, before he could deliver it, his phone rang.

He snatched it from his pocket.

'It's him,' he said. 'It's your idiot boyfriend. What the hell does he want now?'

'Answer,' she said. 'Find out.'

He glared at her, then lifted it to his ear, and walked to the far end of the barn.

Kate watched him, a thin smile on her face.

It would be Phil. She'd spent the last month or so making sure that the rest of her life was disentangled from his, and now, after all that, it was Phil she was relying on to make sure she *had* a rest of her life.

19

Phil sat at the kitchen table, the phone in front of him. May and Gus were standing behind him, listening. Phil had suggested that they didn't speak; for now, it was better if Mike thought that he was only dealing with one person.

He'd looked at the photo of Mike at the Lowry theatre; it was Colin Davidson all right. He'd seen him up close the night Beth disappeared, and he remembered him well; you tended not to forget the more dramatic moments in your life.

Mike's voice came over the phone.

'Who is this?' he said. 'Who are you?'

'You know who I am, I think,' Phil said. 'She'll have said I called.'

'Of course I do. You're the idiot who ran around after her, wondering why she'd dumped you. Is that why you're at her house? Snooping around again?'

Phil blushed. Even though it hardly mattered now, he didn't want May and Gus to hear this.

'That's me,' he said. 'And I don't deny that I didn't get everything right. But ultimately I did it because I loved — I still love — Kate, and I'm not ashamed of that. Not one bit.'

'How about this, then? Your behaviour made it much easier for me to do what I did,' Mike said, a triumphant, mocking note in his voice. 'It made me look mature and grown up and a damn

345

sight more attractive. And, more to the point, it made you easy to blame — I'd been in the house, looking through the files on the computer, and I made a mistake. Switched it off when she never would have done that. She thought it was you, thought that you'd been snooping. Got me out of a bit of a pickle, that did. Not ashamed of that? Even a little bit?'

This conversation was going nowhere. Phil needed to get it back on track.

'You want to talk about shame?' he said. 'I know who you are. And what you've done. Some of it, at least.'

'Yes, you mentioned that. So who am I, do you think?'

'Mark Stevens, for one,' Phil said. 'But you're also Colin, aren't you? Colin Davidson. I met you back then, Colin, and I remember your face. You looked different to Mike Sadler — fatter, hair greasy and swept back, thick glasses, but I remember the night you stood on my doorstep asking where Beth was, and I remember phoning Kate and telling her that there was something not quite right about you — but there's a photo on Kate's phone, and it's definitely you. You'd have been better off not coming looking for her — I'd have seen you eventually — but you couldn't stop yourself, could you? That's your problem, isn't it? You can't stop yourself.'

'Well, well,' Mike said. 'So little Phil isn't the thick as pigshit dickless wonder that Kate told me he was. He has a brain cell or two after all. Not that it'll help.'

'And you're the Strangler too, correct?'

'So it seems.'

'What's all this about?' Phil said. 'What do you want? Maybe I can help you get it.'

Mike laughed. 'Right. You help *me*. Not a chance.'

'Try me. What are you doing this for? Is it for Beth? That's what Kate said.'

'Yes,' Mike said. 'It's for Beth. *She's* what I want.'

'You won't get her. No one knows where she is.'

'I already have her. Kate obliged.'

Phil tapped his foot. So that was what this was about. Mike — or Colin or whoever he was — wanted Beth, after all this time, and somehow he'd staged all this in order to find out where she was. And now he knew; which meant Phil — and Kate — had no bargaining chips.

Unless. An idea started to form. If Kate knew where Beth was, then maybe others did too.

He put the phone on mute.

'May,' he said. 'Are you in touch with Beth?'

May pulled her hair back, fastening it into a ponytail. She nodded. 'On Facebook. I haven't sent her a message, though, not for ages. I don't know how often she uses it. She's not called Beth any more, though.'

'That's good enough. What's her new name?'

'Andrea Berry.'

Phil unmuted the phone.

'There's a problem though,' he said, 'isn't there, Mike? Or Colin. What do you prefer?'

'I don't care. And the only person who has a problem is you.'

347

'Not so,' Phil said. 'You know who Beth is, so you can go after her as soon as we finish talking. But I know who she is as well. Andrea Berry, correct? So what do you think I'm going to do as soon as this call is over?'

There was a long silence. Mike broke it, his voice a low growl.

'What are you going to do?'

'You know.'

'Tell me.'

'I'll tell her that Colin Davidson is coming for her, and she'll disappear again.'

'Then Kate dies.'

'But you don't get Beth. Because as soon as you kill Kate — and by the way, if you do, then I will find you and kill you myself, so all of this will be irrelevant — I tell Beth that you're coming and she'll vanish like a rabbit down a hole. And then the cops find out about you and you'll have to do the same. It won't be easy for you, Mike. It won't be easy at all. But if you return Kate, Beth will never know that you're coming.'

Mike chuckled. 'You're offering me Kate for Beth? Right. But the minute I hand Kate back you'll be straight on the phone to Beth,' he said. 'That's not going to work. Make a better offer, Phil.'

'That's it for now, Mike. That's the best offer on the table.'

'Then it's not good enough.' He paused. 'So we're at an impasse. Kate's with me; Beth's with you.'

'You need to bring her home,' Phil said, his

voice rising. 'You can't — '

'Don't tell me what I can and can't do,' Mike said. 'Let me tell you what's going to happen next. You're going to figure out a way to get me what I want. When you do, call me and we can talk. And in the meantime, no one else gets involved. No cops. Understand? I see a cop and she dies. Got it?'

'Yes.'

'I mean it. No cops. Say it.'

'No cops.'

The line went dead.

Phil looked at May and Gus.

'Well,' he said. His head was spinning and his legs felt weak. 'She's alive, at least.'

'We have to involve the authorities,' Gus said. 'They can trace his phone. Find out where he is.'

'No,' Phil said. 'You heard him. No police.'

'We don't have to send them in. We could ask them to find out where he's holding Kate.'

'Right,' Phil said. 'And they'll stand about waiting while we bargain with the serial killer?' He shook his head. 'No. They'll take over, and Kate will be killed.'

'We have to,' Gus said. 'We have no choice.'

20

Phil paced the kitchen.

'You heard him,' he said. 'Mike or Mark or Colin or whatever the fuck he's called. We can't send the police in. He'll kill her.'

Gus shook his head. 'We have ways,' he replied. 'They'll get a rapid response unit in. Move to the target, throw in smoke grenades. Whatever it takes.'

'Right,' Phil said. 'And they'll get their man. But not before he kills Kate.'

'He won't have time to. We have snipers. We know how to do this.'

Phil stopped. He leaned on his hands. 'Forgive me if I don't share your confidence. And even if you guys *are* so amazing, what if he sees them coming? What then?'

'He won't. They're experienced at this kind of thing.' Gus massaged his temples with his forefingers. 'And my job's on the line. If it came out that I knew about this and didn't tell anyone — '

'Is that what this is about?' Phil said. 'Your job? Well, excuse me for being presumptuous, but I think Kate's life may come first.'

'No,' Gus said. 'That's not what — '

'Gus,' May said. 'She's my best friend. We can't risk it.'

Gus looked out of the window. 'She's my friend too. And trust me, if anything happens to her I'll never forgive myself. But that doesn't

350

change the facts. We have to involve the police. It's the best chance we have. The *only* chance.'

'No,' Phil said. 'We can't.'

'Then what are you going to do, Phil? Storm the place yourself? You're a project manager, for fuck's sake.' Gus stood up. 'Come on, what's your idea? Build a project plan with key deliverables and milestones? Develop a metrics framework and project tracking methodology?'

'Gus,' May said quietly. 'Please.'

'This is what we do, May!' Gus said. 'This is why we have the police! This guy's a serial killer — eight victims that we know of, and counting — and this is a chance to catch him.'

'Kate can't be collateral damage,' Phil said. 'Her safety comes first.'

'And the best way to guarantee her safety is by telling the competent authorities.'

'It's that word that bothers me,' Phil said. 'Competent.'

'Then I come back to my question, Phil. What are you going to do? You don't know where he is and you don't have any way of finding out.'

Phil clenched his jaw, his teeth grinding back and forth.

'What will the police do?' he said.

'They'll locate the phone signal. Send a team in.' He caught Phil's gaze. 'This is the right decision,' he said. 'I promise.'

★ ★ ★

While Gus made phone calls in the yard, Phil and May sat at the kitchen table.

'This is unbearable,' May said, her eyes wet with tears. 'I can't stop thinking of her. What she must be going through.' She brushed the tears away with the back of her hand. 'I'm so worried that we'll never see her again. And none of this would have happened if we'd kept more of an eye on her in Turkey.'

'This isn't your fault,' Phil said. 'It isn't anyone's fault, except his. Except that bastard who took her.'

'I don't know what to do,' May said. 'I feel so powerless, sitting around here, waiting to find out what happens. Whether she lives or dies.'

'I know,' Phil said. 'But there is something we could do. Something we *have* to do.'

'What?'

'We have to contact Beth.'

21

Mike — she still thought of him as Mike and she wasn't ready to make the effort to change that — opened the car door and sat on the passenger seat, his feet on the ground in front of her eyes. He had dust on his shoes and the hem of his jeans and a hard, angry look on his face.

Her ribs ached where he had kicked her. Her nose and cheek throbbed, the result of the stamp on her face.

But she had a feeling this was only the start of the pain. She steeled herself. She could take it.

'What is it?' she said. 'What did Phil say?'

'You told him who I am,' Mike said. 'And he saw a picture on your phone. The one at the theatre.' He shook his head. 'I knew I shouldn't have let that fucking Chinese bitch take it.' He banged his fist on the steering wheel. 'Fuck. The one person who met Davidson saw that fucking photo.'

Ha, Kate thought. *Fuck you, Mr Perfect Plans.* She hid her smile. So Phil knew what was going on. Which meant — what? He'd have told Gus, surely, who'd have told the cops. They'd be coming to get her. But how would they know where to look? Could they trace Mike's phone? She was pretty sure that that was possible. All they would need was some help from the police, and given that Mike was the Strangler, that

353

shouldn't be too hard to get.

'Of course, this changes everything,' Mike said. 'That damn phone. Without that you'd have been found tomorrow morning somewhere near Stockton Heath — I was thinking of somewhere near the bridge at Lumbbrook. Plenty of people walking dogs there. I'd have been questioned, would have my alibi ready, but they wouldn't bother with me, not when they knew it was the Strangler. Then Mike Sadler would quietly disappear, and, a year from now, there would be another serial killer in Wolverhampton targeting women who looked like Andrea Berry.'

He tapped his hand on his knee. 'It was such a good plan. But now — it's over. Busted. I can still kill you — and I will, by the way, whatever happens — and I can still vanish, but there's no way I'll get to Beth. They'll tell her about this and she'll move on. Another new name, another location. And this time, no stupid mistakes, because she'll know I'm out there.' He grinned at Kate, a wide, manic grin. 'Which means you get to stay alive, at least for a little bit longer, until I figure this out.'

It was an improvement, Kate thought. Not much of one, but an improvement. At least now she had some value to him.

'You'd better figure it out fast,' she said. 'They'll be talking to the police right about now.'

She spoke with as much bravado as she could muster, but it took a huge effort. This man was clearly completely crazy, and he was hellbent on getting what he wanted, a large part of which was for her to suffer. When he wasn't smiling, when the mask that allowed him to move around among normal people slipped, she saw how much he hated her, how deep the need for revenge ran. He thought that she and Beth had killed his child, and, over the years, he had twisted the rage that he felt into a worldview that justified murder.

She wondered which came first, whether he was crazy to begin with or whether he had been tipped over the edge by Beth leaving him. And then she remembered the bruises, remembered how Beth had taken photos of her soft drinks in the pub, had disappeared from the Trafford Centre. And she knew that he had been like this from the start.

And she felt very, very afraid.

'The cops?' Mike sneered. 'I doubt it. I made it perfectly clear what would happen if they involved the forces of law and order. And it won't help them if they do. All they have is this phone number. They might be able to find the barn, but if they do, we won't be here.'

She felt the hope drain from her. They — the police, Phil — had no idea what they were up against. 'Where are we going?'

'We're moving on.'

'To where?'

'Nowhere.'

'Nowhere?' Kate said. 'What's that supposed to mean?'

'Like I said, I'm good at disappearing.' He stared at her, his eyes cold. 'I'll be right back.'

★   ★   ★

A few minutes later he yanked open the passenger door. He was holding a loop of heavy plastic twine.

'I need the bathroom,' Kate said. 'I need to pee.'

'Do it there,' he said.

'In the car? In my pants?'

He nodded.

'I don't want to.'

'Then don't.' He grabbed her by the armpit and yanked her to her feet. 'You'll go when you need to. Not my problem.'

He pulled her towards the back of the barn. Ankles still tied, she took small stumbling steps, only staying upright because of his support.

The back of the barn was in shadows. As they approached, she made out a large rectangular shape.

'This is it,' he said. 'The most useful vehicle a man could have.'

It was a motorhome, probably twenty years old. He let go of her and opened the door, then walked behind her and pushed her roughly through it. It was small inside, not much bigger than a transit van. On the left was a seating area, with a sink and two-burner hob. Past that were the driver and passenger seats. To the right was a door; he opened it and dragged her into a cramped bedroom.

Against one wall was a narrow cot; against the other was a metal chair, fixed to the floor.

Kate's legs felt heavy and leaden. She was not an expert in motorhome design, but she didn't need to be to know that the chair was not a standard feature. It had been added, and not to provide additional, comfortable seating for guests. It had been added for another purpose entirely.

And she had a pretty good idea that she was about to discover what it was.

He took her elbow and twisted her so that her back was to the chair.

'Sit,' he said, as though he was talking to a dog. He was brisk now, and businesslike; she got the impression that she was nothing more than a puzzle-piece that he was moving around, a cog in his machine. She was not a person, not any more. She was valueless, and that was the most terrifying thing of all.

'The toilet,' she said. 'I need to go.'

The look he gave her was one of near-disbelief.

'I told you,' he said. 'Do it.'

'I want to use a toilet. I don't want to do it — I don't want to sit in my own urine.' It was a test, she realized, a way to see if he had any human emotion at all.

'Shut up,' he said, and pushed her onto the seat. As he did, she could no longer control her bladder and it let go, a wet, warm stain spreading over her crotch. It reminded her of waking as a child in the middle of the night, after she had wet the bed.

'There you go,' he said. 'Crisis averted.'

He freed her ankles, then took the twine and tied them, one by one, to the metal legs of the chair. He pulled the twine tight and it dug into her flesh; she stifled a cry of pain. She didn't

357

want to give him the satisfaction. With a grunt, he got to his feet, then opened a box in the corner of the room. He took out a thick leather strap, which he wound around her torso, under her breasts.

There was a ratchet on one end; he fed the other end through then yanked it, pulling her upright against the back of the chair. She gasped as the air was expelled from her lungs. When she inhaled, the strap constrained her ribs painfully; she realized she would only be able to take shallow breaths.

He took another, shorter strap from the box, and wound it around her forehead, fixing it to a slit on the wall so that her head was immobilized. He reached again into the box. This time it was a leather gag. He squeezed the base of her jaw to open her mouth, and slid it between her teeth. Then he undid the handcuffs and tied her wrists to the arms of the chair with the twine.

'Good,' he said. 'Time to be leaving.'

He turned his back on her and closed the door. It clicked shut, the thin material vibrating as he walked away.

Seconds later the engine started, and the motorhome began to move.

22

May passed her phone to Phil. They were sitting on a couch in the corner of a coffee shop in the village. The gentle, warm buzz of a Saturday morning seemed totally out of place; it seemed impossible that all these people could be idly going about their business as though nothing was wrong. Phil wondered how often he had been one of those people, ordering a skinny macchiato — or, in his case, a cup of tea — while around him were people in pain: loved ones dying, sons and daughters and brothers and sisters fighting in foreign wars, spouses having affairs. On the outside all was calm; inside, turmoil.

Although he doubted that many people were going through what he and May were facing. Most people — thankfully — would never have to discover just how extreme, just how all-encompassing, this kind of worry could be.

Where was she? Was she alive? In pain? There were so many questions, and no way of answering them. His mind kept skipping from one horrific possibility to another.

Gus was at the house, where a team of police had shown up, some in uniform, some not. DI Wynne had been there; she'd promised Phil, in her practised, measured way, that she and her colleagues would use all the resources at their disposal to find Kate.

And then she'd gone into the house — his

house, until recently — and, in the absence of anything else to do, he and May had walked to the coffee place.

Before they left, May had typed a message to Beth. They'd worded it carefully; they didn't want to spook her. In the end they settled on a non-specific, but somewhat urgent formula.

Hi Beth, May here. Been a long time. Something's come up and I'd like to talk to you. Is there a number I can contact you on? Today, if possible?

May nodded at the screen. 'She's replied. Take a look.'

Phil scrolled through the message.

It's nice to hear from you, May. It has been a long time. Maybe too long. I'm not sure about a phone call, but if I can help, let me know. What's it about?

'She's pretty cagey,' he said. 'Which isn't a surprise. Given what happened to her, I'd be cagey if someone from that time sent me a message which even hinted at something weird going on.'

'So what do I do?' May lifted the coffee and took a sip. 'What I most want to do is smoke. At times like this, I wish I'd never given up.'

'Me too,' Phil said. 'It's weird: I've not smoked for years, but right now all I want is a cigarette. Anything that might help.'

'It wouldn't help, though. It wouldn't make a blind bit of difference.' May tipped her head back and made an exasperated sound. 'What do I say to her? If I say that it's only a chat, she won't believe me; if I tell her what's happened, she'll run a mile.'

Phil drummed his fingers on his mug. 'Maybe not,' he said. 'She might want to, but she might not be able to.'

'I don't get it.'

'How about we tell her that it concerns Colin Davidson and it's something she needs to know. Something important. And that once we've told her, we'll leave her alone if that's what she wants.'

May shrugged. 'Worth a try,' she said. She tapped out a message on the screen, then held it up for Phil to read.

'How about that?' she said.

'Works for me.'

It was about fifteen minutes before Beth replied. They read it together.

It took me a while to decide how to respond. At first I was angry that you mentioned that name to me and I wanted to tell you to leave me alone, but then I realized that it was not you I should be angry at. Don't shoot the messenger and all that. I guess I was shaken to see his name after all this time, although to be honest I suspected it might be about him from the tone of your first message. I've worked hard at forgetting it all, although I've never totally achieved that, and don't suppose I ever will. The truth of what he was — still is, probably, people like him never change — was worse than you can imagine.

May looked at Phil. 'Not now,' she said. 'Not after what we found out.'

That's why, once I was free of him, I tried so hard to stay away. I guess, though, that it hasn't worked. I always wondered whether this day would come. So go ahead, give me your number and I'll call you. I'd prefer it that way around.

May typed in her number and hit send. A minute later, her phone rang. She looked at the screen.

'Withheld number,' she said. 'Must be her.' She put it to her ear. 'Beth?' she said.

A moment later, she winced. 'Andrea, sorry,' she said. 'I'll keep that in mind. And I'm well, thanks for asking. You?'

She listened for a few seconds. 'It's a pretty long story,' she said. 'But here are the highlights.'

Phil listened as she summarized what had happened. She missed out quite a bit, but she got in the main points: his and Kate's break-up, her meeting Mike, him turning out to be the Strangler, and then finally, the bombshell.

'Turns out that Mike wasn't who he said he was,' she said. 'It turns out that he was Colin Davidson, and he was doing all this to get your details — name, location — from Kate.'

There was another pause.

'She didn't tell him. He hacked her computer. Found you on her Facebook account. Anyway, he knows who you are.'

May's face was lined with strain, her eyes red and bloodshot. She put it her hand to her mouth and chewed on her thumbnail.

'And,' she continued, 'he has her. He has Kate with him.' A pause. 'We don't know where. Phil spoke to her, she's alive. But for how long, we don't know.'

She looked down at her feet, tapping her shoes on the wooden floor, listening. Something Beth said made her sit upright. She nodded.

'Of course,' she said. 'Give me an address. We'll be there as soon as we can.'

23

Kate tried to move. She was trapped in a very upright position; it had quickly become uncomfortable; now it was nothing short of agony.

God, her whole body hurt. Every time she took a breath, her ribs were crushed against the leather strap, her knees were protesting at being locked at ninety degrees, her lower back alternated between numbness and bolts of pain that shot down through her buttocks and into her legs. Sciatic pain: her dad got it.

What she had never understood about pain was how exhausting it could be. She wasn't moving, wasn't expending any energy, wasn't out running a marathon or doing a spinning class, but she felt drained, felt as though she had already given everything she had to give to this all-encompassing agony.

And then there was the leather gag, pressing against the sensitive skin on the roof of her mouth. That was painful too, but the pain wasn't the worst thing about it. It was the sense of discomfort, of constantly feeling like she wanted to retch, of wondering whether she might vomit, and die, drowned in her own puke.

There is pain, she told herself. She'd once had a passing interest in Buddhism and the one thing she remembered was that you could somehow diminish suffering by separating it from the self. *There is suffering*, not *I am suffering*. It allowed you to accept it. She tried it again.

There is pain. There is pain.

It wasn't working. She tried to twist her body into a more comfortable position.

That didn't work either. She was well strapped in, and, given the speed and sureness with which Mike had done it, it was evidently not the first time, which meant he probably had more victims than the four women in Sheffield and the four he'd killed here.

Jesus. Had he driven around the country with women trapped in his fucking motorhome? Was she merely one of a whole series to have been in here? One of many women who had been immobilized, in agony, the stench of their own urine filling their nostrils?

For a moment, fear took the place of the pain, then it was back, and worse than before.

And by her reckoning, they'd only been going thirty minutes.

North? South? East, maybe. Probably not West, unless they were heading into Wales. She thought she'd smelled the sea at one point, but that could easily have been her imagination. Or her piss. It was cold now, cold and wet and smelly and uncomfortable.

Anyway, it didn't matter which direction they were heading in. Even if she knew, she had no way of telling anybody. And even if, by some miracle that she couldn't even begin to comprehend, she could get free, then she still might not be able to contact anybody. She was pretty sure she'd seen him leave his phone in the barn, presumably to avoid anyone tracing them with it.

And if he'd left the phone, then he'd left behind any chance of Phil contacting him. So, untraceable, and uncontactable, his plan for her was pretty clear.

This was it. She was going to die, here, in this chair, or in some dark wood or remote cabin. She steeled herself to the possibility; strangely, she wasn't bothered. There was nothing about death that scared her. She wasn't religious; she didn't fear eternal damnation or have any hopes of a joyous, final reward spent at the feet of the Lord. No, like everyone else, she'd rot in the ground or be scattered as ashes in some place that her parents thought she'd like. People died all the time; five in this car crash, twenty in this terrorist attack, a hundred in this bombing raid. Eight at the hands of this serial killer; she'd be number nine.

No, it wasn't death that bothered her. It was the thought of those she'd leave behind, of her parents, suffering the awful fate that no parent should have to: burying their child. She wasn't sure how they'd cope. Her mum would turn inward, bury the emotion, find a way to carry on. Her dad? She didn't know if he'd be able to bear it. Like most of his tough Northern friends, he was, beneath it all, a tender, sweet, loving man. There was a strong streak of sentimentality in Northern men, and it was particularly strong in her father.

This might, she feared, be the end of him.

Tragedy upon tragedy.

Her death bringing about his collapse.

And all because of the bastard driving this

stupid motorhome. God, how she hated him. Hated his selfishness, his simple assumption that he was entitled to whatever it was he happened to want, and that he could do whatever he wanted to get it.

He wanted Beth all for himself? Not to love her but to hit her, bully her, break her. All fine, in his eyes, as long as in the end she was his. And if she wasn't? If she escaped? Why, then kill her and anybody else who you thought might have helped her, along with however many other innocent people you needed to make your plan work.

Yes, she hated him. She'd never known what hatred was, until now. She'd thought it was a stronger version of dislike or distaste, but it wasn't. It was much more than that: she knew that, given the chance, she would kill him without a second's hesitation, even if it bought her a spell in prison; whatever the cost. And more to the point, she would enjoy it. She would take pleasure in seeing his face as she buried an axe or a knife or hammer in it.

But she also knew she wouldn't get the chance. She knew that she was going to die, alone and full of hatred.

And disappointment. There were things she wanted to do. Things she didn't yet *know* she wanted to do, and now none of them would happen.

The motorhome slowed. They'd been moving at a constant speed for a while; probably on a motorway. Kate felt a series of turns. A left, a right, a couple of lefts. She tried to remember

them, but she quickly lost track. After a while,
the road became bumpier.

They were getting closer.

24

Beth lived in a small, Edwardian semi-detached house on the outskirts of Wolverhampton. Her property was well maintained, the garden neat and tidy. It looked like the windows were new, the double-glazing recent.

Other houses in the area were less well-kept, however. There was a general air of scruffiness, the occasional old car on blocks in a driveway, unfilled potholes in the road, hedges untrimmed and growing out of shape.

They parked in the street and walked down the short driveway. The flagstones were neat and recently weeded. There were rosebushes to the left and a waist-high fence separating Beth's drive from the neighbour.

'Nice place,' Phil said. 'I'm glad for her.'

'Me too,' May said. 'I'm only sorry that we're about to ruin it for her.'

They rang the doorbell. It was one of the old-fashioned ones that played an eight-note chime, descending for the first four and rising for the last. The door opened before it was finished.

The three of them didn't speak for a few moments. Phil took in Beth's new appearance; gone was the short, cropped hair he'd last seen her with. Now she had long, black hair — dyed, certainly — cut in an elegant, modern style. She looked strong; she was wearing a pair of jeans and a fitted T-shirt, and the muscles in her

369

forearms were supple and well defined. When she extended a hand to shake, Phil noticed her biceps flex.

He shook her hand.

'Hi,' she said. 'Good to see you, Phil.'

May ignored the hand. She stepped forward, her arms open. 'Beth,' she said. 'I'm so glad to see you.'

Beth hugged her back, hard. 'May,' she said. 'I've missed you. And Gemma, and Kate. All of you. But you know why I had to go. Don't you?'

May pulled back. 'Yes,' she said. 'Yes, I do. And I wouldn't have it any different. And I've missed you too. A lot.'

'Come in,' Beth said. 'I'll put the kettle on.'

They followed her into the kitchen. She gestured for them to sit at the kitchen table.

'Still milk, no sugar, May?' she said. 'And you're milk, one sugar — right, Phil?'

They both nodded. Tea-drinking habits were like fingerprints; they didn't change.

'You look well,' she said. 'Both of you.'

'So do you,' May replied. 'Fantastic, in fact. You're in great shape.'

'I do CrossFit,' Beth said. 'And MMA.'

'MMA?' May said.

'Mixed Martial Arts. It's good for self-defence. I'd had enough of being defenceless, so I decided to take it up.'

She was still Beth, Phil saw, but there was a hard edge to her, a carapace that she had built around herself to hide any vulnerability from the world. She was still angry, but that was no surprise.

370

'Well, it looks like it's a good workout,' May said. 'I'd try it if I wasn't so lazy.'

Beth brought over three mugs of tea. Phil read the words printed on his: *Walsall Triathlon. Finisher, 2014.*

'You do these things too?' he said, gesturing at the mug. 'I didn't know you could swim.'

'I learned. I was scared of the water, but I decided to deal with it.'

Phil glanced around the kitchen. There were no photos of other people. No signs of a boyfriend or a family. In fact, there was very little clutter at all. Too little; she'd tidied up. She didn't want them to know anything about her life. Well, that was fine.

'So,' she said. 'You'd better fill me in.'

★ ★ ★

Between them, Phil and May explained what had happened. There were gaps; they couldn't explain how Mike had been in Turkey and killing the first victim of the Strangler at the same time, and they didn't know the details of what had happened in Sheffield, but they had the broad outline, and that was enough.

As they talked, Beth's expression changed. The hard edge in her eyes slowly dissolved into a blank, disbelieving look. When they had finished, she folded her arms.

'So,' she said. 'He wanted to find out from Kate who — and where — I was and then kill her. And he invented a serial killer so that the police wouldn't suspect him.'

371

'Which he'd done before,' May said. 'In Sheffield. He must have wanted to murder his girlfriend and hit on the serial killer idea.'

'When it worked, he decided to use it again,' Phil said. 'But when he took Kate from her house he left her phone with a photo of them together on it. And now his plan is useless.'

'And he has her,' May said quietly. 'Right now, hidden away somewhere, he has her, and he's wondering what to do.'

'And he's worse than you think,' Beth said. 'Much worse.'

'I think he's pretty bad,' May said.

'It's not what he does,' Beth said. 'It's how he does it. As far as he's concerned, only he counts. Everything — and everyone — else is a tool. He doesn't see people — you, me, Kate — as human. He has no concept of suffering; I don't think he feels fear or pain or worry. He does whatever he wants.'

'Sounds like a psychopath to me,' Phil said.

'That's exactly what he is,' Beth said. 'As you can imagine, I've spent some time thinking about him over the years, and he is a psychopath. It's an overused word, but it applies in his case. He's indifferent to other people's suffering, totally self-obsessed, he does whatever he wants, when he wants, and he never gives up. Add to that his sense of himself as someone special, better than everyone else, and his willingness to use people for his own ends, and you have a classic example of what they call the dark triad.'

'The what?' Phil said.

'The dark triad. It's a combination of personality traits — psychopathy, narcissism and Machiavellianism — that often go together. There's a lot of research about it. I spent some time looking into it; I had a therapist who thought it might help me understand what I'd been through, help me to see that it wasn't my fault, that I was unlucky, and not at fault.'

'You weren't,' May said. 'Of course you weren't.'

'It didn't feel like that at the time,' Beth said. 'People like him are brilliant at manipulating you. He knew exactly how to make me feel like I was letting him down, failing him, bringing the punishment on myself. I felt worthless, and when you feel like that it's hard to find a way out.' She stirred her tea. 'Thank God I did.'

'What about Kate?' Phil said. 'What will he do to her?'

'I don't know,' Beth said. 'I honestly don't know. The question is, what *we're* going to do. You mentioned that Gus was getting the police involved.'

'Mike — Colin told us not to,' Phil said. 'But what could we do? We have no way of knowing where he is. They can at least trace the phone.'

'And then what?'

'Send some people in,' Phil said. He felt sick at the thought; one glance at May told him that she felt the same.

'He won't like that,' Beth said. 'He won't like it at all. When are they doing it?'

May looked at her phone. 'I don't know,' she said. 'Soon. It's been a few hours. I'll ask Gus.'

373

She tapped out a text message. A few seconds later, he replied.

'Holy shit,' she said. 'It's about to start.'

25

'They'll get her out,' Beth said. 'They'll get her out and they'll catch him and this will be over. For all of us.'

Phil nodded. 'They will,' he said. 'I have to believe that they will.'

'And if they don't?' May lifted her tea from the table, then put it down, untouched. 'If they get there and he . . . ' she paused. 'If he's hurt Kate?'

'Then they'll still catch him,' Beth said. 'And it'll be over.'

'But Kate,' May said. 'What about Kate?'

'I know,' Beth said. 'But I guess there is a bigger picture here. The police have to catch this guy. Put yourself in their shoes: he's been killing women in at least two places. They have to act if they get a lead.'

'I know.' Phil stood up and paced the kitchen. 'I know that's right, Beth. But it's hard to see the bigger picture when all I want is to see Kate safe. I know it's selfish, but' — he threw up his hands — 'what am I supposed to think?'

'There's no such thing as selfish in this situation,' Beth said. 'And there's nothing you're supposed to think. No one should have to go through this, and however you get through it is OK.'

'I just want that phone to ring' — he pointed at May's phone — 'and Gus to say it's over and she's OK. I'd give anything. Anything.'

375

'It will,' Beth said. 'Have faith.'

They fell silent. Phil ran through the possibilities in his mind, over and over. They located the phone signal. They surrounded some house — in his mind, it was a cottage by a lake, a cottage that looked like one he'd gone on holiday to with his parents years ago, somewhere in Derbyshire. It was funny how the mind did that, how it dredged up locations from the past when it needed a setting; in this case, a setting for men in black clothes carrying assault rifles to surround, kick the door in, throw flash grenades into the darkness.

He imagined a brief, intense period of shouting and gunfire, and then a pause.

And two of the men in black coming out holding Mike, his arms twisted up his back, his face smeared with dirt, blood on his jeans from a bullet wound.

And then: Kate, walking out, dazed, tears staining her face.

Or: a police officer walking out, grim-faced, shaking his head.

Those were the possibilities. And he had to prepare himself for the second of them.

May's phone rang.

She snatched it up. She said one word:

'Gus.'

Then she answered it.

The world slowed down. Phil studied her face, watching for any sign: happiness, joy, elation. Fear, sadness, grief.

May nodded. Then nodded again.

'So that's it?' she said. 'That's all?'

'What's all?' Phil said. 'What's he saying?'

May locked eyes with him. She was expressionless.

'They found the place,' she said. 'But there was no one there.'

26

The flimsy motorhome door opened. It was ironic that the door to her cell was made of a material she could have kicked her way through, although she wouldn't get the chance, given her current situation.

Mike appeared in the doorway. He was cupping a mug in his hands. It smelled like Bovril.

Jesus. He drank Bovril. She'd always liked Bovril. But now she'd never drink it again. She blinked. It was about all she could do. She'd given up trying to move a while back. There was no position that changed the agony anyway.

He took a slow, slurping sip.

'Your friends didn't listen,' he said. 'They told the police.' He shook his head. 'Idiots. I asked them to do one thing, but they couldn't even do that. My face is plastered all over the news. *If you see this man, please phone us.* That kind of thing.' He rolled his eyes. '*This man is known to be dangerous and might be armed. Do not approach.*'

He raised a finger in a teacherly gesture that said, *But wait, there's more.*

'Watch,' he said. 'You'll like this.'

He stepped back from the doorway. She heard the noise of drawers opening, rubber stretching, the tap running. After a while he reappeared.

Or an old man did.

Balding, white hair on either temple, thick glasses, nostril-hair sprouting, a ruddy complexion on his cheeks.

'Meet Steven Magwith,' he said, in a broad West Country accent. 'Known as Maggs to his friends. Got a passport, National Insurance card, bank account. Lives abroad most of the year, but drinks in a lovely little boozer in Bristol when he's home.'

His voice changed back.

'See?' he said. 'I can vanish' — he clicked his fingers — 'like that. Steven Magwith can move around at his leisure. I can drive my motorhome to all corners of this kingdom and not a soul will notice me. If I wish it to be so, Mike Sadler is, in an instant, no more.' He pointed at her. 'You too,' he said. 'In case you forgot.'

He sat on the cot. Kate followed him with her eyes.

'Quite a few have sat in that chair,' he said. 'Your friend Beth for one. She'll be in it again, someday. In fact, I might not use it again until it's her turn. Then I can tell her that you were her immediate predecessor. There's beauty in that, don't you think? I'm an artist, in many ways. In fact, if I hadn't taken this route, I probably could have been a great artist. Maybe written novels. Or been an actor. Yes — that's it. I'd have been an actor. Maybe I still will, one day.'

He scratched his head and put on a quizzical expression.

'Where's my cider?' he said, cider coming out as *zoider*. 'I love a bit o' scrumpy, me.'

He smiled at her. 'Did you know,' he said, still as Steven Magwith, 'that the actor who played Darth Vader was from the West Country? He was called Dave Prowse, and he had an accent like mine? But then they dubbed James Earl Jones over him.' He laughed. 'Probably a good idea! Not quite right to hear Darth Vader saying, "The force is strong with this one, my luverrr."'

She couldn't believe that she was here, that she was tied to a chair in a motorhome with a man she'd been — until this morning — thinking she might be falling, a little bit at least, in love with.

A man she'd had sex with the night before. A man she'd trusted.

A man who was now wearing a bald wig and speaking in a broad Somerset accent.

He switched back to his real voice, if it was his real voice. There was no guarantee that Mike Sadler was any more real than Steven Magwith.

'That chair,' he said. 'Is a very good way to punish people. Leaves no marks, you see. And from what I understand, it's quite painful. Anyway, I have work to do. I need to have a chat to your friends.'

He took a phone from his pocket. It was a cheap flip-phone, prepaid. He tapped a number into it and lifted it to his ear.

After a pause, he spoke.

'May,' he said. 'Hello. It's me.'

27

May looked down at her phone. It buzzed on Beth's kitchen table.

'Gus again?' Phil said.

'No.' She tilted her head to look more closely at the screen. 'I don't recognize the number.'

'Answer it.'

She put it to her ear.

'Hello?' she said.

Her mouth fell open. She braced her hand against the table.

She looked at Phil. 'It's him. And he wants to speak to you.'

Phil took the phone. He put it on speaker. 'Hello?' he said.

'Phil!' Mike's tone was bright and cheery, as though he was greeting an old friend who he hadn't seen in a while. 'How are you?'

'Not that great,' Phil said. 'But I imagine asking after my wellbeing is not why you called.'

'You imagine correctly. Although there's no need to be rude. I was simply being polite.'

Phil ignored him. 'Where's Kate?'

'With me.' His tone darkened. 'I see you ignored me and went to the police. I'm all over the news. Did those plods trace my phone and come looking for me? Is that what happened?'

'Yes,' Phil said. 'You weren't there.'

'Of course I wasn't. I knew you'd tell them, even though I asked you not to, which is why I've moved on.'

'Where are you now?'

'Somewhere. Near or far. Home or away. You'll never know.'

'Is Kate OK?'

'I wouldn't say OK,' he replied. 'She looks a little fatigued. Drained, almost. But then constant agony can do that to a person. She's tough, though. Hasn't complained once. Not that she can, of course. She can't make *any* noises, if I'm honest.'

'What have you done to her?' Phil said. His fist clenched and unclenched on his leg, bunching up his jeans. 'Is she alive?'

'Yes, of course. You think I'm some kind of monster who goes around killing people indiscriminately?' He laughed, a shy, bashful, aw-shucks chuckle, as though deflecting praise. 'I suppose you do. I suppose I *am* a little itty-bit of a monster, in my own special way.'

'Please,' Phil said. 'Let her go. Leave her somewhere and I'll come and get her. You don't need to kill her.'

'Well, you see, that's not entirely true,' he said. 'Here's what I wanted to happen. I found out where Beth — or Andrea, as I should call her — was, then I killed Kate. Made it look like the Strangler. Then, a year or two from now, a serial killer would start preying on people like Andrea. Eventually, he'd get to her, and I'd get my revenge.'

On the other side of the table, Beth covered

382

her mouth with her hand. She slowly closed her eyes.

'But *now*,' he went on, 'now Beth's going to disappear again. And she did a good job of that last time, so I'm going to have to start all over again. Which, frankly, pisses me off. But it also means I have no use for Kate.'

The doorbell rang. Four descending chimes, four ascending.

May's eyes widened. Beth sprang to her feet. She put the phone on mute.

'Is he here?' she said. 'Is that him?'

A voice came from the phone. 'Hello? Anybody there? Was that the doorbell?' He started to sing. 'There's somebody at the door, there's somebody at the door.'

Phil unmuted the phone. 'Is that you?' he said. 'Are you outside?'

'Take a look,' he said. 'Live a little.'

The doorbell rang again. Mike's voice came from the phone.

'Whoever it is certainly wants to see you.'

Beth opened the kitchen door and walked into the hall. Phil muted the phone, then he and May followed her. She went to a small window and peered out.

'Oh God,' she said. 'Not now. Please, not now.'

28

It was him. Phil could see from the strength of Beth's reaction that it was him. It had to be; she was pale and her hands were shaking. He crossed the hall and joined her at the window.

'Don't worry,' he said, forcing himself to sound a lot more certain than he felt. 'I'm here. It'll be fine.'

She turned to face him, her eyes narrowed in confusion. 'What'll be fine?' she said.

'We won't let him in. We'll call the police and let them sort it out. Or I'll grab a knife, or something.'

Beth shook her head.

'It's not Colin,' she said. 'It's . . . ' she paused. 'Take a look.'

He followed her gaze. Standing outside the front door was a tall woman in black leggings and a red, quilted jacket. She looked to be in her early thirties and in a hurry; she glanced at her watch, and lifted her hand, finger outstretched, to the doorbell.

And next to her was a small boy. About five, Phil thought. He had thick, dark brown hair and a serious, thoughtful expression. In one hand he held a Transformers lunchbox; the other clutched a toy monkey.

Before the woman could ring the bell again, Beth opened the door.

'Hi, Andi,' the woman said, her Brummie accent

384

hurried and exasperated. 'I'm so sorry to do this. I know I said I could have him all day, but Tom called and his dad's not well at all. He's had a stroke, poor duck, and Tom needs me to fetch him from work and take him to the hospital. I've got the car today — ' She looked inside and saw Phil and May. 'Oh,' she said. 'You've got guests? I thought you said you had to finish your assignment? For the anaesthetist exam?'

'I did,' Beth said. 'But something unexpected came up. It's — it's hard to explain.' She paused, and gestured to her guests. 'Phil and May. They're old friends.'

'Oooh,' the woman said. 'From your mysterious past. How intriguing.' She put out a hand. The skin was rough and unnaturally tanned, the fingernails gaudily painted. 'I'm Sandra.'

Beth had squatted and was holding out her arms to the little boy. He stepped into the house and kicked off his trainers, then hugged Beth.

'Hi, Mummy,' he said.

'Hi, Dylan,' Beth said.

Phil glanced at May. Her mouth was slightly open.

'Sorry to do this, Andi,' Sandra said. 'I did send a text, but it all happened so quickly. And now your friends will get to meet your son.'

'Don't worry about it,' Beth said. She glanced at Phil and May. 'Thanks anyway. And good luck with Tom's dad. Give him my best.'

She closed the door behind her friend.

'Dylan,' she said, 'would you go up to your room and choose a book? We can read it together.'

385

Dylan headed for the stairs. When he was gone, May looked at Beth.

'At least now we get to meet your son,' she said. 'I didn't know.'

'That was kind of the reason I asked Sandra to look after him,' Beth said. 'She helps me out sometimes. I didn't want him anywhere near this.'

Phil leaned on the banister. 'How old is he?' he said.

'Nearly five,' Beth replied.

Phil did the maths in his head.

'Is he — '

Before Phil could finish asking the question, she nodded. 'Yes,' she said. 'He is.'

From May's phone on the kitchen table came a voice.

'Hello? Are you still there? Who was it at the door? Anyone interesting?'

Phil picked up the phone and unmuted it.

'No,' he said. 'No one you'd be interested in.'

'I'm interested in *everybody*,' Mike said. 'I'm a real people person.'

'What do you want?' Phil said.

'Nothing,' he replied. 'Nothing you can give me, at any rate. Which means that we're nearly at the end of this call. Before I go, I want you to know that I do what I say I'll do. And when I told you that if you called the police I'd kill Kate, I meant it. I was sort of hoping you would,' he said, 'because then her death would be on your conscience.'

'Why is she so important to you?' Phil said, interested but also stalling for time. 'Why not let her go? It's Beth you want.'

386

Mike laughed. 'You're blind to it, aren't you? The same as the others. The same as Kate. You have no idea what you did to me. But you'll pay. You'll pay with Kate's death.'

'What are you talking about?' Phil said. 'If we — I — did something, at least tell me what it is.'

'You know,' Mike said. 'I wasn't going to. But I think I will. It'll be all the more for you to think about when you're talking to your therapist about this. So let me fill you in: it's because of what Beth did. Of what Kate and you helped her to do. It's because she killed my child. And here's the sweetest part of my revenge, Phil: Kate will pay with her life, whereas you'll have to live with the knowledge that you're responsible for her death. I didn't plan this part, but it's kind of a nice bonus, dontcha think?'

'So,' Phil said. 'This is because of the child. *Your* child?'

'It is. An eye for an eye, my friend. And you can see why you have nothing to give me. Goodbye, Philip.'

'Wait,' Phil said. He paused and took a deep breath. He had mixed feelings about what he was on the verge of doing, but he had no choice.

'I have something I can give you,' he said. 'Something that you might want. That might make you change your mind.'

'No you don't. You have nothing.'

'You sound very sure,' Phil said. 'But your confidence is a bit misplaced.'

'Oh?' he said. 'Then pray, tell me. What is this miraculous gift you have?'

'Your son,' Phil said. 'I have your son.'

387

29

Beth snatched the phone from his hand and broke the connection. She dropped it on the table, then shoved him hard in the chest.

'What the *fuck* do you think you're doing?' she shouted. She grabbed his right arm and twisted it up behind his back, then forced him to his feet. She pushed him up against the fridge door and bent his arm.

'Beth, please,' Phil said. His shoulder felt like it was coming loose in the socket. 'That hurts. A lot.' His breath was coming in pants. 'You're going to dislocate my shoulder.'

'I'm going to dislocate every fucking bone in your body,' she said. 'You told Colin fucking Davidson about Dylan. I've spent five years keeping him secret,' she said, and twisted his arm a bit harder, so that he yelped in pain — 'and you go and put him right in the path of that psychopathic bastard. He's my son, Phil, my flesh and blood, the thing that keeps me going, the reason I didn't kill myself back then and the reason I haven't done since — and I've been tempted. Trust me, I've been tempted. Knowing he's out there, knowing that one day he might find me, waking in the night at every noise, wondering if it's him, if he's in my house ready to do it all again, to hurt me like he used to — it's enough to make me want to end it all, but I didn't, I didn't because of Dylan, because he

388

made it all worthwhile.'

She put a knee in his thigh and pushed, hard. His leg gave way and he slipped down the fridge. As he did, his shoulder wrenched forward and he screamed.

'And you've gone and undone it all. All the protection I'd put in place; you've taken it away.'

She let go of him.

'You're no different to him,' she said. 'You know that?'

'I'm nothing like him,' Phil said.

'You don't think so? You use *my* son to get what *you* want? That's what he does — uses people. Well, I don't play like that any more. I'm going to take Dylan and get out of here. Don't follow me.'

Phil held his elbow, supporting the weight of his arm. Red-hot spikes of pain shot through his back and chest.

'Wait,' he said. 'You're right. I shouldn't have done it. But don't go. Give me five minutes. To explain. And then, if you still want to, you can leave.'

She glared at him.

'Five minutes,' she said.

He sat down, his legs shaking. 'I'm sorry I told him,' he said. 'I'm sorry. But I had no choice, Beth. It's Kate's only chance.'

Beth pointed a finger at him. 'I love her,' she said. 'I love Kate as much as anyone in this world. And there's nothing I wouldn't do to save her. I'd give my own life, in a second. But not my son's. I love him more. And if it's a choice between him and Kate, I choose him every time.

I'm sorry, but it's true.'

'But, Beth,' Phil said, wincing, 'don't you see that this is your only chance too? And Dylan's. What would have happened if I didn't tell him, do you think? You think that would have been it? You think that once he's killed Kate, he's going to stop looking for you?'

'I'd have moved. He couldn't find me last time. I'd have protected my son.'

May put her hand on Beth's shoulder. Beth shrugged it off.

'Beth,' she said quietly. 'Phil's right. He would have found you. He did this time. He killed *four* women to find you. And you could have gone again, but he would have carried on doing whatever it took until he found you again. You know that, don't you?'

Beth stared out of the window. 'I would have protected my son,' she said, her voice not much more than a whisper.

'You couldn't have,' May said. 'This day was coming, sooner or later.'

The kitchen door opened. Dylan stood in the doorway, a book in his hand.

'I got my favourite, Mummy,' he said. '*The Very Wicked Witch*.'

Beth seemed to deflate. She picked him up and hugged him to her chest. 'I love that book,' she said. 'It's my favourite too.' She kissed the top of his head. 'And I love you.'

'I love you, Mummy.' He looked at Phil and May. 'Who are these people?'

'Uncle Phil and Aunty May,' Beth said. 'They're my friends.'

'Why were you shouting?'

'We were playing a game,' Beth said. 'It was a loud game. Sorry, darling.'

'That's OK. Can we go and read now?'

She put him down. 'Go and sit on the couch. I'll be there in a minute.'

'He's beautiful,' May said. 'A beautiful boy.'

Beth nodded. She looked at May, her eyes watering.

'So now what?' she said.

'Now you go and read him a book,' May said. 'We can figure this out when the important stuff is taken care of.'

★ ★ ★

When she had left the kitchen, Phil leaned forward and gingerly stretched out his arm. He massaged his shoulder. 'Shit,' he said. 'That hurt. She's strong.'

May picked up her bag. 'I think I have some ibuprofen,' she said, and handed him a small white packet of pills. 'There you go.'

Phil swallowed two of the pills. 'Thanks,' he said. 'So what *do* we do now?'

May shrugged. 'I guess we call him,' she said.

30

Kate was aware, in amongst all the rest of the pain and discomfort, that she was thirsty. Her mouth was sandpaper dry, and her tongue felt like it was welded to the leather gag. She hadn't eaten or drunk anything since the night before, and most of what had been in her stomach she'd vomited up in the car, an event which seemed very distant.

And maybe it was. She had periods in which she drifted in and out of consciousness. It was her mind's way of avoiding the pain. But from time to time she convulsed in an agony so great that she snapped back to full wakefulness, before slipping away again.

The worst thing was the total motionlessness; if only she could move part of her body, she was sure she could get some kind of relief, but she was strapped so completely to the chair — ankles, calves, thighs, fingers, wrists, arms, chest, head — that only the most minimal movements were possible. A wiggle of a toe, the flexing of a finger, the clenching of her jaw. That was about it, and it was nowhere near enough.

The thin wall vibrated with approaching steps and the door opened. After the darkness the sudden light was dazzling and she closed her eyes. When she opened them, Mike — still dressed as Steven Magwith — was standing in front of her.

He had an odd look on his face: angry, mainly, but with an occasional flicker of something she hadn't seen before, something that, if she wasn't mistaken, looked a lot like joy.

'Did you know?' he said. 'Did you know about him?'

If she had been able to, she would have shaken her head. Not only did she not know, she did not even understand the question.

'They told me,' he said. 'That they have my son.'

Kate's eyes widened. His son? The son that Beth had aborted? And what was more — if they knew this — they were with Beth.

'I don't know whether to believe them,' he said. 'It may be a trick to stop me from killing you, to make me think that they have something to negotiate with.'

He looked at her, deep in thought.

'I can't decide,' he said. 'But if there's a chance . . . ' His voice trailed off. Not for the first time, Kate wondered why this was so important to him, why he had such a need for a child. He was barely human, it seemed to her, but he had this most human emotion at the very heart of him.

In some ways, it highlighted just how twisted he was.

'So,' he said. 'What do you think? Is my son alive? Did you know about this?'

He stepped forward and reached behind her head for the clip that held the gag in place. Then he held her by the jaw and carefully slid it out.

Her eyes watered with the relief. Slowly, she

worked her jaw up and down, loosening the muscles.

'Did you know?' he said.

Her voice was a croak. 'Water,' she said, or tried to. It came out as *waaah*.

He nodded and left the room. When he came back, he was holding a small cup. He held it to her lips and tilted it forwards.

'Not too much,' he said.

It hurt as it went down her throat but she didn't mind; it was the most wonderful, sweet-tasting drink she'd ever had.

'More,' she said.

He lifted the cup again.

'Untie me,' she said. 'Let me move.'

'No,' he said. 'Not possible. Did you know?'

'I need to move.' She hardly recognized her own voice; it was cracked and broken.

'Your head. I'll let you move your head. Then you talk. Got it?'

'Got it.'

He undid the strap around her forehead and stood back. Kate inched her head forwards, the muscles in her neck protesting as she tried to loosen them.

The relief, though. God, the relief. She never would have thought that something as simple as stretching the muscles in her neck could have been so utterly, utterly amazing. It was, by some distance, the best thing she had ever felt.

She looked up at Mike.

'I didn't know,' she said. 'I had no idea.' She thought back to the day of the abortion, of going to the shelter to see Beth, of how she had seemed odd, disturbed. But not sad. And she realized what Beth had done.

'Is it possible?' he said. 'That she didn't go through with it?'

'Yes,' Kate said. 'I think it is.'

'Hmm.' He secured the strap around her forehead.

'No,' Kate said, 'please, no.'

He clipped it shut, then opened her mouth and put the leather gag back in it. Then, distracted, Kate obviously far, far from his mind, he left the bedroom, closing the door behind him.

31

Phil and Beth sat at the kitchen table with the phone in front of them. May was with Dylan in the living room.

Phil dialled the number that Mike / Colin / Mark had phoned from. The call was answered on the second ring.

'You have my son,' he said, wasting no time on a greeting. 'Can you prove it?'

'I'm at Beth's house,' Phil said. 'And she's here with a boy who she says is your son. There's no reason she would lie.'

'But *you* would.'

'Would I?' Phil said. 'Why?'

'So that I don't kill Kate.'

'And then you'd find out I was lying and do it anyway. No — if I tell you that Beth has your son, then it had better be true.'

There was a long pause. 'I want to speak to him.'

Beth shook her head. *No way*, she mouthed.

'No,' Phil said. 'Beth won't allow that.'

'Did you ask her?'

'I don't need to.'

'I want to talk to her.'

Phil looked at Beth. He raised his eyebrows: *You want to?*

She nodded, and leaned towards the phone.

'Go ahead,' she said. 'This is Beth.'

'Beth,' he replied, drawing out the word in a

396

long, breathy sigh. 'Beth. Yes, finally. My little Beth.'

Beth paled, and swayed. Phil gripped her elbow. *You OK?* he mouthed.

She gave him a thumbs up.

'So. You didn't do it, after all. Didn't murder my child.'

'No,' Beth said. 'I didn't. All through my pregnancy I wondered if I'd done the right thing, if I'd regret it, and then he was born, perfect and pink and screaming, and I knew I hadn't. I knew that what I'd done was to make the best decision I ever could have made.'

'I want to meet him.'

'No,' Beth said. 'No way.'

'He's my *son*.'

'No, he isn't. Not in any way.'

'I'll give you Kate. For one meeting with him.'

This was the moment. This was what they had discussed: get him to make an offer, then refuse. Play hard to get.

'No,' Beth said. 'It's not happening.'

Then Phil would try to soften her, try to persuade her. Make it realistic.

'Beth,' Phil said. 'One meeting. That's all. It's no big deal, and we get Kate back.'

'He's my son, Phil. And I don't want him to have anything to do with that bastard.'

The voice came from the phone. 'That bastard who is his *father*.'

'One meeting,' Phil said. 'That's all. Do it for Kate.'

Beth hesitated. 'OK,' she said, acting reluctant, although Phil didn't think she had much

397

need to act. 'One meeting.'

Phil nodded encouragement. This was what they had planned.

'In a public place,' Beth continued. 'For a few minutes. You don't touch him, or tell him who you are. And only after Kate is safe. Then you leave me alone. For ever.'

'That won't work,' he replied. 'You can blame your friends. I don't trust them — if we meet in public there are too many places the police could hide. I'll be too vulnerable.'

'No,' Beth said. 'It's a public setting or nothing.'

'Then nothing.'

She looked at Phil; this was not what they had discussed. They had planned to arrange a meeting in a motorway service station, or a McDonalds, or on a bench is some town centre or other, and then, when he showed up, for the police to grab him. They could be shopping nearby, or having coffee, or dressed as truckers eating eggs and bacon.

But that was no longer on the table.

Beth tried again. 'Public place,' she said. 'Or nothing.'

'Then nothing,' he said again, and laughed. 'I'll bide my time. I'll kill your friend and then I'll find you, Beth, and my son, and I'll take him from you. One way or another. Maybe I'll let you live. Maybe I'll punish you by letting you know that your son is with me.'

Beth glanced across the table at Phil. She had a haunted, distant look in her eyes. Suddenly, she blinked, and straightened in her chair.

'OK,' she said. 'What's your proposal?'

32

His proposal was simple: they would meet at a location that he would specify. The meeting would take place exactly one hour after he gave them the location. They needed to be close to Stockton Heath, as it would be within an hour's drive of the village. Beth was to arrive, alone, with Dylan. Kate would be waiting outside in an open location; Beth would come and meet her, leaving Dylan in the car. Then Kate would go to the car and take Dylan out so that he could run to his Mum.

Through all of this, Mike would be visible and at a distance so that he could not interfere. Once Kate was at the car, he would come over and meet his son.

While the meeting took place, Kate was to stay out of the car and stand with her hands above her head, so that he could be sure that Beth had not brought anything with her — a gun, for example — that Kate could use against him.

In that vein, he wanted Beth to be wearing tight clothes so that he could be sure no weapon could be concealed, and to be empty-handed.

Once the meeting was over, they could leave, unhindered.

That was his offer. His final — his *only* — offer.

★ ★ ★

399

'We need to leave,' Phil said. 'We need to head back home.'

'I have to call Gus,' May said.

Phil shook his head. 'No. He'll get the cops involved again. Not this time.'

'He won't,' Beth said. 'I won't let him. And I have a plan.' She picked up her car keys. 'I'll take my car. I have to stop at work. I need to go to the clinic and pick something up.'

'What?' Phil said.

So she told them.

★ ★ ★

Phil drove back with her, Dylan behind them in his car seat.

'You don't have to do this,' he said. 'You don't have to put yourself at risk. Kate wouldn't ask you to do it.'

'I know,' Beth said. 'But it's not just about Kate, is it? I hadn't fully understood it, until now, but this is never going to end. I have to face it. And if I don't, I'll spend the rest of my life looking over my shoulder, wondering whether Dylan will come home from school, whether his football coach or Scout leader can be trusted, whether he'll be approached one day in the street by a friendly man who says he knows his mum — gives my name, and address, and all kinds of details — and does he want a lift home? He'll never stop.'

Phil nodded. 'But how do you know that won't happen anyway? You let him meet Dylan, Kate is safe, all's good for a while. But he'll still

400

be out there. You'll still be wondering.'

'Yes,' Beth said. 'I know. Which is why this has to be the end.'

33

'I'll admit,' Mike said. 'That I was a bit worried.'

He was sitting on the cot, leaning against the wall, sipping from another mug of Bovril. The warm, meaty smell made Kate want to vomit, despite the fact she was slipping in and out of consciousness.

'I thought that this was going to take a lot longer, that I'd have to find Beth again. But now she's going to come to me, and she's bringing my son as well!' He leaned forward. 'The good news — for you — is that I need your help, which means I have to untie you. A bit, at least. I'll leave the chest strap on, and your hands will stay tied. But I need you to be able to stand up and play your part, so you'll have to stretch your legs.'

He stood up and walked over to her, then knelt down and started to untie the twine that held her legs to the metal chair. When he was finished, he released the strap around her forehead, then loosened the chest restraint a few blessed millimetres.

'The gag remains,' he said. 'I don't want you shouting out warnings to your friend. So, here's what's going to happen.'

He told her what he was going to do. And she knew her friends had no chance.

★ ★ ★

The steady hum from the engine told her that they were on the motorway again. Her legs were straight out in front of her; for the twenty minutes since he'd untied her and started up the engine, she'd lifted and flexed and stretched them, feeling the blood begin to flow again. It had given her a worse case of pins and needles than she had ever thought possible, but it was a welcome pain. She relished every prickle, every buzz.

And her neck and shoulders: she was almost delirious with the pleasure of moving them. She luxuriated in the sensation of the pins and needles, but, as they settled down, her thoughts turned to Beth and her son.

Beth and her son, who were walking into a trap.

Mike had found it very amusing that, because of a hope that they could save their friend, they were going to lose everything. He had no intention whatsoever of handing over Kate, nor of letting them leave. Once his son was with him, Kate would become the latest Strangler victim, and Beth and Dylan would simply disappear.

It was evidence of the stupidity of normal people in letting their emotions guide their actions, he said. People like him ignored emotion; everyone else was in thrall to it. They didn't ask the right questions, took too much at face value. Beth thought that his desire to meet his son was so great that he would hand Kate over in order to satisfy it, and she thought that because she believed in emotions, because that was what she herself would have done.

But she was wrong. His desire to meet his son was very great, but not as great as his desire to get what he wanted, and that was what he was going to do.

Kate flexed her legs. Well, she was going to do something to put an end to this. She wasn't going to sit back and let it happen, not when it was on her account that Beth was doing this.

That was the worst thing about it all: if she had been able to, she would have told Beth to stay away, to leave her to her fate. It was her own fault for trusting him in the first place — God, she'd been stupid — and if someone was going to pay the price for her stupidity then it should be her, and her alone. Not Beth.

And certainly not Beth's son.

Kate felt tears wet her cheeks. They flowed into her mouth, running over the leather gag, their salt taste stinging her swollen tongue.

That poor boy. That poor, innocent child, was going to be left motherless, and at the mercy of his merciless father. What would Mike do with him? She had no doubt that he would soon be introduced to the concept of discipline, Mike-style. Perhaps he'd get his own punishment chair. Whatever it was, it wouldn't be good.

What would the police do, when Beth and her son disappeared? They'd know what had happened; Phil and May and Gus knew about Mike. The question was whether they'd find him. She was pretty sure that Steven Magwith would settle into his life, into the identity that Mike had created for him, with barely a ripple. No one would notice him. They would notice a

404

five-year-old boy, though.

Mike would know that. And so he wouldn't give them the chance to notice him. Was that his plan? To hide his son away in his cellar? And then, after some time had passed, to move again? To a new country, perhaps. Somewhere that the authorities did not pay as much attention as they did here.

The poor child. It could not be allowed to happen.

She had to stop it. One way or another, she had to stop it.

And, dimly, an idea of what she might — possibly — be able to do was forming at the back of her mind.

34

May's phone buzzed.

It was a text message from another new number. GPS coordinates, nothing more. Phil put them into Google Earth.

'Some barn,' he said. 'In the countryside. Not too far from here.'

Gus looked over his shoulder.

'That's where he held her before,' he said. 'That's the place we raided. The bastard's back there.'

He looked at Beth, then May, then Phil.

'I still think we need to involve the police. This is not something — '

'No,' Beth said. 'You had your chance. And if he sees that it's not me, he'll kill Kate. He'll think that he's going away for eight murders, so it might as well be nine. Or he'll escape again. That's what he does. But if I go, there's a chance of ending this.'

'You're a very brave woman,' Gus said. 'Very.'

'It's not bravery when you have no choice,' Beth said. 'This is what I have to do. I should have done it five years ago, and then Kate wouldn't be in this situation, but I didn't. So this is on me.'

'No, it isn't,' May said. 'Not at all.'

'It is. And now I have to end it.' She stood up. 'I'm going to get changed,' she said. 'And then we can go.'

406

Five minutes later she came back into the room. She was wearing a pair of grey yoga pants and an olive green tank top.

'Can't hide anything in these,' she said. 'Just like he wants.'

'He only wants to see your hot body,' May said, and hugged her. 'The fucking pervert. Good luck.'

'Thanks.' Beth let go of her. 'Take care of Dylan,' she said. 'If anything happens.'

'Nothing will happen,' May said.

'If it does.'

May nodded. 'If it does.'

Beth picked up her phone and car keys and turned to Phil and Gus. 'Let's go.'

* * *

They followed her car as the light faded. In the back seat, they could make out the head of the dummy that was supposed to be Dylan. They'd bought a portable DVD player and hung it from the back of the headrest. It was only when they were ready to leave that they realized they didn't have any kids' DVDs, so Dylan was watching *A Few Good Men*. Whatever. It looked, from a distance, like a kid engrossed in an episode of *Fireman Sam* or *Chuggington*, and, in any case, if Mike got close enough to notice what film was playing then they were in huge trouble.

'Think it'll fool him?' Phil said. 'The light will help. At least it's getting dark.'

'It better,' Gus replied. 'It better.'

They continued in silence. After a while they turned off the main road onto a B road. It wound through the flat, featureless landscape of the Cheshire Plains. Somewhere to the east, Phil could see the silhouette of the massive Jodrell Bank telescope. It was no wonder they had situated it here; there was nothing to get in the way of it receiving its radio signals from space. As he looked at it, he felt a mild sense of shame; he'd gone there on a school trip when he was about seven; all he remembered of it was the headmaster — Mr McDonald — making them all stay behind after the show they'd watched in the Planetarium, his face red with anger.

Other members of the audience, he said, came to me after the show and informed me that representatives of this school were talking and laughing throughout the show, and, when asked not to do so, ignored the request. I have never been so embarrassed to be the headmaster of this school, and all of you should be ashamed of yourselves.

Even though he had not been one of the miscreants — he had been thrilled by the show the Planetarium put on — the headmaster's words had stuck with him and ever since he had not been able to think of Jodrell Bank — or astronomy at all, in fact — without experiencing the low-level shame that he felt now. Perhaps without it he would have become a famous radio astronomer; on balance, though, he thought not. His failure to make a mark on the world of cosmic science could not be laid at the door of Mr McDonald.

They turned onto a narrow road, high thick hedges on either side. Tree branches stretched overhead, meeting in the middle to form a canopy that blocked out the little remaining light.

Ahead, Beth's brakelights flashed and she turned to the right. Gus switched off the headlights and pulled into the side of the road, in front of a gate that led into a fallow field. They got out of the car and opened the gate, then walked into the field. The grass was thick and dry and there was a sweet smell; honeysuckle, maybe or something similar.

On the far side they could see the lights of the car moving slowly along the farm track. Phil realized that his legs were shaking.

'I'm fucking terrified,' he said. 'God knows how she feels.'

Gus nodded. 'God knows,' he said.

35

Kate knew now that pain was never going to frighten her again. She'd often wondered how she would get through the pain of childbirth, should that day ever come — it seemed unimaginable, how a baby's head could pass through that particular orifice; the rational part of her knew that it was designed with that purpose in mind, but somehow it didn't seem possible. Now, though, she knew that she'd be fine.

Partly because, if she got out of this, she'd be glad simply to be alive, to have the chance of being a mother, to have the chance of walking down the street; Christ, she'd even be glad to sit through day-long corporate training snooze-fests.

And partly because, after the pain she was enduring right now, nothing was beyond her in the future.

Her legs were better, but one of her knees ached constantly, and when she moved it, it felt as though the bones were grinding against each other somewhere deep inside. Her shoulders and back were sore, too.

Not as sore as her chest, which, after the constant constrictions of the leather strap every time she breathed in, felt as though it had been pummelled with a hammer.

But none of it was anything compared to the blazing pain in her teeth.

Hurt, pain, agony, torment: none of them even came close to describing what she was going through.

Her plan was as follows: the strap serving as a gag was made of leather; leather is chewable; she could chew through the leather. Then, with the gag still in her mouth — she could keep it in there by biting on the broken ends — she would go out to meet Beth. As soon as Beth appeared, she would open her mouth, shake it out, and shout to Beth to run, that it was a trap, to get back in her car and go, as far away as she could, and to call the police and tell them to look out for a motorhome, to put every damn cop in the country on the alert for motorhomes. So they'd find him and that would put an end to it.

True, he might kill her, but at least the pain would be over.

Leather *was* chewable, it turned out. But not without a lot of effort, not without so much effort that first one, then two, then three of her teeth, the big ones at the back, molars or pre-molars, she thought — but she could hardly remember the word because so much of her brain was taken up in screaming *Ouch, what the fuck are you doing that for?* — but anyway, three of those big bastard teeth had broken, snapped off in her mouth, and, because she didn't want him to see them when he came in the room she'd swallowed them, swallowed her own shattered teeth.

She could still feel the sensation as the first one had gone. She'd managed to get some purchase on the leather, get her tooth into it a

411

little bit, and she was working it back and forth, feeling her jaw ache as she did so, and then, without warning there was a loud crack and oh, shit, the pain.

And blood. Blood she swallowed too, but she couldn't stop it from flowing out of her mouth, so she had to bend her head down, use the new freedom he'd given her, and smash her knee against her nose until something inside it broke and it started to bleed.

And she'd had to go on chewing that leather, thinking as she did.

He's a child. A baby.

Not my baby.

But a baby.

Beth's baby.

And somehow she got through the pain. Somehow she carried on until the leather separated and she was able to hold it in her broken teeth.

And she sat back and waited, blood drying on her face.

⋆ ⋆ ⋆

A while later they came to a halt. Mike opened the door.

He frowned.

'What happened?' He leaned forward and examined her. 'Nosebleed? Did you do it to yourself? Think it might act as a warning to your friend?' He laughed. 'I think she already knows what I'm capable of. She was one of the first to find out.'

412

He untied her and dragged her to her feet, then he handcuffed her hands behind her back. He put the leather strap around her chest and attached a chain to the back of it.

'Another aid to discipline I use with my girls,' he said. 'Treat those bitches like the dogs they are.' He gave it a tug. 'Come on, Fido, time for walkies.'

She followed him out of the room, her knee aching, her back in agony. For a second she considered charging at him, knocking him down and trying to overpower him.

But she didn't. She had an alternative plan.

36

He led her to the barn door. It was not yet dark, the time of the evening that her dad called the gloaming, when the sun was still there but was dimming fast. There was a chill in the air, and she shivered. In her mouth the leather strap shifted and she winced as she bit down on it to keep it there. The last thing she needed now was for the strap to fall onto the dusty ground.

He bent down and clipped the chain to a hoop on the thick wooden post that framed the door. He wound it around until it was tight, then secured it, then he walked to the far side of the barn and sat on an old armchair. The red cloth was faded; the stuffing coming out of the arms. It reminded Kate of a couch that she and her university friends had kept outside their halls of residence. On sunny days, they'd sit on it and drink beer and smoke cigarettes; often it was not fully dry and the rain from a day or two before would seep upwards into their clothes.

She ran through what was going to happen: Beth would arrive and walk to her. She would then go to the car and let Beth's son out, so he could go to meet his mum. Then, Mike would get to meet his son, and, a few minutes later, Beth would walk to the car and they would leave.

Mike was to stay seated, a safe distance from Beth and Dylan. If he stood up, Beth would run

414

to the car; she was much closer than him. That was her insurance.

Except that wasn't what was going to happen. Mike had told her what he was going to do, and there was no way that Beth was leaving here alive. It was all a trap.

And she couldn't believe that Beth thought it was anything else. Of all people, she should have known better, after what he'd put her through. But like Mike had explained: people made bad decisions. Beth thought there was a way to rescue her friend, thought she could handle it, thought it was a risk worth taking.

But it wasn't.

And that was the final piece of the puzzle, the piece that even Mike didn't know about.

As soon as she stepped out of the car, Kate was going to open her mouth, spit out the broken gag and tell her friend to get the hell out of there.

She heard the sound of an engine in the distance, then headlights appeared on the dirt track that led to the barn. There was a gate about twenty yards from the barn door; it was closed and padlocked, and that was where the car would have to stop. The side gate was wide open.

It didn't matter. Beth would never get through it. Kate would warn her first.

The car approached slowly, bumping over the rutted surface. As it came near, Kate could make out the driver's head. Hair scraped back; a familiar silhouette.

It was Beth. There was no doubt.

The car reached the gate and did a three-point

turn so it was facing away from the barn. It was a good idea; easier to get away. Kate would have smiled had she not been clenching the gag between her teeth.

Through the rear window, Kate could see a DVD screen on the headrest. So he was here, Beth's son. She'd hoped that Beth wouldn't do it, that she wouldn't put him in harm's way, but that hope was gone now.

This was really going to happen.

But not how Mike wanted. She was going to shout out to her friend, tell her it was a trap, and then she was going to watch her drive away.

And it would be the last thing she ever did. She didn't doubt that. Mike would kill her immediately. She closed her eyes and inhaled deeply through her nose, tasted the sweet summer air. She was ready. And she had no choice. This was a cycle of pain and blood, and it had to end. She'd read the stories: it would continue until a sacrifice was made to end it, and if she was the sacrifice, then that was the way it would have to be. Better her than Beth's boy.

When she looked again, the car door was opening.

37

Beth climbed out of the car. If Kate hadn't seen her silhouette she wouldn't have recognized her; her hair was different, her stance was different, but, most of all, her body was different. She was lean and muscular and languid.

She was wearing yoga pants and a tank top; the only thing in her hands was her phone, which she held covering her palm.

She stood up, and closed the car door.

Kate opened her mouth; the leather strap dropped to the floor and she started to shout.

Or, rather, she croaked. Her throat was so dry that the words would not come out; she worked her jaw up and down and swallowed, then tried again.

'Run!' she said. 'Beth, it's a trap! Run!'

She glanced at Mike; he was staring at her in disbelief. She watched as a look of anger washed over his face.

'He lied,' she called. 'You need to get away from here.'

Beth stood, immobile, by the car. She gave Kate a strange look; it was almost disappointed, as though she wanted her to stop, then she looked at Mike, and her eyes widened.

He was on his feet, a sawn-off shotgun pointing at Beth.

'Don't move,' he said. 'Don't move a muscle. Or I shoot. And the shot from this could scatter anywhere. Like through the back window of that car.' He gestured with the barrel. 'Put your hands up.'

Beth slowly raised her hands.

'Turn around. All the way. Three-sixty degrees. Slowly.'

Kate felt like crying. She'd fucked this up. Her one chance and she'd fucked it up. Beth — and her son — were trapped. Mike had won.

Of course he had. She'd known all along that he would.

'Beth,' she said. 'I'm sorry. You shouldn't have come. Not for me.'

Beth caught her eye. She gave her a nod, and a small smile. She looked, Kate thought, oddly calm.

'Shut your fucking mouth,' Mike said, glancing at Kate. 'I don't want to hear your stupid fucking voice again.'

'Don't speak to her like that,' Beth said. 'I don't like it.'

'Yeah?' Mike said. 'And what are you going to do about it?' He looked her up and down. 'Looking good, Betsy. Remember how I used to call you that? Betsy? You liked it. You liked my little name for you.'

'I hated it,' Beth said. Her voice was flat and emotionless. 'I hated you.'

He ignored her. 'Where was *that* body when I was fucking you?' he said. 'You were such a pudgy little thing back then. It was handy, mind you. You had a bit of self-loathing, didn't you? Lacked confidence. Useful. The confident ones are much harder to break. Your type, though:

418

you're so grateful that anyone gives you a second look you'll put up with just about anything rather than risk being left on the shelf. Any attention will do. Even a good beating.'

'There's no such thing as a good beating,' Beth said. 'Only the shit that bastards like you dish out.'

'Ooh,' he said. 'You're not the lacking-in-confidence type now, are you?'

'As it happens, I am,' Beth said. 'What you did left deep scars. They'll never go away. But I've learned that I'm *wrong* to lack confidence. That's the trick: you can't stop yourself wondering whether you're worth someone's love or whether you can achieve the things you set out to achieve or whether you have anything to give your friends or not, but you can stop yourself letting it get in the way. You can learn to keep in mind all the people who do love you and all the times you did achieve something and all the friends who thanked you for helping them in many, many ways, and then you can silence that doubting voice.'

She smiled a calm, peaceful smile. 'And you know the ironic thing, Colin? The single most important thing in learning that was my son. He loves me, so very, very much. When he wakes up in the morning, all he wants is to get in my bed and feel the warmth of my body, bathe in my scent, let me fold him in my arms and make everything in his world right. Being with me is all he needs. I am everything to him and I'm reminded of it every single moment I spend with him. He's the same to me, of course. He's my world. But I am his too. And that is enough for me: to know, deep down, that I *am* special, that I'm wrong to question myself. And the funny thing is, you gave him to me. You, who did more than anyone else to break me apart, were the person who gave me the means to put myself back together again.'

'Yes,' Mike said. 'The boy. My son. What's his name?'

'You'll never know.'

His face darkened. 'I think your confidence — hard won and well deserved as you might think it is — is misplaced.'

'You'd be wrong.'

'I wonder,' he said. 'If I should let him watch when I kill you? It could be a valuable lesson for him. Show him exactly what his mother was made of.' He laughed. 'Literally!'

'You think I would ever let you near him?' Beth said. 'Do you honestly think that I would ever let you — *you* — near my son.'

'He's my son, too.'

'No, he isn't. He doesn't even know you exist.'

'He will soon.'

'No,' Beth said. 'He won't.'

'What the fuck are you talking about?' Mike said.

Beth nodded at the car. 'Come and see for yourself.'

38

He started to walk towards Beth, the shotgun at hip height, the barrels pointed at her. Kate hadn't ever seen a gun until today; there was something shocking about being in such close proximity to an object designed with the sole aim of wreaking physical damage on another living being. Who was it who had first thought that what the world needed was for them to focus their efforts on creating then refining a means of killing people in a quick, efficient way? What would have happened if they had decided, instead, to write a poem or invent a flower-growing device that everyone could use to surround themselves with fresh blooms?

Nothing, she thought, *because there would always be people like Mike, and they would always find a way to harm other people.*

Beth watched him approach. She didn't move. She stood, hands in the air. Kate couldn't imagine what she was going through, what kind of effort it was taking for her not to react to the presence of the man who had nearly destroyed her.

And who was now threatening to destroy her son.

Except that wasn't what was happening. There was something else going on here. Kate didn't know what it was, but it wasn't what Mike had been expecting.

And she could see that Mike knew it too. He glanced at her as he walked towards Beth. He held her gaze for a second and she saw something in his eyes that she had never seen before. Not fear; she didn't think he felt fear, but the closest thing to it he could experience.

He looked uncertain.

Beth was not doing what he expected. She was not cowering, not simpering and giving him what he wanted. She was defiant. And Kate, too. She'd managed to warn her friend, and now Mike's plan was unravelling.

Halfway to the car, he stopped.

'Get the boy out,' he said. 'I want to see him.'

He was trying to take control of the situation again, but Beth shook her head.

'No. That's not what we agreed. We agreed that she' — she pointed at Kate — 'would be free first.'

'Fuck what we agreed. She' — he too pointed at Kate — 'changed that when she opened her mouth.'

'You were planning a trap,' Beth said. 'You broke the deal.'

He shrugged dismissively. 'I don't care. Deal, no deal, I don't give a fuck. I'm holding this' — he waved the gun — 'so I call the shots. Get him out, or I use it.'

'Then you'll never know what I know,' Beth said.

'What are you talking about?'

Beth nodded at the back seat of the car. 'Come and find out.'

'Is there something wrong with him?' Mike

said. 'Did you give birth to a freak? It wouldn't surprise me. Nothing you did would surprise me.'

He was getting more and more uncertain. Kate swallowed.

'Beth,' she said. 'Get out of here. Leave me. I'll be fine.'

Beth's eyes flicked to her for a second and she gave a small shake of her head.

Stay out of it, she was saying. *There's more going on than you know. Leave this to me.*

Mike swung around so the shotgun was pointing at Kate. 'Another word and you die,' he said. 'One barrel for you, the other for that bitch. Don't give me a reason to do it. I'm tempted enough as it is.'

He turned back to Beth.

'Step away from the car,' he said. 'Stand at the front.'

Beth nodded. She moved a few paces away from the headlights.

'Keep your hands in the air.'

He took another few steps in her direction.

'Pull your pants down,' he said. 'I want to be sure you're not concealing a weapon.'

Beth lowered one hand, keeping the other — the one with the phone — raised. She put her thumb in the waistband of her yoga pants and pulled them over her hips. She turned a full circle.

'OK?' she said.

He nodded, and she pulled them back up.

'Now your top,' he said.

She pulled up her tank top, exposing her lean

423

midriff. She had a tattoo above her hip; Kate couldn't make out what it was. She was wearing a sports bra. Mike gestured to it.

'And the bra.'

She lifted it, exposing her breasts, then turned through another circle. When she was facing him again, she pulled her bra and tank top back into place. The she raised her arm so that both were back above her head.

His eyes locked on hers, he started walking again.

39

He walked through the side gate, making sure he was facing Beth at all times. When he reached the back door of the car, he grabbed the handle.

'Go on,' Beth said. 'Take a look.'

As he opened the door Kate could see the light from the DVD player reflecting on the glass. Mike rested the barrel of the gun on the top of the door, then, keeping it pointed at Beth, he turned to his right and looked into the car.

He let out a roar of anger, then reached in and grabbed the boy. He dragged him out of the car and flung him into the hedge on the side of the road.

Kate gasped, horrified at what he had done, until her brain processed what she had seen and she realized that it wasn't a child, couldn't be a child, it was too light, no one could toss a five-year-old boy so easily.

And she looked at the figure trapped in the hedge and she saw what it was.

A dummy. A crude, basic dummy, hastily thrown together but good enough to be convincing at a distance and through a car window.

Of course she wouldn't bring her son here. Of course she wouldn't put him at risk.

So why *had* she come? Why *had* she shown up, unarmed, when all that could happen would be that Mike would get pissed off and kill them both?

425

'You fucking bitch,' Mike shouted. 'You're fucking dead.'

'Then you'll never see him,' Beth said. 'He'll be gone for ever. I've made arrangements. If I don't come back, then there's a family he'll go to. A family that you'll never find. So go ahead. Kill me.'

He marched towards her, bellowing with rage. When he got to her he jabbed the barrel of the gun hard into her ribs. She grunted, and bent double. When she straightened she smiled at him.

'Go on,' she said. 'Do what you do. Hit me. As much as you want, you useless bastard.'

He swung the gun in a wide arc, slamming it into the side of her head. She collapsed to her knees, her hands on the ground in front of her.

'Get up,' he said. 'I'm not done with you.'

She staggered to her feet and faced him, only a foot separating them. He pressed the gun into her stomach.

'Give me the phone,' he said. 'You won't be needing it. You're probably recording this, or some bullshit like that, but it won't help you. I think I'm going to kill you anyway. I don't think I could stop myself even if I wanted to.'

'As you wish,' Beth said, and held out the hand with the phone in it.

He reached out and plucked the phone from her hand. As he did, she lifted her free hand and knocked the barrel of the gun away from her stomach, then lunged forward, pressing the hand that had held the phone against his ribs.

His eyes widened; the gun fired. Birds flew up

from the hedge, alarmed.

'What?' he said. 'What have you done?'

Then his legs crumbled under him and he fell to the ground. He lay there, convulsing.

Beth put her hands on the car, her legs shaking.

'Holy shit,' she said. 'Holy shit.' Then she vomited. When she looked up at Kate, there were tears running down her face.

'Kate,' she said. 'It's over. It's over.'

40

Beth unclipped the chain from the leather strap and undid the handcuffs — the keys were in Mike's pocket — and hugged Kate.

'What did you do to your mouth?' she said. 'Does it hurt?'

'I'll tell you later,' Kate said. 'And yes, it bloody does, but I don't care. Not now.' She swung her arms, enjoying the freedom to move. She looked at Mike's body, motionless on the ground.

'What did you do to him?' she said. 'Is he dead?'

Beth shook her head. 'Tranquillizer,' she said. 'A very strong one. It was the only thing I could hide. I held the syringe behind the phone.' She looked at Kate. 'Once you warned me, I wasn't sure I'd be able to do it. I had to get close to him, but I couldn't, not after you'd said it was a trap.'

'Shit,' Kate said. 'I'm sorry.' She gently touched her cheek. 'And that's what I ruined my teeth for. To warn you, when you didn't need warning. What a waste.'

'Don't be,' Beth said. 'You were so brave. And it worked. When he pulled out the gun — ' She shook her head. 'I thought it was over.'

'Which is why you told him to come and look at your son?'

'Right. I needed him near me. So I told him to

428

come and see Dylan.'

'Is that his name?'

'Yeah.'

'And was it true? That you'd arranged for him to go with a family?'

'God, no. I only heard about this this morning. He's with May. I was bluffing. To keep him from shooting me.'

There was a loud crashing sound from the hedge. Kate jumped; when she looked over she found it hard to believe what she was seeing.

'Phil?' she said. 'Gus?'

'Yep,' Phil said. 'We're the backup.' He looked at Mike's body, lying on the floor, then at Kate and Beth.

'We heard the shot. Are you OK?'

Beth nodded. 'I think some birds were frightened, but that's about it.'

'What about him?' Gus said. He gestured at the prone form. 'Do we have a problem here?'

'You mean do we have a dead body to worry about?' Beth said. She shook her head. 'No, we don't. But I wouldn't be worrying too much if we did. At least, I don't think so.'

Phil bent down and reached out, ready to take his pulse. Gus put a hand on his shoulder. 'Don't touch him,' he said. 'You and I were not here.' He bent over the body. 'He's breathing.'

'How long will he be out for?' Phil said.

'Another twenty minutes or so,' Beth said. 'Give or take. So we need to move fast.' She looked at Kate. 'Does he have a phone?'

Kate nodded. 'In the motorhome.'

'You call the police, tell them who and where

429

you are. They'll be here right away. We'll tie him up, just in case. The three of us need to get out of here.'

'You're going to leave me?' Kate said. 'I'm not sure about that.'

Beth held her gaze. Her eyes were dark and calm and Kate felt herself gain strength from her friend.

'You'll be fine,' Beth said. 'He'll be tied up and you'll have the shotgun.'

'How do I explain' — Kate gestured around — 'all this?'

'Say he brought you back here to kill you. He told you his plan: fast-acting drug to knock you out, then strangle you, take out your eyes, all the things the Strangler does. You managed to get free somehow — show them your teeth, that should convince them — and you grabbed the syringe and made a run for it. He caught you by the gate, you struggled, in the struggle the shotgun went off and you stabbed him with the syringe.'

Beth hugged her.

'Quick,' she said. 'There's no time to waste.'

★ ★ ★

The police were there ten minutes later. First, a squad car arrived, containing two excited young PCs, who untied the twine that Kate had put around Mike's ankles and wrists, and handcuffed him. Then they propped him up in a seated position against the gate and called for an ambulance.

They offered Kate a drink; she took some water, but even tiny sips brought tears to her eyes.

A few minutes later, another squad car showed up. This one contained DI Wynne.

As she closed the car door, Mike's chin lifted from his chest. He blinked, his eyes unfocused. For a moment there was a confused, bewildered expression on his face, then he became suddenly alert.

He jerked forward, trying to get to his feet. One of the young PCs pressed his shoulders, pushing him back to the ground.

'What's going on?' he said. He stared at Kate. 'What have you done? Where's Beth?'

DI Wynne pointed at the squad car. 'Take him to the station,' she said. 'I'll be right there.'

She walked over to Kate. 'I'm glad you're alive,' she said. 'I was very worried about you. We'll need to take a statement. Not now, of course. But once you've had a chance to rest.' She looked at Kate's swollen, aching cheek. 'What happened?'

'It's part of the story,' Kate said. Her mouth felt like it had been stuffed with cotton.

DI Wynne put her hand on Kate's arm. 'Then later,' she said.

Kate heard the wailing of an ambulance; seconds later she saw its lights turning onto the dirt track that led to the barn.

'Chester Hospital,' DI Wynne said 'That's where they'll take you.'

Kate let the paramedics settle her in a wheelchair and push her towards the ambulance.

DI Wynne walked alongside her.

'I'll call on you tomorrow,' she said. 'If that's OK.'

'Of course,' Kate said. 'Whatever you need to put him away.'

'Oh,' DI Wynne said. 'I think *that's* a foregone conclusion. But we'll talk anyway. Cross the t's and dot the i's, so to speak.'

She watched as Kate was lifted into the ambulance.

'Oh,' she said. 'I do have one question.'

'Yes?' Kate said.

'Who's Beth?'

Kate shook her head. 'Beth? Why do you ask?'

'He wanted to know where she was, when he woke up.'

'Oh,' Kate said. 'I don't know. But he was pretty crazy at the end. Sounds like something that you can dismiss as the ravings of a madman.'

DI Wynne gave her a wide grin.

'I see,' she said. 'I'll bear that in mind. Good luck, Miss Armstrong.'

41

She was going to be fine, although she was going to need some serious dental work.

'I suspect they'll take out what's left of those teeth,' the doctor, a tall man with a goofy smile, said. 'And then they'll put some new ones in there.'

'That's no bad thing,' her dad added. 'Save you having trouble with them later. When I was a kid, I remember people getting a new set of teeth for their twenty-first birthday. Had the real ones pulled out and implants put in. If you didn't, you were in for bloody murder as you got older. Dental hygiene wasn't what it is today.'

Kate's mum rolled her eyes and gave an exasperated shake of the head. Kate knew her dad was only trying to reassure her, but she found it more reassuring that, even now, her parents were still engaged in the good-natured bickering that characterized their relationship. She had wondered as a teenager whether they even liked each other; she realized now that bickering was their way of showing that they still loved each other. It meant they were paying attention, and that they cared. She hoped that she would find a better — or different, at least — way of expressing her love for whoever she ended up with, but if that was what worked for her mum and dad, then who was she to say it was wrong?

433

'Anyway,' the doctor said with a smile, 'we'll give you the names of some dentists. You'll want to get those teeth seen to as soon as you can. Apart from anything else, they're going to be very painful. We'll give you painkillers, but there's no reason to delay.'

'Can I go home?' Kate said. 'Is that it?'

'Not yet,' the doctor said. 'We'll keep you in for a little while longer. Make sure you get hydrated. And I'd like to see you one more time before you go. Keep an eye on you for any signs of shock. But other than that, there are no problems.'

He left, having asked a nurse to explain to her how to use the intravenous morphine drip that was beside her bed. Her mum and dad sat on either side of her, holding her hands. Her mum fiddled with her phone; her dad smiled. When he'd seen her, he'd hugged her — for the first time she could remember in a long time — and kissed her forehead.

That was when it hit her, when she understood how close she had come. She'd known it, of course, but she hadn't understood it, hadn't seen it through other people's eyes.

It could easily have ended differently, and when she thought that, she felt a sudden shortness of breath and a sense of rising panic.

She was lucky to be alive, and it was going to be a while before she truly came to terms with that.

But that was all for the future. For the moment, all she wanted, as the morphine dulled the pain in her teeth, was some sleep.

★ ★ ★

When she woke up, Phil was sitting by the bed, reading the news on his phone. She studied his face in the reflected glare, considered what he had done: without him, she'd probably be dead.

And she felt warmth and friendship and gratitude, but she didn't love him. Not in the way she had done. She'd wondered if she would, but now she saw him, she had her answer.

'Hi,' she said. Her voice was barely above a croak and her teeth throbbed.

'You want a drink?' he said. 'Water?'

She nodded, and he passed her a cup. She sipped it, and then pressed the button for more morphine.

'What time is it?' she said.

'Eleven p.m. They let us stay longer, given the circumstances.'

'Us? Who else is here?'

'May, Gemma, Beth. They're wandering around looking for coffee. Apparently, there's a machine somewhere.'

'So,' Kate said. 'Thanks.' She realized that she still didn't know what had happened. 'You'll have to tell me your story.'

'I got a phone call from Gus — '

'Not now,' she said. 'Later.'

He stood up and looked at her. He loved her still, she could see that. It was written in every muscle in his face, in the part-relief, part-hope, part-sadness of his expression.

He started to speak, then stopped himself, then started again. Then he shook his head, and looked away.

'Go on,' Kate said. 'What is it?'

435

He looked back at her. 'I love you,' he said. 'You know that, don't you?'

'Yes,' she said. 'I do.'

'But you don't love me.' It was part-statement, part-question. She didn't answer.

'It actually *is* over, isn't it?' he said. This was a question, and so she nodded.

'Yes,' she said. 'It is. But I love you too, Phil. Not in the way you hoped, but in another way. And I always will.'

There was the sound of footsteps in the corridor.

'The others are coming,' he said. 'I'll leave you to them.' He paused. 'It might not be enough for me,' he said. 'To be friends. You understand that, right?'

'Yes. I understand.'

'So this might be goodbye. For a while, at least. I'm not trying to be mean. It's . . . it's too much for me to see you.'

'I understand. And thank you, Phil.' She smiled at him. 'Before you go. Is there any chance of a hug?'

He smelled so familiar, so comfortable, so Phil, that for a moment she was tempted to ask him to stay, but, as the door opened, she let go of him and watched him walk from the room.

She wiped a tear from her eye and looked at her friends.

'Oh my God,' she said. 'I can't believe you're here. And I can't believe that *this* is what it took to get us all together again.'

436

42

She ended up leaving the following morning. Beth, May and Gemma had stayed with her for about ten minutes longer before a nurse came and threw them out — in a kind, nursely way — after which Kate went back to sleep. She woke a few times in the night, startled awake by nightmares, and in the morning she was ready to go.

She sat on the couch at her parents' house and sipped a cup of milk and honey. Anything else sent shockwaves through her teeth; she was booked to see a dentist that afternoon and she couldn't wait. She was sick of both the pain and the fogginess that the painkillers — some big yellow pills the doctor had prescribed — caused.

The doorbell rang and she heard her mum answer it. A few seconds later the door to the living room opened.

It was Beth. She was holding hands with a little boy.

'This is Dylan,' she said. 'Dylan, this is Auntie Kate.'

'Hello, Dylan,' Kate said. 'I can't tell you how pleased I am to meet you.'

'Hi,' he said. 'Are you Mummy's friend?'

Kate glanced at Beth. 'Yes,' she said. 'I am.'

Kate's mum came into the room. 'Would you like a cup of tea, B — ' she caught herself just in time: 'Andrea?'

437

'Yes, please. Maybe Dylan could go with you and get a drink? And a biscuit?'

'Of course.' Her mum bent over so her face was level with Dylan's. 'Would you like a biscuit? I've got some very big chocolate ones. Probably too big.'

He shook his head. 'Not too big.'

'Shall we find out?'

They left the room. Beth sat down opposite Kate.

'How are you feeling?'

'Sore. But OK, considering. I'm seeing the dentist later. He's a beautiful boy, Beth.'

'Thanks. I think so too. And he's the reason I'm here.'

'Oh?'

'I knew that Colin — or Mike, if you prefer — was never going to stop. The only way was to face him head on.'

'Which you did. Pretty spectacularly, I'd say. What was in the syringe?'

'A fast-acting sedative. They give it to people before colonoscopies. I thought it was appropriate for that arsehole.'

'You know a lot about that stuff?'

'Trainee anaesthetist.'

'I see.' Kate sipped her drink. 'So. What next for you?'

'Back to Wolverhampton,' Beth said. 'Back to college. I have some exams coming up.'

'As Andrea Berry?'

'Yes. That's my name now, you know? And Dylan — I don't want to have to explain it to him. Not yet, anyway.'

438

'Are we going to stay in touch?'

'I think so,' Beth said. 'I hope so. We should meet up, from time to time.'

'From time to time?' Kate had, she realized, been hoping for more.

'I have a lot of memories,' Beth said, 'that I've worked hard to move on from. And being with you — and May, and Gem — brings it back. I love you guys, honestly, I do. But it's hard. *You* know. You've seen him up close. You know how bad he can be.'

Kate nodded. 'The motorhome,' she said. 'He told me how he used it. Even when I was in agony, I was thinking of you, of what you must have gone through.'

'Exactly,' Beth said. 'And I've dealt with a lot of that. At least, I thought I had, until yesterday, when May and Phil showed up. Which was a shock, as you can imagine.'

'I'm sorry.'

'Don't be. It forced me to do what I should have done years ago, and deal with that bastard once and for all.'

'And you did. He'll never trouble us again. He's going to be in prison for a long, long time.'

'For the rest of his life, according to DI Wynne,' Beth said.

'You talked to her? How did she know you're involved?'

'She's very resourceful,' Beth said. 'And very smart. She told me what he said when she questioned him.'

Kate blinked. 'Are we in trouble?'

'Not according to her. She told me she'd deal

439

with it. I tend to believe her. You'll have to make a statement. You can stick to the story, or we can tell her the truth. Either way, he's not going to see the outside of a prison as long as he's drawing breath.'

'Which will be too soon.'

The door opened and Dylan came in. He had chocolate and a smile all over his face. Kate's mum followed him, a cup of tea in her hand.

'Here you go,' she said.

Beth glanced at Kate. 'We have to leave,' she said. 'But thanks.'

When she had gone, Kate's mum frowned.

'Everything OK?' she said.

Kate nodded.

'As good as it could be,' she said. 'Which is enough for me.'

Later

MASS MURDERER SENTENCED TO LIFE IN PRISON

Judge David Wainwright today sentenced serial killer Colin Davidson to eight life sentences, with a recommendation that he never be released.

Davidson — who used a number of aliases, among them Mark Stevens and Mike Sadler — was found guilty of the murder of eight women during a multi-year killing spree, in Stockton Heath and Sheffield.

Detective Inspector Jane Wynne, leading the investigation, said after the verdict that she was glad to see justice being served. She added that there were suspicions that Davidson had killed other women, but the investigation team had been unable to find proof as yet.

'He is one of this country's most prolific killers,' she said. 'And we live in a safer world now that he is behind bars, and will remain so for the rest of his life.'

Kate had expected to feel some closure when the verdict came; early on she had been involved in the trial as a witness and she had followed it as it progressed.

She didn't, though. She was glad, and relieved, but she didn't feel closure.

What she felt was irrational, she knew that, but she couldn't shake it.

For some reason, she didn't feel it was over.

One year later

The letter came to her home address. She'd moved back in a month after the dental work to replace her teeth. Over the year, the nightmares had become less frequent and, in the last few weeks, she'd even gone on a date.

It was OK. She liked the guy. They'd met in the pub, one on one. It took some courage.

And Gus and May were in the pub, a few tables away, in the event that she needed them.

She got back from work on a Friday evening, and there it was. White envelope, handwritten address.

Sent to Kate Barnstable, not Kate Armstrong.

Odd. But that wasn't the only weird thing about it.

The other weird thing was the stamp.

It was second class.

And it had an unusual postmark. She stared at it.

It was a prison postmark.

She picked it up off the mat and opened it. She began to read. As she did, her stomach shrank and she slumped to the floor, her back against the wall.

Kate, forgive me for writing to you but I do not know Beth's address, so cannot contact her directly, and there is something I need to discuss with her.

I'll get to the point.
I want to see my son.

Kate stared at the wall. The paper shook in her hands as she carried on reading. He was probably banned from writing to her, so he'd used the false name. Typical Mike. She read on.

I have a RIGHT to see him. Not a LEGAL right, maybe, but a MORAL right. I know you will understand this, Kate. You are a good person. He needs to see his DAD. He deserves to know me. And I will get to know him, one way or another. I will write to him, at home, at school, wherever the letters will reach him, and I will tell him who I am and where he can find me. Have you read Harry Potter? The people who he lives with try to stop the letters telling him he is a wizard from reaching him, but in the end they cannot, and they cannot because it is RIGHT for him to know he is a WIZARD.

Just as it is RIGHT for a boy to know his DAD.

It will be better for Beth if she allows this, because then she will be able to control it.

I know YOU will understand this. And that is why I want YOU to talk to her on my behalf. If you don't, then what happens will be on YOUR conscience. You KNOW what I am capable of.

You can write back to me at the address on the top of this letter. Make sure you include my prisoner number, if you want to be sure the letter will reach me. For avoidance of doubt, the number is —

She stopped reading.

He was in prison, locked in a cell, miles away from her, but, with the letter in her hand, he felt so close. It was as though he was in the room with her, right there, grinning like the madman he was. She sobbed, memories of the barn and the motorhome flooding over her.

She shook her head to clear her thoughts. She had to think through what to do. First and foremost, she had to find a way to stop him doing this again.

And then she had to tell Beth. She needed to know.

She picked up her phone and called Gus.

'Hi,' he said. 'What's up?'

'I got a letter,' she replied. 'From him. From Mike. Colin. Whatever he's called.'

'Fucking arsehole,' Gus said. 'He shouldn't be writing to you. What does he want?'

'To see Dylan. He wants me to pass the message on to Beth. I don't know what to do. And I don't want any more letters.'

'I'll deal with that,' Gus said. 'I'll contact the prison authorities and tell them what happened. They won't let him send any more.'

'And what about Beth?'

'I think you should tell her.'

Kate stared at the wall. 'Shit,' she said. 'I'm scared, Gus. Scared that he'll get out and come for us.'

'That won't happen. He's locked up, Kate.

445

Locked up for good.'

'I wish he was gone for good.'

'Yeah. It would be better,' Gus said, 'if one night the wardens happened to forget to lock his cell and he had a nasty accident.'

'Is that possible?'

There was a long pause.

'Anything's possible,' Gus said. 'With the right word in the right ear.'

★ ★ ★

After she hung up with Gus, Kate dialled Beth's number. She was dreading telling her friend about the letter, dreading her reaction, dreading being the one who brought the past flooding into the present.

'Hey, stranger,' Beth said. She sounded bright, happy. 'What're you calling for?'

'I . . . ' Kate didn't know how to say it, didn't know how to pass on the news that would shatter her friend's hard-won peace of mind. 'I . . . '

'Is everything OK?' Beth said. Her tone was alarmed. 'Kate?'

'Yes,' Kate said. 'Everything's fine.'

She couldn't do it. Beth was better not knowing. Mike was gone, safely locked away in prison. There was no point causing Beth the torture of sleepless nights.

She smiled, trying to put some warmth into her voice. 'I wanted to say hi.'

They chatted for a few more minutes, then hung up, Kate relieved she hadn't passed on Mike's message, Beth sounding confused at the

446

strange call from her friend.

Kate picked up the letter and read it again. She could hear his voice in her head, hear his lunatic tone.

He's never going to stop, she thought. *He's going to keep on until he gets what he wants. And I didn't tell Beth, so now it's my problem.*

She thought for a few seconds — only a few, this was a decision that had to be taken quickly, without too much thought, or it would never be taken at all — then called Gus again.

'Hi,' she said. 'I didn't tell her.'

'Oh?' Gus replied. 'She needs to know, Kate.'

'I couldn't. She sounded so happy. She doesn't need to be worrying about this. It's not fair. And there's no threat. He can't get out.'

'Right. He's going nowhere.'

Kate hesitated. 'But if something did happen. If he did get out and come after her and Dylan, then it would be on me, because I didn't say anything. And that can't happen.'

'So you need to tell her,' Gus said.

'Maybe not,' Kate replied. 'I was thinking about what you said. About him having an accident in prison. That it's possible. That *anything's* possible.'

'Yes,' Gus said slowly. 'And?'

'And I was wondering, how possible. If there's a way to make it real . . . '

'Kate,' Gus said. 'If you're saying what I think you're saying — '

'I am,' she said. 'I am. This has to end, Gus. And he deserves it. If anyone does, he does.'

Gus paused. 'Are you sure, Kate?'

'If he'd left us alone, I'd say no,' Kate said. 'But he didn't. He started this. And he won't stop, ever. Beth and Dylan and I deserve to live in peace. So yes, I'm sure.'

'OK,' Gus said. 'Are you asking me to help?'

'I don't want you to do anything that will get you in trouble,' Kate said. 'Tell me what to do, and I'll do it.'

'If I'm going to do that, I might as well take care of it myself,' Gus said. He paused for a long time. 'But you're right. This has to stop. I can help with that.'

'I can deal with it, Gus.'

'I don't doubt that, but it'll be easier if I do it. All I need from you is cash.'

He named a number — a lot, but a surprisingly small amount, given what it represented — and told her to assemble it over a few weeks, so there would be no record of a large withdrawal.

* * *

He came over one Sunday afternoon a few weeks later. Didn't finish the cup of tea she made him. She passed him a fat envelope. He nodded, and hugged her.

Whatever he did, it didn't take long. She read the story on her phone the following Wednesday morning:

BREAKING NEWS: SERIAL KILLER COLIN DAVIDSON FOUND DEAD

Serial killer Colin Davidson is dead. The exact cause of death has not yet been released, but according to a statement from the prison, he committed suicide.

Davidson was responsible for the murders of at least eight women. He operated in Sheffield, and the small village of Stockton Heath. Davidson, also known as, among others, Mike Sadler and Mark Stevens, was one of Britain's most notorious killers. He is survived by his parents.

She was interrupted by her phone ringing. It was Beth.

'Hi,' Kate said. 'Did you see it?'

'Yes,' Beth said. It sounded like she'd been crying. 'It's over, Kate. Finally, it's over.'

Acknowledgements

Warmest thanks to:

My early readers — Jessie, Barbara and Tahnthawan: their careful editorial suggestions — *always kindly delivered* ('*I'm not sure that scene works as well as it could*' or '*you might want to think about how* that character would behave') are invaluable.

Marcus Deck, for his advice on what might or might not be medically feasible.

Norman Banner, for his legal review.

Becky Ritchie, for her support, advice and encouragement. I am lucky to have her as an agent.

Sarah Hodgson, for her invaluable editorial advice. She is patient, thorough and inspiring.

Lucy Dauman, and everyone else at Harper Collins. I continue to be amazed at the work you do in marketing, cover design and all the other things that go into making a book which you mercifully keep hidden from me. Thank you.

We do hope that you have enjoyed reading this large print book.

Did you know that all of our titles are available for purchase?

We publish a wide range of high quality large print books including:
**Romances, Mysteries, Classics
General Fiction
Non Fiction and Westerns**

Special interest titles available in large print are:
**The Little Oxford Dictionary
Music Book
Song Book
Hymn Book
Service Book**

Also available from us courtesy of Oxford University Press:
**Young Readers' Dictionary
(large print edition)
Young Readers' Thesaurus
(large print edition)**

For further information or a free brochure, please contact us at:
**Ulverscroft Large Print Books Ltd.,
The Green, Bradgate Road, Anstey,
Leicester, LE7 7FU, England.
Tel: (00 44) 0116 236 4325
Fax: (00 44) 0116 234 0205**

Other titles published by Ulverscroft:

AFTER ANNA

Alex Lake

A girl is missing. Five years old, taken from outside her school. She has vanished, traceless. The police are at a loss; her parents are beyond grief. Their daughter is lost forever, perhaps dead, perhaps enslaved. But the biggest mystery is yet to come: one week after she was abducted, their daughter is returned. She has no memory of where she has been. And this, for her mother, is just the beginning of the nightmare . . .

CROSS THE LINE

James Patterson

Shots ring out in the early morning hours in the suburbs of Washington, DC. When the smoke clears, a high-ranking cop lies dead. Under pressure from the mayor, Detective Alex Cross steps into the leadership vacuum to investigate the audacious killing. But before Cross can make any headway, a wave of murders erupts across the city. The victims have one thing in common — they are all criminals. And the only thing more dangerous than a murderer without a conscience is a killer who thinks he has justice on his side.

NO TURNING BACK

Tracy Buchanan

When radio presenter Anna Graves and her daughter are attacked on the beach by a crazed teenager, Anna reacts instinctively to protect her baby. But her life falls apart when the schoolboy dies from his injuries. The police believe Anna's story, until the autopsy reveals something more sinister. The evidence seems to connect Anna to a decades-old serial murder case. Is she really as innocent as she claims? And is killing ever justified, if it saves a child's life?

THE LONG COUNT

J. M. Gulvin

Marion County, 1967: Texas Ranger John Quarrie is called to the scene of an apparent suicide by a fellow war veteran. Although the local police want the case shut down, John Q is convinced that events aren't quite so straightforward. When his theory is backed up by the man's son, Isaac — just back from Vietnam — they start to look into a series of other violent incidents in the area, including a recent fire at the local Trinity Asylum and the disappearance of Isaac's twin brother, Ishmael. In a desperate race against time, John Q must try to unravel the dark secrets at the heart of this family, and get to the truth before the count is up . . .

UNDERTOW

Elizabeth Heathcote

My husband's lover. They said her death was a tragic accident. And I believed them . . . until now. Carmen is happily married to Tom, a successful London lawyer and divorce with three children. She is content to absorb the stresses of being a stepmother to teenagers and the stain of 'second wife'. She knows she'll always live in the shadow of another woman — not Tom's first wife Laura, who is resolutely polite and determinedly respectable, but the lover who ended his first marriage: Zena. Zena, who was shockingly beautiful. Zena, who drowned swimming late one night. But Carmen can overlook her husband's dead mistress . . . until she starts to suspect that he might have been the person who killed her.